THE FURIES OF ROME

Robert Fabbri read Drama and Theatre at London University and has worked in film and TV for 25 years as an assistant director. He has worked on productions such as *Hornblower, Hellraiser, Patriot Games* and *Billy Elliot.* His lifelong passion for ancient history inspired him to write the Vespasian series. He lives in London and Berlin.

Also by Robert Fabbri

THE VESPASIAN SERIES

TRIBUNE OF ROME
ROME'S EXECUTIONER
FALSE GOD OF ROME
ROME'S FALLEN EAGLE
MASTERS OF ROME
ROME'S LOST SON

Coming soon ...

ARMINIUS

SHORT STORIES

THE CROSSROADS BROTHERHOOD
THE RACING FACTIONS
THE DREAMS OF MORPHEUS
THE ALEXANDRIAN EMBASSY

Coming soon ...

THE IMPERIAL TRIUMPH

THE FURIES OF ROME

ROBERT
FABBRI

First published in hardback in Great Britain in 2016 by Corvus,
an imprint of Atlantic Books Ltd.

This paperback edition published in Great Britain in 2016 by
Corvus, an imprint of Atlantic Books Ltd.

Map designed by Jeff Edwards

10 9 8 7 6 5 4 3 2 1

A CIP catalogue record for this book is available from the British Library.

Paperback ISBN: 978 0 85789 973 6
E-book ISBN: 978 0 85789 972 9

Printed and bound in Great Britain by Clays Ltd, St Ives plc

Corvus
An imprint of Atlantic Books Ltd
Ormond House
26–27 Boswell Street
London WC1N 3JZ

www.corvus-books.co.uk

For my cousin, Aris Caraccio, his wife, Nathalie, and their children, Mathilde, Arthur, Victor and Margaux; as well as my uncle, Giuseppe 'Pino' Caraccio, with much love.

Also to George and Ice, their Corsa hounds upon whom – with a lot of latitude! – Castor and Pollux are based.

N
BRIGANTES
Mona
Lindum
Venta Icenorum
Durobrivae
Veronae
ICENI
Camulodunum
Verulamium
TRINOVANTES
Londinium
Calleva
Rutupiae
REGNI
Isca Dumnoriorum
Please note that this is the probable coastline in 1st century AD

PROLOGUE

ROME, NOVEMBER AD 58

FEW ENJOYED NERO'S feasts; each seemed interminable and this occasion was no exception.

It was not because of the endless courses, all exquisitely presented, paraded out by dozens of scantily clad – if clad at all – slaves of either sex or none. Nor was it the conversation: anodyne, occasional and humourless; neither was it the entertainment, which had been a repetitive series of heroic odes in the Emperor's favourite styles, both in Greek and Latin, performed with the sickening smugness of a lyre-player who doubted not his own ability and knew himself to be high in the Emperor's favour. Even the vulgarity of the size of the dinner – thirty couches, each with three guests reclining at their own low table, arranged in a 'U' shape around the entertainer – could be forgiven as it had become the norm in Nero's reign.

No, it was none of these things that made Titus Flavius Sabinus loathe every moment of the gathering and pray to his lord Mithras for its end. It was a completely different factor: it was the fear.

The fear swathed the room like an invisible, gladiatorial net, with lead weights holding it down to the ground and the *retiarius*, wielding it, pulling on the drawstrings so that it entrapped all within its grasp, making escape impossible. Most of the guests were entangled in this net of fear although none would let it show in their outward behaviour; recently, after four and a half years of Nero as emperor, the élite of Rome had begun to learn that to show fear in front of him was to encourage him into worse excess.

It had not always been so: in the early years of his rule Nero had shown restraint – at least in public – although he had raped and then poisoned his adoptive brother, Britannicus, the Emperor Claudius' true blood heir who had been passed over because of his youth. However, that outrage, or the fratricide part of it at least, could be justified by political necessity: had he lived, Britannicus could have become a figurehead for dissension that may have turned into conflict; his death, it was argued, prevented the possibility of another civil war and therefore his sacrifice was made for the good of all. Because of that, people were willing to overlook the boy's murder on the eve of his becoming a man on his fourteenth birthday.

After the death of his only serious rival – as well as the elimination of a couple of lesser ones – Nero had settled down to a life of pampered luxury, leaving the running of the Empire mainly to his former tutor and now advisor, Lucius Annaeus Seneca, and also the prefect of the Praetorian Guard, Sextus Afranius Burrus, preferring instead to indulge in his two passions, chariot racing and singing, both of which he, naturally, conducted in private. It was unthinkable for a patrician, let alone the Emperor, to be seen indulging in either of those demeaning pursuits in public, and so Nero, aware of the dignity of his position, had not displayed his taste for the activities of freedmen and slaves to anyone outside a very tight inner circle on the Palatine Hill. As far as the people of Rome were concerned, the Golden Emperor, as they liked to think of their Princeps, whose hair blazed with the colour of the dawn, was an upright and generous ruler – as witnessed by the magnificence of the games and public feasts that he provided. Outwardly he was soberly married to Claudia Octavia, Claudius' daughter, and conducted himself in a very worthy and Roman fashion – the fact the marriage was technically incestuous was quietly forgotten, again for the greater good – but inwardly it was quite a different story.

However, now, to those close to Nero, it had become clear that only he could curb his own behaviour; but if he chose not to then that was his prerogative. Seneca and Burrus, who between them had taken on the task of moulding the young Princeps into a temperate and just ruler, could do nothing to restrain the desires within Nero that had grown with each of his twenty-one years.

And his desires were great.

Too great to be satisfied by the patrician rigidity of his young wife, reclining to the left of her husband with the blank look on her face that she had worn for the past four years since Nero had humiliated her by taking a freedwoman to his bed and withholding from her the chance to produce an heir. But even the charms of the freedwoman, Acte, had not been enough to fulfil the lust of a young man who had come to realise that he could do anything that pleased him to anyone he chose.

It was now becoming clear that many things pleased him and ordering the élite of Rome to join him for lavish dinners at a few moments' notice was, however inconvenient, the most innocuous; there were far darker activities that pleased Nero even more. One of those activities, Sabinus guessed, as Tigellinus, the prefect of the Vigiles, approached his couch, the Emperor was going to indulge in, yet again, later.

Dark-eyed and sharp-featured, Tigellinus leant down to whisper in Sabinus' ear. 'The Quirinal from the fourth hour.' With a smile like a rabid dog's snarl, he patronisingly patted Sabinus on the cheek before walking away.

Sabinus sighed, reached for his cup, downed its contents then held it behind him for a naked slave boy, smeared all over with silver lacquer, to refill as he turned to his corpulent neighbour, keeping his voice low. 'You should get home quickly as soon as the dinner finishes, Uncle, if it ever does. He's planning on going out again tonight; Tigellinus just informed me that there are to be no patrols of his Vigiles around the Quirinal Hill after the fourth hour of the night, apart, of course, from the one that shadows Nero to keep him safe.'

His uncle, Gaius Vespasius Pollo, flicking a carefully tonged ringlet of dyed-black hair away from his kohled eyes, looked at Sabinus, alarmed at the lack of Rome's Night Watch in his neighbourhood. 'Not the Quirinal again, dear boy? The area is still reeling from his rampage through it last month.'

Sabinus nodded, thoughtfully sipping from his replenished cup. 'One tenement block and two houses burnt to the ground, half a dozen rapes, countless broken bones and several murders as well as the forced suicide of Julius Montanus for daring to try to defend himself when set upon by what he thought was a slave in a ridiculous wig.'

Gaius' jowls and chins wobbled in indignation; he reached for another anchovy pasty. 'A man of senatorial status ordered to kill himself for apologising when he recognised that his attacker, whom he now had in a headlock, was in fact the Emperor; it's too much. It's been going on for more than a year now; how much longer will we have to stand for this sort of thing?' The pasty disappeared whole into Gaius' mouth.

'You know the answer to that: as long as Nero subjects us to it. It's his idea of fun, and with his friend Otho and other young bucks encouraging him it can only get worse.' Sabinus looked over at the tall, well-built and exceedingly handsome man reclining to the right of the Emperor: three years older than Nero, Marcus Salvius Otho had been the Emperor's lover on and off since Nero's tenth year.

'And as the Urban Prefect, responsible for law and order in Rome, it's you who's made to look stupid, dear boy.' Gaius joined in the rapturous applause led by Nero, weeping freely, for the conclusion of the performer's latest rendition.

Sabinus raised his voice over the exaggerated adulation. 'You know perfectly well there's nothing I can do about it. Tigellinus tells me where he's withdrawing his patrols from so that I can order a century of one of the Urban Cohorts to be on standby in the area in case Nero needs to be extracted in a hurry or his activities cause a riot. He claims he tries to keep the violence to a minimum.'

'My flabby arse he does!' Gaius scoffed and reached for another pasty. 'The more violent it becomes the happier he is because it adds another element of fear for us all and the more we fear Nero the more secure his position becomes and Tigellinus' with it. Thankfully, I've got four of Tigran's lads waiting to escort me home; although since he took over from Magnus as the leader of the South Quirinal Crossroads Brotherhood I'm obliged to do more favours in return for the service. And it's all because you're failing in your duty.'

A disturbance at the far end of the room saved Sabinus a blustered answer; to the not-that-well-hidden outrage of most present, the Emperor's mistress, the freedwoman Acte, entered, garbed, coiffured and bejewelled with a vulgarity that was unsurprising in one newly come to money and position. Pausing as her entourage of attendants – and again there was vulgarity in their number – unnecessarily adjusted her costume and her intricate and towering arrangement of blonde hair as well as putting a final touch to her excessive make-up, she glanced around the chamber with a haughty triumph, until her eyes fell on Nero. Slapping away the women surrounding her, she glided towards the Emperor.

A tense silence fell on the room; all eyes went to the Empress.

'I feel that it is time to take my leave, dearest husband,' Claudia Octavia said, rising with fluid elegance to her feet. 'I caught a faint whiff of something that doesn't agree with me and it would be best if I were to lie down and let my stomach settle.' Without waiting for Nero's leave, as his attention was on the sheerness of Acte's attire and the lack of anything beneath it, Claudia Octavia progressed with rigid-backed, patrician dignity from the room.

'She has the support of many,' Gaius whispered to Sabinus, 'Calpurnius Piso, Thrasea Paetus, Rome's dourest Stoic, and Faenius Rufus, for example.'

As Nero made a great fuss of greeting his slave-born mistress and Acte made it a point that all should see how favoured she was, Sabinus glanced over to three middle-aged senators on a couch opposite him, their visages clouded with disapproval as they witnessed the supplanting of the daughter of the previous Emperor by a coarsely arrayed sexual-acrobat; their wives, on the couch next to them, pointedly refused to look in the direction of such an affront to female pride. 'I was going through Faenius Rufus' annual report as prefect of the grain supply and it would seem that he's hardly used his position to enrich himself, just a few kick-backs here and there.'

'He's always had a reputation for honesty to the point of recklessness, dear boy; he has the morality and sympathies of an upright republican of old – a Cato not a Crassus. And as for Piso and Thrasea, the gods alone know what they must think of the Emperor behaving in such a way to a daughter of the Claudii, even though her father was a fool who drooled. And what they all think of Nero's rampages through the city I wouldn't try to imagine, if *I* were *you*.'

Sabinus did not answer but, rather, devoted his attention to his cup, frowning at his perceived inability to keep the better quarters of Rome safe as the lyre-player launched into yet another ode. Since his recall, almost two years previously, from the provinces of Moesia, Macedonia and Thracia, where he had been serving as governor, and his surprise appointment as the prefect of Rome, the magistrate overseeing the day to day running of the city, Sabinus had been trying, to no avail, to work out who had used their influence to secure him the position; neither his uncle nor his brother, Vespasian, could help him in uncovering the identity of his anonymous benefactor. Naturally Sabinus found it disconcerting not knowing whose debt he was in and when it would have to be repaid, but he was very happy with the position and the status that it conferred on him: he was one of the five most influential men in the city after the Emperor himself – officially, that was.

Unofficially there were others who had closer access to the Emperor's ear than he did, namely Seneca, Burrus and the consuls, but the main two were Otho and Tigellinus. Although Sabinus was his superior, in that the Vigiles, as well as the Urban Cohorts, were under the command of the prefect of Rome, Tigellinus was impossible to control. He had used his unabashed depravity to ingratiate himself with the Emperor whom he had recognised immediately as a kindred spirit; it had been Tigellinus who had held Britannicus down whilst Nero had buggered him at what was to be the boy's last and fatal dinner in this very room. This inability to control his underling was taking the gloss off Sabinus' status; he felt it made him look as if he condoned all the violence that had gradually increased as more and more young men realised that with the Emperor running amok in the city they too had licence to do the same.

'I assume from that exchange earlier,' a voice said, impinging on his thoughts, 'shall we call it an exchange? No, we can't because you didn't say a word back to Tigellinus, did you, prefect? So let's say it was a command, yes, a command, prefect, from your underling. I assume from that command, Nero's going out again tonight.'

'Very astute, Seneca,' Sabinus said without bothering to look round.

'Another triumph for Roman law and order; it makes me wonder if I was right to take the very substantial bribe I was given to have you confirmed in your post. Perhaps for the good of all I should have taken less money and got someone more competent.'

Still Sabinus did not look round. 'When did you ever do anything for the good of all?'

'That's harsh, Sabinus; I've moderated the Emperor's behaviour for the past few years.'

'And now you can barely restrain him. I suppose you enjoy making me look stupid as the Urban prefect. By the way, who did bribe you on my behalf?'

'I've told you before, that as a man of a strict moral code I could not possibly divulge such confidences; without the appropriate, what's the best word ... er ... inducement, yes, that's it, inducement. Anyway, that's by the by; it's about your enquiry that I wanted to speak to you.'

'Oh, yes?' Still Sabinus did not turn.

'Yes. The consulships are all spoken for ...'

'Bought, you mean.'

'Don't be ridiculous; the Emperor does not buy his consulship.'

'More's the pity for your purse.'

'I'll ignore that. Three years' time is the earliest that your son-in-law could expect one and the price is non-negotiable: two million sesterces.'

'Two million! That's twice the threshold for admittance into the Senate.' This time Sabinus did turn round but only to see the portly form of Seneca walking away; he watched as Nero's chief advisor sidled up to Marcus Valerius Messalla Corvinus, Sabinus' and Vespasian's sworn enemy since he had abducted Sabinus' late wife, Clementina, and taken her to Caligula for repeated and brutal rape. His outrage at Seneca's price was immediately replaced by curiosity. 'What's Corvinus negotiating with Seneca about, Uncle?'

'Hmm, what, dear boy?'

Sabinus repeated the question.

'A lucrative governorship. It's rumoured that he's trying to get Lusitania because of the tax possibilities on the garum trade; as you can imagine, there's a lot of money in fish sauce.'

'It makes you wonder where he's getting the money to bribe Seneca with.'

'That's easy; if Corvinus doesn't mind paying the exorbitant interest rates, Seneca will lend him the money for his own bribe, provided he can get someone to stand as a guarantor; which will be yet more expense for him but well worth it if he gets Lusitania.'

And that was how it now worked, Sabinus reflected: Seneca, it seemed, cared only for amassing a fortune from his position much to the private amusement of the few who had read his philosophical tracts. However, Seneca was not unusual in this; his predecessor, Pallas, the Flavian family's chief supporter during Claudius' reign and the early part of Nero's, had made his fortune as Claudius' most trusted advisor before he had fallen from Nero's favour at the same time as his lover, Nero's mother, Agrippina; he was now exiled to his country estates, no longer playing a role in imperial high politics. Pallas was more fortunate than Narcissus, the man he had outmanoeuvred and replaced; Narcissus had been executed, despite his fortune – or, it could be argued, because of it.

Unable to think where he would come up with the outrageous amount Seneca was asking for his son-in-law, Lucius Caesennius Paetus', consulship without borrowing it from the man himself – something he would never allow himself to do – Sabinus cast his mind back to the issue from which he had been dragged away when the Emperor's summons to dinner had arrived that afternoon. Some of the duties of the prefect of Rome were less onerous than others and the questioning of prisoners who posed a threat to the security of the Empire was one of the more pleasant tasks;

and when that man was no longer a citizen and therefore Sabinus had a freer rein then it could be a positive pleasure. That pleasure was made all the sweeter in this case by the fact that this was not necessarily an imperial matter as the man in question had been sent to him by his brother, Vespasian, to be incarcerated and questioned as a favour that he needed to repay; although what that favour was owed for and to whom, Sabinus knew not.

'My friends,' Nero's husky voice cut through the applause for the latest ode that had finally ground to an end, drawing Sabinus out of his thoughts. 'I would that we had time for more of this sublime gift of the gods.' Nero raised a hand to the heavens and gazed after it for a few moments, his expression composed into one of deepest gratitude; he then looked over to the lyre-player and inhaled, long and deep, his eyes closed as if he were smelling the sweetest of scents. 'Terpnus, here, has received the blessing of Apollo with his honeyed voice and skilled fingers.'

There were general mutterings of agreement from the audience, although those with a true ear for music found Nero's statement exaggerated.

Nero nodded at Terpnus before drawing himself up and filling his chest with air. Terpnus plucked a chord and then, to everyone's astonishment, some more obvious than others, Nero let out a note, long and quavering; it was reasonably close to the chord that Terpnus had plucked but not nearly as strong nor as constant. Nero's audience, however, chose to interpret the sound as a harmony of infinite and intricate genius rather than the lamentable discord that was the reality; they burst into unrestrained applause as soon as the note died a miserable death on the Emperor's lips. Ladies who had suffered violent rape at Nero's hands and those others who feared it would soon be their turn clapped demurely whilst their husbands cheered the man who would sully their womenfolk and steal their fortunes and their lives. Sabinus and Gaius joined in the lauding wholeheartedly, refraining from catching the other's eye.

'My friends,' Nero rasped, 'for three years now Terpnus has been training me, bringing out the innate talent within your Emperor. I have lain with lead weights on my chest; I have used enemas and emetics as well as refraining from eating apples and other foods deleterious to the voice. I have done all these things under the guidance of the greatest performer of the age; so, soon I will be ready to perform for you!'

There was a momentary silence as the hideous thought of breaking the taboo against people of consequence – let alone the Emperor – performing in public sank in, before the audience burst into rapturous cheering as if Nero had just announced the very thing that each had desired most in life and yet, up until now, none had thought it possible to attain.

Nero stood, side-on, left hand on his heart and right hand extended to his guests; tears trickled down the pale skin of his cheeks to catch in the wispy, golden beard that grew thickest under his chin, which, despite his youth, had begun to sag with the weight of good living. Thus, he let the adulation wash over him. 'My friends,' he said eventually, his voice imbued with rich emotion, 'I understand your joy. To be finally able to share with me my talent as expressed through my voice, the most beautiful thing I know.'

Acte, now in Claudia Octavia's place, looked less than impressed by this assertion.

'As beautiful as my new wife, Princeps?' Otho asked with a note of drunken laughter on his voice; his closeness to Nero for so long meant he was the only man in Rome with licence to exchange banter with the Emperor.

Nero, far from being aggravated at his announcement being interrupted, turned and smiled at his friend and sometime lover. 'You've boasted all evening of Poppaea Sabina's charms, Otho; when you bring her to Rome I shall sing to her and then you can judge the relative beauty of your new wife and my voice.'

Otho raised his cup to Nero. 'That I shall, Princeps, and I shall ravage the winner; she will be here in four days.'

This produced raucous and ribald cheers from the young bucks who considered themselves part of the Emperor's close associates; they were soon stilled by a withering look from Nero that, once silence had returned, transformed into an expression of abject humility. 'Soon, my friends, I shall be ready for you;

until then I shall practise more. Adieu.' With mannered gestures to Acte, Otho, Terpnus and his young sycophants to follow him, Nero turned and left the room, bringing the dinner to an end and taking with him, much to the relief of all those remaining, the fear.

'I'll be fine, dear boy,' Gaius insisted as he and Sabinus came to the Forum Romanum, its flagstones wet from a light drizzle, glowing in the light of the many torches of their bodyguards and those of other groups passing through on their way home. 'It's only half a mile up the hill and, besides, I've got Tigran's lads looking after me.'

Sabinus looked dubious. 'Go quickly anyway.' He slapped the shoulder of the largest and most bovine of the four men with flaming brands accompanying them. 'Don't pick any fights, Sextus, and keep to the better-lit thoroughfares.'

'No fights and keep to the better-lit thoroughfares; right you are, sir,' Sextus said, slowly digesting his orders. 'And give all the lads' greetings to Senator Vespasian and Magnus when you see them.'

'I will do.' Sabinus clasped his uncle's forearm. 'We leave for Aquae Cutillae at the second hour of the day, Uncle.'

'I'll be at the Porta Collina, waiting with my carriage. Let's hope my sister can hang on for the two days it'll take us to get there.'

Sabinus smiled, his round face, semi-shadowed in the torchlight, was thoughtfully sad. 'Mother is very resolute; she won't cross the Styx until she's seen us.'

'Vespasia has always been a woman who enjoyed trying to dominate her menfolk; it wouldn't surprise me if she died on purpose, before we arrived, just to make us feel guilty at being forced to delay our departure by a day.'

'It couldn't be helped, Uncle; the business of Rome takes priority over personal affairs.'

'It was ever thus, dear boy, ever thus. I shall see you tomorrow.'

Sabinus watched his uncle make his way through a colonnade, into Caesar's Forum at the foot of the Quirinal and then disappear from sight, with his bodyguards surrounding him like four torch-bearing colossi, warding off the dangers of a city made feral by night.

With a prayer to his lord Mithras to preserve his dying mother for just two more days, he turned and headed the few paces to the Capitoline Hill and the Tullianum at its base.

'How is he, Blaesus?' Sabinus asked as the iron-reinforced wooden door to the prison was opened by a heavily muscled, bald man, wearing a tunic protected by a stained leather apron.

Blaesus shrugged. 'I haven't touched him, prefect; I hear the odd moan from down there but other than that he's been quiet. He certainly hasn't volunteered to talk, if that's what you're asking.'

'I suppose it was.' Sabinus sighed as he sat down on the only comfortable chair in the low-ceilinged room and looked at a trapdoor towards the far end just visible in the dim light of an oil lamp set in the middle of the sole table. 'Well, we'd better get him up then and carry on. I think we'll try slightly stronger encouragement this time; I need the answer tonight as I'm leaving the city for a few days tomorrow morning.'

Blaesus beckoned to a corner. A hirsute giant of a man, dressed only in a loincloth, unfurled himself from where he had been curled up on a pile of rags in the shadows; he held a bone in one hand whose provenance Sabinus did not like to guess at. 'Down you go, Beauty,' Blaesus said as he hauled on a rope that raised the trapdoor. 'Bring him up and don't bite him more than once.'

Beauty grunted, his face, flat as if it had been pummelled by a spade, cracked into a leer and he nodded furious understanding of his instructions, dropping his bone. Sabinus watched the monstrosity lower himself through the floor and out of sight, revolted by his grossness and briefly wondering what his real name was before deeming it far beneath his dignity to ask.

A cry of pain echoed around the bare stone walls, emanating from the cell below, which was the only other room in Rome's public prison; the cry was followed by a deep snarl, which Sabinus took to be Beauty encouraging his charge to move. A few moments later, the head of the only occupant of the Tullianum appeared through the hole in the floor, his arms pulling himself up, wriggling his body in his desperation to get away from the hideous beast below him. After a couple more racing heartbeats of scrabbling, the terrified prisoner emerged, whole but naked, from the dark pit below, his long hair and moustaches matted with filth.

'Good evening, Venutius,' Sabinus crooned as if the sight of the prisoner was the most pleasing thing in the world. 'I'm so pleased that you managed to avoid becoming Beauty's dinner; now perhaps we can get back to what we were discussing this afternoon.'

Venutius drew himself up; the muscles in his chest, thighs and arms were sculpted and pronounced, and, despite his nudity, he managed to exude an air of dignity as he looked down at his gaoler. 'I have nothing to say to you, Titus Flavius Sabinus; and as a citizen of Rome you can do nothing to me until I've exercised my right to appeal to the Emperor.'

Sabinus smiled without humour. 'You betrayed that citizenship when you led the Brigantes in revolt against Rome; your citizenship, as I told you earlier, is revoked and I don't think you'll find anyone who would argue against a traitor having his legal protection removed. The Emperor is unaware of your presence in Rome, which is just as well for you as I believe he would order your immediate execution. So, I'll ask you again, nicely, and for the last time: who gave you the money to finance your rebellion in Britannia?'

Venutius flinched and moved away from the trapdoor as Beauty reappeared, snarling softly to himself in what could be described as a form of singing as of one happy in his work. 'I'm protected by someone very close to the Emperor; you can't touch me,' Venutius said once Beauty had retrieved his bone and retired to his rags to gnaw on it.

'And I've been asked by someone very close to the Emperor to find out where all your cash came from.' That, Sabinus knew, was a lie; however, it was close enough to the truth for it to be believable. 'And that someone is very anxious to find out quickly; tonight in fact.' Sabinus nodded to Blaesus.

'Beauty!' Blaesus shouted in a commanding voice. 'Put the bone down.'

The monster growled deep and long, as he, with obvious reluctance, complied with his master's will.

'He'll start getting hungry soon if he's not allowed to gnaw on his bone,' Sabinus observed to Venutius, who looked sidelong at the hair-covered thing in the corner, concern showing in his expression.

A couple more growls caused Venutius to glance at Sabinus before looking back at Beauty. 'No one financed my rebellion, it was my own money. It was after my bitch of a wife, Cartimandua, replaced me as her consort with that upstart, Vellocatus, I decided to have my revenge and remove her; which I did with pleasure.'

'But it cost a lot of money to raise so many warriors and to keep them with you; and then taking on the survivors of Cartimandua's army was yet more expense.'

Beauty growled again and let out a reverberating fart as he got to his feet, slavering at Venutius.

Venutius spoke quickly: 'I found Cartimandua's hoard, there was plenty in it; all freshly minted silver denarii – tens of thousands of them – as well as hundreds, perhaps thousands of gold aurei.'

'Roman coinage that you then used to rebel against Rome,' Sabinus observed as Beauty began to lumber across the room.

Venutius' face now registered an unusual thing to see in the expression of a Britannic chieftain: fear. 'I couldn't stop once I defeated Cartimandua. My men were stirred up to it by the druids; Myrddin, the chief druid of all Britannia, came amongst us. To keep my position I had to lead a rebellion against Roman rule.' Venutius started to back away from Beauty, who glanced over to his master for reassurance that he was, indeed, doing what was expected of him.

Blaesus smiled, inclining his head at his pet to encourage him.

Venutius now had his back to the wall; Beauty, snarls grinding in his throat, was almost upon him. 'I didn't have any choice.'

'Yes you did; you could have fled here to Rome, to your benefactor, and thrown yourself at the mercy of the Emperor. Instead you used all that newly minted money against the Emperor and now you try to blame the druids.'

With a surprisingly agile bounce, Beauty pounced on the Britannic chieftain, his snarl turning into a hunger-fired roar. Venutius screamed as he was thrown flat on his back with the monster astride him, clawing at his chest.

Sabinus got to his feet and stood over the scene from which nightmares are woven, his face unmoved by the potential horror. 'So where did that money come from?'

'It was a loan!' Venutius screamed as Beauty's jaws opened, teeth honed by bone, and his head dropped towards him.

'And your wife's?'

'The same; now call this thing off!'

With a guttural rumble of satisfaction, Beauty clamped his teeth into the muscular flesh of Venutius' pectoral and, shaking his head like a beast at its prey, began to rip at it.

With cries that would have disturbed the peace of Hades, Venutius howled for mercy, sobbing with the terror of being devoured by a thing. As Beauty's jaws worked, so did Venutius' shrieks increase, his fists beating uselessly on the beast's furred back and head, his eyes looking up at Sabinus, pleading.

'Who gave you and your wife your loans?' Sabinus asked with an enquiring furrowing of his brow.

Beauty wrenched his head back and blood arced above it, black drops in dim light.

Venutius stared in horror at the lump of dripping meat dangling from the hideous, masticating jaws. His eyes rolled as he watched Beauty chewing on his own precious flesh; then he screamed once, even louder than previously: 'Seneca!'

PART I

Aquae Cutillae, November AD 58

CHAPTER I

SHE WAS DYING; there was no doubt about it in Vespasian's mind as he looked down at his mother, Vespasia Polla. Late afternoon light, seeping through the narrow window above her bed, illumined the small bedroom, simply furnished, that was to act as the starting point for Vespasia's last journey. Her face, with skin the texture and hue of wrinkled tallow wax, was peaceful: her eyes were shut, her thin lips, dry and cracked, trembled apart with each irregular breath and her long, undressed grey hair lay spread upon the pillow, arranged so by one of her body slaves in order that there would still be feminine dignity in death.

Vespasian increased slightly the pressure on the frail hand that he held in both of his as he said a prayer to his guardian god, Mars, that the messenger he had sent to Rome had made good time and his brother and uncle would arrive before she had need of the Ferryman's services; he promised a white bullock to the deity should this be so.

Vespasian felt a hand on his shoulder; he looked up to see Flavia, his wife of nineteen years, standing next to him.

His prayer had been so intense that she had entered the room without his noticing. Her make-up and jewellery were lavish and extensive; they were complemented by a high and ornate coiffeur and a crimson stola and saffron palla of the finest wool that allowed her comely form to be admired. Vespasian felt a twinge of annoyance at his wife for coming into a dying-chamber dressed as if she were about to entertain guests of the highest rank, but refrained from saying anything as he knew that dressing down would never have occurred to Flavia; instead he focused on family matters: 'Are the boys still out with Magnus and his new hunting dogs?'

'Titus is but Domitian came back with one of the hunting slaves half an hour ago sulking because Magnus had stopped him from doing something; what, I don't know. He then pinched and scratched his sister.'

'Domitilla's had worse from him.'

'She's twice his age and soon to be married; she shouldn't have to take that from a child of seven. I've given him to his nurse, Phyllis, she can restrain him, and I've promised him that you'll give him the thrashing of his life once ...' Flavia trailed off knowing exactly what was preventing her husband from disciplining their youngest son immediately. 'May Mother Isis ease her passing. Shall I send for the doctors again?'

Vespasian shook his head. 'What can they do? Cutting out the swelling in her stomach will kill her quicker than leaving it in. Besides, she sent them away last time.'

Flavia could not resist a snort. 'She always thought that she knew best.'

Vespasian gritted his teeth. 'If you insist on carrying on a pointless feud with a dying woman, Flavia, it would be better to do so in the privacy of your own room and your own head. I am not in the mood, nor do I have the time, for women's petty quarrels.'

Flavia tensed and took her hand from Vespasian's shoulder. 'I'm sorry, husband, I meant no disrespect.'

'Yes you did.' Vespasian returned his concentration to his mother as his wife left the room at an irritated pace; her footsteps faded into the courtyard garden beyond.

For a few days over forty-nine years now, Vespasia Polla had been a part of his life and, as he again squeezed her hand, he thanked her, for he knew that neither he nor his brother would have reached the consulship had it not been for her drive and ambition for her family. His father's side of the family were respectable, rustic equestrians; Sabine in ancestry and accent. Vespasia, however, came from a family that could boast a senator who had reached the rank of praetor: her older brother, Gaius Vespasius Pollo. It had been that connection she had used to launch the career of her sons in Rome and it had been Gaius' relationship with the Lady Antonia, niece to Augustus, sister-in-law to

Tiberius, mother of Claudius, grandmother of Caligula and great-grandmother of Nero, that had propelled them into the mire of imperial politics in which they had managed to swim not sink – just. Both had reached the pinnacle of the Cursus Honorum, the succession of military and magisterial ranks that were the career structure for the élite in Rome, which was far more than most New Men from non-senatorial families could expect; indeed, Sabinus had progressed from the consulship to being a provincial governor and was now the prefect of the city of Rome. Yes, Vespasian reflected, rubbing the thin crown of hair that was all that remained on his otherwise bald head, Vespasia could be proud of her achievement for her family.

Yet there was one thing that she had left undone in Vespasian's eyes: she was going to her grave with a secret; a secret almost as old as him. That secret had been enforced by an oath administered, at Vespasia's insistence, to all who had been a witness to the incident – Sabinus, aged almost five, included. It had occurred at Vespasian's naming ceremony, nine days after his birth and it had to do with the markings on the livers of the sacrificial ox, boar and ram; what these markings were, no one had been able to tell him because of the oath. He knew, though, that his parents had believed the marks prophesied his future for he had overheard them discussing it, in vague terms, as a youth of sixteen; but what was prophesied, he knew not. And now his mother was going to the shaded land beyond the Styx without releasing people from that oath. However, due to certain strange occurrences and prophecies that Vespasian had been subject to throughout his life, he had formed a reasonable idea of what the omens may have predicted for him all those years ago; and it was an idea that was as outrageous as it was implausible with the political settlement as it was and the Principate in the hands of one family.

But, should that line fail, what then? If the Emperor were to die childless whence would a new emperor come?

It had been to this end that Vespasian had been instrumental in bringing about a state of war, still continuing, between Rome and Parthia over the nominally autonomous kingdom of

Armenia. The war was seen by the powers behind the throne as a good thing to help secure the young Emperor Nero's position and Vespasian wanted Nero's position to be secure; he wanted Nero to rule for some time because he had a suspicion, no, it was more than a suspicion, it was a feeling bordering on certainty, that Nero would run to excesses that would make the depravities of his predecessors seem as mere foibles to be shrugged off with indulgence. If that were to be the case then Vespasian doubted that Rome would tolerate another emperor from the same unstable family. And so to whom would Rome look to fill that position? The candidate would have to be of consular rank with a proven military record and there were many men in Rome like that, Vespasian included; but, Vespasian had reasoned, if it were to be someone like him then why not him?

And that was what Vespasia was taking to her grave: the confirmation, or not, of Vespasian's suspicions; and he knew that even if she did regain consciousness he would never be able to get her to change her mind.

'Master?' A voice intruded into his inner thoughts.

Vespasian turned; his slave stood silhouetted in the doorway. 'What is it, Hormus?'

'Pallo sent me to tell you that your brother has arrived.'

'Thank Mars for that. Have our finest white bullock prepared for sacrifice as soon as Sabinus and my uncle have seen my mother.'

'Your uncle, master?'

'Yes.'

'There must be a misunderstanding; it's just your brother arriving, your uncle is not with him.'

Although the atrium of the main house on the Flavian estate at Aquae Cutillae benefited from the underfloor heating of a hypocaust and, despite a raging log fire in the hearth, the chamber still felt chill after the warmth of Vespasia's dying-chamber. Vespasian rubbed his arms as he followed Hormus across the floor, decorated with a pastoral mosaic illustrating the various ways that the family supported itself through working the land. Before they reached the front door, Pallo, the aged estate steward, came in from outside and held it open for Sabinus, dusty and dishevelled from travel.

'Is she still here?' Sabinus asked without any pleasantries.

Vespasian turned and fell in step with his brother. 'Just.'

'Well, just is good enough. I don't think I've ever made the journey from Rome in such quick time.'

'Did you leave Uncle Gaius behind you on the road?'

Sabinus shook his head as they passed through the *tablinum*, the study at the far end of the atrium, and then on out into the courtyard garden. 'I'm afraid not; he wasn't well enough to make the journey.'

'What's the matter with him?'

Sabinus looked at his brother as they paused outside Vespasia's room, his eyes full of concern; although whether that was due to their mother's imminent death or their uncle's illness, Vespasian could not tell. 'I'll tell you after we've watched Mother ... ' He left the sentence unfinished; they were both only too well aware of what they were going to watch their mother do.

Vespasian opened the door and allowed Sabinus to step in first; as Vespasian followed, Vespasia surprised them both by opening her eyes. Her lips twitched into a weak smile. 'My boys,' she croaked, 'I knew that I would see you both together before the end.'

The brothers went to her bedside, Sabinus taking the chair and Vespasian standing at his shoulder.

Vespasia reached out a hand to each of her sons. 'I'm proud of your achievements for our family; the house of Flavius is now a name to be remembered.' She paused for a couple of uneven, wheezed breaths, her eyes flickering between open and closed; neither Vespasian nor Sabinus attempted to interrupt her. 'But it does not stop here, my sons; Mars has spoken. Sabinus, I've left a letter for you safe in Pallo's care; take it, read it and act upon it when you see fit.' Another struggle for breath made the siblings hold theirs until she managed to carry on: 'Although I won't release you from the oath you made all those years ago, the secondary oath that your father made you both swear, not just before Mars but before all of the gods including Mithras, to help each other does, as he rightly claimed, supersede it should it become necessary.' Her hands squeezed those of her sons as her frail frame was wracked by a series of coughs, each more rasping than the previous.

Vespasian raised a cup of water to her lips and she drank, immediately gaining relief.

'And it will become necessary, Sabinus,' Vespasia continued, her voice markedly weaker. 'Because you will need to guide your brother.' She fixed her watery eyes on Vespasian. 'And you, Vespasian, will need to be guided. Indecision could be fatal.'

'I believe that I know the contents of the prophecy, Mother,' Vespasian ventured. 'It's that—'

'Don't try to guess, Vespasian,' Vespasia cut in, her voice now barely more than a whisper. 'And certainly never make your thoughts public; indeed, the fact that there were portentous omens at your naming ceremony should never even be admitted outside the family. You may think that you can guess at the meaning, but I tell you, you can't. There were three livers, three different signs; I've written them all down in Sabinus' letter to refresh his mind as he was so young at the time.' Her eyes closed with the effort of speech, but she pressed on. 'It's what, when and, most importantly, how.'

'Then tell me now, Mother.'

Vespasia seemed to consider that for a few moments as she laboured to draw more breaths. 'To do that would be to tempt the gods. For a man to know the exact course, timing and mode of his destiny would mean that his decisions would be shaped by something other than his own desires and fears; it would unbalance him and ultimately bring him down. A prophecy made is not necessarily a prophecy completed.'

'I know,' Vespasian said, thinking back to what Myrddin, the immortal druid of Britannia, had said to him when he had tried to kill him. 'A man can always accept death voluntarily.'

'A man can also push too hard for the fulfilment of a prophecy. By trying to make it so he can alter the timeframe so that the various factors that are needed to bring it about are no longer in conjunction and so therefore the whole thing can never be. I made all the witnesses swear that oath for two reasons: firstly so that it would never reach the ears of those who would jealously guard their position and, secondly, to prevent you from knowing the details in order that you would always follow your instincts rather than a course that you thought had been fabricated for you; that way would have ended in failure and death.' Vespasia opened her eyes, the strain of her many words showing in them and telling also in the shallowness of her breathing. 'What you may suspect will come to pass may indeed be so, Vespasian; but it's Sabinus who holds the key as to how and when. And to prevent you from acting precipitously he will guard that knowledge until such time that he deems you ready to receive it, using the oath that your father made you swear to each other. You are bound together now, my sons; now that I am gone, only between the two of you will you have the power to make this family one of the great families of Rome.'

Vespasia's eyes ranged slowly from one son to the other and, as the siblings met her gaze, they both bowed their heads in acknowledgement of her wishes; whilst they did so they felt her grip on their hands strengthen a fraction and then release. When they raised their heads again, they met with the blank eyes of the corpse that had been their mother.

'I'll not! I'll not go! She was never nice to me.' Domitian faced his parents, standing in the tablinum, looking up at them, defiant, his fists clenched, ready to strike. Phyllis, his nursemaid, stood behind him with a hand on each of his shoulders.

'You mean she tried to discipline you,' Vespasian said, attempting to keep his voice level in the face of such insubordination from his youngest son, 'which is exactly what I will do if you refuse to go and pay your respects to the body of your grandmother.'

'You're going to thrash me anyway for what I did this afternoon, so why should I?'

'I'll thrash you twice as hard and for twice as long if you don't.'

The child responded to this threat in an age-old fashion: he stuck out his tongue and then tried to wriggle free of his nursemaid's clutches. Phyllis, although no more than twenty, was wise to the tricks of young boys and had the child by the hair before he had gone two paces.

'Bring him here,' Vespasian said, unbuckling the belt about his waist.

Phyllis, sturdy and with an attitude that would brook no nonsense from children, hauled the writhing Domitian over to his father who pointed at a table. 'On that.'

Grappling with the twisting child, Phyllis managed to manoeuvre him so that he lay on his belly on the table; she had him pinned down by the shoulders, in what was almost a wrestling move, but his legs were free to kick. But Vespasian did not care, such was his anger with his son; it was an anger that was not novel, due to Domitian's constant wilfulness. He wrapped the buckle end of the belt about his right wrist, grasped the other end in his hand, doubling it over, and caught the flaying legs with his other hand, holding them down. With the combined grief of mourning a mother and the outrage at his child for refusing to show due respect to her in death, he thrashed Domitian until the boy's howls brought concern to Flavia's eyes and he restrained himself.

Panting, Vespasian lowered the belt. There was a giggle from behind him and he turned around to see his daughter, Domitilla, peering through the curtains that separated the room from the atrium.

'Thank you, Father,' Domitilla said, favouring him with a radiant smile that put him in mind of Flavia when he had first met her in Cyrenaica, 'that served the little beast right.'

Crowded around the body in the death-chamber, Vespasian stood with Sabinus, Flavia and his three children – Domitian snivelling quietly and Titus, his eldest son, still in his hunting clothes – in contemplation of the deceased, who remained exactly as she had died, untouched until the ritual of death could commence. Outside the room all the family's freedmen and slaves had gathered in the dusk-swathed courtyard garden, ready to play their part in the lamentation.

After a respectable period of reflection, Sabinus, as the eldest blood relative present, stepped forward and knelt down next to Vespasia. 'May your spirit pass,' he whispered before leaning over her, kissing her lips and then pulling the palm of his hand over her eyes, closing them for the last time, thus sealing the passing of the spirit. 'Vespasia Polla!' Sabinus cried, 'Vespasia Polla!'

Vespasian and the rest of the family joined in the calling of the deceased's name and were soon followed by the men in the household outside as the women began to wail in grief, the sound echoing around the house as it grew in intensity and conviction.

Vespasian shouted himself almost hoarse calling his mother's name, but to no avail as she had already begun her final journey and was now beyond hearing.

When Sabinus deemed the grieving to be sufficient, he got back to his feet and placed his hands under the arms of the corpse as Vespasian took hold of the ankles; between them they lifted Vespasia from the bed and laid her on the ground. This final duty done, the menfolk left the corpse in the charge of Flavia and Domitilla, along with the rest of the women for washing and anointing before being dressed in her finest attire and then brought into the atrium to lie in state with her feet pointing towards the front door.

'So it's to be tomorrow then,' Magnus, Vespasian's friend of many years despite their very different social status, said as Sabinus concluded the final prayer at the household altar in the atrium, having placed a coin under the tongue of his dead mother.

'Yes,' Vespasian replied, pulling down the fold of his toga with which he had covered his head during the religious ceremony. 'Pallo is going to have the slaves work all night to build a pyre for her and assemble her tomb.'

Magnus' lined and battered face, moulded over sixty-eight years, creased into a questioning aspect; his left eye, a crude glass replica, stared at Vespasian with the same intensity as his real one. 'Assemble her tomb? Do you mean you've already commissioned it? Before she was even dead?'

'Well, yes, evidently, otherwise the slaves wouldn't be able to put it together tonight.'

'Wasn't that a bit previous, if you don't mind me saying, sir? I mean, what if she had got better? Might it not have looked as if you were actually hoping that she would die and were so keen on the idea that you'd got everything ready because you couldn't wait?'

'Of course not; a lot of people order tombs in advance because you can get a better price from the stonemasons if you're not in a hurry for it.'

Magnus scratched his grey hair and sucked the air through his teeth, nodding his ironic understanding. 'Ah, I see, economising in death; very wise. After all, she was only your mother; you wouldn't want her to cause you too much unnecessary expense now, would you?'

Vespasian smiled, used to his friend's criticisms of his use – or lack of it – of his purse. 'It makes no difference to my mother whether her ashes are placed tomorrow in a tomb or if they hang about in the casket for four or five days while a stonemason builds exactly the same tomb for twice the money.'

'I'm sure it don't,' Magnus agreed as the rest of the family started to make their way, past Vespasia's body seemingly at sleep on her bier, to the *triclinium* where the household slaves waited to serve dinner. 'But perhaps propriety should occasionally take precedence over thrift, at least in matters concerning the death of family members; you don't want to set a bad example to the next generation as we're none of us getting any younger, if you take my meaning?'

'Oh, I do, indeed; and if by that you're implying that my children might not give me the respect that I deserve in death then you're wrong: Titus and Domitilla will do me proud with my tomb.'

'How do you know?'

'Because I ordered it at the same time as I ordered my mother's and got a discount for commissioning two at once!'

Magnus could not help laughing at his friend's self-admitted parsimony. 'I notice you didn't include Domitian in the list of children doing you proud in death.'

Vespasian shook his head with regret as he looked over to his youngest son being led, firmly by the wrist, off to his room by Phyllis, his protests falling on deaf ears as all the family were now as used to them as they were to the spatter of the fountain in the *impluvium*. 'I mustn't write him off but I can't see how he'll ever have respect for anyone or anything that doesn't in some immediate way benefit him.'

'I'd have thought that was an attitude to be proud of in a son; it'd hint at a ruthless ambition.'

'Normally I would agree with you, Magnus; why should anyone waste time on something that was going to prove of no use to them? However, you will have noticed that I used the word "immediate" and I'm afraid that is what Domitian's real fault is: if the gain is not immediate then he doesn't see the point of it. He has no patience and cannot take a long view. In other words, there is no innate cunning for planning and manoeuvring, which is one of the main requisites for success and survival in society; without that he doesn't stand much chance.'

Magnus took a moment in sombre thought before turning his one good eye to Vespasian. 'Do you want to know why I sent Domitian back to the house this afternoon?'

'Do you think I should?'

'It'll probably make you angry, but yes, I think you should; but don't punish the boy for it.'

'Go on then.'

Magnus gestured with his head to Titus to come and join them. 'Tell your father what your younger brother did this afternoon.'

Titus, now eighteen and the image of his father with a powerful chest, a round face with a dominant nose, large ears and eyes that normally twinkled with good humour, looked worried.

'It's all right,' Vespasian assured him, 'I'm not going to do anything about it.'

Titus seemed dubious. 'Well, if you're sure. It's hard to say exactly how it came about but we'd been out hunting for a good three hours without a scent of anything and Domitian was being his usual self, complaining that the dogs weren't trying hard enough, our horses were too slow, the slaves too loud and Magnus was useless at hunting and kept on making the wrong decisions and going the wrong way. Suddenly Castor and Pollux raised their muzzles in the air, got a scent and then bounded off up the hill covered with scrub just beyond the lower pasture.'

'A good place for deer to hide in if they've been disturbed on our grazing,' Vespasian commented.

'Indeed, Father, which is why we went back there, having had no luck the first time around. Anyway, sure enough, a buck and his two does broke from cover and raced on up the hill with the dogs howling in pursuit. But one of the does was heavily pregnant and soon fell behind and Castor and Pollux were on her before Magnus could call them off in order to leave us with a clean kill. Magnus got there quickly and hauled his dogs away but the doe had a lot of bite injuries and the stress had put her into labour.' Titus glanced at Magnus, who urged him on with a nod. 'Well, neither Magnus nor I could kill the doe whilst she was giving birth, it just didn't seem right, I don't know why, so we withdrew a bit and waited as nature took its course. Eventually the thing was done and the fawn was tottering around whilst its mother, despite her wounds, licked it clean. So we decided that the best thing to do was to let the pair go and hope that they would both provide good sport in the future.'

Vespasian felt himself starting to tense up, hoping that what he had just imagined was not going to be the end of the story.

'We hadn't been gone long when Magnus noticed that Domitian was no longer with us; none of the slaves had noticed him go so he must have just let his pony slow so that the hunting party gradually outpaced him.'

Vespasian felt his stomach start to churn now he began to be sure that the story would sicken him.

'Well, we rode back to where the doe had given birth and sure enough Domitian was there, but there was no sign of the doe.' Titus paused and looked at Magnus again.

'The truth, Titus,' Magnus said, 'don't spare him.'

Titus swallowed. 'But the fawn was there, stumbling around; and we could hear Domitian laughing and as we got closer we could see what was amusing him so: he had taken the creature's eyes. It had been alive for less than half an hour and it had been blinded.'

Vespasian fought to contain the rage that welled within him. His throat tightened; the ending was even worse than he had imagined. 'How?'

Titus grimaced and again looked at Magnus, obviously unwilling to go on.

'With his thumbs,' Magnus said in almost a whisper, 'they were covered in blood.' He grabbed Vespasian's arm to restrain him. 'Don't! We told you because you promised to do nothing about it.'

Vespasian struggled against Magnus' grip. 'I'll thrash the little shit to within an inch of his life.'

'No you won't, sir; he's been thrashed enough today from what I hear. But I agree he does need to learn a lesson.'

Vespasian ceased fighting Magnus and let his body relax; his face, however, remained in the strained expression that he had developed during his time as legate of the II Augusta. 'What would you suggest?'

'After the funeral tomorrow morning we should all go out hunting; is there a decent-sized wood on the estate?'

'Yes, over on the eastern edge.'

'Good, because I reckon that with the help of a wild boar we could show him the difference between taking life for amusement or sport and wanton cruelty.'

'Seneca?' Vespasian spoke the name aloud for the second time since hearing it from Sabinus; and still it made no sense.

They were sitting in his private study – a room off the atrium – and were enjoying the warmth of a brazier and a fine vintage of their own estate's manufacture after what had been a subdued meal for obvious reasons.

'That's what he said,' Sabinus confirmed, 'and I've got no reason to suspect he was lying. He was being eaten at the time, after all, and by a creature that would make you believe that it wouldn't finish until every last morsel was tucked away.'

'But why would Seneca want to finance a rebellion by the Brigantes?'

'Venutius didn't say that he financed the rebellion as such; he said the rebellion was financed by a loan from Seneca. I don't imagine that our Stoic friend questioned Venutius too closely as to what he was planning to do with the loan; he doesn't care for niceties like that. All he's concerned about is the exorbitant interest that he charges. He seems to think that he can get away with even higher rates if he lends to provincials.'

'I know; and from all accounts he does.' Vespasian took a sip of wine and remained for a few moments in contemplation. 'What have you done with Venutius?' he asked eventually.

'Nothing; I left him with Blaesus and his pet. I imagine that he'll behave himself with the threat of being Beauty's supper hanging over him.'

'And no one else knows that he's there?'

Sabinus shook his head. 'So, are you going to tell me what this is about?'

Vespasian shrugged and placed his cup down on the desk between them. 'As I told you, I'm doing a favour.'

'Who for?'

'Domitilla's future husband, Quintus Petillius Cerialis.'

'Cerialis?'

'Well, his older brother, actually.'

'Caesius Nasica? Wasn't he the one who defeated and captured Venutius in the first place with the Ninth Hispana? If he had him then why didn't he ask him anything he wanted to know in Britannia rather than send him all the way to Rome? I'm sure they've got plenty of hairy beasts that are only too happy to rip chunks out of people there.'

'I'm sure they have, and worse, as we both know. But the new Governor of Britannia wanted Nasica to get Venutius away from the province as soon as he could because he knew that Cartimandua would find a way to murder her former husband, even if he were kept in secure custody. She's a woman who will never relent until she's had her way.'

'Why worry about her killing him?'

'Because without him Governor Paulinus would have nothing to threaten Cartimandua with: if she doesn't behave herself then he can replace her with an equally legitimate king.'

'Even though Venutius has already rebelled once and now has a hunk of muscle missing from his chest and so would probably be looking out for revenge and therefore the first thing that he'd likely do as king is rebel again?'

'Even then, because it won't come to that as Cartimandua wouldn't dare call his bluff for fear of actually losing her power. Don't forget that, at present, Britannia is not viable as a province. It costs us far more to keep it pacified than what we claw back through taxes and it's not even half conquered yet. We've got to keep as many tribes as we can subdued, by whatever means possible, in order to stand a better chance of defeating the others one by one and thus making the province feasible. There are certain people who feel that we should pull out of Britannia altogether for the financial good of the rest of the Empire; however, another ignominious retreat like that, a mere fifty years after the withdrawal from Germania Magna having been defeated by Arminius in the Teutoburg Forest, might give encouragement to other disaffected areas. Judaea springs to mind, Pannonia is often restless and there always seem to be disturbances in northern Hispania. If we still want to have an empire in fifty years' time then, however misguided the original invasion was, we can't afford to lose Britannia.'

'Indeed; I understand. We keep Venutius safe in Rome as a guarantee that the Brigantes don't cause any trouble whilst Paulinus struggles on with the rest of the conquest and Rome isn't forced into a humiliating retreat with dangerous repercussions. But why the secrecy? It sounds to me as if you're helping Paulinus and Nasica formulate imperial policy without reference to the Emperor; and even though Nero takes very little interest in policy unless it concerns the filling of his treasury or the boosting of his vanity, what you're doing is dangerous.'

Vespasian tapped the side of his forehead with his forefinger and leant across the desk, the flickering lamplight playing in his eyes and warping the shadows on his face. 'Information,

Sabinus; information buys patronage and Paulinus wanted to know something. We've now found out where Venutius' money came from, which is something that we wouldn't have been able to do if he was passed on immediately to the Emperor because Seneca would have intervened to protect his reputation. I can convey that information to Nasica, who will in turn tell Paulinus who will then have leverage enough over Seneca to ensure that he doesn't have to pay a massive bribe if he desires another lucrative position after Britannia. Although how he suspected that the source of the money was someone so close to the Emperor as Seneca, I don't know, but Nasica said that he was adamant that Venutius be kept and questioned in secret. I was happy to help because Nasica's time with the Ninth Hispana will be at an end in a year or so and Paulinus has promised to use his influence to make sure that Cerialis takes over his older brother's position.'

Sabinus finally understood. 'Ah! So you're ensuring that your soon-to-be son-in-law has the status that you feel your daughter deserves; very commendable, but what about the risk of going behind the Emperor's back?'

'If no one knows that Venutius is in Rome then there's no risk of that ever being found out. Once we've buried Mother, I'll come back to Rome with you and take him off your hands.'

'What will you do with him?'

'Something that he really won't like: I'm going to give him to Caratacus; I'm sure that he'll enjoy keeping, in a very small little cell, the man who, along with his former wife, betrayed him to us and I know that he'll take extra special care that he doesn't escape.'

Sabinus grinned at his brother. 'I'm sure he will; no one will find him there. Then, once that matter is out of our hands, we can think about how to avenge the outrage perpetrated upon our uncle.'

With the day's events having been so draining, Vespasian had practically forgotten about the non-appearance of Gaius. 'What happened to him?'

'It was one of Nero's rampages.'

'He got Gaius?'

'Gaius said that it wasn't Nero himself but rather Terpnus the lyre-player; although Nero encouraged him on whilst Otho, Tigellinus and some others held Tigran's lads at knifepoint.'

'Terpnus beat up Gaius?'

'Yes, and pissed all over him and then left him lying in the street, unconscious, with the haft of a flaming torch stuffed up his arse, which they, apparently, considered to be hilarious.'

The brothers looked at each other over the table and reached a silent, mutual agreement before both picking up their cups and downing the contents in one.

'We'll organise it through Tigran,' Vespasian said, wiping his mouth with the back of his hand. 'I'm sure that after his lads have been so humiliated he'll be only too keen to ensure that Terpnus loses the ability to play the lyre.'

CHAPTER II

A DAMP MIST SWIRLED around the front door as Vespasian and Sabinus stepped out of the house the following morning soon after dawn. Sabinus held the waxen funeral mask of their father who had died, seventeen years previously, far to the north in the lands of the Helvetii; Vespasian held the newly crafted one of Vespasia. Following them came the rest of the family displaying the funeral masks of their ancestors and then the body, borne on a bier by the household freedmen. The slaves came last; the household ones and the exterior ones, who could be trusted, free; but the field slaves, whose lives were one long blur of pure misery, remained shackled under the eyes and whips of their overseers.

Crows cawed from up in trees whose topmost branches were barely visible in the weather conditions that seemed to Vespasian to have been sent by the gods specifically with a funeral in mind.

With sedate dignity the procession made its way around the house, past a paddock where Vespasian's five grey Arab chariot horses grazed on the dew-laden grass, and on to where the pyre had been built near Vespasia's newly constructed tomb. Next to it was that of her husband, whose ashes she had brought with her when she had returned to Aquae Cutillae, soon after his death.

As the light grew with the sun cresting the peaks of the Apennines, in whose western foothills the Flavian estate was situated, the bier was placed upon the pyre; Pallo then led a fat sow, coloured ribbons tied around its neck, up to the brothers standing next to the pyre with folds of their togas covering their heads in deference to the deities about to be invoked. Pallo's son, Hylas, followed his father with a tray upon which was placed the necessities for sacrifice.

Sabinus held out his hands, palms upwards, and kept his gaze to the ground; with a voice made flat by the dampening mist, he intoned the ritual ancient prayer to Ceres, the agricultural goddess who was always addressed at funerals.

The sow remained calm during the prayers and hardly stirred as Sabinus took a salt cake from the tray and crumbled it over its head and then poured a libation over the crumbs. It stared at Sabinus with dark, unquestioning eyes as he approached it, with the sacrificial blade in his right hand; it did nothing to try to escape as he lifted its snout with his left hand. It was not until the blade bit into its throat that it recognised the danger it was in but by then it was too late and the blood was pouring from the wicked gash in powerful, heart-pounding spurts. As its veins emptied, so its strength faded and within a score of heartbeats its front legs buckled and its snout crashed into the bloodied earth whilst its hind legs shuddered their last, eventually weakening under the weight they still supported so that they too collapsed and the dying beast rolled onto its side, its limbs twitching feebly.

At a nod from his brother, Vespasian took a flaming torch from one of the freedmen and thrust it into the oil-drenched wood of the pyre. Deep in its centre it was constructed of brushwood and small kindling; this caught with growing fury, emanating heat outwards that transferred into the larger logs around the edge; they soon began to smoulder and then eventually burst into flame, sending spirals of black smoke skywards. With tears welling, Vespasian watched the smoke, the by-product of his mother's physical form's consumption, ascend and then disperse on the breeze. The constant that had been there for him and his brother throughout all their years, the woman who had helped shape their lives by her ambition for the family, had departed; now he and Sabinus were responsible for taking the family forward and he prayed that they would not be found wanting. He lowered his head, a tear fell, and he felt the weight of familial responsibility pass onto the shoulders of his generation.

The sow had been turned on its back and Sabinus was making the belly and chest incisions as the first flames licked Vespasia, and her hair and clothes began to crackle and smoke. As he worked to remove the heart, fire caught all along the corpse and the skin started to blacken and blister. With a prayer to Ceres asking that she deign to accept the sacrifice, he threw the heart onto the pyre so that it landed next to the corpse, hissing and spitting now as it began to be consumed. With a few more incisions of the razor-sharp blade, the liver, richly brown, emerged from the chest cavity, dripping with blood. Sabinus examined it and found it to be perfect; he showed it to the congregation, so that they too could witness it as being so, before throwing it, after the heart, into what was now a raging conflagration hiding all signs of the melting corpse. Now the only evidence of Vespasia was the smell of crisping and then burning meat as the mourners took steps back to avoid the scorching heat.

The sacrifice made and the goddess appeased, Hylas began to butcher the sow; Sabinus apportioned a small amount to the dead but the most part to the living. With the meat divided and Vespasia's share given to the flames, she was left to burn to ashes as her family departed with their portion of the offering that would provide an ample meal for all later in the day when they returned from the hunt.

Vespasian urged his horse to the crest of the hill and then pulled it up; the beast snorted, breath steaming from flared nostrils, and pranced a couple of high steps as it settled. Vespasian let the pressure off the reins and gazed across the valley of lush pasture, edged by a wood to the right, to the scrub-covered hill on the other side of a gully, on the far side.

'The last time that we were both here together,' Sabinus said, bringing his mount to a halt next to him, 'I had to save you from being strangled to death by a mule thief, you little shit.'

Vespasian laughed at the title by which Sabinus used to address him in youth and cast his mind back to that time when the brothers had, with the help of Pallo and six of their father's freedmen, ambushed and killed a band of runaway slaves who had been stealing mules from the estate. It had been the day after Sabinus had returned from his four years as a military tribune serving with the VIIII Hispana in Pannonia and Africa and it was probably the incident that had begun the siblings' journey from mutual detestation to mutual respect. It had also been the day after he had overheard his parents mentioning the prophecy made at his naming ceremony.

Whatever it was, it was a long time ago but the memory was still clear in Vespasian's mind for it had been the first time that he had come close to death and would have died had it not been for his brother. 'That's where you crucified that boy,' he said, pointing to an area of pasture, just to the right of the wood, in which they had hidden, waiting for the runaways to take the bait of tethered mules with seemingly no minders about.

'Where *we* crucified the boy,' Sabinus reminded him as Titus and Magnus joined them. 'We all did it together; although I do remember you complaining that it was a waste of money crucifying what could be a hard-working field slave.'

The terror on the boy's face and the bestial screeches he had howled as the nails were hammered home had ingrained themselves on Vespasian's memory; it had also been the first time he had witnessed an execution of that sort and, although the boy had been thoroughly deserving of his fate, Vespasian had tried to argue for his life as he had felt an empathy towards him because of their similar ages. However, Sabinus had insisted on the boy's death and they had left him shrieking on the cross with the dead bodies of his comrades and mules beneath him; his cries had followed them most of the way home until they had been suddenly curtailed, most probably by friends finding him and putting him out of his misery.

'I'll let Castor and Pollux loose,' Magnus said, dismounting and taking the leads, from a couple of mounted slaves, of two huge and sleek, black hunting hounds, broad shouldered, with almost square heads and sagging, dripping lips that barely concealed fearsome, yellow teeth.

'They'll be as useless as they were yesterday,' Domitian stated with certainty as he looked down at the beasts from the back of his small pony that was barely taller than the dogs.

Magnus ignored the remark as he rubbed Castor and Pollux's flanks and lavished praise for their beauty upon them; the dogs responded with slimy licks and much tail wagging, evidently genuinely fond of their master. With a final scratch behind the ears of each of the beasts, Magnus detached their leads, slapped them both on their rumps and sent them lolloping across the hill towards the wood to do what they did best: hunt. Behind them the hunting party kicked their mounts into action and cantered after them with Magnus, having remounted, bringing up the rear with Domitian.

Vespasian, with Titus and Sabinus to either side of him, gripped the flanks of his horse with his thighs, feeling the ease of its movements whilst enjoying the wind on his face; his mind was now off the funeral of his mother whose ashes were still too hot to collect. His bow and ash-shafted hunting-spear rattled in their holsters attached to the rear of his saddle and his cloak flapped behind him, pulling at his throat as he watched the two hounds disappear under the eaves of the wood with the two hunting slaves in close pursuit. He followed them in; moisture, collected on the naked branches, dripped down upon him as he slowed his horse to a trot, mindful of its footing amongst the tree roots. From further ahead came the deep-throated barks of Castor and Pollux, although the dogs themselves were now out of view. Seeing that the undergrowth was still thin and the lie of the fallen-leaf-covered ground was clear, he urged his horse into an easy canter, following the direction of the dogs' noise, across the line of the hill, deeper into the wood as Titus whooped with excitement next to him. The hunting slaves could just be glimpsed through the cover, fifty or so paces away, expertly weaving their horses between the trunks as they tried to keep pace with the dogs. Glancing back, Vespasian could see Magnus and Domitian, who was struggling to keep up on his pony, passing under the first of the trees. His horse navigated its own twisting path through the obstacles with Vespasian just guiding it in the direction of the barking. From up ahead came a shout followed by a human cry of fear. Vespasian could see the hunting slaves change direction and head downhill as Castor and Pollux's barks became fiercer with growls rolling in their throats.

Vespasian tugged on the left rein so that his mount followed the slaves downhill, a sense of urgency growing unbidden within him as he ducked and dodged overhanging branches; Titus and Sabinus came with him, their heads low about the horses' necks.

A guttural, rattling snarl accompanied by a human howl of pain followed by the growl-barks of dogs fighting caused Vespasian to lose all caution and accelerate his mount forward as something unseen fizzed past him. He crashed through the wood, branches whipping about him, as the canine frenzy became increasingly more savage; the hunting slaves had dismounted, at least that's what he assumed, as he glimpsed their horses running off unaccompanied. Breaking out into a small clearing he saw a flurry of shiny black fur twisting and writhing on the ground on what looked to be, at first glance, a red mattress but after a moment he realised was the bloodied body of a horribly mauled man; the sheen to the dogs' pelts was his blood. Just next to the carnage, one of the hunting slaves knelt over his companion who lay on his back; an arrow protruded from his shoulder and another was stuck in his gut. As Vespasian jumped from his horse and rushed forward, the kneeling slave juddered and went suddenly rigid, his eyes wide open; he dropped his companion's hand and, with a slow start that quickly accelerated, keeled over to lie on his side exposing a shaft buried in his temple as yet another unseen object hissed within a couple of paces of Vespasian's head.

'To your left, Father!' Titus shouted.

Vespasian glanced in that direction to catch glimpses of a couple of figures, dressed in the colours of the forest, pelting away, bows in hand, jumping obstacles and swerving around trees. 'After them, Titus,' he ordered as he ran towards the dogs, hoping that there may be a little life left in the victim; enough, perhaps, to answer a few questions. But whether there was or not he could not tell and he did not dare risk coming between Castor and Pollux and their prey, so reluctant did they seem to desist from their ravaging; one, although Vespasian could not tell which, so covered in gore were they, had an arrow embedded in its hind left thigh.

'I'll sort them out, sir,' Magnus called, jumping from his horse and putting two fingers to his teeth as Sabinus went crashing through the wood after Titus. A shrill whistle rent the air, changing note up and down; the dogs reacted immediately, the snarls tailing off and their bloodied teeth leaving the fresh meat of their victim who was, much to Vespasian's annoyance, obviously dead. They turned to look at their master and immediately the one with the arrow wound began to whine. 'What have they done to you, Castor, you poor boy?' Magnus said, getting down to his knees and taking his wounded dog's head in both hands. He looked down at the mangled corpse of the dogs' victim and spat at his ripped face. 'Whoever you are you deserved what you got for shooting one of my dogs, arse-sponge!'

Magnus eased Castor around and examined the entry wound, pulling gently on the shaft; the hound whimpered but made no move to savage its master for causing it more pain. Looking relieved, Magnus hugged the dog and kissed its broad shoulders whilst tightening his grip on the arrow. 'You'll be fine, Castor; it went in at an angle and hasn't touched the bone.' Castor yelped, brief and high-pitched, as his body stiffened; his head turned, jaws open, and began to lunge at Magnus. But Magnus held up the arrow and the hound checked itself, recognising that its master had done it a service and not a mischief and, rather than attack Magnus, it licked his face before turning its tongue's attention to the open wound. 'That's a good boy,' Magnus said as if talking to a favoured slave or a small child.

A groan from behind him took Vespasian's attention away from Magnus and his dogs as he remembered that one of the hunting slaves was still alive. He lay, breathing in ragged gasps, lying on his back staring up at the canopy, a hand clutching each of the arrows piercing him.

'What happened?' Vespasian asked, kneeling down next to him.

The slave turned frightened eyes onto his master. 'The dogs got their scent, master. There were four of them butchering a wild boar carcass. But they ran when they heard us. Three escaped.' He indicated with his head to the savaged man. 'He was the fourth. As the dogs brought him down, Gallos and me went after the other three but ...' He looked miserably at the two shafts piercing his body.

Vespasian squeezed the slave's arm. 'Lie still; we may be able to save you if we get you back soon, before you've lost too much blood.'

The slave nodded, smiling faintly, evidently aware of the remoteness of that possibility as Vespasian suddenly realised that there was somebody unaccounted for. 'Where's Domitian, Magnus?'

Magnus stood and looked around. 'I don't know, sir; the last time I noticed him was when the dogs went crazy, he was behind me.'

Vespasian looked back in the direction whence they had come; there was no sign of his young son or his pony. Hoof-beats from down the hill to his right gave him a moment of relief until he saw Sabinus returning, alone and at speed.

'Where're the boys?' Vespasian asked.

Sabinus pulled his mount up to a skidding halt. 'Titus is fine; he had his horse shot from under him but not before he brought one of them down; he's stayed with the bastard. You need to come quickly as we have rather a delicate situation on our hands.'

'Shit!' Vespasian swore as the reality of the predicament that Sabinus had explained to him became apparent. He stood at the eastern edge of the wood looking down the slope to the gully that was the limit of the Flavian lands.

'You see?' Sabinus said, dismounting next to him.

'The bastards!' Magnus growled, hauling a straining Pollux back by the lead; Castor stood gingerly on three legs next to him, shivering slightly and making no attempt to pull his master away down the hill.

'What do we do, Father?' Titus asked; his left hand had a firm grip of the hair of a man kneeling in front of him and his right hand held a blade to his throat.

'Nothing hasty; keep your prisoner alive and safe and in full view of those cunts.' Vespasian stared at the two men, just a hundred paces away; one held a bow ready to release an arrow at him whilst the other held a squirming small figure by the throat and grinned. Domitian's shrieks of fear and protest echoed around the valley; his pony lay dead halfway down the hill close to the body of Titus' horse.

'Give us one good reason why we shouldn't fillet the boy,' the man holding Domitian shouted.

Vespasian stepped forward and held out his hands to show that he was unarmed. 'If you do then things will go badly for your friend here.'

'What if he ain't our friend? What if we really don't like him?'

'What if we really don't care for the boy? What if we could well afford to lose a slave born on the estate? A slave we haven't even had to pay for.'

'Slave? If this is a slave then you're far too generous with your clothing; his tunic is very finely spun.'

'I like my boys to be well dressed; now I suggest we have a simple exchange of prisoners and be on our separate ways.'

'I'm not a slave,' Domitian shrieked; his high voice sharp with indignation. 'Tell them to let me go, Father, and then crucify them.'

'Father, eh?' the man holding Domitian said with a leer, picking the boy up off his feet and looking closely at his face. 'Well, well; looks like we've struck lucky, Tralles.'

'It certainly does, Cadmus,' his bow-wielding companion agreed, 'it certainly does.'

'So that leaves us in a very interesting position, I'd say. I wonder what those fine gentlemen up the hill think.'

Vespasian took another few paces forward. 'Where do you come from and what do you want?'

'I don't think that you're in the position to be asking us questions,' Cadmus observed, allowing Domitian's feet to touch the ground again. 'But seeing as you did ask, we want you to release our mate and then we'll start talking about how much you're prepared to pay for this little runt.'

'If you think that I would be that stupid then we could be here for quite some time. Here's what I'm prepared to do: you release my son and I'll release your mate.'

'And how do we profit from that?'

'With your lives. Harm my son and you'll be dead within a hundred heartbeats; sorry, you'll be caught in that time and then you'll start dying. You'll be dead within five hours, perhaps a few more.'

Cadmus laughed, hollow and without mirth. 'You'll not catch us; once we're across the gully and on that hill we'll travel much faster than you ever could.'

'I'm sure you will if you get across the gully; but can you do that before the dogs catch you? Unless I'm completely mistaken, you're on foot; you won't make it and you'll suffer a very unpleasant last few hours.'

Cadmus looked at his companion whose bow began to waver as if he were not sure where to aim it.

Vespasian pressed his case, taking advantage of their uncertainty. 'So, it's like this: touch the boy and you're dead, release him and one of you will live whilst the other will have a swift death.'

The two brigands stared back up the hill frowning as if they had not heard correctly.

'That's right,' Vespasian said, 'my terms have just gone up; because you seem unable to come to a sensible decision one of your lives is now forfeit and that'll be the slowest of you.' He pointed to Pollux still straining on his leash. 'I'll tell you what: I'll make things easier for you. Titus, bring our friend here.'

Titus brought the prisoner to his father who, without hesitation, pulled his knife from his scabbard and, yanking the man's hair back, ripped his throat open and then stood, holding him up so his companions could see as the blood poured forth. 'He was lucky,' Vespasian shouted, 'because that was an easy death.'

This was too much for the brigands who turned and fled, dropping Domitian on his arse and loosing a wild shot that buried itself in the ground ten paces in front of Vespasian.

Magnus slipped Pollux's leash and the hound bounded off down the hill, barking deeply and accelerating at a considerable pace as Vespasian, Sabinus and Titus reached for their horses' reins, remounted and moved off in a single motion. Magnus hurtled after them on foot.

One glance at the four-legged hunter behind them was enough for Cadmus and Tralles to start hauling at one another, trying to make the other fall behind. With Vespasian, Sabinus and Titus in pursuit, Pollux sped past Domitian, who was threatening all manner of high-pitched retribution to his erstwhile captors, and quickly gained on the two fleeing brigands, now just twenty paces from the gully.

With a backhanded swing, Tralles brought his bow crashing across the bridge of Cadmus' nose, sending him, with a terrified howl, tumbling to the ground and, within a few quickening heart-beats, right into the jaws of Pollux.

Whether the hound had sensed, and therefore been angered by, the worry that Cadmus had caused his master and his master's friends or whether its canine mind had set itself on some course of revenge for the harm done to its companion or whether it was just that its blood was up after the fury of another chase was uncertain; what was certain, however, was the viciousness with which Cadmus was attacked. Not even in the circus had Vespasian witnessed such a blur of claw and jaw as the brigand was bitten, torn, mauled and ripped to the accompaniment of human and bestial cries of pain and anger, respectively, that were so similar and intense as to meld perfectly until it was impossible to tell man from hound as one complemented the other in macabre harmony.

Vespasian sped down the hill. 'See to your brother, Titus,' he shouted as he passed his younger son whooping and clapping at the sight of the blood and flesh flying from the two beings joined in the frenzied and savage dance of hunter and prey. 'Call Pollux off, Magnus!'

Magnus whistled as he ran, the notes rising and falling, but to no avail as they did not penetrate the noise emanating from the hound and its victim. It was Sabinus who got there first but, as he dismounted, Pollux briefly took his attention away from a writhing Cadmus to turn and roar a warning at him not to interfere; Sabinus did not need to be told twice nor did Vespasian, once he arrived, feeling it wise not to try to do anything whilst waiting for Magnus to get there other than watch the beast gnaw, with satisfied guttural growls, on the forearm of the screaming Cadmus as he held it over his face to protect what was left of it.

'Off, Pollux! Off!' Magnus yelled as he came panting down the hill; he tried another shrill whistle that this time seemed to penetrate the hound's consciousness as it began to cease. 'Get off him, you disobedient dog.' Magnus reached down and grabbed Pollux's collar, hauling him off the mangled Cadmus who, apart from his boots, was now as good as naked, his clothes bloody rags and his skin shredded and smeared in gore; he was, though, unbelievably, still alive and stared in horror, with his one remaining eye, at the dripping jaws of Pollux who was being reprimanded as if he were a puppy who had peed on his master's foot.

'You do as you're told next time, you bad boy,' Magnus scolded, smacking his dog on the muzzle causing it to whimper and hang its head, looking up at its master with sorrowful eyes.

Sabinus looked to where Tralles was making his way swiftly up the hill and away. 'Do you think Pollux could catch him, Magnus?'

'Don't,' Vespasian said before Magnus could reply. 'I gave my word that one of them would live.'

Sabinus grunted. 'As you wish; it was your son that was in danger.'

Vespasian knelt down next to Cadmus and asked conversationally: 'What were you doing on my estate, Cadmus?'

Although obviously in great pain, Cadmus formed his ruined face into a sneer.

Vespasian sighed, irritated; he stuck a finger into a rip in Cadmus' cheek and pulled, tearing it open even further. 'Do you remember what I said just now about you having a very painful last few hours? Well, there's a taste of it. Now, I'll ask you again: what were you doing on my estate?'

'Hunting.' Cadmus spat out the word.

'An expensive and painful trip.'

'As it will prove to be for you.'

'I doubt it.'

'Oh, but I don't; not once the Cripple comes back to this area and hears of this. He'll avenge me and he's a very patient man the Cripple is; he doesn't mind if things don't move fast because he can't either. So speed is never an issue for him, you see; he'll take his time.'

'Which is more than you will,' Vespasian observed as Titus arrived with Domitian.

Immediately the boy leapt forward, not towards his former captor but at Vespasian, landing on his back and beating him about the head and shoulders. 'You would have let them kill me! You didn't try to buy my life!'

Titus pulled him off as he shouted accusations and tried to claw at his father's face.

Vespasian stood, turned and slapped the boy about the ears until he stopped his noise. 'Listen, son; it was your pride that put you in the greatest danger. I could have made them believe that you were an unimportant slave despite your dress, but you just couldn't bear it, could you? No, you just had to let them know how important you were and in doing so upped the stakes. We could have had a very neat little exchange of prisoners if you had kept your mouth shut but you just couldn't, could you? You couldn't see beyond the immediate present and your pride wouldn't allow people, people who don't even matter, to think that you were a slave. Therefore, you forced me into a position where I had to out-bluff them and that could have gone very, very wrong and you would have been the first to die, you stupid little boy. You've as much sense of strategy as one of Magnus' dogs! And that's being kind.'

The vehemence of the diatribe shocked Domitian into silence.

'I hope that one day you'll be able to look back at this and learn from it.' Vespasian turned back to Cadmus. 'I'll forego the pleasure of your lingering death because I think that you might just have been instrumental in teaching my son an important lesson.'

'Very gracious of you,' Cadmus whispered, the pain evidently now flooding through him as the shock of the attack wore off. 'But don't expect the Cripple to hold that into account; he's not known for his mercy as none was ever shown to him.'

Vespasian knelt again, drawing his knife. 'And if I ever come across him he certainly won't be receiving any from me.'

'Let me, Father,' Domitian demanded whilst Titus held him back.

Vespasian turned to his younger son. 'You will do nothing, Domitian, other than what you are told and now I'm telling you to keep silent.' He put the knife to Cadmus' chest and rammed it through his heart.

The last of the scalded bone fragments were consigned to the urn atop the heap of fine ashes and Sabinus replaced the lid. Using a taper, Vespasian melted wax so that it fell around the rim of the urn, sealing it. Once the wax had solidified, Sabinus placed the urn into the opened tomb and then began a series of prayers before that too was closed and Vespasia's passing was complete. The brothers could then walk away, their duty to their mother done.

But Vespasian had one more thing to do in honour of his mother. 'Hormus,' he called to his slave standing with the rest of the household, 'come here.'

'Yes, master,' Hormus replied, as if he was reviewing in his head incidents in which it could be said that he had been at fault that day.

As Hormus approached, Vespasian drew a scroll and what looked like a piece of felt from the fold of his toga. 'Hormus, you have been my slave for fourteen years now and served me faithfully.'

Hormus' eyes filled with tears as he and all present could guess what was about to happen.

'You have passed the age of thirty and are now eligible for manumission.' Vespasian handed Hormus the scroll that confirmed his freedom and the felt hat, the *piletus,* which was the physical sign of it. 'Take these in honour of my mother and may you, in her memory, carry on serving me with the same faithfulness as a freedman as you did when a slave.'

Hormus fell to one knee and kissed his master's hand. 'I shall, master, as all the gods are my witnesses, I shall.'

Vespasian stroked Hormus' hair and then helped him up. 'Your first duty as a freedman is to supervise a slave to pack my things as we're leaving for Rome.'

'Yes, master; it'll be my pleasure.'

Vespasian pointed to the five Arab greys grazing in the paddock next to the house, his pride and joy since receiving them as a gift, five years previously. 'And tell Pallo to have the stable slaves ready my horses for the journey.'

'Indeed, master; will they be going back to the Greens' stable?'

Vespasian beamed at his treasures: 'Yes, and so much the better for some time out in the country. Magnus will see to their return.'

Hormus inclined his head and went about his tasks.

'That was a surprise,' Sabinus said as the rest of the household returned inside.

'He deserved it and I thought that here and at this time was a suitable place to do it.'

'Yes, here was a good place to choose,' Sabinus said, looking around at their land. 'I don't know when I'll get the chance to come back here again, what with my duties in Rome and my estate at Falacrina.'

'I'll come as often as I can to make sure that prayers are spoken over the tombs; and I'm sure that Uncle Gaius will want to come out here as soon as he can to pay his respects to his sister.'

'Once justice has been seen to be done.'

'Indeed, Sabinus; once justice has been seen to be done. We've much to do in the coming days.'

PART II

Rome and Baiae,
November AD 58–March AD 59

CHAPTER III

'DEAR BOYS, I shall get over the bruising, and the cuts will heal as will the soreness from the splinters in my ... well, you know where; I've had one of my boys try to remove them all but I think he's missed one.' Gaius helped himself to another consoling honeyed cake, popping half of it into his mouth, and then shifted the position of his ample posterior on the deeply cushioned wicker chair, wincing as he did so. 'But what I'll never get over is the humiliation of it all: left unconscious in the street with a torch ...' Gaius shook his head unable to complete the sentence. 'As, apparently, some wag said: like a crude, lopsided model of the Pharos lighthouse protruding from its island in Alexandria.'

Vespasian and Sabinus leant back slightly in their chairs as a blond-haired youth of outstanding beauty set down another platter of cakes on the table, fresh from the oven by the smell of them; the slave's short tunic exposed more than was decent as he leant over.

'That will be all, Ludovicus,' Gaius said, eying the revealed flesh appreciatively before resuming his outraged expression and devouring the other half of the cake. 'It's all round the Senate and beyond; I'm a laughing stock. I've even heard people refer to me as the Pharos behind my back!'

'And there was no question that it was Terpnus who did it?' Vespasian asked once the slave had withdrawn to wait upon his master by the lamprey pond in the middle of Gaius' courtyard garden in his house on the Quirinal Hill.

'None. He was wearing a wig and had a cloth tied around his face but I recognised his voice – I'd just been listening to it for hours. Nero was wearing a curly blond wig and the theatrical mask of a slave in a comedy but he ululated, high-pitched, constantly, like some crazed Fury, if Furies can be male, which I don't think they can. All the others had disguises of varying competence but on such a dark night they were hardly needed; it was their voices that gave them away. But it was Terpnus, may Mars rot him, who committed all the outrages done to my person, including the ...' Unable to vocalise the basest of the outrages, Gaius fortified himself with one of the freshly baked cakes and washed it down with some reviving wine. 'But worst of all was that I was prevented from seeing my sister at the end. Did she ask after me?'

'Yes, Uncle,' Sabinus lied; Vespasia had never quite accommodated herself to her brother's lifestyle, although she had found his status very useful.

'Magnus is here with Tigran, master,' Gaius' steward announced from the door leading into the tablinum.

'Send them through, Destrius,' Gaius said through a mouthful of cake, sending crumbs spraying over the table.

Destrius, a few years older than the slave boy waiting upon them and elegantly handsome rather than ravishingly beautiful, bowed and retired back through the cotton curtains that billowed, after his passing, gently in the fading sun.

Within a few moments Magnus came through them with a man of eastern appearance: a dyed and shaped beard, trousers and an embroidered knee-length tunic with a loose belt, studded with silver discs, from which hung a curved dagger in an ivory and silver scabbard; soft calf-skin slippers and a cap of the same material, covering his ears, completed his attire. Judging by the richness of the rings on his fingers, Vespasian could see that Tigran had done well since taking over as the *patronus*, the leader, of the South Quirinal Crossroads Brotherhood from Magnus seven years previously.

'The horses are back with the Greens,' Magnus said straightaway to Vespasian, forgetting his manners, such was his excitement at the prospect of his favourite team competing in the Circus Maximus again for his beloved Green racing faction after a rejuvenating country break.

'We'll talk about that later,' Vespasian said, indicating with a nod to his uncle the real reason why he had been summoned.

'Oh! Yes; right you are, sir.'

'Magnus! Good to see you,' Gaius boomed, not getting up.

'And you, sir,' Magnus replied, embarrassed by his misplaced enthusiasm.

'And, Tigran, thank you for coming.'

Tigran touched the palm of his right hand to his heart. 'I cannot ignore the summons of my patron.' He nodded at the Flavian brothers. 'Senator Vespasian and Prefect Sabinus.'

'Sit down, gentlemen, and help yourselves to cakes.' Gaius signalled to the slave boy. 'Wine for my guests, Ludovicus.'

'Yes, that's how Sextus described it to me,' Tigran said after Gaius had recounted the incident in full, not sparing his own blushes, 'and I would dearly love to avenge your humiliation, Senator Pollo, as well as redress the insult to my brethren who were held at knifepoint and prevented from protecting you. However, the way I see it is that it would be impossible to do anything unpleasant to Terpnus without running the risk of hurting Nero.'

'Then hurt Nero,' Magnus suggested, 'and hurt him permanently, if you take my meaning?'

'It would mean certain death,' Sabinus said. 'Nero is very well protected. For a start he's always with Tigellinus, Otho and a half dozen others and then there's a unit of Vigiles following his rampage around ready to step in if anyone looks like threatening him; not to mention the Urban Cohort century that I have to have positioned close by. No, you would be killed the moment you tried to attack him.'

'And even if you did murder him and escape with your life at the time,' Gaius said, raising a forefinger in the air and waggling it, 'although there are many who wish for that at the moment, you wouldn't find his successor showing you any gratitude at all; remember what Claudius did to Caligula's assassins.'

'Those that were caught that is,' Vespasian pointed out, looking meaningfully at his brother who had been the one conspirator whose part in the assassination of Caligula had been covered up and kept secret by Narcissus and Pallas in return for the Flavian brothers' help in securing Claudius' position.

'Indeed, dear boy. But the point is that whoever benefits from Nero's death will execute his murderers as it would not do for people to be seen to assassinate an emperor and live; that would be a very unwise precedent to set. The only person who can get away with killing an emperor is the man who succeeds him.'

'I see your point,' Magnus mumbled from behind his wine cup.

'So the question is, how to get Terpnus away from Nero,' Tigran said, running his beard between his fingers.

'He very rarely leaves the Palatine except in Nero's company,' Sabinus informed them, 'such is his dedication to sycophancy.'

'Very commendable,' Gaius observed without irony.

Tigran frowned. 'I could try an arrow shot from a distance.'

Sabinus shook his head. 'No; if you wounded him his companions would get him back to the Palatine, and if you killed him outright it would be very unsatisfactory; the whole point of this is to have revenge by ensuring that Terpnus never plays the lyre again but lives, so that his loss eats away at him.'

Tigran pursed his lips, deep in thought. 'I shall give it serious consideration, gentlemen,' he said eventually. 'You say, Prefect Sabinus, that you have some advance knowledge of when and where Nero's rampages are going to take place.'

'That's correct; it's so that I can order a century of one of the Urban Cohorts to be standing by in the area.'

'Then perhaps you would be so good as to send word to me next time you hear that the Viminal is due to be targeted; especially the western part.'

Sabinus nodded his assent.

Tigran got to his feet. 'My thanks for your hospitality, Senator Pollo. Senator Vespasian, Sextus and four of my brethren are waiting for you outside to help you with that bit of business that Magnus mentioned to me; I trust that they will serve you better than they did your uncle the other night.' With a nod to Sabinus and Magnus, Tigran left the garden.

'Do you think he'll come up with an idea?' Sabinus asked.

Magnus grinned. 'I'd say he's already got one and he plans to execute it on the West Viminal Brotherhood's territory to lessen the chance of retribution falling in his direction; but what it is I couldn't guess. That's the thing about Tigran, he doesn't let on too much, not until he has to, that is. It's what's made him so successful, even more so than I was as patronus.'

'He certainly has more rings than you. So the horses are fine?'

'Yes, the faction-master said that they were in great shape and he'll race them as soon as possible.'

'Good, I'll go and give them a turn or two around the Flammian Circus as soon as I can.'

Gaius looked horrified. 'You don't race them yourself, dear boy, do you?'

'Of course not, Uncle; I just enjoy driving them, in private, obviously. It's good exercise and very invigorating.'

'Let's hope you don't start singing as well.'

'One bad habit is enough, Uncle.' Vespasian got to his feet. 'Come, Sabinus; Sextus and the lads are outside and if we're going to relieve you of that inconvenience we should go now that it's starting to get dark.'

'And why should I not just strangle the treacherous bastard?' Caratacus asked, the ruddiness of his clean-shaven, oval face accentuated by barely supressed ire. 'He and his bitch-queen, Cartimandua, broke every law of hospitality to hand me over to you Romans.'

'*Us* Romans, Tiberius Claudius Caratacus,' Vespasian reminded the former Britannic chieftain. 'Seeing as you are now a citizen and hold equestrian rank, I think you should count yourself as one of us. We don't discriminate against race, as you know – we've even had consuls of Gallic descent – so, as far as I'm concerned, my friend, you are Roman, and therefore you will help me do what is best for Rome and that is to keep Venutius safe so that Paulinus has something to threaten your bitch-queen with.'

Caratacus smiled at his former adversary as they looked down at the filth-encrusted figure of Venutius glaring up at them from inside a cage placed in the corner of Caratacus' cellar in his house on the Aventine Hill. 'I suppose I still get the pleasure of keeping his confinement as uncomfortable as possible.'

'So long as he's kept alive and doesn't have any more bits missing than he already does, then you can do what you will.'

'You'll pay, traitor,' Venutius hissed, grabbing the bars of his cage.

'Me? A traitor?' Caratacus kicked at the cage, catching one of Venutius' hands under the sole of his sandal, cracking a couple of fingers. 'I was resisting the invaders up until the moment that you gave me to them.'

'It was nothing to do with me,' Venutius said, grimacing as he held his broken fingers tight beneath his armpit. 'It was all Cartimandua's doing.'

'She's your wife, and a husband is responsible for the actions of his wife.'

'She *was* my wife until she went to the bed of my armour-bearer, Vellocatus.'

Caratacus sneered. 'That's not what I heard, Venutius. I heard she took Vellocatus into your bed, dishonouring whatever honour was left in it. But it is nothing to me what your domestic arrangements are or have been. You were the King of the Brigantes when I sought refuge there and therefore you,' he pointed with his forefinger at his betrayer, 'were responsible for my safety. *You* should have controlled your wife.' He turned on his heel. 'Come, Vespasian, let's waste no more time on, what we would call in our language, a pussy-whipped weakling.'

Vespasian followed Caratacus out and up the stone steps thinking the term appropriate for one who had allowed his wife to dominate him so. 'There is one thing, though, my friend,' he said as they came out into the moonlight of the stable yard behind Caratacus' house.

'No one should know?' Caratacus questioned with a grin.

'Exactly.'

'That was obvious when you surprised me with him. I still get to know about most things of importance that occur in my homeland; I had heard that Venutius had rebelled against

Cartimandua and that he had replaced her on the throne. And I had heard that Myrddin had encouraged him to carry on his rebellion and take it against Rome but he had been defeated by the older brother of your future son-in-law.' Caratacus shrugged and held out his hands as they entered the house through the back door. 'And then you turn up with him in the night; I had not even heard that he had left Britannia and yet suddenly he's here in Rome, in a cage and guarded, not by soldiers of the Urban Cohorts, but by what I assume are your own personal militia.'

'They're members of the South Quirinal Crossroads Brotherhood who have a strong connection with my family through my uncle.'

'Well, I hope they'll see you back to the Quirinal in one piece. The streets are far from safe these days.'

'I know; my uncle was attacked a few nights ago and outrageously treated.'

'Take my advice, my friend, and leave now. I shall rudely not offer you refreshment of any sort so that you can get on your way. We can carry on our reminiscing about our respective parts in the invasion of my island another time; in daylight hours.'

Vespasian grasped Caratacus' proffered forearm and clenched it, happy not to have to refuse any hospitality as he had plans for the rest of the evening and they did not include refighting old battles. 'Thank you, I always look forward to our talks, Caratacus. I'll be in touch with you once I've been told what we should do with Venutius.'

Caratacus looked puzzled. 'I thought Paulinus wanted him kept in Rome.'

'Yes, he does, for now; but since he's given up the information Paulinus wanted perhaps he might be of more use elsewhere.'

Whether or not Nero had been out on one of his rampages that night Vespasian did not know, for he passed with his escort peacefully between the Aventine and Quirinal Hills by way of the Forum Boarium and the Forum Romanum. His mind, however, was not at peace as he fretted on the truth of what Sabinus and his mother had said on the night of her death. He had not gone into assisting Paulinus with his eyes shut; he had been well aware that what he had been asked to do was indeed, as Sabinus had put it, dangerous. Nevertheless, he had acquiesced, ostensibly for the furtherance of the career of his future son-in-law; but although that had been a strong factor in his calculations, it had not been his overriding reason. That had been far more self-seeking.

For over four years now Nero had been emperor and during that time his degeneration had been slow but palpable; however, in recent months it had been accelerating as he had made the transition from youth to man without the benefit of the restraint of the Cursus Honorum. It had not been Nero's lot to work his way up the ladder, commanding and being commanded in differing ratios the higher one climbed. No, Nero had found himself at the top without ever having to obey an order; he had achieved absolute power but had never felt the threat of such power. He knew not what it meant. And it was because of this that the murmurings against him had grown stronger with every year that passed of his reign; conspiracy was in the air and that was to Vespasian's advantage if his suspicions concerning the omens at his naming ceremony were correct. Therefore, if Paulinus was part of a conspiracy against Nero he was happy to aid it provided his actions could remain secret, which he felt, by giving Venutius into Caratacus' charge, they could.

But Sabinus was right, Vespasian accepted: what he was doing was dangerous; but what concerned him more was his mother's observation that: *for a man to know the exact course, timing and mode of his destiny would mean that his decisions would be shaped by something other than his own desires and fears; it would unbalance him and ultimately bring him down.* Had his decision to act as he had done been motivated by what he thought was prophesied for him, and in which case was he guilty of trying to force it to come true and thus putting it at risk? Or had it been a decision influenced solely by the opposing forces of his genuine fears and desires? Only Mars knew the truth of it and he was unlikely to share it with him as that was always the way of the gods.

Thus his mind whirred as he walked, unsure in his course one moment and then confident the next, as was ever so when contemplating things that are not fully understood. So it was that he came to the Quirinal but it was not to his house in Pomegranate Street that he went but, rather, to a smaller house a couple of streets away.

'Thank you, Sextus,' Vespasian said, handing the ox-like brother a couple of silver denarii, as they waited for the door to be answered, 'buy the lads a few jugs with this.'

Sextus' dim eyes lit up. 'We'll be able to take it in turns with a whore as well as drink our fill for that; thank you, sir.'

The image that his tip had conjured was not pleasant but Vespasian managed to keep his expression dignified as he acknowledged the profuse thanks of the other three lads before turning his back on them as the door was opened by a huge middle-aged Nubian who smiled a white-toothed greeting at him as he bowed. 'Good evening, master; the mistress is entertaining. I will send word that you are here.'

Vespasian acknowledged the doorkeeper with a nod and then stepped through the vestibule and on into the brightly lit atrium belonging to his mistress of many years and the true love of his life: Caenis, the former slave, secretary and surrogate daughter of the Lady Antonia and then secretary to Pallas and then Narcissus and now to Seneca. She was a woman of high intelligence, political cunning and rare beauty whom he had first glimpsed as he had entered Rome as a lad of just sixteen and who had been his lover since soon after that day; his lover and his mistress but never his wife due to the Augustan law prohibiting the union of senators and freedwomen. He sat next to the impluvium watching the water spurt from the fountain, forming droplets in the air that fell like golden gemstones glinting in the lamplight to spatter softly into the pool. How different would his life have been if not for the existence of that law; how different might his children have turned out. Then he dismissed the thought from his mind, as there was one thing of which he was certain and that was he could never regret marrying Flavia, for to do so would be to regret his children and that he could not do – not even Domitian.

It was but a short while until a woman's footsteps echoed through the marble columns and Vespasian drew himself out of his introspection and got to his feet. Caenis, her eyes of sapphire, her skin of cream and her lips so full and inviting, smiled at him and walked quickly into his embrace. He buried his face in her hair and inhaled the musk of her perfume.

'I'm so sorry for your loss, my love,' she whispered, 'I've grieved for you and for Vespasia. To lose a mother is a sore hurt as I found out when mine was ripped from me at such an early age and then again when my mistress, Antonia, who had taken her place, took her own life.'

He kissed her brow. 'It's done and she has passed. Sabinus and I have mourned her and placed her ashes in a tomb next to our father; we can do no more now other than honour her memory.' He pulled back and looked Caenis in the eye. 'And try to forget all the annoying traits in her character,' he added with a grin, 'and how she could manage to get on my nerves just with one look of disapproval.'

Caenis laughed.

'Still, at least it has simplified my life in that I won't have my mother and my wife constantly vying with one another for my attention by pursuing petty female arguments and then coming to me for adjudication.'

'What about your mistress? Where does she fit in the battle for your attention?'

'First and foremost, my love, and I adjudge you to be the most beautiful and attentive.'

'Not attentive enough, it would seem.'

'How's that?'

'I didn't realise that you were back in Rome and I have a couple of dinner guests.'

'I know, the doorkeeper told me; but he didn't say who.'

'He wouldn't know who as they are here incognito.'

'How intriguing.'

'All the more so seeing as when you arrived unexpectedly they said that they would very much like to talk to you if you would put old differences that you have with one of them behind you.'

'Now you really have got my attention.' He creased his brow quizzically. 'Who?'

'Pallas and Agrippina.'

Vespasian made polite enquiries as to the health of the other two guests on the opposite side of the table as slave girls took his toga and sandals, washed his hands and feet and shod him in soft slippers before helping him to recline on a couch next to Caenis and then spreading a napkin before him upon the fine upholstery. All the while he was trying to work out just what it was Agrippina could want of him seeing as she had been his sworn enemy since marrying her uncle, Claudius, and becoming the most powerful woman in Rome. It had been Agrippina who had blocked his career: she had been responsible for his not getting a province to govern, as was his due once he had served as consul. It had also been her doing that his term as consul was just for the last two months of the year, which had been an insult he had been forced to bear. As to her lover, Pallas, he had been Vespasian's greatest supporter in Claudius' court even though he was cuckolding the Emperor by sleeping with Vespasian's greatest enemy.

'I was sorry to hear of your mother's death,' Pallas said, although his face, grey-bearded Greek style, showed no sign of sorrow; in fact, it showed no sign of anything as it remained, as always, impassive. 'She was a fine, respectable woman.'

Vespasian dried his hands on the napkin. 'Thank you, Pallas; she thought very highly of you.'

Agrippina, unsurprisingly, made no gesture of condolence but, rather, nibbled on a chicken thigh. Her dark eyes regarded Vespasian with a cool disinterest that he felt to be a vast improvement on the venom they used to hold when looking at him in the past.

'How is life in the country, Pallas?' Vespasian asked after the pause in the conversation had stretched almost to embarrassment.

'Dull,' Agrippina answered, surprising Vespasian, 'and for the most part pointless.'

'I'm sorry to hear that; I have always had a great fondness for my estates.'

'I can tell your attachment to all things rural by the Sabine burr that affects all your vowels; it's like talking to my swineherd – not that I ever do, naturally.'

Vespasian let the insult wash over him, helping himself to a portion of the chicken.

Pallas put a hand on Agrippina's arm. 'That is not, my dear, how to go about enlisting someone's help.'

That Agrippina should wish to seek his help came as a mild shock to Vespasian; he glanced at Caenis who inclined her head a fraction to signal that she knew and approved of what was to be asked of him.

He took a sip of wine and swilled it around his mouth leisurely; swallowing, he dabbed his lips with the napkin, taking his time, before looking up at Agrippina. 'Why should you think that I would wish to help you and why would you, of all people, wish to seek my help?'

Agrippina's cold eyes lingered on him and her nose twitched in distaste. 'Because, sadly, it would seem that only you are in a position to help us.'

'If that were so it would make me doubly determined to refuse your request; you who's done all you can to block my career.' Vespasian let his hatred show upon his face. 'You, who had the governorship of Africa taken away from me. You, who arranged it that I should have the least prestigious consulship imaginable, and what had I done to deserve that? Offered Messalina a sword so that she could take her own life when I accompanied Burrus and his execution party to where she was hiding in the Gardens of Lucullus; what was wrong with that?'

'It showed sympathy to her; Burrus confirmed that to me later.'

'Burrus was lying to ingratiate himself with you; but I suppose that seemed to work seeing as it was you who got him appointed as the prefect of the Praetorian Guard. But I would no more have shown sympathy to that Fury than I would for the one who replaced her – you. I offered her the sword so that she could finally be in the same situation in which she had placed so many other people, and I enjoyed watching her cowardice at the end and the disbelief on her face when Burrus ran her through. It had nothing to do with feeling pity for her and it certainly did not mean that I would rather not have you as empress, which was the insinuation that I'm told you read into it.' He glanced at Pallas who had furnished him with that information; the Greek was still expressionless. 'What difference does it make to me which Fury is in the Emperor's bed, when she has the time in her busy sexual schedule, that is?'

This was too much for Agrippina; she threw the chicken thigh at him, hitting him on the forehead. 'How dare you speak to me like that, you country-upstart!'

'I'll speak to you however I like seeing as you're the one asking me for the favour.'

'You Sabine mule-herder! My family was—'

'I don't believe that this is getting us anywhere,' Pallas interjected, putting a calming hand onto Agrippina's arm. 'We came here to ask Caenis to intercede with you, Vespasian, on our behalf and then, when you turned up unexpectedly, we thought that we would speak to you directly; I apologise if that seems to have been an unwise decision.' His grip tightened on Agrippina as he restrained her. 'I can understand your reluctance to help us, especially in the light of that display. However, I would appeal to you, Vespasian, to grant us this favour for my sake, considering everything that I've ever done for you and your brother to help your careers.'

'Like sending me off to Armenia on a mission that ended up with me in a cell for two whole years of my life? Or almost getting Sabinus and me killed by hairy-arsed barbarians in Germania Magna? I don't call that being helpful.'

'I got your brother his position as prefect of Rome; surely that's a favour worth repayment?'

Vespasian hid his surprise but his curiosity was piqued; he and Sabinus had been unable to ascertain the identity of his brother's benefactor. It had not occurred to them that it would be the marginalised Pallas. 'I don't believe you.'

The corner of Pallas' mouth twitched up into the closest he ever came to smiling. 'Just because I'm banished from Rome doesn't mean that I've lost all my influence; don't forget, my twelve years as secretary to the Treasury and after that as chief secretary left me a very wealthy man. With more than three hundred million sesterces to my name I'm probably the wealthiest person after the Emperor, certainly wealthier than Seneca, which is a fact that I exploit often, seeing as he will do anything for money. I bought Sabinus' position for ten million sesterces, which I considered to be a bargain.'

'Ten million!' Vespasian could not conceal his confusion. 'Why did you do that?'

'For precisely a situation such as this. The position was coming vacant and no one else was prepared to pay the amount that I offered Seneca, as well as forwarding a sound political argument as to why Sabinus should get the position.'

'Which was?'

'That he had done very well in Moesia and Thracia, perhaps too well, and it would be better if he were brought back to Rome and honoured with a position that would keep him in the city where the depth of his ambition could be monitored. The negative arguments always work better than the positive when dealing with people anxious to hang onto power.'

'As you should know only too well, Pallas.'

Pallas surprised Vespasian by breaking into a genuine half-smile, something he had rarely seen before. 'Indeed; and Seneca quite understood the argument, just as he understood the ten million. So he added the money to his ever-growing fortune and took the argument to Nero; Sabinus was recalled from his province and made prefect of Rome.'

'Very neat; but to what end?'

'To this very end: we need your help and your family owes me a favour.'

'Sabinus owes you the favour, not me.'

'But you are better placed to deliver what we need.'

'In what way?'

'You know Cogidubnus, the King of the Regni and the Atrobates, very well from your time in Britannia.'

Vespasian took a moment to register the Britannic client king whom he had not seen, and had barely thought about, in more than ten years. The man he had defeated on the Island of Vectis off the south coast of Britannia and who had subsequently become his ally and friend. The man to whom he owed his life. The man who had helped him to rescue Sabinus from the druids. 'But my brother also knows him.'

'He does indeed, but as prefect, Sabinus cannot go more than a hundred miles from Rome without the Emperor's permission.'

Vespasian began to have a nasty suspicion that Pallas was once again going to coerce him into doing something against his will. 'Whatever it is I'm not interested, Pallas.'

'What we want,' Agrippina said, taking absolutely no notice of Vespasian's remark, 'is for you to go back to Britannia and speak to Cogidubnus on our behalf.'

'Why?'

'Shortly after I married Claudius, Pallas and I made some investments in the new province; large investments in estates and mines. Their value was low at the time but with good estate managers and mine supervisors we've made them very profitable and they must have tripled in value. We only bought in the Regni and Atrobates' lands as those tribes were very pro-Roman and Cogidubnus was friendly.'

'And he needed the money,' Pallas added, 'in order to start a programme of building works in our style, including his new palace.'

Vespasian could well imagine the proud Britannic King wanting to build a Roman-style residence that he felt was fitting for the monarch of the united tribes. 'So what would you have me do, in the unlikely event that I would agree to do your bidding?' The question was levelled at Pallas as he certainly was not going to do Agrippina's bidding.

'We want you to use your friendship with Cogidubnus to persuade him to buy our investments back.'

'At the current market value,' Agrippina insisted.

Vespasian looked at her for a moment in disbelief before breaking out into laughter. 'You want me to travel all the way to Britannia to try to persuade an old friend, whom I haven't seen for years, to buy back the property he sold you for three times the amount you paid him? Is that what you're asking?'

'Of course,' Agrippina snapped. 'He should be honoured doing business with the mother of the Emperor.'

Vespasian ignored Agrippina's arrogance and looked, instead, at Caenis. 'Were you really going to come and put this daft proposition to me?'

Caenis smiled and stroked his arm so that the hairs rose. 'Of course, my love.'

'Whatever for? You must have known I would reject it out of hand.'

'For a start they've paid me very handsomely to do so.'

'How much?'

'My love, does everything have to come down to money? No, this payment was in a far more valuable currency: information.' She patted a cylindrical, leather scroll-holder next to her.

'Just because you've been paid to present this proposition to me doesn't mean I'll accept it – or even listen.'

'If you don't listen you won't hear the really interesting part.'

Vespasian turned back to Pallas. 'So what's the really interesting part?'

'Ah, I was coming to that.' Pallas paused for effect, taking a sip from his cup and swilling it around his mouth in the manner that Vespasian had done earlier. 'In going you will repay the favour I did Sabinus and that is all very well; but even if you did agree to go I can see by your laughter that your heart would not be in it because you don't think that there is any chance of success.'

'Who's ever going to buy back something for three times the amount he was paid for it?'

'We will take double.'

'Three times!' Agrippina almost shrieked.

'Double, my dear,' Pallas countered, 'and we would still have done well on the deal. Cogidubnus will see that the property is worth more than that so he would be more likely to agree to the deal.'

Agrippina seethed quietly to herself, her eyes boring into Vespasian.

'Although, of course your opening offer will be three times,' Pallas continued, 'but if you get double then the really lucrative part from your point of view will be your reward.'

Vespasian was now becoming interested. 'Which is?'

'Seneca's greed is such that if I can purchase Sabinus' position as prefect of Rome then it would be easy for me to get him to make you governor of Africa.' He looked at Vespasian with his eyebrows raised questioningly.

Vespasian's heart jumped; and then he cursed Pallas inwardly for always knowing what strings to pull to manipulate him as if he were a puppet. 'Africa?'

Pallas inclined his head. 'The very province that was taken away from you.'

'What if Seneca doesn't agree?'

'For another five million sesterces, which is a fifth of the profit that we'll make on the deal should we only double our money, Seneca will do anything. You can't go until the sea-lanes open again next year, so if you're interested come down to Agrippina's estate at Bauli on the Bay of Neapolis after the ides of March and we will give you the deeds to all the properties. Then you can take a ship from Misenum to Forum Julii on the south coast of Gaul as soon as the equinox has passed and the sea routes open.'

Vespasian was shaking his head, unable to believe what he was just about to say. 'All right, Pallas, I'll do it. But one question: why are you both so desperate to sell?'

The Greek stroked his full beard. 'I would have thought that was very obvious: the Emperor's spending is becoming more and more profligate at the same time as the demands of keeping the province subdued are becoming increasingly unaffordable. Put the two things together and what is the obvious conclusion?'

It was not what Vespasian wished for; quite the reverse, in fact. 'But we can't withdraw from Britannia; it would destabilise the whole Empire.'

'Not if we turned it into three client kingdoms with Cogidubnus the king of the southern one, Cartimandua the queen in the north, and Prasutagus of the Iceni, king in the east. Then we could save face by claiming that our mission had been a success and that all the kingdoms nearest the Empire were now our clients, trade had been established and so there was no more need to spill Roman or Britannic blood. That's what I would do and I don't think it'll be long before Nero realises the same thing: it's time to leave Britannia.'

CHAPTER IV

NERO'S EXPRESSION WAS one of ill-concealed lust as he looked Poppaea Sabina up and down.

Otho, next to her, laughed uneasily, the hollowness of it echoed around the cavernous atrium of the imperial palace on the Palatine. 'What did I say, Princeps?' Otho asked. 'Is she not a rare beauty?'

Nero was too distracted to answer.

Acte, who had accompanied the Emperor into the room, stood behind Nero, ignored and seething.

Rather than blush demurely and keep her eyes to the floor, Poppaea Sabina held herself erect, thrusting out her breasts and looking Nero in the eye, her lips, parted and loosely pouted, moist and inviting.

She was, Vespasian thought as he watched the meeting with two score or so other senators who had been summoned to judge between the woman and the voice, indeed a beauty, despite her face being dominated by a strong, straight nose. Her skin was almost milk-white, as if it had never once been exposed to the sun; and it was said – according to Gaius, next to him, whispering in his ear – that she bathed in milk every day to preserve its hue. Black hair ringletted and then pinned atop her head in three ascending crowns contrasted dramatically with her alabaster tones. But it was her eyes that captivated: dark almonds at once innocent and yet full of carnal knowledge, they were an open invitation to both protect and ravage and freely admitted that nothing was too base and nothing too depraved for Poppaea Sabina. She was, in short, designed for pleasure: a sensual vessel to be steered to the port of any of one's desires, however remote, however hard to gain. All those watching the meeting could see her for what she was and they also knew that she had ensnared the Emperor with just one quiver of her lower lip.

Nero tentatively held out a hand and brushed the backs of his fingers along a smooth cheek; the sensuous sigh that issued from Poppaea was audible to all, and none in the room – with the obvious exceptions of Gaius and Acte – could be unmoved by it; many hearts raced and many scrotums tightened.

Nero finally managed to tear his eyes away from the overt promise of unrestrained passion before him and looked at his long-time friend, Otho. 'Now you will judge.' He gestured to Terpnus to approach with his lyre.

Vespasian and his fellow senators braced themselves for the shocking sight of the first man in Rome behaving like a slave or freedman.

A chord was plucked; its sound melodic. A note, in some way related, rumbled in Nero's throat and he launched into a ballad of love that none had ever heard before – or, at least, if they had it was not recognisable.

For how long Vespasian stood and endured he could not tell; all he was aware of was the most excruciating embarrassment of all the witnesses to this bizarre behaviour. Only Poppaea and Otho seemed unaffected: she, appearing to fellate Nero mentally with the wanton poise of her lips and slight movement of her head and he, staring at the Emperor as if enraptured by the feeble series of seemingly random notes that passed his lips. Terpnus plucked away, beaming at his pupil with the pride of a *grammaticus* watching his favourite pupil reciting a long passage of Homer in Greek, whilst Acte endeavoured to attract Nero's attention by flaunting her genitalia, clearly visible through the sheer material that passed for clothing, in his eye-line.

But her endeavour was to no avail as Nero's gaze was fixed on Poppaea's lips and there was no doubt in anyone's mind, as the ode scraped on, what they would be doing before the day was out.

Eventually the ordeal came to a close as the last note expired with a weak growl and Nero looked to his audience who immediately broke out into rapturous applause, some even managing to squeeze out a tear or two, although perhaps they had been aided by the eye-watering ineptitude of the performance. Nero, though, was weeping for joy and taking Terpnus to the imperial bosom and bestowing kisses upon his mentor as he too was overcome with the emotion of it all.

The celebrations went on for an age as none wished to be the first to stop applauding and Nero showed no sign of feeling that he had been lauded enough. He wept and he hugged and he made shows of modesty and surprise and gratitude, each with what seemed to be a well-rehearsed pose until eventually he could refuse no more and, signalling for silence, repeated his triumph.

This time many in the audience copied their Emperor and wept freely as his performance rumbled on whilst the rest stood with expressions of delight or gratitude firmly etched on their faces to cover their disbelief at the depth of Nero's delusion. There was even less to recommend the ballad on a second hearing than there was when it was fresh to their ears; the tune was monotonous and the couplets rarely rhymed or scanned correctly. And it was on the second hearing that Vespasian realised what they were listening to. 'It's his own composition, Uncle,' he whispered to Gaius.

'Dear gods, you're right,' Gaius muttered through the clenched teeth of his fixed grin, his lips barely moving. 'Let's hope we're the only ones to notice.'

On Nero forged, his voice weakening and growing huskier with each verse, Poppaea's bosom heaving next to him as she stared into his face with undisguised animal desire, her thumb toying with the tip of her tongue whilst her spouse continued to regard the Emperor in wonderment.

As the final verse was laid to rest and Terpnus melodramatically plucked the last chord, Gaius stepped forward. 'A composition of your own making, Princeps,' he shouted just as the applause began. 'Inspirational! We are blessed that you have shared it with us.'

There was a pause in the applause as the rest of the audience realised that this was the reality of the affair: Nero had indeed written the ballad, which perfectly explained the direness of its quality. They began to shout out their admiration for his talent and ask why he had kept it from them for so long; but they were too late. Nero, beaming with joy, walked up to Gaius and took him by the shoulders; for a few moments he stared at Gaius as if he were the rarest and most beautiful gem.

'The Pharos is right,' Nero declared, 'it was indeed my own composition.'

'A work of genius, Princeps,' Gaius affirmed, ignoring the use of what he hoped was not becoming his nickname.

'*We* were overwhelmed,' Vespasian put in, 'when *we* realised that it was so.'

'And you, Vespasian,' Nero said, turning to him, 'you too recognised it as being my own work?'

'It was unmistakeable, Princeps,' Vespasian replied, truthfully.

'And my voice?'

'Beyond description, Princeps; in a category of its own.'

'You have both earned my gratitude.' Nero turned to Otho as senators congratulated Vespasian and Gaius through gritted teeth at their audacious sycophancy, wishing that they had had the sense to see the ballad for what it was. 'So, Otho, now has come the moment when you must judge: Poppaea's beauty or my voice; which of the two do you deem the most beautiful?'

Otho had no doubt. 'Your voice, Princeps; your voice every time. How can mere womanhood compare with a voice lubricated with ambrosia?'

Poppaea held the same view. 'My beauty is nothing in comparison to the voice of a living god, Princeps.' She ran the tip of her tongue lightly along her upper lip and looked at Nero with smouldering, half-closed eyes in a vain attempt to prove the fact that her looks were as nought compared to Nero's voice and were unable to move anyone in such a degree.

This, however, was more than Nero could bear. 'Otho, you said that you would ravage the winner, so, therefore, I declare it a draw.' He took both Poppaea and Otho by the arm and led them, with undignified haste, towards his private chambers whence, Vespasian assumed, they would not emerge for some time.

With a howl of rage, Acte stamped her foot, tearing at her elaborate coiffure and throwing hairpins after the retreating trio. No one took the slightest notice of her as her time was now over.

'That was, how should I put it, a flagrant, yes, flagrant is the perfect word, a flagrant piece of sycophancy that has probably done you both a great deal of good.'

Vespasian turned in the direction of the voice. 'Thank you, Seneca. I'm surprised that you didn't think of it first.'

Seneca's flabby features took on a conspiratorial aspect and he placed an arm around Vespasian's and Gaius' shoulders. 'It wouldn't have worked for me seeing as I was already privy to the secret, having sat through the whole thing four times yesterday and failed to find a way of persuading the Emperor to keep his genius to himself. Let us hope for dignity's sake that this is the most public stage on which he ever decides to perform.'

Vespasian declined to offer an opinion on the subject.

'Yes, you are unfortunately right,' Seneca said, reading Vespasian's silence correctly. 'The question is: how do we limit the damage that this will cause to the, what's the best word in this case, decorum, yes, that will do nicely, the decorum of the Principate?' Seneca paused but did not seem to be expecting an answer. 'One thing I will suggest is that your flagrant sycophancy has made it much more likely that Nero will pluck up the courage to perform in public sooner than he would have done had you stayed quiet.'

'Had we stayed quiet, Seneca,' Vespasian replied, 'then some other sycophant would have done the very same thing. We just took advantage of the situation because, as it may have escaped your notice, neither of us seems to be in the greatest of favour with the Emperor at the moment.'

'Which is exactly why I have taken you aside.' Seneca beamed in an avuncular manner at each of them. 'I have a little proposal that will help your standing in Nero's eyes; a mission that, now he has bestowed his favour upon you, he will be only too pleased to see you perform. Who knows, but it may even get your son Titus that posting as a military tribune that you both so wish for.'

Vespasian remained non-committal. 'Oh yes?'

'Yes, and with a chance to see real action on the Rhenus in Germania Inferior; interested?'

'Obviously.'

'Good. I want you to organise a meeting; no, that isn't the correct word. A reconciliation, yes, I want you to organise a reconciliation; and when I say "I", I mean "we".'

'"We" being you and Burrus?'

'Oh, no, no, no. "We" being the Emperor and me, or, rather, the Emperor.'

'With whom does he wish to be reconciled?'

Seneca looked at Vespasian as if he were an idiot of the highest standing. 'His mother, of course. He feels that it's high time that he and Agrippina sorted out the differences between them, permanently.'

'Very admirable. I wonder what she would have made of his performance just now?'

Seneca winced at the memory of Nero's antics. 'I'm hoping that if a reconciliation can be reached then Burrus and I will have an ally in Agrippina to prevent that sort of thing getting out of hand.'

'I'd say it was out of hand already,' Gaius remarked, seeming to forget that he had praised and encouraged the Emperor in a self-seeking, sycophantic frenzy. 'As are his attacks on respectable citizens; what are you going to do about them?'

'As *pharos* I can see, there's nothing I can do.'

Gaius' jowls wobbled with indignation at the pun.

Vespasian had to restrain himself from chuckling. 'So what do you want me to do, Seneca?'

'I would like you to act as the intermediary between Nero and Agrippina.' He paused and looked at Vespasian with his eyebrows raised meaningfully. 'Seeing as you're invited down to her estate at Bauli after the ides of March next year.'

'You're invited down to that Fury's nest?' Gaius spurted, his previous indignation quickly forgotten. 'And you've agreed to go?'

'I'll explain later, Uncle; I haven't had time to tell you because it only happened last night.' He returned Seneca's meaningful look. 'Well?'

Seneca shrugged as if his knowledge of a secret meeting so soon after it was arranged were nothing out of the ordinary. 'I keep abreast of such matters.'

'But only Agrippina, Pallas, Caenis and I were present when the arrangement was ...' He paused for a moment's reflection; his stomach churned as he felt the full force of betrayal. Neither Agrippina nor Pallas would ever share their plans with Seneca. 'Of course. Caenis is now your secretary.'

Seneca smiled, neither confirming nor denying Vespasian's supposition. 'The Emperor was speaking to me only yesterday about looking for a suitable way of conveying the invitation to Agrippina in a manner that she would not find suspicious and it occurred to me, as I watched Nero fall for your flattery, that you were the perfect man for the job seeing as you are already invited to Agrippina's estate in just under four months' time, by which point the Emperor would have had as long as he needs to make the preparations. Although, I have to say that I think that Pallas and Agrippina are acting a little too precipitously – yes, that's the perfect word in this case – they are acting precipitously in trying to sell their property in Britannia back to Cogidubnus; there's still a lot of money to be made in that province yet. Wouldn't you agree?'

Vespasian was too mentally winded to answer; the thought of Caenis' possible betrayal was all consuming.

Seneca pressed on regardless. 'The invitation will be for Agrippina to come to a dinner of reconciliation with Nero at his seaside villa at Baiae, just along the coast from hers. He wants to treat her with all the courtesy and consideration with which a son should. In fact, he even plans to send his own ship for her equipped with every luxury to make her journey as pleasant and convenient as possible. The ship will, obviously, be at her disposal to take her home again at the end of the dinner. So will you do it?'

Vespasian had barely heard a word that Seneca had said, so strong was the image of his lover whispering his secrets in Seneca's ear.

'Will you do it?' Seneca repeated.

'Dear boy,' Gaius said, 'you're being asked a question.'

Vespasian frowned. 'What was that, Uncle?'

'Seneca is giving you a way to ingratiate yourself with the Emperor and his mother, albeit some time hence; will you do it?'

Unfocused, his eyes gazed around the room before alighting on Seneca. 'Yes, I'll do it; of course I will. I've spent my life doing things I don't want to for other people, why should this be any different?'

Seneca smiled benignly and patted Vespasian on the arm. 'At the moment the Emperor plans to travel down to Baiae on the ides of March and arrive three days later. The dinner will be the evening after. I will have his invitation to Agrippina drawn up once his plans are confirmed nearer the time and delivered to you before you leave. Caenis will, no doubt, be drafting it: I'll have her bring it to you.'

'No you won't! Not if you don't want the invitation ripped up and thrown back in her face. I'll send my freedman, Hormus, to pick it up from her.'

'As you wish.' Seneca turned and walked away leaving Vespasian feeling sick.

'Dear boy—'

'Not a word, Uncle; not one fucking word,' Vespasian snarled as he stormed off.

'All I'm saying is that you have no proof that isn't circumstantial,' Magnus said as a burly, pale-skinned Britannic masseur kneaded his left shoulder.

Vespasian grunted and squeezed his eyes shut as his deep massage almost crossed the boundary between pleasure and pain; he was finding it hard to relax beneath the expert hands of his masseur. 'Who else could it have been?'

'What if Seneca has a spy in Caenis' household?'

'How could she fail to find out about that given as she's his personal secretary?'

Magnus let out a low, vibrating growl of contentment, like an oversized-cat's purr, as his masseur began pummelling up and down the length of his spine with the edges of both hands. The growl continued for the length of the procedure and a touch beyond. 'At least give her the chance to defend herself. Ow!' He looked back at the Briton. 'Easy with the use of the knuckles, you pale bog-dweller, you haven't got any fog to hide in here if you piss me off.' With a grunt of satisfaction as the slave eased off the pressure, he settled back on the leather upholstered couch. All around them male citizens of Rome of all classes enjoyed having their muscles toned in the high-domed room at the centre of the baths of Agrippa on the Campus Martius; their shouts, curses, growls and chat echoed off the marble and tiles of the walls, floor and dome of the huge chamber, providing an aural backdrop of such a blur that it melded with the consciousness to become almost unnoticeable. 'I mean: what if she really didn't have anything to do with it? What then? When the truth of the matter all came out you would look very stupid, so stupid that she might never want to talk to you again, if you take my meaning?'

Vespasian did but it did not sway him. 'Do you really consider it's possible that either Agrippina or Pallas would let on to Seneca that I was coming down to Bauli, next March, to pick up some land deeds in order to take them to Britannia and sell them back to Cogidubnus, not even a day since the arrangement was made? Bollocks.'

'Why don't you take the horses for a spin around the track because your head evidently needs clearing?'

'My head's perfectly clear.'

'Well, have it your way; but if it were me then I would do a bit of sniffing around first before I decided, on the basis not of solid proof but of being unable to see any other possibility, that the woman who I've loved for most of my life has betrayed, to one of the most unscrupulous men in Rome, information about me that he could have got in half a dozen other ways.' To emphasise his point, Magnus turned his face away from Vespasian and concentrated on grunting with pleasure at the efforts of his now-forgiven masseur.

Vespasian kept his eyes shut and prayed to Mars that his friend was right; however, it seemed such a far-fetched possibility that after a few moments contemplating it he could no longer countenance the idea.

It had to be Caenis.

Miserably he turned and, beating away his masseur with a backhanded slap to his chest, gathered his towel and went to find solace in the heat of the *caldarium.*

It was with his head in his hands and a slave wafting the heat down upon him with a wet towel that Sabinus found Vespasian in the hot-room half an hour later. He stood, looking down at his brother, and tutted. 'Magnus told me that you were here and he warned me about your condition but he evidently played it down. That really is a despicable display of self-pity, if I might say so.'

'Piss off, Sabinus.'

'If you really want me to, I will and leave you to wallow in your unfounded misery.' Sabinus laid a towel down next to Vespasian on the marble bench and sat. He signalled to the slave to pour oil over him and rub it in. 'So, tell me,' he said once the task was complete and he was at leisure to enjoy the heat.

And Vespasian did. He told Sabinus of his surprise conversation with Pallas and Agrippina at Caenis' house, and then his meeting with Seneca.

When Vespasian had finished, the brothers sat quietly for a while as people came and went around them, gossiping, conversing, arguing or in silence.

'So Pallas is my secret sponsor, I didn't see that; but it makes sense in that it keeps him actively involved and he can exploit Seneca's greed and he knows that we are the closest things he has to friends now that he's so out of favour, in that he saved my life.'

'I saved your life.'

'True, but he was the one who persuaded Narcissus not to have me executed before you had the chance to do your bit. But that's not what interests me; no, it's not his reasons for paying Seneca a vast amount of money to get me a very lucrative and powerful position and seeming to gain nothing from it himself other than a mediocre favour from you that is really not worth one million, let alone ten. I just assume that he's playing a long game and trying to get as many people indebted to him as possible to help protect him when Nero finally tries to take his fortune – which he will. What is really interesting is who told Seneca that you were going to Bauli?'

'Caenis, of course!'

'If you don't have anything sensible to say then I suggest you be quiet and let me think, seeing as you're obviously incapable of that function at the moment.'

Vespasian shrugged and the brothers lapsed back into silence as Sabinus took a strigil and began to scrape the oil, sweat and dirt from his arms and legs.

'There's something not quite right here,' Sabinus observed after a while.

'Nothing's quite right.'

'Oh, do be quiet; I'm not talking about your suspicions about Caenis, which, had you paid any attention to what she has done for you in the last thirty and more years, you would realise are completely unfounded. No, I'm talking about Nero wanting to be reconciled with his mother when all she wants is to share his power. She'd try to usurp it if she weren't a woman.'

Vespasian raised his head from his hands and looked with scorn at his brother. 'She *is* a woman so that's a stupid thing to say.'

'No it isn't. She wanted him to become emperor solely so that she would get power, and since he's denied it to her she has done nothing but insult him to the extent that she openly takes antidotes claiming that the offspring of her womb is trying to kill her. And, so the gossip goes, she has been right to do so on two or three occasions; not to mention her bedroom ceiling collapsing in mysterious circumstances last year when she was staying at the palace.'

This cheered Vespasian; his face brightened. 'Adding matricide to fratricide and multiple-incest with your mother and stepbrother; Nero really is deteriorating, even by Julio-Claudian standards.'

'Yes; but think: if he succeeds in killing her he just gets rid of a disapproving nuisance; ultimately she can do him no real harm.'

Vespasian smiled in slow understanding. 'But who really gains from Nero's crime of matricide?'

'Exactly, brother; feeling better?'

'Much better all of a sudden. There are two obvious people who would appreciate Nero's successful attempt at matricide. Pallas because he's tied to Agrippina, and if she were to disappear then he would have a better chance at re-ingratiating himself with the Emperor and regaining some power without Nero always being reminded of his hated mother.'

'And Seneca?'

'Because all her very considerable wealth would go to Nero and therefore it would keep Seneca's growing fortune safe from him for at least a year or two; it'll buy him more time to make further investments in far-off provinces like Britannia, keeping his money well away from Rome and Nero's clutches.' Vespasian paused and shook his head, looking incredulously at his brother. 'This isn't about getting money out of Britannia; this is about collusion to matricide. Pallas admitted to me that he's in contact with Seneca when he said he had bought your position from him personally. So Pallas and Seneca could have planned this together, both understanding that it would be for mutual benefit and neither of them being able to organise it on his own. Seneca knows of Nero's plan to kill his mother and wants it to succeed without being seen to have helped. Pallas needed to find a way of sending his lover to her death at the hands of her son without her suspecting a thing.'

Pausing again, Vespasian contemplated the refined thinking that had gone into the two former rivals' plan. 'It's beautiful and so completely deniable at every stage should anything go wrong. Pallas uses his knowledge as the former secretary to the Treasury to persuade Agrippina that they need to pull their money out of Britannia, which is very feasible given Nero's profligacy. He then persuades her that I am the only man who could convince Cogidubnus – again, feasible – and then makes an arrangement for me to travel to Bauli conveniently nearly four months hence so that Nero has had the time to make all his preparations, whatever they are. At Bauli I pick up the property deeds before sailing from Misenum but it so happens that the Emperor, who would have had to give me permission as a senator to travel to Britannia, upon realising that I'm going to see his estranged mother on the way decides to use me as the bearer of his invitation for that same evening as if upon a whim; the most natural thing in the world to do as if it were an impulsive invitation rather than something that has been planned so far in advance. Agrippina is far more likely to trust an impulse rather than a long-standing invitation when there has been time to plot.'

Sabinus slapped his brother on the back. 'You see? It must have been Pallas who told Seneca that you would be coming. In fact, it was probably the other way around: Seneca told Pallas when he wanted him to have you down at Bauli so that whatever Nero's planning is ready. Seneca didn't give you this errand as a favour because you pleased Nero with your flattery, he just used that to make it seem even more spur of the moment, less like a set-up; you had been chosen for the job some time ago by both he and Pallas together. Who better than the person trusted with doing Agrippina's business in Britannia bearing the invitation from her son for a grand and seemingly impulsive reconciliation? Why would you be part of a plot against her and your former patron, Pallas, if you had been promised a governorship if you succeeded in his mission for them? You had to have the Emperor's permission to travel so it would be no secret to Nero that you are sailing from Misenum, so he just used you as a convenient way of sending his invitation. It's perfect, completely innocent.'

'But how will he do it?'

'What? Kill her? It'll seem to be an accident so that Nero can dodge the stigma of matricide. It'll happen after a *very happy* family dinner at which there will be many witnesses as to the joyful reunion of mother and son who have never been seen to be so happy in each other's company. Then, tragically, on that night of all nights, a terrible accident, months in the making, occurs to sunder them for ever.'

Vespasian gave a few slow nods. 'Nero will be sending a ship for her that will take her home afterwards.'

'A ship is full of dangers. And I would be willing to wager that once Pallas receives news of his unfortunate lover's death, he will cancel your trip to Britannia as being unnecessary until her estate is sorted out. All that wanting to sell property back to Cogidubnus and giving you the deeds at Bauli is nothing more than a plausible ruse to get you down there knowing that you wouldn't accept an invitation from Agrippina.'

Relief surged through Vespasian with the same intensity as despair had only a few short hours earlier; relief that the darkness that had entered his world when Caenis had seemed to leave it was gone. 'How could I have ever suspected her?'

'Because Pallas and Seneca made you; they didn't give a fuck about your feelings or hers even though she has served them both loyally – well, almost loyally.'

'Conniving cunts! I'll have them.'

'One day perhaps, but not in the near future.'

'You're right; but in the meantime it's to my advantage to make sure that their scheme works and that Agrippina ends up at the bottom of the Bay of Neapolis. But perhaps not as cleanly as Nero might have hoped; it would be awful if he ended up getting sympathy from the mob for killing his own mother.'

'Indeed, and to do that properly you have to play your part well; and to play your part well you have to make them believe that you suspect nothing.'

'Of course.'

'Which means you must revert to the disgusting state of self-pity that I found you in. You have to seem to Seneca's and Pallas' spies that you are distraught by what you see as Caenis' betrayal; the betrayal that they made you believe was true. But more than that, you have to make Caenis believe that you think that she's betrayed you.'

Vespasian swallowed as he realised the truth of what his brother had just said and then his stomach lurched as he understood what the reality of it would be: when he next saw the woman he loved he would have to shun her and continue to do so for over three months.

CHAPTER V

VESPASIAN CROUCHED NEXT to Sabinus and Magnus in a shadowed alley just off a side street of the Via Patricius, the main thoroughfare leading up to the Viminal Gate and on to the Praetorian camp beyond it. All three wore deeply hooded cloaks even though the moon was not far from new and very little light made it through the drizzle-laden cloud cover. They were armed with knives and cudgels and Magnus had brought Castor and Pollux along as insurance against the venture getting completely out of hand, but none of them expected to be obliged to defend themselves as they were here to observe only. However, none of them had expected to end up in this filth-encrusted alley to which they had moved only recently after a messenger for Tigran had arrived at their last and more salubrious hiding place in the back yard of a tavern two streets down from their present location.

Further up the alley, almost at its junction with the side street, they could just make out the silhouetted huddle of a dozen of Tigran's brethren all wearing actors' masks as Nero was purported to do when on a rampage. Vespasian wondered just how Tigran expected to achieve the vengeance on Terpnus with so few men when the Vigiles shadowing Nero's latest storm through the city would number at least eight and Nero's cronies would be about the same amount. Not to mention the century from one of the Urban Cohorts that Sabinus was obliged to put on standby close to the area to extract Nero if necessary. He had muttered his misgivings to his companions.

'It's all right, sir,' Magnus whispered next to him, 'Tigran knows what he's doing.'

'I'm sure he does,' Vespasian replied as a drunk tried to turn into the alley and was knocked insensible by one of the brethren.

'I just wish that I knew what he was doing too; if this is a shambles and Sabinus and I get caught we'll be lucky to get away with committing suicide and our families keeping our property.'

'Oh, and what about the rest of us?'

'Insignificant enough not to be noticed if two senators are caught waylaying the imperial progress through the Viminal.'

'I thought that you two just wanted to observe?'

'We do,' Sabinus hissed, 'but if it goes wrong we may well get caught up in it.'

'If you're worried about that then you shouldn't have come; you could have waited at home for the trophy Tigran promised to bring Senator Pollo.'

'Then I would have missed seeing the fear in his eyes.'

'In which case stop complaining.' Magnus pulled his cloak closer about his shoulders to protect himself from the steadily increasing rain and then wedged himself deeper between Castor and Pollux to gain some benefit from their body heat.

Vespasian shifted his position, rubbing his stiff thigh, as he strained his ears in an attempt to hear beyond the cries and shouts of the throng of people frequenting, even at the eighth hour of the night, the brothels of either sex for which the Via Patricius, thirty paces to his right, was famed. He shivered and thanked Mars that the chance of revenge, which had obliged him to stay in Rome, had finally come; once it was done, and Nero's birthday had been celebrated in five days' time, he could remove himself from the city more often and stay on his estates until it was time to go to Bauli, thus reducing the chances of contact with Caenis. He would, of course, have to be in Rome for certain occasions and festivals but he hoped he could keep these visits to a minimum.

In the twenty or so days that had passed since he and Sabinus had guessed at the unlikely alliance between Pallas and Seneca, he had done just as his brother had suggested and moped about as if he was in the depths of self-pity. He had obeyed any summons from the Emperor and had attempted to act the part of a man putting a brave face on things, especially when Seneca was present, which was most of the time. The one luxury he had allowed himself was to spend more time at the Green racing faction's stables, on the Campus Martius, with his team of Arab greys. Since receiving them as a gift from Malachus, the King of the Nabatean Arabs, in return for him interceding with Seneca concerning the jurisdiction of Damascus, Vespasian had become a proficient driver of a four-horse racing chariot. He took out much of his frustration at not seeing Caenis by hurling his team around the Flammian Circus, next to the Greens' stables, in private sessions with one or two of the team's drivers.

As for Caenis, he had ignored her letters and on one occasion had actually turned about when he found himself approaching her in a corridor of the palace; she had called after him but he had ignored her in a scene that had been witnessed by at least three palace slaves and a couple of equestrians waiting for an interview with Epaphroditus, one of Nero's rising freedmen. The incident, he knew, would get back to Seneca without a doubt, having had such a wide audience and Epaphroditus being such a renowned gossip. Although it had pained him to do it, he consoled himself with the thought that he would hurt a lot more if he still believed her guilty of betrayal; betrayal as false as the two men who had insinuated it.

Pallas had slipped back out of Rome with Agrippina and they had returned south to her estate at Bauli. Vespasian now knew that Pallas had in fact run little risk in returning to the city against the will of the Emperor: Seneca must have been complicit in his coming and going so that he avoided the attentions of the Urban Cohort guards on the gates who would have been briefed to look out for him. Vespasian bristled as he thought of Pallas whom he had once considered a friend, whom Caenis still considered a friend. That he could try to poison their relationship with false suspicions of disloyalty he felt was itself the ultimate act of betrayal; now any shred of loyalty he felt to the once-powerful Greek freedman had evaporated and there remained only a desire for vengeance. But first he was to avenge his uncle and that, he hoped, would be a pleasure; again he concentrated on distinguishing between the multitude of sounds coming from the Via Patricius.

But when the noise that he was listening for came, it was not from the direction of the main thoroughfare but, rather, off to his left. He heard it again, closer this time; the sound that Gaius had described to him: high-pitched ululations. Nero was approaching, causing havoc and carnage, freely and at will, as he passed through the city in which he was supposed to be the final arbiter of justice. Tonight, Vespasian hoped, they would put an end to that by frightening him off.

A couple of figures dashed past the head of the alley, fleeing as if in fear of their lives as the ululations came closer. Tigran made a couple of calming motions with his arm to steady the lads around him. Castor and Pollux pricked up their ears. A screech of pain rent the air and the ululations paused to be replaced by rhythmic clapping in time to hoarse chanting, occasionally broken by a woman's pleas for mercy. But mercy was not to be shown to this victim and her cries became weaker in inverse proportion to the strengthening of clapping and chanting; as they came to a crescendo the ululating recommenced, piercing and wild, chilling the blood like the war cry of some hitherto unknown barbarian tribe. And then it began to come closer, the rattle of hobnailed soles accompanying it along with the whooping of hunters who have spotted fresh quarry. Vespasian did not have to wait long before he saw what had caught the attention of Nero's gang: a huge man, dressed in a toga and holding a flaming torch aloft came pelting past the alley at a speed that belied his bulk followed by three women.

'Good lad, Sextus,' Magnus muttered, 'nice, tempting bait.'

As Sextus passed, the ululations drew almost level and then the corpulent silhouette of Nero, accompanied by a posse of whooping shadows, sped past. Two heartbeats after the last one passed Tigran leapt up and dashed into the road but, instead of following Nero, he turned left with all his brethren following. Vespasian moved up to the end of the alley as mortal screams and the clash of weapons came from his left. He peered around the corner to see Tigran and his brethren at close quarters with the surprised Vigiles shadowing the Emperor; three, including their optio, were already down and the other five were wavering under an assault of nailed cudgels and honed blades. The crossroads brethren were showing no sign of easily forgiving the insult perpetrated on their fellows a month previously. With two swift swings of a club, Tigran stove in the face of another as a further member of Rome's law-enforcement fell to his knees with his belly ripped open. This was enough for the last three; they turned and fled rather than give their lives protecting rapine and pillage.

Turning the other way, Vespasian could make out the large shape of Sextus slashing his torch and roaring at a couple of Nero's companions, supported by three other figures who, whilst dressed in women's clothing, were wielding blades in a decidedly masculine manner. Between them they blocked the side street and there was now no escape for the Emperor's rampaging party as Tigran led his brethren back past the alley and completed the trap.

Nero turned this way and that, desperately looking for a place to hide but there were none, just brick walls and shuttered windows to either side. One of his companions stepped forward, his face covered with a scarf; he held out his sword to show that he was not about to use it. 'I advise you to let us go,' he said and Vespasian recognised the voice of Tigellinus. 'You don't know who you are dealing with.'

'I'm well aware who you are, Tigellinus,' Tigran said from behind his mask, 'in fact we came looking for you.'

Tigellinus stepped back, stung by the unexpected use of his name. 'Then you know who else is here?'

'Yes, we do; and we've come for him.'

Nero yelped and fell to his knees, shuddering with sobs, the tips of his fingers touching the eye-holes of his gurning comic-actor's mask as if catching the tears issuing from them. 'Mercy, mercy; grant your Emperor mercy.'

'Of course, Princeps,' Tigran replied with a surprising amount of respect in his tone, 'we have not come to harm you; only to ask you to keep to the Palatine in your future night-time escapades. You may go if you leave us Terpnus.'

Nero looked from side to side as if he were trying to spot a trap, before bounding to his feet. 'Of course, take him!' he said, then turned and grabbed the unfortunate musician and shoved him towards Tigran. Two of his brethren secured Terpnus up against a wall as he attempted to wrest himself free.

Tigran nodded at Sextus and his cross-dressed support. 'Let them go, lads.'

They stepped aside and Nero darted through the gap followed by his companions; only Tigellinus hesitated. 'I'll find you,' he spat.

'No you won't, Tigellinus, because you don't even know where to start looking; and if you start to get close I'll find you first.'

Tigellinus stared at the expressionless mask, hawked and spat at Tigran's feet before turning and walking away at a dignified pace.

Tigran slowly revolved his head until the menacingly still mask faced Terpnus.

'What do you want with me?' Terpnus asked, his voice weak and shaking.

Tigran remained silent as he lifted his hand and ripped off the cloth tied around his captive's face.

Terpnus' lips quivered and his brow was bunched with fear. 'What do you want?' he asked again, his voice weaker.

'Not your life, you will be pleased to learn.'

Terpnus' features relaxed.

'Just your talent. Sextus, you know what to do.'

Terpnus looked momentarily confused as the bovinesque brother approached him and then shook with fear as Sextus grabbed his right wrist and pressed his hand flat on the wall, his torch casting flickering light onto the scene.

'No, please!' Terpnus screamed as a short axe flashed in Tigran's fist. He tried to bunch up his fingers but Sextus' strength was too much for him and the pressure kept his hand pressed to the wall with his fingers splayed.

Golden in the torchlight, the axe glistened as it fell; it struck the wall with a metallic ring, chipping into the brick. There was an instance of silence and then a howl that morphed into a wail of despair as Terpnus watched his thumb fall to the ground. The axe blade had turned red; Tigran raised it for a second blow, adjusting the angle. Down it fell leaving an arc of dark droplets in its wake. The wailing did not cease but rose in pitch as the forefinger and middle finger flew, rotating, back towards Terpnus' face, one striking him on the cheek, his eyes following it in disbelieving terror. Once more the axe swished through the air, severing the final two digits. Sextus let go of the wrist and Terpnus gazed at his maimed hand in wide-eyed horror, the wail now gone and replaced with a silent scream.

'That feels much better,' Sabinus muttered to Vespasian.

'It certainly does, brother.'

'I've got one refinement that I think will gratify our uncle more than having those trophies that Tigran promised.' Sabinus strode forward and picked up the thumb and forefinger. 'Bend him over, Sextus.'

Sextus grinned, took Terpnus by the back of the neck and forced him to double up. Tigran understood what was to happen and aided it by ripping off the musician's exposed loincloth. Without ceremony, Sabinus rammed the severed thumb, lubricated with its own blood, into the man's anus and followed it with the forefinger as Terpnus' whole body shook and heaved in shock. Tigran collected the other three digits, which soon disappeared the same way before Sabinus cracked his knee into Terpnus' face, flattening his nose. 'That's the last time you humiliate a member of my family, you disgusting bastard!' With a nod of thanks to Tigran he turned and walked towards the Via Patricius with Vespasian and Magnus following him hauling Castor and Pollux away from the rain-diluted blood with which they were slaking their thirst.

'You shouldn't have spoken to him,' Vespasian said as they turned onto the bustling thoroughfare alive with brothel frequenters and delivery carts, banned from the city during the daylight hours, 'he might have recognised your voice.'

Sabinus shrugged. 'He wouldn't have noticed my voice; he was too busy wondering which hurt the most, his hand, his nose or having four fingers and a thumb shoved up his arse.'

'That'll make for an interesting morning shit,' Magnus mused. 'I suppose it adds a whole new sense to sitting on one's finger, if you take my meaning?'

Vespasian ignored the remark. 'Even so, Sabinus, I think you should avoid Terpnus for a while; you're going to have to be careful at Nero's birthday celebrations in five days' time just in case he hears your voice and it sparks a memory.'

And so it was with feigned surprise that Vespasian and Sabinus heard about, and then discussed, the tragic and brutal attack that had been perpetrated upon the most talented lyre-player of the age with the other guests at the many festivities that marked Nero's birthday two days after the ides of December.

'It happened right here on the Palatine apparently, under our very noses,' Marcus Valerius Messalla Corvinus said pointedly to his companion as he passed Vespasian, Sabinus and Gaius standing watching the sun descend over the Circus Maximus from a terrace in the imperial residence. 'And just what the prefect of Rome thinks he's doing allowing that sort of violence so close to decent people's homes, I don't know.'

'I think it's time he was replaced, Corvinus,' his companion replied, equally as loud.

'I completely agree with you, Pedanius, I have already suggested as much to Seneca and the Emperor; in fact I think that I shall mention it again to Nero when he arrives this evening and recommend you for the post in gratitude for your ... er ... help in securing me the governorship of Lusitania.'

'I'm sure that I'll make a better job of it than the present incumbent.'

'That won't be difficult.'

'Ignore it, dear boy,' Gaius said as Corvinus and Pedanius walked off laughing. 'They know perfectly well how and where it happened.'

'Besides,' Vespasian pointed out, 'no one believes the official version of events.'

Sabinus spat over the balustrade into the garden below. 'It doesn't matter what they believe when the official account is held up as the truth; yet again it makes me look stupid.'

Gaius grabbed a pastry from the tray of a passing slave. 'I hope you're not regretting avenging my humiliation in such a pleasing manner.'

'Of course not, Uncle,' Sabinus replied, looking in through the terrace doors over to where Terpnus sat, glancing every few moments in disbelief at his bandaged, mutilated hand. 'Just the sight of him gives me a warm feeling, but it's tempered by shits like Corvinus and Lucius Pedanius Secundus stirring their venom in public.'

'And Corvinus walks into a governorship immediately after he's consul,' Vespasian said with more than a touch of bitterness.

'He didn't walk in; he paid for admission and it cost him a fortune, dear boy; Seneca's interest rates are exorbitant and he had to go to Pedanius to have him be the guarantor of the loan, thereby humiliating himself by publicly admitting that his family did not have the resources any more.'

'Nor do we; I can't afford to pay Seneca for a governorship.'

'Yes, but we never could afford it. Corvinus' family always used to be able to but now can't. But he was so desperate to restore his finances with a province that he put his dignity aside and borrowed the money. But I don't suppose he cares now as he has his governorship.'

'And he enjoys flaunting it in front of me at every opportunity; I much preferred it when he was dead.' Corvinus had long ago reneged on an oath to conduct himself as a dead man in Vespasian's presence in return for Vespasian saving his life after the downfall of his sister, Messalina; a deed that Vespasian now regretted.

A shrill shriek from above them, causing all three to look up, cut through Vespasian's regret. A vase hurtled from the balcony above to smash with a ceramic clatter on a paved path.

'Then get rid of him!' a woman's voice raged. 'And then get rid of your dull and sour wife! You will make me your Empress whatever your mother says.'

'Careful, Poppaea.' Nero's husky voice was unmistakeable. 'Your beauty and versatility in bed do not make you immortal. I do what I want when I want and take no direction from anyone.'

Whether the chill note of warning in Nero's voice frightened Poppaea into submission or whether she just changed her tactics was uncertain; however, it was not long before the distinctive sound of urgent rutting came from the balcony.

'I think I'll go back in,' Gaius announced, none too keen on the sound of Poppaea's evident female pleasure.

The brothers followed him in.

'That Terpnus business has reflected very badly on you, prefect,' Tigellinus sneered with his rabid-dog snarl of a smile stretched across his sharp features; Otho stood next to him.

'Where were your Vigiles, Tigellinus?' Sabinus retorted. 'You should have had ample to spare seeing as you told me that the Viminal was being kept clear of patrols because of … well, you know why.'

'I do.'

'So let's stop pretending that Terpnus was attacked on the Palatine, shall we?'

'I know perfectly well that he wasn't because I was there, as you know. The question is: who else was there?' The rabid-dog snarl widened. 'Eh?'

'Eh, what?'

'I'll tell you something interesting. I've had a couple of the West Viminal Crossroads Brethren hauled in for questioning and even under the strictest inducements they knew nothing about Terpnus' fingers.'

'So?'

'So, I'd say it wasn't them; but then who else could it be? Now, you're the only person I told that the Viminal was to be targeted just so you could have the usual century from one of your Urban Cohorts standing by just in case. Who did you tell, prefect? Eh? Who should I question next, I wonder? Eh?' With that he walked abruptly away.

'A tricky situation, perhaps?' Otho questioned before following Tigellinus.

'I'll get a message to Tigran to lie low for a while,' Gaius said as Tigellinus and Otho disappeared into the crowd of guests, passing Faenius Rufus, Thrasea the Stoic and Gaius Calpurnius Piso.

Vespasian rubbed his bald pate and looked even more constipated than usual. 'We'll have to find some way to put him off the trail.'

'We believe, prefect, that what happened the other night,' Rufus said, sidling up quietly to Sabinus, 'was perhaps no more than a form of justice. Someone is to be congratulated.'

Sabinus looked quizzically at the man he considered honest to the point of recklessness. 'I'm afraid I don't understand what you mean, Rufus.'

'Your feigned ignorance does you credit, Sabinus,' Thrasea said.

'But it does not fool,' Piso affirmed, his voice lowered beneath the surrounding conversations. 'We all know that the Emperor was waylaid on one of his disgusting rampages and that Terpnus paid for an outrage that he'd perpetrated on a man of some influence as it was obviously an arranged attack. What we're saying is that there are more than a few who welcome this development and hope that it will serve to curb some imperial excess. Furthermore, we know that there was no way that the attack could have been accomplished without at least the tacit approval of someone like yourself, for example.'

Sabinus was about to protest his innocence but Piso cut him off. 'Say nothing, prefect; but if you ever want to talk ...' Piso smiled and walked away with Rufus and Thrasea.

'That was indiscreet of him,' Vespasian observed.

'Was it, dear boy? I'd say he'd made a couple of very pertinent assumptions from the facts as most people know them and came to the right conclusion. It's good to know that there are people thinking the same way as us, but let's hope that not everyone is as astute as Piso and Rufus, especially Tigellinus. However, I wouldn't advise going for a little chat with him as he advocates, just in case he's made false assumptions about, but the same suggestion to, other people less of our way of mind.'

Before Sabinus could express a view, the assembly broke into applause as Nero and Poppaea Sabina appeared on the stairs, their rutting evidently concluded in quick time.

At the halfway point, Nero paused and soaked up the welcome for more than a few moments. Eventually, satisfied, he held up his hands for quiet. 'My friends, it is not often that I change my mind; indeed, having never been in error there has not been occasion for me to do so. However, I believe that I may have overlooked one thing when I was confirming an appointment.'

Vespasian felt Sabinus tense next to him; he glanced over to Pedanius who was looking intently at the Emperor, his interest evidently piqued.

'It was an easy thing to overlook as I who have so much of it don't consider it in others. However, this time I deem myself to be at fault for not taking it into account: money.'

Vespasian was now convinced that somehow the Emperor had got wind of Pallas' ten million sesterces bribe. But would that matter?

'When one lacks money one can't act in the way that a Roman noble should in whatever position he finds himself and so therefore it is better if I relieve Marcus Valerius Messalla Corvinus of his position as governor of Lusitania, as I now know that his six months as my colleague in the consulship cost him far more than he made and his family finances are now below that required of the senatorial order.'

There was a low gasp from the assembled and all eyes turned to Corvinus who stood, rigid, jaw jutted, his face red with fury.

Sabinus visibly relaxed.

'But I am not insensible to the lineage of this great patrician family, so therefore I propose that the Senate should vote him an annual stipend of half a million sesterces so that he can enjoy his poverty in dignity and still retain his senatorial rank.'

The use of public funds in such a way seemed to be the most natural thing in the world and Nero was roundly praised, as Corvinus' countenance eased into gratitude now that he would have a substantial income for doing absolutely nothing.

'His luck makes me sick,' Vespasian hissed at Gaius, venom in his voice.

'Indeed, dear boy, and he won't even have the difficulty of getting Seneca to pay back his bribe money as it was Seneca's anyway.'

'So who should take his place?' Nero continued. 'There seems to me to be only one option and that is my good friend, Marcus Salvius Otho.'

The look on Otho's face made it clear that he did not think he was the only option to go and govern a province about as far away from the pleasures of Rome as it was possible to get, even though it was a lucrative posting.

'And so, Otho, I wish you joy of your appointment and promise that I will look after your wife, Poppaea, until your safe return. Although I think that in the circumstances a divorce would suit better all round. Now go.'

Otho stepped forward. 'But, Princeps—'

'Go! And don't come back until I recall you.'

If he ever does, thought Vespasian, as Otho realised that there was nothing he could do to resist Nero's will without losing his life.

Poppaea Sabina watched her husband go in triumph, holding onto the Emperor's arm. Victorious, she looked to Vespasian, as one of the three obstacles to her becoming empress was removed from Rome leaving just Nero's wife, Claudia, and his mother, Agrippina; both of whom were doomed by the ambition of the new Fury at Nero's side.

'Master,' Hormus said as Vespasian walked through his front door a couple of hours later, leaving his escort of Tigran's brothers to make their way home in the chill mist of a December night. 'I'm sorry but I couldn't stop her. She insisted.'

'Who insisted, Hormus?'

'Caenis, master.' The freedman wrung his hands, not daring to meet his patron's eyes as they passed through the vestibule and on into the atrium. 'She came an hour after you left, tricked her way past the doorkeeper by saying that she had an important message for you from Seneca that she personally had to leave in your study and then refused to leave, even though I told her that you had given orders that she should be refused entry.'

Vespasian looked around the atrium but could see no sign of Caenis. 'Where is she?'

'I'm sorry, master, but she's with the mistress.'

'With Flavia!'

'Yes, master; her shouting disturbed the mistress who came to see what was going on; when she saw it was Caenis she insisted that they wait for you together in the triclinium and that I should have dinner served there for them both.'

Vespasian was horrified. 'They've been closeted together for almost three hours!'

Hormus cringed, wringing his hands so that his knuckles were white. 'I know, it's terrible. I'm so sorry, master.'

Vespasian swallowed and looked towards the closed door of the triclinium. The only other time he had seen his wife and mistress together was when they had both suffered the indignity of having their houses searched in the wake of Caligula's assassination; it had not been a comfortable experience. And, although Flavia and Caenis had maintained cordial relations and had even become friendly towards one another whilst Vespasian had been away in Germania and Britannia for six years with the II Augusta, to the point that his two elder children referred to Caenis as 'aunt', the thought of seeing them both together was not a pleasant one, especially when he had so flagrantly avoided Caenis and had given her no good reason for doing so. He had purposely kept her completely unaware of his motives for his behaviour in order to keep the pretence complete but now he would have to explain.

He steeled himself, walking slowly to the triclinium door, and, with a brief pause as his hand gripped the handle, opened it.

'There you are, at last,' Flavia said, her tone implying that he was late for an appointment that he himself had made. She was reclining on a couch with Caenis next to her; the remains of a large meal was laid out on the table before them. 'Where have you been?'

'You know perfectly well where I've been, Flavia, as well as you know it's not fitting that you should even ask.' He broke off a hunk of bread and dipped it into a bowl of oil before sitting down on an unoccupied couch; Caenis kept her eyes lowered, not meeting his look. 'How are you, Caenis?'

With a suddenness that surprised both Vespasian and Flavia, Caenis threw her cup, shattering it against the wall in an explosion of shards and wine. 'What have I done?' she almost screamed.

'Nothing, my love, nothing.'

'Then why have you cut me off? What did I do to deserve you turning around when you saw me coming the opposite way down a corridor? Why haven't you responded to any of my notes? What is going on? Have you found a younger mistress? Am I too old now that I'm fifty-three? Have I aged like milk rather than wine?' Her eyes had filled with tears and Vespasian wanted only to take her in his arms to comfort and reassure her; but he could not do so in front of his wife. The fact that Caenis was here with Flavia was a sign as to how desperate she had become.

'I've had no choice and I've been unable to communicate with you for fear of a spy in one of our households getting wind of the fact that I know it was not you who betrayed me to Seneca.'

'Of course I wouldn't betray you to Seneca, even though I work for him.'

'Yes, I know that now but I didn't when he told me that he knew I was going to Bauli the morning after our conversation with Pallas and Agrippina; then it seemed that it had to be you.'

Her face was set hard, as hard as her voice. 'So what made you change your mind?'

And then he let it all tumble out: Pallas' ruse, sweetened with the promise of a governorship, for getting him down to Bauli and the whole disgraceful tale of matricide and how he was going to help facilitate it because ultimately the abhorrence that people would feel towards Nero for the crime would be to his advantage and it would also earn Titus a good posting as a military tribune.

'Blessed Mother Isis,' Flavia whispered when he had finished; her face left him in no doubt about her feelings for his story.

Caenis was equally as disgusted. 'You've buried your own mother last month and now you're going to help Nero to kill his? Have you no respect for the sanctity of motherhood? That is one of the crimes that can never be assuaged; it is an affront to every god, not just Isis or the great mother Cybele, but all of them. History is full of examples of men who have done wrong to their mothers and none of them comes to a happy ending. The plays written about them are all tragedies; have you ever thought about that? Not one comedy amongst them. Yes, Agrippina is a Fury who deserves all the ill that could possibly come to her but if she ends up being murdered by her own son then she will be remembered with sympathy rather than scorn. And all those who helped Nero commit such a terrible act will share the odium attached to it. So I advise you, Vespasian, to think again.'

Vespasian sat, looking first at his mistress and then his wife; he did not detect an iota of sympathy for his position in either of them. 'I can't refuse Seneca now; I've already said that I would take the invitation to Agrippina when I go to collect the land deeds.'

Caenis shook her head, looked away and with marked petulance ripped off a hunk of bread; but Flavia continued to stare at him, her face thoughtful as if making a difficult decision. 'Titus' posting is assured?' she asked eventually.

'In as much as anything can be.'

'Then you cannot go back on what you have promised Seneca, otherwise this family's rise will be at a standstill. He has to progress up the Cursus Honorum soon, else his career will founder as it's almost two years since he finished his time with the junior magistrates of the *vigintiviri*. The question is: are we buying his advancement with a crime against the gods? And if so, will the gods' wrath rebound onto him with some apt act of retribution?'

'What do you mean? His son will kill him?'

'Son, daughter, nephew, whatever.'

'More likely to be his brother.' Vespasian instantly regretted the remark as once again he felt he was doing Domitian down.

'I don't know; but what I am sure of is that the gods have a tendency to have the last word and their sense of humour is known for being macabre.'

Vespasian did not like this line of reasoning as he was afraid that Flavia might have a valid point: the gods were well known for their ability to punish with unpleasantly dark humour. 'So what do you recommend, Flavia?'

Flavia looked at him in surprise. 'I do believe that is the first time you have ever asked me for advice, my dear. In the past you have always gone to Caenis for that.'

'That was for political advice,' Caenis said, chewing on some bread. 'This is a religious matter and your devotion to Isis makes you the ideal person to recommend a course of action.'

'Thank you, my dear; that is very gracious of you.'

The two women smiled warmly at one another, causing Vespasian to shiver.

When they had finished being polite, Flavia thought for a few moments, running her forefinger along her lips. 'I have worshipped Mother Isis for most of my adult life and therefore she has an interest in my family and especially in Titus, my firstborn. This crime that you've bought Titus' advancement with is an affront to motherhood so therefore we need to appease the goddess who represents motherhood for my family.'

Vespasian found himself agreeing with his wife. 'That makes sense; I shall organise a sacrifice immediately.'

'No, husband; do it in a couple of months' time, just before you set off, to keep the sacrifice as fresh as possible in the goddess's mind.'

'If you say so. What do you think will be appropriate? A white ox? A sow?'

'No, husband; this has to be something very personal; you have to show the goddess that you really need her protection for our son. You have to make a huge sacrifice, a personal sacrifice.'

Vespasian knew where she was going and tried desperately to think of some alternative, anything, but failed. 'Are you sure, Flavia?'

'Yes; I can't see any other alternative; it only has to be one of them but it has to be the fastest.'

Vespasian's heart sank. 'It shall be done.' He reached across the table and took Caenis' proffered hand, wondering just how he was going to stomach sacrificing to Isis the fastest of his team of Arabian racing horses.

'Are you sure you want to go through with this?' Magnus asked as he stroked the muzzle of the fine Arab stallion that had had the misfortune to be pronounced the fastest of the team by the Green faction stables that housed and trained Vespasian's horses;

the beast gave a snort and rubbed itself hard against Magnus' hand. 'I mean, what if Flavia had just suggested this because she's jealous and thinks that you give more attention to the horses than you do to her?'

'Of course she didn't; she knows just how much these animals mean to me.' Vespasian's voice was tight with emotion; he had grown fond and proud of his pets, as he thought of them. In the five years that his Arabs had raced for the Greens in the Circus Maximus they had competed on twenty-three occasions and had won a staggering nineteen of those races; they were the best team in the Greens' stable and, arguably, the best team in Rome. It had squeezed his heart every day for the last two months knowing that he would have to give one of them to Isis, but he could perfectly understand Flavia's reasoning and cursed the machinations of Pallas and Seneca for having brought him to this situation now that the day was finally here. 'At least I'll still have four to race as a team,' Vespasian said ruefully, stroking the flanks of the beast that steamed as a result of the last run around the circus that he had insisted it had. He took the halter and walked towards the open gates of the Flammian Circus and then on to the Temple of Isis where Flavia and Caenis awaited.

'I beheld a great wonder in heaven, a woman clothed with the Sun, with the Moon at her feet. And on her head was a diadem of the twelve stars. Hear me, O Mother Isis, hear and save. O Queen of love and mercy, whose raiment is the Sun, who is crowned with stars and shod by the Moon, whose countenance is mild and glowing, even as grass refreshed by rain.'

Vespasian stood with a fold of his toga draped over his head as the priestess of Isis continued to recite the ancient prayer calling upon the goddess to hear their supplication. Next to him the magnificent stallion skittered occasionally; the beat of its hoofs hitting the marble floor echoed around the dim, columned interior of the temple, fugged with incense. Flavia held her palms across her chest as she faced the statue of Isis wearing a dress of the same rich blue as the goddess's; her eyes were brim with moisture, although whether it was from communing with her goddess or from the heavy smoke of the burning incense, Vespasian did not know. Magnus stood just staring at the stallion; his one good eye was also glistened with tears but Vespasian knew that this was a genuine show of feeling for the demise of the beast who had, along with its team mates, won Magnus more money in bets than any other horse in his long experience of betting on his beloved Greens. It was a sombre atmosphere in which the priestess finished the prayer and the time for the despatch came closer.

'Mother Isis, hear us,' Flavia pleaded, holding out her hands in supplication. 'Accept this sacrifice and hold your hands over my son, Titus; keep him safe from the crime that is to be committed. Take this stallion, Mother Isis, star crowned, in atonement for my husband's small part in this affront to motherhood. Take, hear and save.' Flavia bowed her head and re-crossed her arms on her chest as the priestess began a chant in praise of the goddess being invoked.

Vespasian glanced at Magnus; the time had come. Four acolytes, youths dressed in Isis-blue tunics decorated with the twelve golden stars of the goddess arranged in a circle, came forward from the shadows, two bearing a great bronze basin that they set upon the ground before the stallion, who looked down at it curiously, checking whether it contained food or water – it did not.

The third acolyte handed Magnus the stunning-mallet and the fourth gave Vespasian a foot-long curved bronze blade with an ivory handle inlaid with silver moons and gold suns. The stallion took no notice of this development and stamped its foot a couple of times as if impatient as to how long things – whatever they were – were taking.

Vespasian moved forward to be level with the horse's neck as two of the acolytes held the beast's halter, worrying it so that it began to pull against them. Vespasian and Magnus shared another quick look; Magnus' right arm arced in a blur of motion. There was a crack as the mallet slammed into the stallion's forehead just above the eyes. Its front legs shook and the animal staggered but remained upright as Vespasian rent a gash, slow and deep, across its throat, releasing a torrent of warm, irontanged blood that turned his arm red as it gushed down to be collected in the basin. Too dazed by the blow to comprehend in its equine mind what was occurring to it, the stallion just stood, trembling as the blood cascaded down, splashing its fetlocks. Its eyes rolled back so they were nothing but white and its mouth and nostrils foamed red; its plight must have then become clear to it for it began to struggle against the halter and kick out with its back legs. But to no avail, the acolytes held firm and the beast's struggles diminished as its strength waned until, with a hideous gurgle from the gaping wound, its front legs collapsed and its head sank to the floor just as the basin, now full, was dragged out of the way. Death followed slowly but surely as the back legs lost their power and the stallion fell onto its side, its eyes still rolling. Vespasian fought back the tears that Magnus was now openly shedding as the horse made pitiful attempts to lift itself back up, each more feeble than the last, until it lay still, its chest barely rising and falling.

And then that too became still.

Vespasian performed the rest of the sacrifice in a haze of misery, barely aware of removing the heart and liver to the accompaniment of the prayers and chants of the priestess and Flavia and hardly remembering the pouring of blood libations on the altar and at the goddess's feet. But still it was done and it was done well so that the procedure did not have to be repeated and he should lose another of his prized possessions. It was with relief that Vespasian completed the ceremony in the knowledge that Isis had accepted the sacrifice, but it was with foreboding as to what was to happen that Vespasian walked with Magnus down the steps of the temple and began his journey south to assist in a matricide.

CHAPTER VI

'I DON'T BELIEVE IT!' Agrippina threw down the invitation, which she had barely glanced at, and stared at Vespasian; he could feel the venom. 'My son has tried to poison me twice to my certain knowledge and would have succeeded had it not been for a friend writing to warn me and to advise me as to which antidote to take. And then, the last time I slept under his roof the ceiling of my bedchamber mysteriously collapsed; I would have been crushed had it not been for the fact that my bed was next to a tall and sturdy piece of furniture. After going to all this trouble why would he want to be reconciled with me and pretend that we are a loving mother and son?'

'Perhaps he feels the anger of the gods at attempting such a hideous crime,' Pallas suggested, 'and he wants to make up for such deeds by showing you the filial honour that you deserve, which is why he has, seemingly spontaneously, chosen to invite you to celebrate the feast of Minerva with him.'

Vespasian was not astonished by Pallas' brazen lie as he stood before the couple sitting in the shade of an olive tree on a terrace overlooking the Bay of Neapolis with the hulking presence of Vesuvius in the distance; it was what he had become used to in the years of wading through imperial politics. It was what came next that caused him to start.

'Besides,' Pallas went on, 'when you're with Nero he would hardly dare to kill you in public and receive the opprobrium of all for being a matricide; so if there is to be an attempt on your life then it will be aboard the ship. I suggest that Vespasian and Magnus accompany you there and back with your freedman, Gallus, to defend you against any assassination attempts out at sea.' Pallas looked at Vespasian innocently. 'You'd be only too pleased to do that for me, Vespasian, wouldn't you?'

Vespasian gritted his teeth; he could not let on that he knew what was to happen. 'Only too pleased, Pallas.'

'There you are, my dear; problem solved.'

Agrippina did not seem convinced and gazed out over the sea, glimmering with warm afternoon sun and speckled with fishing boats; in the distance a trireme pulled south, headed for one of the ports at the other end of the bay. 'I don't know, Pallas; I don't trust this, it's too sudden and has no logic to it. Last time I saw him, at the beginning of the month, we had a major row about how he was comporting himself with Otho's wife, Poppaea Sabina, now that he's as good as exiled Otho by sending him to govern Lusitania. I tried to explain to him that if he divorced Claudia Octavia he would be losing quite a substantial piece of his legitimacy as she is Claudius' blood-daughter. He laughed at me and showed no inclination to reconciliation, quite the opposite in fact; he told me that he would sleep with whomever he wanted to and would marry Poppaea even if it meant having Claudia executed and ordering Otho to commit suicide if he continues refusing to divorce Poppaea. And he threatened to kill me, yet again, if I tried to interfere.'

'Perhaps he's realised that even an emperor has to keep up appearances.'

'No; I didn't bring up my son to worry about what other people think. I brought him up to take what he wants and not to care about others. I brought him up to be emperor. When he was a babe I had his horoscope cast by two different astrologers; both said that he would become emperor and both said that, once he did, he would kill me. I replied: "Let him kill me so long as he becomes emperor." I'm starting to think that I spoke rashly.'

Pallas scoffed. 'I've never believed in the ridiculous Babylonian so-called science of astrology. Augury, yes, because that is interpreting the will of the gods at this present moment through bird flight or lightning or whatever; and their will changes as circumstance does. To think that the course of one's life is completely mapped out by the position of the planets at the moment of your birth is ludicrous; it means that the gods have no influence upon how we lead our lives because it's been pre-ordained.'

Vespasian enjoyed Pallas' reasoning and watched carefully as Agrippina tried to refute it in her head.

'But he did become emperor,' she pointed out.

'Of course he did, but that was not because the planets had pre-ordained it; it was because you and he desired that event more than anyone else and had the will to dispose of all that stood in his way.'

As Agrippina digested this, a skein of geese came into view, flying in formation from the direction of the Emperor's villa at Baiae. 'What would an augur say about that?' she asked pointing at the birds.

Pallas shrugged. 'I'm not in the college of augurs and nor have I ever taken much interest in the science. What do you think, Vespasian? Do you have any experience in augury?'

'I do,' Vespasian lied, knowing that Agrippina was yet to be convinced. 'I once considered applying to Claudius for a position in the college of augurs but then ...' He looked with regret at Agrippina. 'Well, then I fell out of favour. However, my reading of that sign would be that, in conjunction with the ship sailing south, the geese returning north would mean that you will go south to Baiae and return north to Bauli without any incident.'

Agrippina watched the geese fly overhead; as they did so the formation changed and another took the lead at the apex of the 'V'.

'Renewal,' Vespasian found himself saying, astounded by his unabashed dissembling; the signs of bird flight had always been a mystery to him. 'It's quite clear that you will come back after there has been a renewal.'

Pallas took up the theme. 'Which fits in perfectly with the Emperor's stated aim of this dinner. A reconciliation; a renewal of trust.'

Agrippina's dark eyes bored into her lover. 'Is that what you really think or are you just trying to persuade me to my death?'

Pallas did not show what he thought; he rarely did. 'Don't go then, my dear, and see what happens if you refuse the Emperor's invitation and hospitality. If, however, your fears are founded and he has decided to kill you, then kill you he will, whether you get on the ship he's sending or not.'

This clinched it for Agrippina; she nodded slowly as her mind ran over the logic of the argument. 'Yes, my dear, you're right; I have to go if I want the chance of any power ever again. For too long have I been excluded, my opinion not registered; this is a final opportunity and if my son plays me false then I shall go out with defiance, but if he's genuine then I shall do everything within my power to draw him to me and keep him captivated. I shall accept the invitation.'

'You have made the right decision,' Pallas said, although he knew that to be a complete lie.

What he was unaware of, however, was that Vespasian knew that too.

Magnus sniffed the air as the trireme slipped along the coast, its oars rising and dipping in time to the high-pitched call of the stroke-master's pipe; lights began to twinkle in the luxurious villas along the shore as dusk fell on the holiday playground of the wealthy. 'I'd be happier if this ship was taking us all the way back to Rome rather than dropping us off at what I can only assume is going to be a venomous dinner, if you take my meaning?'

'I do indeed, but I don't think Nero will try poison.' Vespasian looked over to Agrippina reclining on a sumptuous couch on a dais in the bow of the ship watched over by her bulky freedman, Gallus. She was dressed for seduction, in the finest of everything; each item, whether it be jewellery or a garment, had been chosen to accentuate her still very desirable femininity; a femininity she evidently planned to use on her own son in a final attempt to lure him back into her incestuous clutches. Two braziers kept her warm as her body slave, Acerronia, attended to her coiffure, maintaining it from any damage caused by the slight breeze.

'Well, I ain't going to be tucking into any tasty morsels there.'

'Don't worry, you won't be invited to. I can't see Nero wanting to recline to dinner with the likes of you when he's got his mother to kill. You'll be perfectly safe.'

'What about you?'

'I imagine that I'll be asked to join them as one of the witnesses to the great reunion so that I can swear to just how well they were getting on together before she was so tragically taken from the Emperor.'

Magnus contemplated this as the landing jetty on the shoreline of the grounds of Nero's villa came into view. Two great torches flamed at its end and within their light half a dozen silhouetted figures stood. The trireme's *trierarchus* began calling out a series of orders in fluent Nautic; the ship slowed and then, as the larboard-side's oars were hauled in, it slewed around until, with considerable grace, it nudged the jetty and came to a creaking rest.

'Mother, my darling! You've come at last.' From within the group of silhouettes Nero, with Burrus next to him, emerged, his arms extended towards Agrippina, still in her position in the bow of the ship. 'Let me help you.' He moved to board the vessel but the gangplank had not yet been fixed in place. 'Herculeius! How dare you keep the woman who bore your Emperor waiting?' He clapped his hands, staccato, and the trierarchus issued a stream of nautical oaths and speeded up the process of lowering the gangplank by kicking the nearest sailor up the backside and clouting another couple around the ears so that they stumbled and nearly dropped their load.

Eventually, and with a few more bruises inflicted, the gangplank was in place and Nero rushed up it, knocking an unfortunate sailor off the side so that he fell onto the jetty, his right leg slipping between it and the hull of the ship as it bobbed gently back and forth against it, crushing the limb; his screams were ignored as the Emperor helped his mother to her feet and took her into the warmest of embraces.

'Oh, Mother, my darling Mother, it has been too long; a whole month,' Nero crooned in a voice loud enough for Vespasian to hear despite the agony of the injured sailor. 'How this misunderstanding between us has been allowed to fester, I don't know.' He threw back his head with his right hand placed languidly on his brow in the manner of an actor in a tragedy. 'I blame myself, Mother, and I promise to do all in my power to make it up to you.'

Agrippina, who had hitherto done nothing to express joy or otherwise at the reunion with her son, allowed herself a smile. 'In which case, my sweet boy, you will be doing a lot seeing as you have so much power; enough to share some with your mother to make up for your negligence.'

Nero laughed off Agrippina's naked appeal for a position at the heart of his regime and, with formal elegance, escorted her from the ship; Burrus and the three Praetorian centurions accompanying him to guard Nero and his mother snapped salutes as the injured sailor was hauled away by his comrades, still howling with pain.

Vespasian and Magnus followed the imperial couple at a discreet distance down onto the jetty where Seneca was waiting. 'How is she?' he asked in a whisper, his eyes showing apprehension in the torchlight. 'I mean, has she indicated any, how shall I put it, reluctance, yes, reluctance that's it; has she indicated any reluctance to be reconciled with the Emperor?'

Vespasian played the innocent, pretending that he had not guessed, along with his brother, the real reason why Agrippina had been invited here and just who was aiding the Emperor in committing matricide in order that he too could benefit from Agrippina's death. 'She knows that whether the Emperor is playing her false or not is irrelevant, as if he's not then this her last chance at power, and if he is then she's doomed never to be back in favour with him anyway.'

Seneca chuckled. 'Sensible vixen to calculate in such a way; but I think that she'll be pleasantly surprised as the Emperor is entirely genuine in reaching out his hand in friendship – no, love, yes, love, that is the just word in this case.'

'Is it? How gratifying,' Vespasian said without feeling the least bit gratified by the lie given by Seneca concerning the Emperor's alleged motives.

'Yes, it is, isn't it?' Seneca chuckled again and slapped Vespasian on the back. 'I do love a family reunion; it makes for such a happy occasion. Come, my dear Vespasian, you must join us in recognition of your part in bringing about this joyous event. I believe you've met Vologases, the Great King of Parthia?'

'I did, a few years ago now. Why?'

'Excellent, excellent. Come, we have much to discuss and to celebrate.'

And so, with a 'what did I tell you?' glance at Magnus, Vespasian accompanied Seneca towards Nero's seaside pleasure villa.

And pleasure was indeed the watchword in this palace of delights that the Emperor had stuffed full to the brim with luxury. Every imaginable taste could be catered for whether it was for the flesh of either sex or none, be it thin, fat, deformed, old, or, indeed, young. But if carnality was not your whim then music, theatre, gourmet cuisine and the finest wines were also on offer. However, if you were more of the outdoor type then there was a stable filled with some of the finest horseflesh money could buy, ready to be driven about the oval track Nero had had constructed at the rear of the villa. There was even an exercise area next to the bath-house, not that Nero exercised that much but he did appreciate, from time to time, watching others do so; especially should they be at the peak of physical condition. Any pleasure could be indulged in in this villa, any pleasure, that is, save one: there was no death for amusement – although there was death as punishment. Nero had recently decreed that gladiatorial contests should not be to the death and should instead be about the beauty of combat, the elegance of sword play, the skill of the fighter, and to that end he had banned all gladiatorial blood from the arena. It also had the gratifying side effect for the profligate Emperor of allowing him to put on ever grander displays without having to pay the gladiatorial schools for the lives of their dead property. To most people's surprise, Nero kept up this regime in the privacy of his own domain but there was so much else to distract his visitors that no one seemed to mind unduly. But, of course, they were still only too well aware that should they displease the Emperor during their visit then the moratorium on death was only for amusement, not punishment; no, for the élite of Rome to be in the presence of the Emperor always involved the presence of fear and not even Agrippina was exempt from it.

And so to cover her fear, so that her son would not notice it, she allowed herself to enjoy the fruits of Baiae.

Nero, however, had not brought his mother to Baiae just so that she could indulge in the pleasures that it offered; far from it: he had brought her here to woo her before witnesses. His objective was that by the end of the evening she would feel completely relaxed and at ease in his company and he went about this mission with an extraordinary energy. It was he who served her the first cup of wine, making a point of tasting it first to show that whatever she may have thought him guilty of in the past he was not trying to poison her this evening. It was Nero who deferred to her on the choice of music that the ensemble of musicians, placed discreetly behind intricately carved wooden and ivory screens, should play. Nero himself chastised a slave who had been clumsy enough to brush against Agrippina's arm as he served her water for her second cup of wine; and to show his filial concern for the presumption of one so far beneath his mother, Nero ordered the hapless man to be flogged then and there until the whiteness of his ribs could be seen through the tattered flesh and streaming blood. Yes, Nero was the model son trying to make every effort to ensure that his mother had the most relaxing and carefree of evenings.

And Vespasian observed all this along with a couple of dozen other senators, summoned to bear witness to the joyous occasion. He watched the solemnity with which mother and son said prayers and made sacrifices to the goddess Minerva; and he, along with his colleagues, stood with a fold of his toga covering his head, partaking in the ceremony, as the would-be murderer performed the rites sacred to the virgin goddess of music and poetry alongside his intended victim. He partook of a meal of such extravagance that even Caligula might have felt a twinge of envy, joining in the toasts and savouring recipes of Nero's own concoction as they were entertained by troupes of dancers and acrobats from all over the Empire. He listened intently as Nero praised his mother, calling her the best of mothers and affirming that any good son should tolerate outbursts from their parents and try to soothe their behaviour. He and the rest of the witnesses pretended not to notice the salacious kisses exchanged by the reconciled couple and they feigned not to see the lingering caresses that also passed between them; but they applauded wholeheartedly when Nero raised Agrippina to her feet and announced that they would leave the company for a short while so that they could walk and talk in private around the gardens. When the imperial couple returned, not long later, Vespasian and the others welcomed them back with equal enthusiasm and tried not to think about how the grass stains came to be on Agrippina's stola around the height of her knees and why her hair on either side of her head was ruffled as if it had been subject to a fierce grip.

Soon it was time for the parting and Nero spilled many tears at the thought of being separated from his mother but extracted a solemn promise from her that she would allow him to return the visit the following evening. 'Mother, you have made me the happiest of sons,' Nero declared looking to the heavens, his left arm raised.

Agrippina played her part and cradled Nero's chin in the palm of her hand and, pulling him close, kissed him full on the mouth. 'To be reunited with her son after an estrangement is a mother's dream.'

This sentiment was commended by all present and joy seemed unconfined.

'Anicetus!' Nero called, once he was able to master the emotion of the moment. 'Where are you? Is it here?'

A man stepped out of the shadows, a man whom Vespasian was sure had not been there before. He wore the uniform of a prefect and Vespasian knew him to be a freedman of Nero's and recently appointed the commander of the fleet at Misenum a few miles north up the coast.

'Well?' Nero enquired.

'Princeps, it has arrived and it is splendid.'

Nero clapped his hands together like an excited child. 'Excellent!' He turned to Agrippina. 'Mother, I have had a beautiful thing created for myself but, despite its beauty, it cannot please me nearly as much as you responding so favourably to my overtures of peace; it makes me so happy to know that there is nothing but love between us now. So therefore, Mother, come and see what I've had crafted for my pleasure that I now, spontaneously, give to you in celebration of our peaceful accord.' He took Agrippina by the hand and led her from the hall; Vespasian and the other senators followed in close attendance.

Through the villa Nero led them and then on out into a night chilled by a freshening wind. Across the lawns they went, down towards the sea. And there at the jetty, on the opposite side to the trireme upon which they had arrived, was moored another vessel. Even in the light of the two torches still flaming at the jetty's end, Vespasian could see that it was painted white and its metal fittings were gilded. And he could see why this evening had been almost four months in the preparation: it was magnificent. At its prow was a swan's neck and head, elegantly carved and covered with white feathers each individually attached. Amidships were two wings, one on either side; again these were feathered. Protruding from the stern and forming a covered seating area was the tail of the bird so that the whole vessel resembled a swan swimming.

Cries of wonder and disbelief that such a thing could have been conceived, let alone built, erupted from the senators, and Vespasian did not hold his contribution back even though he knew that this was not what it appeared to be. However, one glance at the genuinely pleased smile written all over Agrippina's face told him that she suspected nothing; she evidently thought that Nero had been sincere and her desirable femininity had truly secured their relationship and this gift was the proof of it: how could something so extravagant, so beautiful, so elegant be anything other than what it seemed: a gift from an Emperor to his mother? It did not cross her mind that this was to be the instrument of her death. She flung her arms around Nero's neck and kissed his cheeks and he, in turn, cupped her breasts in his hands and bent to nuzzle them. Mother and son parted on the best of terms as all present would be able to bear witness to.

'You should have seen it arrive,' Magnus said, appearing next to Vespasian. 'I really thought it was a monstrous swan at first, until I saw the oars sticking out.'

Vespasian looked at the vessel, impressed at the effort that Nero had gone to in order to hide his true intentions. 'He must be very keen for people not to suspect him one bit over her death.'

'He's going to kill her in that? How?'

'I imagine he'll sink it.'

Gallus, Agrippina's freedman, helped her aboard and Acerronia, her slave, went ahead to plump up the cushions on the couch beneath the swan's tail. As Agrippina stepped onto the deck she turned. 'Where is Vespasian? He and his man are meant to be accompanying me.'

Vespasian jolted; he had no intention of getting on that ship. He stepped further back into the shadows.

'Where're Vespasian and his man?' Agrippina repeated with more truculence.

'Shit!' Magnus whispered. 'Are we going to have to go too?'

Nero looked around. 'Vespasian?'

Vespasian was unable to hide any longer, not with the Emperor calling for him. 'I'm here, Princeps,' he said stepping out from the crowd.

Nero beamed at him. 'There you are; you and your man will accompany my mother.'

Vespasian swallowed. 'As you wish, Princeps.' He began to walk forward.

'Princeps,' Seneca said, putting a restraining hand on Vespasian's shoulder. 'I was very much hoping to keep Senator Vespasian here with me for the rest of the evening, as I was hoping to ... er ... what's the best way of putting it?'

'Just put it anyway you like,' Nero snapped, evidently irritated, 'but put it quickly as my mother is waiting.'

'Borrow him, Princeps; yes, that's exactly it. Borrow him.'

'Borrow him? What do you mean by that?'

'I was hoping that he could give me some insight into the mind of the Parthian King, Vologases, seeing as he is the only senator to have met him and we are thinking of sending an embassy to him to discuss the Armenian question very soon in light of Corbulo's recent successes with our legions out there and to demand that he refutes his younger brother Tiridates' claim to the throne.'

Nero thought for a few moments. 'Why now?'

'What better time than the present, Princeps? It'll give us more time to draft a speech for the ambassador to read out.'

This made sense to Nero and he acquiesced. 'Very well, you can *borrow* Vespasian, but his man has no need to stay; he can accompany my mother to ensure her safety.'

Seneca inclined his head. 'Indeed he can, Princeps.' He looked at Magnus and gestured him towards the ship.

'I guess I don't have a choice,' Magnus muttered to Vespasian under his breath.

'I'm afraid you don't, old friend.'

'Well, there's always a first time to learn how to swim.' Magnus patted Vespasian's shoulder and walked towards the ship.

Vespasian watched his friend ascend the gangplank, which was drawn up after him. With a series of nautical orders ropes were cast off and the ship was pushed clear of the jetty. Oars appeared from within the vessel and the stroke-master's shrill pipe got them beating in slow time. The graceful vessel rowed off into the night as the wind freshened even more and the waves got up so that the white swan swam on white horses. Soon it was but a shadow out to sea and then Vespasian could see it no more.

Once Agrippina had gone, Nero's creatures came out: the people with whom he enjoyed amusing himself but whom he would rather hide from his mother lest they sway her mood and spoil his deception. Vespasian entered the atrium and sat in a corner with Seneca, watching them emerge from wherever they had been secreted: battered charioteers, actors and the more raucous sort of musician as well as deformed things of either sex who were there to be enjoyed by whoever felt the need. Of Nero, however, there was no sign, which presented a difficulty to the senators, who did not know whether they had been dismissed or were required to wait for the Emperor to return. They milled around the atrium in small groups drinking wine, which was circulated by slaves, and talking in hushed tones as Burrus walked amongst them laughing and joking with each group and assuring them that the Emperor would be down soon.

Now that he and Seneca were relatively secluded, Vespasian felt free to talk. 'Why did you do it?'

Seneca was a picture of innocence. 'Do what, my dear fellow?'

'Prevent me from getting on a doomed ship while I have to watch my friend walk to his possible death.'

'Doomed? Who said anything about it being doomed?'

'Oh come on, Seneca; don't think that I don't know just what has been going on. How you did nothing to stop me from believing that Caenis had betrayed me to you so that your real motive for getting Agrippina here and your co-operation with Pallas for doing so could be kept hidden.' He waved a hand towards the senators. 'Assembling a load of witnesses to watch the happy reunion and then see the tears and anguish of the Emperor when he receives the news that his darling mother has gone the way of the Ferryman so that no one can accuse Nero of such a disgusting crime. You and Pallas have formed an alliance to get rid of Agrippina for your mutual benefit and the Emperor's convenience; you used me as your tool, and yet rather than discard me when Agrippina unexpectedly gave you the chance to be rid of someone who may well have seen through the plot, you save me. Why?'

Seneca chuckled, genuinely amused. 'Well, well; I did question Pallas when he assured me that you would never suspect the real motive for the reconciliation. He evidently underestimated you. But I didn't. I was sure that you wouldn't be able to believe that Caenis spied on you for me so it was a certainty, in my opinion, that you would realise the true nature of the plot—'

'It was my brother, actually.'

'Whoever; but don't worry, Titus will still get his posting in Germania. The point was that I wanted you implicated so that I would have a certain amount of, what's the best way to describe it? Leverage! Yes, leverage; I needed to get a certain amount of leverage over you.' Seneca beamed broadly at Vespasian, a picture of contentment. 'Which I now have.'

'You're even more involved than I am in Nero's matricide, should the crime become public.'

'Perhaps so, but that would take a lot of proving; and yet there are plenty of people who can swear that it was you who, how shall we put it? Enticed, yes, there are plenty of people who can swear that it was you who enticed Agrippina to her death. And of course the crime will become public knowledge; it's a stupid plan that Nero and Anicetus have come up with but I couldn't dissuade Nero from it because I had to pretend to him that I had no notion of the scheme. A lead-weighted, collapsing awning in the form of a swan's tail, on a ship that is designed to fall apart at probably around about now; ridiculous! Of all the fifty or so crew aboard only twenty are in on the plan; but what about the others? Some of them will survive and the whole foolish affair will be revealed, and then what?' Two raised eyebrows. 'Hmmm?'

Vespasian did not need to think for too long to have the answer. 'Nero will be looking for scapegoats.'

'Yes, anybody who can be used to divert attention away from him will be in danger. You see, Vespasian, I've known Nero a long time and I know that at heart he does have some form of a conscience, in that he doesn't like people to think badly of him, which is a burden in someone becoming so prone to … what should I call them … despicable, yes, that will do nicely, despicable deeds; although, he does seem to have stopped his rampages through the city since that business with Terpnus.' Seneca scrutinised him intently, giving Vespasian the impression that he knew more about the incident than he, Vespasian, would wish. 'So, apart from Anicetus, who Nero finds very useful for the more hideous of his crimes, everybody involved in the plot's days are numbered, as are the men's on the ship, should any of them survive, and then of course, if that doesn't satisfy Nero, I could point out to him that there is you.'

'Not you or Burrus?'

'My dear fellow, as I said: I, like Burrus, had no notion of the scheme and Nero knows that. Now, I can use my influence with Nero to save you and that's the leverage, I think we decided that was the right word, that's the leverage that I now have on you.'

Vespasian groaned. 'What do you want?'

'Well, for a start, I want Venutius, the Britannic King that you've got tucked up nice and safe with Caratacus, to be delivered secretly into my custody so that he can't go spreading his tittle-tattle about me lending him money.'

Vespasian looked at Seneca in astonishment.

'Don't act so surprised, Vespasian; don't you think that when a man seriously in debt to me goes missing I wouldn't take the trouble to find out where he is?'

'I suppose you would; so you have some form of a conscience as well, Seneca?'

'Not when it comes to how I make my money. Nevertheless, I do want to be seen as someone who is civilised, thoughtful and erudite, so lending large amounts to warlike Britannic kings and queens might be ... misconstrued, shall we say?'

'We shall; it wouldn't really sit well with your philosophical treatises, from what I hear of them. Very well, I'll get Venutius for you.'

'As soon as we get back to Rome.'

'Agreed; but that'll be it.'

Seneca beamed again. 'Will it? I don't think so, my dear fellow; Nero has a very long memory.'

Before Vespasian could object, Nero came into the room accompanied by Poppaea Sabina whom he had also taken care to hide from Agrippina. 'Friends,' he declaimed in his husky voice, 'we shall sacrifice again in thanks to Minerva, the goddess of two of my passions, music and poetry, and also to the gods of my household, for the safe delivery of my mother to her villa. May they hold their hands over her as she sails.'

And so all joined Nero in the prayers around the *lararium* and as Nero pronounced the auspices good that the goddess would, indeed, hold her hands over Agrippina, a dishevelled man burst through the door escorted by a couple of Praetorian Guardsmen.

'Princeps, Princeps!' he called, interrupting the prayers. 'A tragedy has occurred.'

Nero flung his hands in the air, melodramatically rolling his eyes, doing his best impression of someone receiving awful and unexpected news; Vespasian found himself cringing at the sight. 'What is it, man? Out with it!'

'The Augusta's ship has gone down and—'

The howl that Nero let fly was of titanic proportions and it echoed around the columns of the atrium, louder and stronger than any sound he had ever made before. Senators immediately rushed to support their Emperor in his grief as Vespasian prayed to Mars for Magnus' deliverance, but without much hope.

'Minerva!' Nero wailed. 'Cruel goddess to accept the sacrifice to protect my mother and then to renege.'

'But, Princeps! Princeps!' the messenger shouted over Nero's robust lamentations. 'The Augusta, she's safe, she managed to get ashore.'

The change was almost instant; Nero went from red-faced grief to pale fear. 'What?'

Poppaea screamed.

The messenger seemed confused by the reactions but pressed on with his news. 'The Augusta managed to swim to safety.'

Burrus stepped forward. 'Are you certain?'

'Yes, prefect, she was seen swimming away from the ship and was picked up by some fishermen who took her to her villa at Bauli.'

'Then surely that's good news, Princeps,' Burrus said, turning to the Emperor.

Vespasian felt a small hope for Magnus now that he knew there were boats in the vicinity of the wreck.

Poppaea grabbed Nero's arm and whispered urgently in his ear.

Panic was now in Nero's eyes. 'You're right; she'll kill me! She'll arm her slaves or send soldiers; the legions have always loved her because she is Germanicus' daughter.'

'It would seem that Minerva did answer Nero's prayers after all,' Vespasian observed dryly to Seneca.

'I don't think she was meant to,' Seneca muttered as he went forward. 'Princeps! Whatever is the matter? You must be confused; your mother has been saved. It is good news, surely?'

Nero turned with wild eyes to Seneca and then rushed towards him, grabbing his shoulders. 'No, don't you see? It was all an act; I planned to kill her. I wanted her dead.' He glanced back at

Poppaea. 'We wanted her dead; she was meant to drown on the ship, not escape. She'll know it was me, she will, and she'll want her revenge because she's a beastly woman when roused and her desire for vengeance knows no end. She'll kill me!'

Seneca tried to pull the rambling Nero from the room as all who had witnessed the outburst realised the significance of what had been said and what a hideous crime their Emperor had attempted. It had become public knowledge even sooner than Seneca had predicted.

Nero resisted all attempts to remove him from the room. 'What shall I do, Seneca, Burrus, my friends, my protectors? I don't want to die; it wouldn't be fair if I should die and she should live. What should I do? I know, I'll take a ship to Alexandria and hide from her there. Have my things packed at once.'

'Princeps, who is the Emperor?' Seneca asked.

Nero calmed, the answer clearing his mind. 'I am.'

'Indeed; so let us act in the manner of an emperor. An emperor hides from no one. An emperor issues commands. An emperor is above the law because he is the law.'

'He's right,' Poppaea hissed. 'Act before she does; send someone to execute her.'

'But I can't do that in cold blood; what would people think?'

Burrus had no doubt. 'She's plotting against you with people who would have rather seen Germanicus on the throne. The people will praise the gods for your safe delivery from the murderous conspiracy hatched by your own mother. They'll applaud your resolve for the sake of the peace of the Empire. I'll have the Praetorian Guard reaffirm allegiance to you immediately and you can distribute a donative to them in gratitude and this whole affair will turn into a triumph for you, Princeps.'

Nero pulled himself together, nodding gravely. 'You're right, both of you.' He smiled at Poppaea. 'And you, my sweet dove, thank you.' Looking around the room he soon found who he sought. 'Anicetus, this is your failure.'

The prefect of the Misenum fleet paled as Nero approached him, and then looked with relief at the door as the second interruption of the evening was escorted in by smart-stepping Praetorians.

'Who is this?' Nero demanded.

'My name is Agermus, Princeps,' the new arrival replied. 'I am a freedman of your mother's. She sends me with a message to say that she is well, having escaped from the unfortunate foundering of your beautiful gift with nothing but a minor wound to the head. She knows that you will be mortified to hear of the accident but she entreats you to in no way blame yourself as she is sure that you could have had nothing to do with the canopy collapsing and killing Gallus nor did you have knowledge of the men who battered Acerronia to death. She begs to be excused your visit tomorrow as she feels that she must take a few days to recuperate.'

'Lies!' Nero screamed, moving next to Anicetus. 'All lies; she's sent you here to kill me, hasn't she? Admit it.'

'P-P-Princeps, no.'

Nero grabbed Anicetus' sword in what he hoped was a surreptitious manner and approached the freedman so that their faces were a hand's breadth apart. 'Admit that you were sent to kill me.'

'No, Princeps, never.'

There was a metallic clang and Nero stepped back; at Agermus' feet was the sword.

'Then what's that that has just fallen out of your tunic?' Nero demanded.

Agermus looked in horror at the weapon. 'That's not mine, Princeps, you dropped it.'

'Me! Why would I drop a weapon so close to someone sent to assassinate me? I'd be mad to do that. Burrus, have him taken away and executed.'

As the pathetically framed man was dragged away pleading in desperation for his life, Nero turned back to Anicetus. 'It's your duty to remedy this; do you understand?'

The prefect just nodded, dumbly.

'Take the trireme and a century of marines and go now.'

Anicetus saluted and turned smartly on his heel.

Nero addressed the senators. 'Agrippina has directly threatened the life of your Emperor; you were all witness to it.'

No one objected to that interpretation of events.

'You can all see that after the kindness that I have tried to show her here and despite it, she does this.' Nero pointed to the sword still lying where he had dropped it. 'She cannot be trusted and therefore I have no alternative. And, Vespasian,' Nero growled, turning to him. 'I think that Seneca's finished borrowing you now; seeing as you're part of all this you can go with Anicetus to make sure that he does the job properly this time and then keep the villa closed and stay there so that no one sees her body until I arrive soon after dawn.'

Thus, a couple of hours later as dawn revealed a sky clear of cloud, Vespasian found himself walking with Anicetus and Herculeius, the trierarchus, along the jetty at Bauli; behind them a century of marines was disembarking from the trireme. Up ahead, becoming ever more distinct in the growing light, lay Agrippina's villa. No one spoke as there was nothing to say, no debate; should they not complete the task that they had been assigned by their Emperor then their lives would be forfeit.

Vespasian recalled when he had been present at the execution of Messalina, which had been, in part, brought about by Agrippina so that the way would be clear for her to marry her uncle, Claudius, and thus become the most powerful woman in Rome. He smiled inwardly at the dark justice of fate: Agrippina's death had been decreed by Poppaea Sabina, the woman who would now move to become the most powerful of her sex in Rome; with Agrippina gone there would be nothing to stop her from having Nero divorcing Claudia and so leaving the way clear for her to become empress.

'You're looking grim.'

Vespasian turned towards the sound of the familiar voice, letting Anicetus and Herculeius go on ahead. 'So you learnt to swim after all, did you?'

Magnus was sitting, leaning against the hull of an upturned fishing boat. 'Didn't need to in the end; it turned out that swan wings are very buoyant. Me and a few of the lads clung onto one and kicked our way to shore.' He eased himself up and fell into step beside Vespasian. 'I waited here for you because I guessed that when Nero found out what a shambles his attempt at staging an accident was he'd send a party to do it properly and, being already implicated, you'd be part of it.'

'Well, you were right. I heard roughly what happened; so how did Agrippina get away?'

Magnus gave a grim little laugh. 'A lucky piece of selfishness by her slave. After the canopy had come down, crushing Gallus but missing the two women on account of the high-backed couch that Agrippina was reclining in, the ship started to take in water. Some of the crew were part of the conspiracy but most of them were just shit-scared. Anyway, the bastards who were trying to sink the ship must have had some mechanism to scuttle it that hadn't completely worked so they started to try and capsize it by all going onto one side. This helped and water started flooding in. At this point Acerronia, who was evidently unaware that this was an attempt on Agrippina's life, started to shout out that she was Agrippina and that the crew should save her. This surprised the assassins as they'd thought that Agrippina was dead beneath the canopy and were now trying to sink the ship so that there'd be no evidence as such; so they battered Acerronia to death with oars whilst Agrippina managed to slip over the side in the dark. Anyway the ship eventually went down, the assassins, and those of the crew who could, swam for the shore whilst me and the rest of the lads floundered around waiting for Neptune to suck us under; only he didn't but sent us a swan wing to float on instead, which I felt to be very decent of him. I shall be sacrificing a swan to him as soon as I have the chance.'

'That's the least you can do.'

'Two, then.'

'That should do it. Sounds like it was more than a shambles. Why put a high-backed couch on board for Agrippina to recline on when you're trying to crush her with something falling from above? Especially when the last time you tried the same trick she was saved by a high-backed piece of furniture.' Vespasian shook his head in disbelief. 'If they had gone about it properly I wouldn't be having to be part of finishing off the job.'

'Yeah, well, no point in moaning about it now.'

Vespasian's attention was taken by a fugitive fleeing from the house, now only fifty paces away.

'Get her!' Anicetus shouted at the marine centurion.

Two men were despatched and quickly ran the woman down and dragged her, writhing, back. They threw her on the ground; by her attire she was obviously a slave. She was young and not unattractive, if slightly plump, with a shock of angry-red hair.

Anicetus slapped the woman a couple of times across the face. 'Where were you going?'

'Please, master; I saw you coming and was just trying to get away.'

'Who do you belong to?'

'Agrippina, master.'

'Is she in there?'

'Yes, master; she's locked herself into her bedroom.'

'And you were deserting your mistress and running away, were you?' Anicetus drew his sword. 'You know the penalty for that, don't you?'

'Wait,' Vespasian said, putting an arm across Anicetus. He looked down at the slave girl. 'Is Pallas still in there?'

The girl looked with terrified eyes at the sword, unable to answer.

'It's all right; you won't come to any harm. Anicetus, put that away, this girl is now under my protection.'

Anicetus did as he was told.

'What's your name?'

'Caitlín, master.'

'So, Caitlín, has Pallas left?'

'Yes, master,' the girl said, watching the sword go back into the scabbard. 'He left as soon as the mistress departed for Baiae yesterday evening.'

'What a surprise. Magnus, you look after her; bring her with us and make sure that she comes to no harm.'

'That'll be my pleasure,' Magnus said, eying the girl's full figure with the appreciation of a connoisseur.

Vespasian nodded to Anicetus. 'Deploy your men.'

'Centurion Obartius!' Anicetus called. 'Have your lads surround the villa and bring me anyone who tries to get out.'

Obartius saluted, issued a stream of orders and the marine century split up into eight-man sections, obeying Anicetus' command.

'Right, let's get this done,' Vespasian said once the men were all in position.

Anicetus led Obartius and eight marines up to the front door; it was locked. Without ceremony two of the men shoulder-barged their shields into it; after three hits it cracked open. Anicetus led them in. The atrium was deserted; very few lamps were lit so despite the growing light outside it was shadowed with gloom.

'Which way?' Vespasian asked the girl.

She pointed a trembling finger down a corridor that ran off the left-hand side of the atrium. 'Down there at the end, on the right, master.'

The marines clattered down the corridor, hobnailed sandals sparking on the marble in the half-light. The same two marines hefted their shields against the door at the end and within moments it was hanging off its hinges.

There was a screech from within as the marines piled through the doorway. Vespasian followed Anicetus and Herculeius in to see Agrippina standing, four-square, facing up to the marines; defiant to the end.

A slave girl nipped out of a door behind her but Agrippina disdained to follow. 'Are you deserting me too?' she yelled after the fleeing slave, before looking back to Anicetus and levelling her voice. 'If you've come to visit the patient on behalf of my son, I can report to you that she is fully recovered. But if you have come to commit a crime, did the order come from Nero?'

But neither Anicetus nor Herculeius bothered to answer as they moved towards her, the trierarchus brandishing a club, the other, his sword. The club arced round towards Agrippina's head but she ducked and it just caught her a glancing blow.

'Strike here, Anicetus!' Agrippina screamed, ripping her stola open so that her stomach was exposed. 'Strike me in the belly because that is what bore Nero!'

Straight and true, Anicetus plunged his blade into her womb and, straining, forced it up, slicing through flesh and muscle, laying her open. Agrippina stared at her murderer, her body tensed rigid, her mouth firmly shut as her nostrils flared with deep breaths sucked in against the pain.

And Vespasian watched in horror and awe as she voluntarily submitted to disembowelling in a last act of defiance against the son she had borne, the son to whom she had given sovereignty, for whom she had murdered her uncle-husband, Claudius, her second husband before him and many others. There she stood with blood pouring down her legs and innards slopping out of the hideous wound; but still she stood. And then Anicetus, in an act of mercy for a woman who had so bravely met her end, angled his sword up and pierced the heart that had been filled with the overbearing pride of being a daughter of Germanicus. With a long exhalation that was no louder than a sigh, Agrippina's eyes rolled up and a trickle of blood slipped from the corner of her mouth; she slid off Anicetus' blade and collapsed back onto the bed, staring sightlessly at the ceiling with a faint smile on her lips as if her last thought had been of the guilt that her son would for ever feel.

There was complete silence in the chamber for many speeding heartbeats as all contemplated the enormity of the crime that had just been perpetrated.

Vespasian was the first to rouse himself. 'Obartius, have your men seal off this room and then do not allow anyone into the villa until the Emperor arrives. I'm going to wait for him outside.' He turned about and walked at pace back out into the corridor.

Magnus came hurrying after him, still holding the red-headed slave girl by the arm, her eyes brim with the horror of what she had just witnessed. 'What shall I do with her?'

'Bring her with you if you want, Magnus; one slave won't be missed even if they do an inventory of Agrippina's possessions. Once I've fulfilled my duty to the Emperor and he's seen his mother dead, that's enough for me; we're going back to Rome and then straight to the baths. I've got a lot of filth to sweat out and it's not just other people's.'

PART III

ROME, AD 60

CHAPTER VII

THEY TURNED TOGETHER, and then stretched their legs: four Arab stallions in a line, galloping in harmony. Their manes flowed behind them, sweat sheened their coats and dust from the sand-track flicked up from their pounding hoofs as the light racing chariot skidded around the one hundred and eighty degree turn in their wake.

Vespasian gave the team a lick of the four-lash charioteer's whip over their withers, not so much that they needed reminding of their duty of speed but more out of habit at the start of a new lap. With only one left to go of the seven in total he was in the lead in this two-team race and he intended to keep it that way – until coming down the final straight where he would, of course, allow the Emperor to pass him and win – just. It always took fine judgement. Not that there was anything at stake that Nero wanted to claim by coming first, it was just that no one had ever beaten Nero at anything in his life so there was no sure way of knowing how he would react to losing; Vespasian was certainly not going to be the first person to find out.

Wind rushed past his head, hammering grains of sand into his face, stinging his squinting eyes and drying his throat; he felt the stallions extending their stride as they straightened up for the dash to the next turn at the far end of the *spina*, the central barrier down the middle of the circus built by Caligula for his own private use on the far side of the Tiber at the foot of the Vatican Hill.

It was here that Nero enjoyed the privacy that he still felt that he needed in order to pursue his passion for chariot racing, and it was to here that Nero had taken to ordering Vespasian to bring his four remaining Arabs on a regular basis so that they could race together.

Vespasian hauled back on the reins, wrapped about his waist, putting more pressure on the left-hand side so that the inner horse slowed more than the outer. Its job was to be sure-footed as it guided its three team mates around the turn whereas the outside beast, taking a longer way round, needed the ability to keep its footing and greater pace as the corner was negotiated so that the team rounded the bend as one, in a line and not as a ragged disorder of horse-limbs that would come to grief with the slightest bump. Again Vespasian flicked the whip but not so hard this time as he was aware of Nero's chariot just behind him, no more than a length away; this was how Nero liked it and it was worth getting it how Nero liked it as it made him much more amenable to favours asked after the race – and Vespasian had a big favour to extract from the Emperor.

Since the 'suicide' of Agrippina – as Nero liked to think of it in his state of deep delusion – Vespasian had found himself becoming a favourite of the Emperor's. As to the reason, he was not quite certain but he assumed that it was to do with the fact that he was the only witness left to Agrippina's death, apart from Anicetus who was fiercely loyal to his patron and so would never divulge the truth. Herculeius, Obartius and the eight marines who had accompanied them had disappeared and Vespasian assumed that they were dead as Nero had given Anicetus orders, upon his arrival at his mother's villa a couple of hours after her death, that they were all to be arrested and kept in close confinement; that had been the last he had heard of them. Magnus and the plump, red-headed slave girl's presence at Agrippina's assassination had not been noticed by Nero, and Vespasian thought it best to keep it that way; as did Magnus who had kept the girl for himself and was, from all accounts, putting her to extremely good and frequent use.

Vespasian had then accompanied Nero to examine Agrippina's corpse. The Emperor had studied it, stroking the limbs and running the tips of his fingers over the contours of the face and breasts and remarking over and over how he did not realise that he had such a beautiful mother. He then announced to the members of her household and the rest of the marines that

Agrippina had committed suicide out of remorse for making an attempt on his life and showed them, from a distance, the wound to her belly as if it were proof of the act. After that he ordered that her body be unceremoniously burnt on a dining couch and her ashes entombed nearby, again without ceremony, before returning to Baiae and going into mourning, bewailing her tragic suicide just when they were getting along so well. However, he had not dared to go back to Rome for a couple of months, fearing what the people might think. It was to this end that he had kept Vespasian, a man of proconsular rank and therefore, obviously, of unimpeachable character, as the only witness, giving him instructions to tell Nero's version of events whenever he was asked about Agrippina's death and say that it was indeed a suicide and he had arrived there, tragically, just too late to prevent it. No one, of course, believed him but no one questioned his story or, indeed, blamed him for sticking to it as all knew that to do otherwise would mean certain death. Indeed, the Senate had accepted, almost unanimously, Nero's version of events as presented to it in a letter written by Seneca; only Thrasea the Stoic had walked out of the chamber in silent protest and had remained absent from the assembly ever since.

And so, Vespasian assumed that the likely reason for his being so favoured by the Emperor was that as the only 'witness' to the mode of Agrippina's death, Nero liked to keep him close in order to add strength to his delusion that he had not murdered his mother; as far as Vespasian was concerned, the Emperor could think whatever he liked if it kept him from going the same way as Herculeius, Obartius and the eight marines who had accompanied them.

As to how Pallas had fared since being liberated from the encumbrance of Agrippina, Vespasian knew only that he was still exiled to his country estates and was still managing to retain his considerable fortune. Whereas Seneca had made good his promise and Titus was now a military tribune in Germania Inferior, Pallas had reneged on his; he had not made any attempt to secure Vespasian the governorship of Africa. This rankled with Vespasian as he considered that an agreement was an agreement and the fact that Pallas had, as suspected, cancelled his trip to Britannia was not his concern; Pallas should still, in all honour, fulfil his side of the bargain. His lack of progress since stepping down as consul was made all the more bitter by the fact that Aulus Vitellius had been given Africa and it was rumoured that his brother, Lucius, would take over from him next year.

Ululations from behind – the same as those that Nero used to make when rampaging through Rome – told Vespasian that the Emperor was gaining on him and pulling his chariot out into the straight in preparation for passing him. He pulled slightly on the reins, equal pressure on each, so the team slowed infinitesimally but enough. The ululations increased in volume as Nero drew level, his team disordered and failing to gallop in time. Vespasian made a great show of brandishing his whip but took care that none of the strokes should make contact and cause his Arabs to accelerate. Hard he worked at it, time and time again, furiously arching his back and then bringing the whip down, overarm, but flicking his wrist up at the last moment so the lashes never touched. Nero looked over to him, grinning and whooping furiously, whipping his team without mercy so that, despite their chaos, they eased ahead of Vespasian's now cruising Arabs. On went the Emperor, his fist punching the air as he crossed the winning line and the seventh dolphin, used to mark the laps, dipped to line up with the six others on a pole, high above the spina, next to the towering obelisk that Caligula had had brought over from Egypt.

Nero had won, yet again, and Vespasian was very pleased to see him do it.

'You make the same mistake every time, Vespasian,' Nero asserted, unwrapping the reins from around his waist as Vespasian drew up his team next to the Emperor's chariot. 'You drive your horses far too hard for the first six laps and then they're blown by the final one. I, on the other hand, with my eye for the subtleties of the track, conserve my team's strength, nursing them through the opening laps, just sitting behind you, ready to pounce at the last moment; which I do to great effect. It takes a great skill to have that judgement.'

'Indeed it does, Princeps, and you are blessed with it in abundance,' Vespasian agreed, with all solemnity, as he too attended to his reins; grooms ran up to hold the teams steady as the two charioteers dismounted. 'I so wish that I could learn to judge the pace correctly but just when I think I've got it right your extraordinary talent beats me yet again.' He shook his head in a creditable display of disbelief. 'I hope that I can better you next time.'

'You can try, Vespasian, you can try,' Nero said jovially, taking a towel from one of the grooms; he was never more pleased than when boasting of his prowess on the track having won yet another race, and this, Vespasian had noticed, showed in his far more straightforward conversation and manly deportment. 'But I think that by the time men get to your age, fifty-one? Fifty-two?'

'Fifty-one this coming November, Princeps.'

Nero started to walk towards the gates, rubbing the sand from his face with the towel. 'Well, by the time men get to that age they're too set in their ways to learn much. And seeing as you don't possess my natural talent I don't hold out much hope for you. A shame really, as I believe that you have the better team.'

'You do, Princeps?' Vespasian hoped that his tone sounded as if he had never even countenanced the possibility.

'Of course; they're eight-year-old Arabs in their prime who run beautifully together; I'll prove it to you that they're the best. Next time we race I'll take your team and you can choose any of mine and I'll wager I'll beat them. How much shall we have on it?'

Vespasian's dry throat dried even more. 'A bet, Princeps?'

'How about ten thousand?'

'Ten thousand sesterces, I ...'

'Of course not; denarii.'

If Vespasian could have swallowed he would have; the biggest bet he had ever laid in his life had been one sestertius on his team the first time they had raced in the Circus Maximus; the thrill of winning two whole denarii when they had come in first had not been enough to tempt him from being so reckless with his money ever again. 'Could we, perhaps, bet with something other than money, Princeps?'

Nero threw the towel back to the groom. 'Like what?'

Again Vespasian wished he could swallow; he was at a loss for an idea.

'So it's agreed then,' Nero carried on when Vespasian failed to furnish him with another form of currency. 'Twelve thousand denarii from the loser to the winner; we'll do it next time I'm in the mood for it.'

Vespasian nodded blankly, registering Nero upping the wager and wondering how his innate parsimony would allow him to deliberately lose a race to the Emperor; he was sure that even driving his team of Arabs the Emperor's ability to race chariots was only slightly greater than his talent for singing. But for Nero it was the delusion that counted.

Suddenly remembering the objective of the morning, Vespasian steeled himself to get the favour he desired from Nero. 'Princeps, as you may know, my daughter is to be married in a couple of days now that she is of an age. Her husband-to-be was a praetor last year.'

Nero thought for a few moments. 'Quintus Petillius Cerialis, yes, I granted him an audience yesterday. I hope you don't expect me to be coming to the wedding?'

Vespasian held up both hands as they approached the gates. 'No, Princeps, no; I would never expect you to do anything. Should you wish to attend the festivities then we would be the most honoured family in Rome but should you wish to confer some mark of distinction on the couple, merely a ...' Vespasian trailed off hoping that Nero would fill in the rest of the sentence.

And he did as the gates were swung open for them. 'A wedding present! I must think of a suitable wedding present for the couple.'

'A wedding present, Princeps? That would be a great distinction; such an honour.'

'Yes, it would be, wouldn't it? Have you any suggestions?' Nero asked as he walked out onto the open ground beyond the gates where his litter and Praetorian Guard escort awaited him, all snapping smartly to attention at the bellowing of their centurions.

'Me? Well, let me see.' Vespasian knew that he was getting close to his objective and just had to play the next few lines carefully. 'What did Cerialis come to see you about, yesterday, Princeps, if I might ask?'

The transformation that came over Nero by stepping out of the masculine environment of the racetrack and back into his world of art and creative pretence was palpable. He struck a pose, suggesting thought, before answering. 'Oh, just the usual: he offered me his greetings and complete loyalty and then gave me a present of an amber ring. Oh yes, and he passed on a letter from his brother, Caesius Nasica, the legate of the Ninth Hispana in Britannia.'

'He's ... er ... he's coming back to Rome soon, I believe.'

'He is; and Suetonius Paulinus, the Governor of Britannia, has written to me with a few suggestions as to who should ...' Nero took an inspirational pose. 'Wait! Cerialis' name was on that list.'

'Was it now?' Vespasian said, knowing perfectly well that it was and that had been Paulinus' repaying Vespasian the favour he owed him for dealing with Venutius even though the Britannic chieftain was now in Seneca's custody; the other names on the list were mediocrities or plain no-hopers.

'Perfect! That will be the ideal gift,' Nero announced as the curtains to his litter were drawn back for him, 'I will confirm Cerialis as the new legate of the Ninth Hispana; I shall have his Imperial Mandate sent to your house on the day of the wedding. He can leave for Britannia once he's done his duty by your daughter, provided it doesn't take more than a moon.'

Vespasian's gratitude was genuine and his expression told no lie. 'Princeps, he'll be entirely in your debt.'

'The whole of Rome is in my debt.' Nero clapped his hands and the litter rose, lifted by bearers chosen for their bulk rather than their good looks. 'It is all mine.'

Vespasian watched the Emperor depart, contemplating the frightening truth of that simple statement.

Vespasian listened to the ribald comments of the young, male wedding guests with a mixture of amusement and paternal outrage at such things being said about his daughter as she was led off by Flavia and the other women to prepare herself for the consummation of the marriage in her new husband's house on the Aventine.

'I am a very lucky man,' Cerialis, Vespasian's new son-in-law, admitted, watching his bride walking away.

'You are indeed, Cerialis. I didn't get mine until I was thirty-two; you've managed it just before your thirtieth birthday.'

Cerialis' well-formed face – high cheekbones, prominent nose, firm mouth and intelligent, dark eyes – betrayed momentary confusion. 'Quite so,' he said, knowing that his father-in-law had been married at the age of twenty-nine just like him. 'You had to wait a long time for your legion; I am very lucky.'

'Very lucky, indeed,' Vespasian confirmed as the bridal party disappeared down a corridor, 'it took a few favours called in but we got there; so don't fuck it up. Britannia has plenty of scope for military glory but it also has plenty of scope for making a balls-up of everything and coming back in disgrace; I should know as I was within a hundred heartbeats of having my legion hit in the flank, whilst deploying forward, by that man over there.' He indicated with his head to Caratacus who was drinking wine and conversing with Sabinus and his son-in-law, Lucius Caesennius Paetus.

Cerialis was interested. 'And what saved you?'

'Who, more like.' Vespasian pointed out Hormus chatting with Magnus and Tigran on the fringe of the reception, the realm of the less prestigious guests. 'That man over there.'

'Your freedman?'

'He was my slave at the time. An oil lamp in my tent rekindled itself mysteriously and he told me that his mother used to believe that when things behave in a strange way, like that, it's the gods giving us a warning that we've overlooked something. I didn't take much notice at the time, but as I was leading the legion out of the camp to attack the hill fort we'd invested I realised that I had overlooked something and that something was in the north. I just managed to have the legion form up facing in that direction as thirty thousand hairy-arsed savages appeared out of the night, led by Caratacus. It was a very nasty moment; we beat them off but not before I had to send a young tribune to his certain death leading a suicidal cavalry charge that bought me the time I needed for my reserves to arrive. He went without a complaint and we buried him with great honour.' Vespasian slapped Cerialis on the back. 'So, my boy, be prepared for nasty decisions and look out for candles and lamps rekindling all by themselves.'

Cerialis grinned; it was a pleasant sight. 'I will, Father; and I shall make you proud to have me as a son-in-law.'

'I'm sure you will. And by the way; I knew exactly what you were referring to when you first said that you were a lucky man.' It was Vespasian's turn to grin, the strained expression on his face lighting up. 'You played along perfectly, well done; I think we might enjoy each other's company, you and I.'

'I hope we'll have ample opportunity to do so, Father.'

'We will, I'm sure; but not too much, as you should be off winning a name for yourself and making my daughter proud of her husband. And you're right: you are a lucky man.'

A cheer erupted from the younger male guests and Vespasian looked round; Flavia was standing at the end of the corridor. He smiled at Cerialis. 'Well, my boy; time to go and get me a grandson.' He gripped Cerialis' proffered forearm before the younger man walked off to his awaiting bride to the percussion of slow clapping echoing around the atrium. He followed his mother-in-law out of sight and the guests settled down with more wine to wait for the announcement confirming the successful conclusion of the business at hand after which they would depart.

'I suppose it's best not to think about what's happening at the moment,' Vespasian said as he joined Sabinus, Paetus and Caratacus.

Sabinus laughed and threw an arm around Paetus' shoulders. 'Someone's got to do it and it's as well that it's someone you like, as with Paetus and my daughter, and not just a political union with some flaccid patrician from a family that's seen better days.'

'I suppose you're right,' Vespasian agreed half-heartedly, trying not to picture the scene in Cerialis' bedroom.

'Of course he's right,' Caratacus affirmed. 'What use are daughters anyway unless they produce sons?'

Sabinus took a firm grip of Paetus and shook him. 'Especially sons of consuls.'

It took Vespasian a few moments to realise just what Sabinus had implied. 'Really?'

'Yes,' Paetus agreed, his face breaking into a toothy grin, reminding Vespasian of his father, his long-dead friend. 'Nero is coming to the Senate tomorrow to announce the consuls, praetors and governors for the coming year; I'm to be Publius Petronius Turpilianus' junior colleague for the first six months.'

Vespasian was genuinely pleased despite the fact that Paetus had exceeded him by becoming a consul in January, thereby having the year named after him and his colleague. 'Congratulations, Paetus, how did you manage that?'

Paetus looked to his father-in-law but said nothing.

'Well?' Vespasian asked Sabinus.

'There was no way that we could afford to bribe Seneca so I did a trade with him,' Sabinus admitted. 'I've been the prefect of Rome for four years now and Lucius Pedanius Secundus, Corvinus' crony, has been agitating endlessly for the position, so I went to Seneca and offered to step down, pointing out that if I stayed he wouldn't be getting any bribe money from selling the post for the foreseeable future. He said that he could just remove me and sell the post anyway, to which I replied that if he did that who would ever trust him enough to offer him a large bribe again anytime soon?' Sabinus tapped his temple to indicate his own perceived cunning. 'So I said, instead of selling the junior consulship, for however much, why don't you just give it to Paetus and sell the prefecture for a lot more instead? Being a reasonable businessman he saw the logic and we had a deal.'

'Very good, Sabinus; very well played,' Vespasian said, full of admiration for his brother.

Only Caratacus looked less than impressed. 'I still fail to understand how you Romans can consider that achievement of power by anything other than strength of arms to be honourable.'

Sabinus scoffed. 'It's where you get to that counts, not how you get there; and it's not "you Romans", it's "we Romans", as we keep on having to remind you, Tiberius Claudius Caratacus, ever since you were brought to Rome, pardoned and given citizenship.'

'What good is citizenship to me?' The former Britannic King's eyes flashed for a moment before they resumed their normal mild aspect. 'Prasutagus of the Iceni has been granted citizenship and he is free to stay in the province of Britannia. Yet I, who am also a citizen, cannot leave Rome without the Emperor's permission, which means that I'm a prisoner here.'

Vespasian was stunned by Caratacus' outburst. 'I thought that you had accustomed yourself to that, having had your life spared.'

Caratacus' expression soured. 'I had; up until yesterday.'

'What happened then?' Vespasian asked, frowning as he could think of nothing special occurring the day before.

'Yesterday Seneca released Venutius and procured a pardon for him from the Emperor; he is free to go back to Britannia with his citizenship restored.'

Vespasian, Sabinus and Paetus were all lost for words.

'Why?' Vespasian eventually managed to ask.

'You tell me, Vespasian; all I can say is that I perceive it to be a grave injustice if the man who betrayed me, the man who rebelled against Rome, is free to go back to our own land and yet I, I who have sworn my loyalty, must remain here as a virtual prisoner.'

'It must be about money,' Sabinus hypothesised. 'Seneca, as we all know, does nothing unless it's for money. As we also know, Venutius owed him a substantial amount numbering in the low millions and I suppose there was no possibility of him retrieving that and the interest whilst Venutius was being watched over by you, Caratacus, which is why he put pressure on Vespasian to have you hand him over.'

'But he won't get his money back at all if Venutius goes back to Britannia and on up to the unconquered tribes in the north and starts to stir them up against us. If anything he risks losing all the other loans that he has made in the province by causing another revolt.' It made no sense to Vespasian but it did keep his mind off what was happening to his daughter only a few dozen paces away.

'That's just the point,' Caratacus said, after taking a large draft from his cup. 'The price for Venutius' freedom was that he pay back his debt to Seneca by borrowing from other sources; he's done that and Seneca's destroyed the debt marker.'

Vespasian looked at Sabinus; they both saw the logic of the move. 'That means that if Paulinus was planning on using the information that we provided him with, that Seneca's loan had helped fund Venutius' revolt, then he'll be disappointed as there's now nothing that can prove it any more.'

Sabinus shook his head. 'He's covered his tracks perfectly and will no doubt invest the returned loan somewhere just as dubious.'

Vespasian found it hard not to admire the lengths that Seneca would go to in order to keep his reputation clean whilst at the same time indulging in some of the worst excesses of usury that he had ever heard about.

Eventually there was another raucous cheer, far more boisterous than the one that followed Cerialis' departure, announcing the groom's reappearance, smiling broadly and wearing only a tunic; behind him came two female slaves holding up a bloodied sheet as proof the wife had been a virgin and that was now no longer the case.

'Family and friends,' Cerialis called over the hubbub; it soon died down. 'I have taken possession of my bride and her dowry.' He paused for another bout of cheering. 'Tomorrow I shall hold the formal wedding dinner here in my home. I invite you all to come along two hours after the Senate has risen for the day.' With that he turned and, at some pace, walked back to his new bride.

'Furthermore, after I had Artaxata raised to the ground so it could no longer be held against us and had taken possession of Tigranocerta,' Cossus Cornelius Lentulus, the junior consul, declaimed, reading aloud from a despatch, 'urgent news reached me. Tiridates, the younger brother of Vologases, the Great King of Parthia, was advancing across the border from Media into Armenia in another attempt to claim the Armenian crown; and this in spite of the diplomatic efforts of the embassy that we sent to Vologases last year. I despatched one of my legates, Verulanus, ahead with the auxiliaries whilst I followed on with the legions by a series of forced marches.' Lentulus paused as the assembled senators rumbled their agreement to the wisdom of that course of action.

'Speed, you see, Cerialis,' Vespasian said to his son-in-law, sitting to his right, 'always speed in reaction. I've known Corbulo for almost thirty-five years and I've never seen him dither once. Hit the bastards before they get a chance to consolidate.'

Cerialis nodded thoughtful agreement while Paetus, seated on Cerialis' other side, wrinkled his nose. 'He's just doing what anyone with any sense would do.'

Vespasian did not bother arguing as he knew that it was pointless when discussing Corbulo with Paetus. Paetus had never got on with the dour and rigid patrician when he had served under Corbulo's command in Germania Superior as he, Vespasian, had seen at first hand, much to his amusement.

'Thus I forced the Parthians' withdrawal,' Lentulus continued, 'subjecting those whom I caught, as well as any towns that held out against us, to wholesale slaughter and burning and so managed to have Armenia completely under Roman control when Tigranes, of the Cappadocian Royal House, whom our Emperor, in his wisdom, has chosen to be our puppet-king in Armenia, arrived in the country. I have installed Tigranes on the throne, have overseen his vassals swear the oath to him and he in turn to Rome. I have left him with a garrison of two cohorts of legionaries, three of auxiliaries and two cavalry *alae*. As well as that, I have requisitioned fifty talents in gold and one hundred talents in silver that will pay for all our expenses incurred during the struggle; this I have sent overland for fear of shipwreck. I have now withdrawn back into Syria to take up the governorship left vacant by Ummidius' death.' Again a pause for more protestations of approval from the full Senate House. 'I commend myself to my Emperor and my esteemed colleagues in the Senate.' Lentulus rolled up the scroll with a flourish. 'That completes the despatch from Gnaeus Domitius Corbulo, proconsul of Syria.' He turned, beaming, to Nero, his senior colleague in the consulship for the first six months of the year, who sat at the head of the long oblong chamber. If he was expecting fulsome praise from the Emperor to be heaped upon Corbulo for what sounded like a very neat and clinical job in wresting Armenia back into the Roman sphere of influence and at the same time adding to Nero's much depleted treasury, he was sadly disappointed.

Nero's hands were gripping the arms of his curule chair so intensely that his knuckles were white.

'I propose a vote of thanks,' Lentulus ventured, his voice trailing off to almost a whisper.

'There'll be no vote,' Nero rasped. 'Why should the Senate thank one of its members for doing a job that any one of us could have done?'

'Indeed, Princeps,' Lentulus agreed as a chorus of voices supported the Emperor's decision.

'Corbulo better watch his step,' Gaius, sitting to Vespasian's left, whispered in his ear, 'it doesn't do a man any favours to be seen to be doing too good a job in a military capacity. Emperors tend to be thankful that the job is done but not grateful to the man who did it. It doesn't matter that Nero's spending more and more on grandiose building projects and Corbulo's just provided the finances to make his new baths on the Campus Martius even more lavish. Remember what happened to Germanicus? If only half the rumours at the time were true then he met his end because of Tiberius' jealousy.'

Vespasian could but agree. 'The trouble with Corbulo is that his innate patrician arrogance won't let him play down his part; he needs everyone to know just what a glorious victory he has gained.'

'Well, dear boy, if he carries on sending despatches like that then it'll be an inglorious death that he gains and he'll have no one to blame but himself.'

'I think you may well be right, Uncle,' Vespasian agreed as the Father of the House called upon the Senior Consul and First amongst them to make the statement that he had prepared.

'In addition to these appointments to the consulship and praetorship,' Nero declaimed in his husky voice, 'I have a list of suggestions for next year's aediles and quaestors, which I shall give to the Father of the House so that you, Conscript Fathers, can vote on them as is your right.' A round of thankful applause followed for the crumb of autonomy offered by the Emperor to the body that once proudly voted on all its own decisions and appointments. Nero accepted it, smiling benevolently as if it were one of the most beautiful sounds he had ever heard. Eventually, much to everyone's relief, he carried on: 'And so I come to the governorships for next year: Lucius Vitellius will replace his brother, Aulus, in Africa.' Nero paused, evidently delighted by the murmur of surprise that echoed around the chamber.

Vespasian found himself struggling to keep his temper as he looked over to the smug and porcine younger Vitellius brother.

'I reconfirm Marcus Salvius Otho,' Nero continued, 'in his position as governor of Lusitania.'

'So Otho is doomed to stay in Lusitania until Nero either murders him or forgives him,' Vespasian observed, trying to take his mind off Africa, 'even though he's complied with his wishes and has divorced Poppaea.'

'That's no surprise,' Gaius whispered as Nero carried on with the list of appointments to the imperial governorships and confirmations of those already in place, 'his presence back in Rome would prove an inconvenience for Nero. What is surprising is that Nero still hasn't divorced Claudia; perhaps he's realised that losing the legitimacy that Claudia gives him might be a precarious move to make, having killed his ...' Gaius dried as he realised that Nero had stopped talking and was looking directly at him and Vespasian; all eyes turned on the two of them. 'My apologies, Princeps,' Gaius stammered; Nero was not used to people whispering whilst he was talking as he expected everyone's full attention all of the time. 'We were just commenting on ... on ...' He trailed off, unable to think of a reasonable excuse.

'*I* tell you when to comment,' Nero said, his voice dangerously quiet. '*I* tell you when to talk and *I* tell you when to shine, *Pharos*!'

Gaius went red as the whole Senate erupted into sycophantic laughter at Nero's use of what had now become, to one and all, Gaius' nickname.

'And finally, I appoint Servius Sulpicius Galba,' Nero continued once the mirth had died down, 'governor of Hispania Tarraconensis.'

Vespasian glanced at the bald and gaunt Galba, sitting opposite, and wondered how he managed to get the posting as it was well known that Galba espoused ancient values and would never demean himself by buying a position.

'And so, Conscript Fathers, I commend these appointments to the House and ask that you vote them into being.' Nero sat down having requested this unnecessary formality.

And now it was the turn of the Senate of Rome to debate the Emperor's appointments; and they did, at length and with fulsome praise for his wisdom, no one daring to leave until, finally, Nero departed, before the House divided on the matter, evidently having had a surfeit of flattery, which, for him, was unusual.

The vote, once all had spoken and had their remarks placed on the record for all to read in the future, was unanimous and, at last, Rome's élite were free to file out.

'That was an extremely nasty moment, dear boys, I don't mind telling you,' Gaius said as they came out into the Forum, 'very nasty indeed; I felt like I was ten and under the withering stare of my grammaticus.'

Sabinus laughed. 'Well, Uncle; if you and Vespasian had not been so busy talking in class then you would have noticed something very interesting.'

'The only thing I noticed was that I didn't get Africa,' Vespasian grumbled.

'Do stop going on about that. That was not what I was talking about. What you obviously didn't notice was that Nero mentioned every province except one.'

'Yes, I noticed that,' Cerialis said, frowning.

Vespasian was unimpressed. 'So? He probably just forgot it.'

'He was reading from a list,' Sabinus pointed out.

'Then he missed it out by mistake.'

'Really? The Emperor forgot the most important province at the moment by mistake? I doubt that very much.'

'All right then, which one?'

'Why do you think Cerialis noticed it?'

Vespasian did not need to think for too long to work that out. 'Ah!'

'"Ah!" indeed, brother. Now why do you think Nero didn't reconfirm, or name a replacement for, Suetonius Paulinus as governor of Britannia?'

CHAPTER VIII

'AND WHAT MAKES you so sure, my love?' Vespasian sat with Caenis the following day, in the cool of her garden, escaping from the worst of the midday sun.

Caenis took a sip of her pomegranate juice as she contemplated her answer. 'I suppose it's because for the last two months, Seneca has written to every one of his debtors in Britannia changing the terms of their loans; he's given them the choice between immediate repayment or a rise of five per cent on the interest.'

'Five per cent!'

'I know; even by his standards, it's iniquitous.'

'What are people choosing to do?'

'I've no idea, as none of them have responded yet to any of his letters; that's why he keeps on writing. I think he's starting to get desperate. The trouble for him is that with Nero getting increasingly more profligate, he daren't bring too much cash back to Rome; Nero would have it off him as soon as he heard about it.'

Vespasian could appreciate Seneca's dilemma. 'And yet if he leaves it invested in Britannia and *if* the Emperor does decide to withdraw from the province after all then he's as good as lost it all. But that is a very big if.'

Caenis did not look so sure. 'Is it? I was doing a transaction with the Cloelius Brothers' banking business in the Forum Romanum a couple of days ago and Tertius told me that they've given instructions to their agents in Londinium to stop issuing any more loans in the province and where possible to recall all those who have in any way fallen behind on their payments. They've stopped short of calling in every loan that they've made, like a few of the less respectable Londinium bankers have begun to do, but Tertius says that unless there is a clearer sign from the Emperor that he intends to stay in the province then the Cloelius Brothers will have no choice but to take their money out. Although, he did say that he had heard that Suetonius Paulinus was planning an invasion of the Isle of Mona in an attempt to wipe out the druids altogether. He thinks that if this can be achieved then resistance to our rule would decrease significantly and the province would stand a chance of being financially viable – eventually.'

'He was very free with his thoughts; what did he want in return?'

Caenis smiled, her eyes flashing sapphire in the sun. 'You always assume that someone wants something if they let slip a bit of information.'

'Well, they normally do in my experience.'

'And you're right, this was no exception. Tertius was very keen to know what Seneca was planning to do.'

'So you told him about his dilemma?'

'No, my love; I told him nothing, but I did promise Tertius that should I hear that Seneca plans to take his money out then he would be the first to know. He was so pleased that he refused to charge a fee for taking deposit of my five thousand aurei.'

'Five thousand! You could almost pay a legion for six months with that. Where did you get it all?'

'As Seneca's secretary it's even more lucrative charging for access to him than it was for Pallas or Narcissus. Corvinus gave me a hundred aurei the other day to get him an immediate appointment with him; which I was only too happy to do.'

Vespasian was always interested when his enemy's name came up in conversation. 'What did he want?'

'I knew that would get your attention.' Caenis took another sip of juice and then, with a mischievous look in her eyes, placed the cup down on the table, very slowly.

Vespasian laughed. 'Stop teasing, woman, otherwise I'll show you just what a large amount I pay for access.'

'That's a big promise and very tempting; I think I'll take you up on that.'

'Not until you've told me why Corvinus wanted an urgent meeting with Seneca.'

'Ah, yes; all that talk of access drove it from my mind. Well, remember that Nero granted him a stipend of half a million sesterces a year, ostensibly to raise his family's fortune to above the minimum level required for a senator but in fact to buy him off for having his province taken away so that Nero could send Otho as far away from Rome as it's possible to get within the Empire?'

'Of course I do, the bastard hasn't stopped smirking since.'

'He has now; Nero's withdrawn it as a luxury that he can ill afford.'

'Ha!' Vespasian clapped his hands in delight. 'That's the first sensible thing that I've heard Nero do for a long time.'

'I thought that would please you, my love.'

'Did Seneca promise to help him?'

'Yes; he said he'd try to get Nero to change his mind for an annual payment of three hundred thousand.'

'More than half the stipend! This just gets better.'

'Corvinus flew into a rage and so Seneca showed him the door saying that if he was willing to take a hundred per cent of nothing rather than two fifths of something then he was even more stupid than people thought.'

'That must have stung seeing as stupidity is one thing of which you cannot accuse Corvinus.'

'Quite; and he realised that he was indeed being stupid so he agreed, grudgingly, to Seneca's terms.' She tilted her head at an angle and looked at him out of the top of her eyes in an excellent impression of a coy innocent. 'Now, what do you mean by "paying me a large amount for access", sir? How large?'

Vespasian reached across the table, grabbed her wrist and pulled her over to him so that she landed, giggling, on his lap; negotiations began in earnest.

However, before the deal could be concluded there was the sound of a throat being cleared coming from the doorway into the tablinum. Caenis dropped what she was doing and looked up to see her steward.

'I'm sorry to interrupt, domina,' the steward said, his embarrassment palpable, 'but Magnus and another gentleman are here for the master. They say it's of the utmost urgency.'

Caenis got up off Vespasian's lap. 'Very well, show them out here and bring wine for them both; I don't imagine that Magnus has much of a taste for pomegranate juice.'

'Yes, domina,' the steward said, bowing and turning to go.

Caenis looked down at Vespasian and frowned; he followed her gaze, grinned and then adjusted his tunic so that what had caught her attention could no longer do so as Magnus along with Tigran were shown into the garden; the steward followed with a slave girl carrying a tray with a jug of wine and some cups.

'I hope we didn't interrupt anything,' Magnus said as he took Caenis' hand in greeting.

'Nothing that can't be revived later, Magnus,' Caenis said as Tigran took her hand and mumbled his greetings. 'Sit, please, gentlemen.'

'Well, it's like this,' Magnus said after they had been served wine and the steward and slave girl had retired. 'They've got Sextus.'

Vespasian looked at Magnus, his mind still on other things. 'Who's got Sextus?'

'The Vigiles,' Tigran said, 'they grabbed him this morning.'

'Why?'

Magnus took a slug of his wine and wiped his mouth with the back of his hand. 'We think it's to do with the Terpnus affair.'

'But that was over a year ago; surely that's been forgotten by now?'

'I don't think Tigellinus forgets things that easily; especially as he was deeply humiliated.'

'Then why has it taken him so long to haul Sextus in?'

'I had all the lads involved in the business leave Rome straight after Senator Pollo warned me that Tigellinus was investigating it,' Tigran explained. 'I sent them down to Pompeii; Cassandros, my second in command, has a cousin who's very influential there, shall we say.'

'I see,' Vespasian said, understanding perfectly, his heart beginning to race. 'And now they're back.'

Tigran nodded. 'Yesterday. I thought that it would be safe after so long.'

Vespasian saw the implication immediately. 'Mars' arse! Tigellinus was waiting for him to arrive back in the city and took him the moment he did so?'

'That's what it looks like,' Magnus muttered.

'The bastard knows; I can feel it.'

'That's what we think too. As soon as I was sure it was the Vigiles who had him,' Tigran continued, 'I went to Magnus to ask his help and advice. Sextus is tough but I don't think he will be able to hold out that long against specialist interrogators; they'll have broken him by this time tomorrow and then Tigellinus will know not only that it was the South Quirinal Crossroads Brotherhood who attacked the Emperor on the Viminal, but also that the prefect of Rome and an ex-consul were with us.'

Vespasian felt the colour fade from his cheeks, his expression more strained than ever. 'That's something to be avoided at all costs; it would be the end of us and our family.' And so soon after becoming the generation responsible for it, he added in his head.

'Which is why I thought that you could get Sabinus to put pressure on Tigellinus to release Sextus,' Magnus suggested.

'That won't work,' Caenis said, shaking her head. 'Tigellinus doesn't take any notice of anyone other than the Emperor and the only other man who could have him killed.'

All three men looked at Caenis, trying to work out who that was.

'Burrus?' Vespasian said eventually, the sick feeling in his stomach alleviating slightly with a glimmer of hope. 'Of course, the Praetorian prefect could have Tigellinus on trumped-up charges of treason any time he wanted.'

Caenis smiled. 'Yes, but would he want to? Or to put it another way: what would make him want to?'

Vespasian looked despondent, the glimmer fading. 'I have absolutely no influence over Burrus at all, quite the reverse, in fact, as it was him who suggested to Agrippina that I had shown sympathy towards Messalina at her execution.'

'You might not have any influence over him but I'm pleased to say that, thanks to Pallas and Agrippina, I do and it will be a pleasure to exercise it.'

'What have you got over him?'

'Ohh, something he really won't like.' Caenis rose to her feet. 'I'll just get my secretary to make a copy of a letter whilst I call for my litter and get changed; I think a visit to the Praetorian Guard's camp is in order.'

Caenis' litter passed through the Viminal Gate; Vespasian, walking next to it, nodded at the Urban Cohort centurion on duty and then wiped the sweat from his forehead with a handkerchief, pulled from the fold in his senatorial toga. Magnus and Tigran did their best to keep their faces averted from the guards as they came through behind the litter. Up ahead, about two hundred paces away, lay the brick-built walls of the Praetorian Camp; massive structures in their own right but dwarfed by the Servian defences of Rome.

'I can't say as I'm all that keen on going in there,' Magnus muttered as they passed through the obligatory crowd of beggars that infested every gate, waving their mutilated limbs or displaying virulent skin diseases in the hope that revulsion would stir pity and generosity in the hearts of the passers-by. A small boy, holding his begging bowl between two stumps, accosted him importunately, causing Magnus to have to step aside to avoid tripping over the child. 'Fuck off!' Magnus clouted the boy on the side of the head, toppling him and sending his bowl flying through the air to disappear into the crowd. 'Just fucking sitting around here all day and annoying respectable folk; why don't you work like the rest of us?' Magnus stalked on muttering, his mood worsening the closer they came to the gates of the camp.

'Senator Titus Flavius Vespasianus and Antonia Caenis here to see Sextus Afranius Burrus, prefect of the Praetorian Guard,' Vespasian informed the Praetorian centurion in charge of the four men blocking their entry to the camp.

Cold eyes scrutinised Vespasian with no particular urgency as the centurion tapped his vine-stick repeatedly into the open palm of his left hand, his burnished bronze scale-armour almost blinding in the burning sun. He pulled a grudging salute as if he were unable to understand why such an illustrious member of the

Praetorian Guard should have to salute a senator rather than the other way around. 'Wait here.'

This was too much for Vespasian, who jumped forward and caught the man's elbow as he turned, restraining him. 'Listen here, lad,' he hissed in the man's ear, 'you might think that being in the Praetorian Guard makes you ever so special but you're wrong. Not only am I a senator and a good twenty years older than you but I'm also an ex-consul and have commanded a legion for six years during which time I actually *saw* combat on a regular basis, all of which makes me far superior to a parade-ground soldier like you. Now, if you choose to leave me waiting on the doorstep like some tradesman whilst you go off to see whether the man I've come to see is busy or not then that's your decision; but between you and me, I can tell you it'll be the last decision that you ever make. Common legionaries in the Second Augusta, fighting the painted savages of Britannia, don't need to make decisions as they're all made for them in order that they can spend all their time concentrating on getting killed or having a limb lopped off. Do I make myself clear?' Vespasian pulled back, allowing the man to turn and face him.

The centurion opened his mouth to speak but Vespasian's intense stare made him think better of it; his eyes shifted nervously, left and right, to his men who were all studiously transfixed by something in the middle-distance. 'Let the senator and his party pass,' he ordered with as much dignity as he could manage. 'And escort them to the tribunes' mess and tell the steward to serve them whatever they require.'

'That was a very wise decision, centurion,' Vespasian commented as he was allowed into the camp. 'If that is the calibre of your decision making then I can see that you are well qualified to make many more.'

With a blank expression, the centurion snapped a very smart salute, turned stiffly and then stamped off.

'That seemed to work,' Caenis said with an amused expression as they came out into a street running between long, two-storey, brick barrack blocks with tiled roofs that seemed to be home to hundreds of crows. 'What did you say to him?'

'Oh, nothing too threatening, my love; I just pointed out that people who are lucky enough to have the ability to exercise a modicum of free will, and then abuse it, generally seem to lose it.'

'How very astute of the centurion to see the truth of what you were saying and modify his behaviour accordingly; I do hope Burrus is just as sensible.'

'Why is a prisoner of the Vigiles any concern of yours, Senator Vespasian?' Burrus asked, surprising Vespasian by addressing him formally and with a certain degree of respect in his tone.

'He is of interest to some associates of mine who would rather he didn't share his knowledge with someone like Tigellinus.' Vespasian knew that sounded lame; however, Burrus seemed to take it at face value, or, at least, had the good manners to pretend to do so.

'I see.' The prefect frowned whilst considering what to say next. He leant forward in his chair and rested his elbows on the desk; bellowed orders and the crash of drill came through the opaque-glass window behind him. He looked hard at Vespasian and then at Caenis sitting next to him. 'Forgive me, but I really don't see what this has to do with me; as prefect of the Praetorian Guard I have absolutely no influence over the Vigiles or their prefect.'

Caenis presented Burrus with her sweetest smile. 'We quite understand that, prefect; technically you have no power over how the Vigiles run themselves.'

'So why are you here then?'

'Because, if you chose to, you could make life very difficult for Tigellinus; even impossible, I would suggest, to the point where he would be obliged to terminate it. No one likes their life to be impossible, do they, *prefect*?'

'I see.' Burrus frowned in thought again.

Vespasian kept his face straight, enjoying the subtlety of Caenis' implied threat. The speed with which Burrus had seen them had hinted at an anxiety to get the interview over with as quickly as possible and Vespasian knew that was nothing to do with his own presence. As a veteran of imperial politics himself,

Burrus would be only too aware that Caenis did not come asking for something unless she felt sure that she had the means to get it. They had barely enough time to be served their wine in the tribunes' mess before a very respectful secretary had invited them to follow him to the prefect's quarters in the praetorium at the heart of the camp. Magnus and Tigran had been more than happy to keep the jug of notably tolerable Falernian wine company and await the result of the meeting in the mess.

'And why would I choose to make Tigellinus' life impossible – assuming that I could, that is?'

'I'm not saying that you should make his life impossible; the threat should be enough. We want to avoid any unpleasantness. As to why, prefect?' Caenis bestowed another radiant smile upon Burrus. 'I don't know about you but I always find it much better when someone else's life is made impossible rather than my own; wouldn't you agree?'

Burrus swallowed; it seemed to Vespasian that he evidently believed that whatever Caenis would threaten him with would be viable. 'And ... er ... what incentive would you have for me to help you out in this matter?'

Caenis pulled a scroll from beneath her palla. 'This is a copy, prefect, which I had my secretary do just before I left my house; the original is stored very securely.'

Burrus unrolled the scroll and read its contents, his face seeming to fall with every sentence. When he had finished he laid it down on the desk and tapped his fingers together. 'Where did you get this?' he asked.

'I should think that's obvious.'

'Agrippina?'

'Who else could have had such a document?'

'And how did you come by it?'

Vespasian recalled the cylindrical document case that Caenis had said contained the payment from Pallas and Agrippina for her to present their request for help from him.

'Now that is a rather strange tale, prefect. My price for a favour is either cash or information; I have never had any leverage on you, so when approached by Pallas and Agrippina for a favour, you were my price. Agrippina gave it to me in return for me presenting Vespasian with a proposition from her and Pallas. However, that proposition was nothing but a ruse to get Vespasian to deliver the invitation that lured Agrippina to her death; a plan, I believe, that you acquiesced to, having, as we both now know, sabotaged the previous two attempts.'

Vespasian was now confused: how did Caenis know that?

Burrus could not resist a smile. 'Are you saying that she gave you this document in return for facilitating her own demise?'

Caenis joined him in his amusement. 'Yes, prefect, I found it a delicious irony when I realised it myself. But then I understood how that came about and my respect for Pallas' subtlety increased even further, if that is possible.'

Vespasian was desperate to discover the contents of the letter but knew better than to show his ignorance of the matter.

'You see, prefect,' Caenis continued, 'Pallas has never forgiven either you or Seneca for his banishment. He knew perfectly well that Agrippina could never use this document whilst she still lived for she couldn't possibly let on to Nero that she knew of its contents as it would've meant certain death to her. So it was easy for Pallas to get her to part with it because if it came to the Emperor's attention from any other source, she could legitimately deny all knowledge of it, saying that it must have been intercepted before it reached her or that it was a fake.'

Burrus completely understood. 'But now she's dead she can't do that so the Emperor will assume, correctly, that she did receive it and it is genuine.'

'And you will be dead; as you well know because you wrote and sent it.' Another sweet smile lit up Caenis' face. 'And so Pallas gets her to give it to me, in payment for a favour that seals her fate, which thereby makes the document so toxic that you would do almost anything to get the original back. I thought it was a work of genius.'

Even Burrus could appreciate the finesse and shook his head slowly in wonder. 'So if I induce Tigellinus to give up this ... Sextus?'

'That's right, prefect, Sextus along with any notes taken whilst interviewing him; and make it clear to Tigellinus that what he's investigating is best left alone.'

'Then I'll get the original back.'

'You have my word on it, prefect.'

'And you aren't afraid that when it's all over I might be very angry and seek revenge on you?'

Again Caenis smiled. 'I don't think you'll want to do that, prefect; after all, everyone is happy: Sextus has been released and Tigellinus knows never to try to investigate that matter again and you have the original copy of your letter to Agrippina warning her that Nero was going to attempt to poison her and telling her what antidotes to use. I think that we can leave it there, don't you, prefect?'

Burrus rubbed the back of his neck, sucking the air through his teeth, as he looked at the copy. 'I did it out of loyalty to her, you know; she did get me the Praetorian Guard, after all.'

'Very commendable, prefect; and I suppose it was out of loyalty of a different sort that you assisted in her murder.'

'I didn't assist; I just knew about it and did nothing to stop it or warn her this time.'

'What made you change your mind?' Vespasian asked, feeling better now that he understood what Caenis had over Burrus.

'What?' Burrus looked at Vespasian in surprise as if he had forgotten his presence in the room. 'Oh, for a couple of reasons: he was going to do it no matter what, so it was best that it could at least look like an accident; although that went wrong too. Plus the fact that Agrippina had made it clear that she would never support him divorcing Claudia because she believes that being married to Claudius' daughter gives Nero legitimacy that he would not otherwise have as Claudius' adoptive son. Should Agrippina have made a public display against Nero by supporting Claudia it could be very dangerous for my position; both women are, or were, very popular with the people and, more importantly, the army, so it could easily have led to a rebellion and then where would I be? Leading ten thousand parade-ground soldiers against frontier legions; not a happy prospect.' Burrus got to his feet, pushing his chair back behind him. 'Still, it's done now and once I have that letter back I can forget about Agrippina completely. So, if you would excuse me, I've got to go and mention to Tigellinus that his life might just become intolerable and will carry on being so until he forgets everything concerning Sextus and whatever investigation he's involved in. I shall bring Sextus to your house, in an hour or so, personally in order to take receipt of what's mine.'

Caenis stood, gracing Burrus with yet another beaming smile. 'Prefect, we look forward to seeing you there. You know where I live?'

'I'm the prefect of the Praetorian Guard; I know where everyone who matters lives.'

'Indeed. Would you care to stay for dinner?'

'Let's not go so far as to pretend that we're friends, Antonia Caenis.' With that he stomped from the room leaving Vespasian looking in awe at Caenis; relief coursed through him.

'We'll make a special sacrifice to our crossroads *lares* if Sextus is released before he's been made to talk,' Tigran said, looking much relieved at the news.

'He's a tough lad, Sextus is,' Magnus assured him, his face flush from a very convivial time with the Falernian. 'He wouldn't have talked yet.'

'It won't matter if he has,' Caenis said from within her litter. 'Burrus will make sure that Tigellinus can do nothing with the information.'

'What's he going to threaten him with to ensure that?'

'That's his business; but I'm sure it'll be good. He's going to get any notes that may have been taken when interviewing Sextus and make his displeasure felt. Tigellinus fears Burrus so much that that will be sufficient.'

'You showed no fear of him, though, did you, Caenis?' Vespasian said, still in a state of advanced admiration for the feat he had just witnessed.

'I may have showed no fear, but I felt it. That could have gone very wrong.'

And Vespasian knew that she was right; to coerce the prefect of the Praetorian Guard was not a thing to be undertaken lightly. Had he, Vespasian, tried it alone he would probably find himself with a treason charge hanging over his head by now; but Caenis was a different prospect. She was Seneca's secretary and had been Pallas', Narcissus' and Antonia's before that and she was known for having an encyclopaedic memory. Who knew what dangerous items of information were stored in there, garnered over almost forty years at the heart of imperial politics? Then, of course, there was Narcissus' private cache of files that he had entrusted to her safe-keeping when he fell from favour; after his execution she and Vespasian had gone through them, keeping the more interesting documents and burning the rest. The difference between them was that whereas Vespasian could remember which documents referred to which people, Caenis would be able to quote whole sections. No, Vespasian thought, Burrus would have been foolish to try to call her bluff; but Caenis well knew that just because a course of action was considered to be foolish did not necessarily prohibit someone reckless from pursuing it and had Burrus not calculated cautiously then they could have ended up in a very nasty situation. However, Caenis' calm use of implicit threat had been sufficient to convince the prefect that he should subject himself to her will. Vespasian had never seen the like of it and his eyes had been opened to Caenis' strength. The woman he loved, he had realised, was stronger even than him; a ruthless negotiator with a store of information on most people to be used in order to get at their weak points. She was not someone to cross and he thanked Mars that their relationship had been strong enough for her to forgive him for the time when he had been forced to avoid her. He knew he would never have been able to achieve what she had just done and he and Sabinus would have been doomed and the house of Flavius would have sunk back into the mire of obscurity.

Burrus arrived at Caenis' house, as he had promised, bringing a battered-looking Sextus with him and left almost immediately, without formalities, with the original copy of his incriminating letter to Agrippina.

'How did it go?' Vespasian asked Sextus as soon as Burrus was out of the door; although judging by the bruising he thought it a mildly silly question.

Sextus leant against the wall, rubbing his swollen right eye carefully. 'It weren't good, sir, not good at all.'

'Did you talk, though, brother?' Magnus asked as a slave brought Sextus a cup of wine; Caenis signalled the slave for another one.

'What do you mean, Magnus?'

'Did you say it was the South Quirinal Crossroads Brotherhood that did Terpnus' fingers?'

Sextus looked at his wine, shamefaced, and then downed it in one. 'I think I did, brother; I'm sorry; they were threatening to do to me what we'd done to Terpnus and once I let on that I knew what it was I couldn't deny it. I'm not so bright, you see.'

No one argued with that assessment.

'And what about Sabinus and me, Sextus,' Vespasian asked, 'did you mention that we were there?'

'No, of course not, sir.'

'Good man.'

'But I did tell them that the attack was revenge for Senator Pollo having the torch shoved … well, you know where.'

Vespasian, Caenis, Magnus and Tigran groaned as a loud knock came from the front door. Caenis' doorkeeper opened it to reveal Hormus, Vespasian's freedman.

'I hoped I'd find you here, master.' Hormus looked pale; in his hand he had a scroll.

'What is it, Hormus?'

'This just arrived, sir.'

Vespasian took the proffered scroll and looked at the seal and felt his heart jump; perhaps Burrus had not done what he had promised after all, or he had been late. 'That's Nero's seal,' he said, showing Caenis the offending article and then opening it and reading. 'This is an imperial summons for tomorrow morning; I'm to wait at home and a messenger will be with me at the third hour of the day to tell me where to present myself to Nero.'

CHAPTER VIIII

THE LAST OF his clients stepped out through the vestibule and Vespasian felt a relief that his morning *salutio* was over; he leant back in his chair at his desk in the tablinum and looked down at his desktop, covered with scrolls and wax tablets. It had been a busy morning as there had been much business to take care of. Vespasian wanted his affairs in order and, to that end, Hormus and the four slaves who worked under the freedman as secretaries were still occupied writing out, in longhand, letters that he had dictated to them between seeing clients. All of these letters Hormus was to send should the worst come to the worst. The first was to Titus, in his province of Germania Inferior, advising him to throw himself at Nero's mercy at the first possible opportunity should he, Vespasian, be condemned. He had written also to his stewards on the estates, making arrangements for them to have access to cash should he be indisposed – as he thought of it – and Titus, still far away in Germania Inferior, unable to release the necessary funds quickly; to facilitate that he had written to the Cloelius Brothers in the Forum authorising his stewards to make withdrawals there in person. He had also authorised his uncle to withdraw on Flavia's behalf; he knew that to give someone as profligate as Flavia complete access to all the family finances would be enough to send them back down to equestrian status. He had learnt this possibility the hard way upon his return after six years away with the II Augusta to find Flavia ensconced in lavish comfort in the imperial palace and spending money as if she were as wealthy as her friend – and, as it turned out, lover – Messalina. No, he would not make that mistake again; if, indeed, it was there to be made.

Vespasian was only too aware that there may not be anything left for her to spend anyway. If the summons was for him to appear before Nero to answer accusations that he was responsible for ordering the attack on Terpnus and therefore, by implication, an assault on the Emperor himself then that would be seen as treason; if found guilty, which he was sure that he would be, and he was not shown the mercy of being allowed to end his own life then execution would bring complete confiscation of his property and, therefore, who had authorisation to withdraw cash was immaterial. He carried on making the arrangements anyway, just in case he managed to escape with mere banishment, denied fire and water for four hundred miles around Rome.

He had one slight hope: as soon as he had received the summons he had sent a message to Sabinus, explaining what had happened and his worry that either Burrus had not kept his word or that Tigellinus had taken his evidence to Nero either before Burrus threatened him or despite the prefect's threats. He asked Sabinus if he had received an order also to appear before Nero; he had not. That did not stop Vespasian from fearing the worst, nor did it prevent Flavia from assuming that the worst had come to pass solely as a result of Vespasian's selfishness. And as she barged, without leave, into the tablinum, Vespasian hoped that he would be able to keep his temper enough to prevent himself from throttling her; something, he reflected as she opened her mouth, that as her husband he would be well within his rights to do.

'Just when I thought things couldn't get any worse,' Flavia screeched, her voice tight with anger and her eyes dull with insomnia, 'I find out that Magnus is taking possession of our strongbox.'

'My strongbox,' Vespasian reminded her truthfully. 'And how did you find that out?'

'Because he's here with that big brute who alerted the Emperor to your selfishness and Hormus has just sent a couple of slaves to fetch the box for him. How am I meant to live in the style that a woman of my status deserves to if I can't have access to that box after you're ... well ... after you're dead?'

Vespasian rose to face his wife over the desk. 'Because,

woman, with that strongbox under Magnus' guard I have a chance of preventing your total impoverishment.'

'How will it prevent that if I don't even have access to it?'

'Firstly, if my property is confiscated they won't get the contents of that box because Magnus has it and they don't know about it; and secondly, if you were to have it then within a month, knowing you, there wouldn't be anything left in it and I might as well have just left it here for the Emperor to seize. At least this way Magnus can give you a monthly income.'

The idea of being doled out money by Magnus was too much for Flavia and she reached for the inkpot on Vespasian's desk and threw it over his toga.

'That is not helpful, Flavia,' Vespasian said through gritted teeth.

'Getting yourself executed and turning me into an impecunious widow isn't helpful either but you've still gone and done it.'

'Flavia, I would remind you that I'm still here and very much alive.' He slapped her across the face to prove the point. 'Now calm down, woman.'

Flavia shook her head, blinking her eyes rapidly, her chest heaving as she put a hand to her reddened cheek. 'You just hit me!'

'And I'll do it again unless you calm down, Flavia; this isn't the time for self-pitying hysterics. You need to think clearly as the messenger will be here in half an hour and you should be gone by then; you should have already left. Tigran's lads are still waiting around the back to take you to Domitilla's house. I told you to take Domitian and get away from here.'

'Skulk out of my own home by the back door? Who do you think I am?'

'I think you're my wife who should obey my every order.' Vespasian paused for an exasperated deep breath in an attempt to calm himself. 'Flavia, you must go and you must go now. By this evening we'll know what is happening.'

'By this evening you'll be dead.'

'That may well be so and if it's indeed the case then you stay with Domitilla. Hormus will look after the house until such time as it is seized along with all our slave-stock—'

'The slaves!' Flavia looked horrified; she had evidently only just realised that the slaves, as they counted as property, would be taken and sold. 'But who will do my hair in the mornings?'

'That will be the least of your worries as I'm sure that Domitilla will lend you one of her girls. If my property is taken then you must stay at Domitilla's, out of sight for as long as possible; don't draw attention to yourself and most certainly do not petition the Emperor or Seneca or anyone. Just keep your head down and with a bit of luck you will be overlooked and allowed to live.'

The thought of being overlooked did not go down too well with Flavia. 'Like an inconsequential nobody?'

'Not *like* an inconsequential nobody, my dear, but *as* one, because that is your best chance of survival. Nero has already taken to having some of the families of men he's executed put to death; I believe it makes him feel better knowing that there isn't anyone left to resent him for the execution. He can't bear the thought that anyone should think badly of him, therefore he'd rather have them dead. And so, Flavia, please take Domitian and go now.'

'Domitian's run off.'

Vespasian groaned.

'His nurse said that he thought everything that was happening was an attempt solely to make him even more miserable and he wasn't going to stay around and let the soldiers take him just because he had an idiot for a father.'

Vespasian shook his head. 'Well, let him go; I haven't got time to worry about that little pest. If I don't get a chance to say goodbye to him he won't notice and I won't care. He'll turn up soon enough if I survive, and if I don't then I'm sure he'll arrive at Domitilla's as soon as he realises that fending for oneself involves doing more than pulling the wings off flies and the legs off spiders all day long; or taking the eyes of newly born fawns for that matter.'

Flavia stared at Vespasian for a few moments and then, without saying goodbye or wishing him luck, turned and stormed from the room.

'That seemed to go well,' Magnus said, popping his head around the door. 'But, seriously, sir: why don't you make a run for it?'

'What's the point, Magnus? The Emperor is everywhere. I'd have to live incognito in some shithole with hardly any money so that I didn't draw attention to myself and be in constant fear that someone might recognise me. That would be no life. For me it's either living here in Rome as well as my status and wealth allow or living as a governor in one of the provinces; if I can't do either of those then I'm better off dead.'

Magnus grunted. 'Well, if you say so; but I thought that you intended to die in your bed and I've never heard of a dead man making his way back into favour, if you take my meaning?'

Vespasian did but he did not agree with it.

'You will present yourself to the Emperor at the Temple of Neptune on the Campus Martius, Senator Vespasian; he's making his way there now and is expecting you to join him immediately,' the Praetorian centurion barked having performed a crisp salute.

'Very well, centurion,' Vespasian replied, his heart beginning to race. The Temple of Neptune did not sound good; temples were often used as courts. Vespasian had witnessed Sejanus' downfall in the Temple of Apollo. He glanced at Hormus, standing next to him; his face was ashen. 'I shall go immediately.'

The centurion saluted once more, spun on his heel and began to stamp back across the atrium towards the vestibule.

'Wait!' Vespasian called after him; the centurion halted. 'I just need to give my freedman some instructions.'

'That's fine, senator,' the centurion said over his shoulder and carried on. 'I don't have to wait for you.' With that he disappeared into the vestibule.

Vespasian heard the doorman perform his duty and the centurion was gone; he looked at Hormus, frowned and then walked to the front door, signalling for the slave to open it. A quick glance up the street told him that the centurion was not waiting outside with his men but, instead, marching away, further up the Quirinal, in the opposite direction from the Temple of Neptune.

'That's a relief,' Vespasian said, coming back into the atrium, 'it seems that I'm not to be escorted, for which small mercy I'm grateful. That would have been a humiliation hard to bear.'

'Indeed, master,' Hormus said, his voice thick with emotion.

'My will is lodged in the House of the Vestals, Hormus; should I be allowed to keep my property and the worst happens then retrieve it from them and have it read out here. If I'm not allowed to keep my property then let in whoever comes to seize it without any argument and get off to Domitilla's house to join the mistress. Understand?'

'Yes, master,' Hormus said, miserably wringing his hands.

'Just remember, Hormus, that you're a freedman; no one can do anything to you unless you give them just cause.'

'Yes, master.'

'If I don't come back, serve the mistress well.' Vespasian patted his freedman's shoulder, adjusted his toga and, with a deep breath, turned and walked out of his house for what he hoped would not be the last time.

The morning was humid and sweat soon ran down Vespasian's face and back as he walked at a calm pace down the Quirinal. He reviewed his life as he went, objectively, and found himself unable to justify throwing away all that he had achieved just for the pleasure of a little revenge; he and his brother should have got at Terpnus in a different way that did not involve a direct threat to the Emperor. But it was too late to change things now, so all he was left with was the bitter taste of regret for a future that he had dared to imagine but was probably not to be. Yet again he wondered if he had made his decision to attack Nero's rampage because he had felt insulated from retribution as he considered his future to be prophesied and in the hands of the gods; his mother had said on her deathbed that a man should always make his choices by balancing his desires with his fears and this he had patently not done. Any reasonable man would have seen that fear of Nero far outweighed desire for vengeance for the outrage perpetrated upon his uncle. Tigran and his brethren had far less reason to fear Nero as they were from the underbelly of Rome and lived according to different rules to the élite and with very little regard for the Emperor other than enjoying his largesse; their desire to avenge their humiliation was, therefore, not balanced out by their fear of someone so remote to them as Nero. He, Vespasian, on the other hand, lived in the small section of society that revolved around the Emperor who held sway over everyone and everything by the fear that he generated; no, he had been foolish and influenced by his probably erroneous belief in a predestined future. He wished that he had paid more attention to his mother's warning as he entered Caesar's Forum; if he survived this day he swore to himself that he would.

Sabinus was at his desk, in his capacity as Urban prefect, beneath the equestrian statue of the long-dead dictator. Vespasian walked towards his brother who waved away the various petitioners surrounding him and hurried to join him.

'Well?' Sabinus asked.

'Well what?' Vespasian said with a shrug.

'Well, do you really think that this is about the Terpnus affair?'

'I'm sure it is; Sextus told Tigellinus that Terpnus lost his fingers in revenge for his treatment of Gaius.'

Sabinus screwed up his face, inhaling sharply. 'Then why aren't I joining you?'

'Who knows, Sabinus; who can really understand what goes on in Nero's head?'

Sabinus rubbed his forehead, thinking; sweat beaded on his brow. Brightening suddenly, he indicated to either side of his brother. 'Look!'

Vespasian frowned and looked about. 'What at?'

'Exactly. Nothing. There's no one there. No escort so you're not under arrest.'

'Do I need to be? Where's there to hide? Perhaps Nero's just giving me the chance of suicide.'

'And you're not taking it?'

'What if I'm wrong?'

Sabinus nodded his understanding. 'May my lord Mithras and your Mars hold their hands over us, brother; we'll need them looking over the family today.'

On his brother's face, Vespasian saw the fear that all in Rome's élite felt; the fear of Nero. The fear that preyed on one's mind, day in and day out, ever present, ever gnawing, clouding one's judgement and preventing coherent thought. 'What will you do?'

Sabinus took a deep breath. 'What can I do but carry on in my duty, waiting to see what happens?' Taking Vespasian by surprise, he squeezed his shoulder in the first ever physical show of fraternal affection.

Vespasian mirrored the gesture, holding his brother's gaze for a few moments.

With a resigned smile, Sabinus walked back to his desk to disappear in amongst a swarm of petitioners all insisting that theirs was the most pressing problem. Vespasian turned and headed on through Caesar's Forum cursing Nero and those who supported him in power; those men who were responsible for the intolerable way that people of his class were forced to live. Once again the élite of Rome were in the savage grip of a monster who knew no limits to his power and enjoyed searching for them. It was intolerable and surely it could not continue thus? Yet, as Vespasian walked through the Gate of Fontus, under the shadow of the Capitoline Hill, and out onto the Campus Martius, he could see no escape from Nero short of his assassination and then who would take his place? There were no direct male descendants of the Julio-Claudian line left and Nero himself was, as yet, childless.

So what would happen if men like Piso and Rufus gathered malcontents in a successful conspiracy against Nero? The answer was obvious to Vespasian: there would be a rush to claim the Purple by the generals in the field; those men lucky enough to have the command of legions. And of them there was one stand-out candidate after his recent despatches to the Senate: Corbulo. Corbulo with the Syrian legions behind him and his kudos high, having won glory first in Germania and then in Armenia, would be foolish if he did not make a bid for empire. The Egyptian legions and the Moesian would rally to him making him the king of the East. Suetonius Paulinus in Britannia could not oppose him without losing the new province and the Governors of the two Germanias would not be able to agree as to which of them should receive the backing of their legions, so the legions themselves would more than likely back the man who had commanded many of them to victories only a few years previously. How could anyone compete with Corbulo's record?

A bitter smile crossed Vespasian's face as he remembered thinking at his mother's deathbed: *if it were to be someone like him then why not him?*

No, it was not to be him; Corbulo was the best and obvious choice and Corbulo could do it, Vespasian was now convinced of that. And that thought sealed Vespasian's conviction that he was doomed as he mounted the steps of the Temple of Neptune His mother, indeed, his whole family, had been mistaken about the prophecy and he cringed inwardly at the thought that he could ever have considered entertaining such grandiose ambitions for himself.

'Ah, there you are at last.' Nero's voice was husky from much talk already that morning; he was accompanied by a couple of dozen senators whom, apart from Caratacus, Vespasian recognised as being mostly the same men as witnessed Agrippina's last supper. 'I hope you brought the money.'

'The money, Princeps?'

'Of course, the twelve thousand.' Nero looked at him as if he were being deliberately obtuse.

Vespasian felt his knees buckle; he stumbled, saving himself from crashing to the floor by supporting his weight on the plinth of a statue of the host deity. His head span and he sucked in a couple of quick, deep breaths as he realised what all this was about and the relevance of meeting in the Temple of Neptune, the god, amongst other things, of horses. All that anguish had been over a chariot race, a race he was obliged to lose and with it twelve thousand denarii. 'It's lodged with the Cloelius Brothers in the Forum,' he improvised.

'Good, you can pick it up after the race.'

Vespasian noticed that Nero had made no mention of where his twelve thousand was lodged, no doubt because he did not expect to lose as he never had.

Nero peered at him. 'Are you feeling all right? I don't want you saying that you lost because you were ill as we know that wouldn't be true.'

Vespasian felt his equilibrium returning and took on his most sincere expression as he looked up at the Emperor. 'I'm fine, Princeps; it's just ... er ... nerves at competing with someone of your talent; I always get them.'

'Of course you do. We'll sacrifice a bull to Neptune Equester before going to my circus on the Vatican. All my teams are waiting there for you to choose your favourite. Your Arabs are being fetched from the Greens' stables at the moment.'

'Very good, Princeps; I am honoured that you should go to such trouble on my behalf.'

'It's for everyone here, Vespasian.' Nero gestured with an arm around the chamber to include all within. 'I intend to show people just what can be achieved by a man of my skill driving a less-favoured team against my best team driven by a man of your meagre accomplishment.'

There were sage nods and murmurs of impatience from the assembled senators, all of whom, like Nero, chose to ignore the fact that Vespasian's Arabs were one of the most successful teams in Rome.

But then, Vespasian reflected, that was all part of the delusion.

Vespasian had never seen all of Nero's racehorses assembled together before; lined up in one long row they were an impressive sight. However, as he moved along the teams of varying coats and builds he saw nothing that could compare to his Arabs who, having arrived, stood opposite the parade, observing without a great deal of interest.

'Would you like some advice?' a voice asked from behind his right shoulder.

Vespasian turned to see Caratacus. 'You're here to witness Nero's triumph on the track too, are you?'

The former Britannic chieftain smiled. 'Who would wish to miss the opportunity to witness a master-class in charioteering? But I got the impression that it wasn't what *you* were expecting when you entered the temple.'

Vespasian stroked the muzzle of a chestnut mare before moving on to an all-black team. 'I thought I was coming to be condemned; I know I didn't hide my relief very well when I realised that the worst that was going to happen today was to lose twelve thousand denarii to Nero.'

'I won't ask what's on your conscience; but I would say that losing twelve thousand is a lot better than losing your life. It must be your lucky day.'

Vespasian smiled as he moved on to a team of greys. 'That's one way of looking at it, I suppose. Another way is ... well, it's best not to say anything about he who weighs us down with constant fear.'

'A policy that I too follow; especially as I'm making every effort to ingratiate myself with our multi-talented Emperor.'

'Oh, why so?'

'Well, apart from the usual reasons, he is in the process of considering appointing me as king of the eastern client kingdom in Britannia after the legions pull out.'

'Pull out? Nero's not serious, is he?'

They carried on walking down the line of horseflesh examining muscle tone and hoofs. 'Yes, he is; the freedman Epaphroditus, Nero's new secretary, approached me about it yesterday. His belief is that if Suetonius Paulinus can destroy the druids on Mona and kill Myrddin himself then an honourable peace can be achieved. That's what Venutius' release was about, to send him back to Britannia, in the Emperor's debt, and use him as a counter to his ex-wife's ambitions; either he or she will have the northern kingdom, Cogidubnus will be king in the south and either Prasutagus of the Iceni or myself will get the east. But seeing as Prasutagus is in increasingly poor health and with only a wife and daughters to inherit from him, I think that I should be in luck.'

'So he would restore you to the Catuvellauni throne and everything will be as it was before.' Vespasian had completed his inspection of the teams and doubled back to four bays that had caught his eye. 'Who else knows this?'

'Just Seneca at the moment. Nero's made his final decision, but is yet to make the announcement; that won't happen until next year when the legions begin to withdraw. What a waste of blood the whole exercise would have been once he does pull out.'

'We should never have gone in in the first place. Augustus always maintained that your fog-bound island was not worth even one drop of legionary blood; it was just selfish politics that caused it.'

'And now it's selfish politics that ends it, so that Nero has more money to spend; did you see his new baths that he's constructing next to Agrippa's old ones?'

Vespasian had passed the building site on his way to the Vatican. 'The finest of everything, Nero boasted as we went past; not at all cheap.'

'But cheaper than maintaining four legions and their auxiliaries in Britannia.'

Vespasian had made his choice. 'I shall take these, Princeps,' he called to Nero.

Nero looked pleased. 'A fine choice, Vespasian; we shall prepare.'

'It was a good choice,' Caratacus affirmed, 'they might have a chance of beating your Arabs; not that you would let them, obviously.'

'Obviously.' Vespasian looked Caratacus in the eye. 'If Nero did make you Rome's client king, would you stay loyal?'

Caratacus inclined his head a fraction. 'Technically, yes, just so that Rome had no reason to come back. As you say, things would go back to how they were before the invasion. We would still trade with the Empire; we would still be at peace with the Empire and we would still send our sons to Rome for education. The only difference would be that we'd go back to fighting amongst ourselves, otherwise we'd get bored.' Caratacus grinned and slapped Vespasian on the shoulder. 'Good luck losing your race.'

'Thank you, my friend; and good luck winning your kingdom.'

Vespasian steadied his team, with the reins wrapped round his waist, as they waited on the starting line in front of the circus gates, about fifty paces from the start of the spina. Unlike the Circus Maximus, Nero's circus did not have starting boxes; the race, therefore, would start at the drop of Nero's handkerchief, which, seeing as Nero had already taken his team up to a canter and was now ten lengths away, seemed delayed. Vespasian waited, trying not to think about the money.

As Nero neared the spina he dropped the handkerchief; Vespasian whipped his team forward and enjoyed the surge of energy created by the four bays as they eagerly accelerated after the Arabs. From the small group of spectators there were cheers of varying enthusiasm, more because they felt that it was expected of them rather than for any tension or excitement generated in a race whose conclusion was in no doubt.

But Vespasian was not going to trail meekly behind the Emperor, shadowing him in the fifteen-length lead that he had given himself by his blatant cheating; no, the contempt he felt for that pathetic manoeuvre of Nero's had decided him to make a race of it and then to lose in the last lap. He cracked the whip over the withers of his team and screamed encouragement at them as they stretched their necks, their nostrils flaring and their eyes wild. On Vespasian urged them up the track, towards the first turn, spitting out the dust kicked up by Nero as he yelled and bawled. Despite the fact that he was only an amateur, he knew well enough how to handle a team he had never driven before, and he quickly had them in hand so that they worked and responded as one. By the time Nero had rounded the far end of the spina, Vespasian had almost halved the lead, whooping and grinning broadly as the wind pulled at his tunic and flicked grains of sand into his face. With the deft tugs on the reins that he had learnt to perfect in the past years, he slowed the team in precise order so that they glided with grace around the turning stone placed at the extreme of the spina.

Brandishing the four-lash whip and shaking the reins, he pressed his team on to greater efforts and, coming out of the turn exactly in line with their hoofs beating virtually in time, they shot forward, each free to exert itself to the utmost, unimpeded by its fellows. Down came the distance between him and Nero and, in inverse proportion, up went the volume from the few senators and stable hands watching.

They were willing him on to win, he was sure of it; although it could never really be proven that they had not been cheering for Nero.

But Vespasian, despite his excitement, was not about to oblige them with a victory. Yet still he gained on the Emperor and, as the first of the seven bronze dolphins dipped its nose and the second lap began, Vespasian was less than ten lengths behind. Up the back straight they surged, Nero whipping his Arabs and casting glances over his shoulder, paying little heed to the performance of his team, which had now begun to lose the rhythm that a successful combination so needed if they were to be able to act in unison. Vespasian continued to chase down Nero as they approached the far turn for the second time; the Arabs bundled round, the light chariot slewing behind them, spraying sand up at forty-five degrees in a great arc before just righting itself. Without any thought for harmony between beasts and vehicle, Nero whipped his team on, looking nervously behind. His wheels bounced once and then twice, up off the track, as the team accelerated without the chariot being in perfect alignment; but as Vespasian came out of the turn, now just seven lengths behind, Nero's vehicle was running smoothly once more.

Vespasian felt the joy of the chase well up within him, and the fear of Nero that dwelt in the hearts of every one of his subjects seemed to dissipate as he slowly gained on the Emperor, who had now let his Arabs' discipline degenerate to the extent that their heads were all moving in different times.

On they powered, Vespasian's bays, eating up the lead that his own Arabs, being so inexpertly handled, could not hope to maintain, despite the serious whipping that Nero was administering. They thundered past Caligula's obelisk at the halfway point of the straight and careered on towards the second turning stone. Nero, once again, glanced backwards and then thrashed his whip cruelly down onto the Arabs' withers as they went into the turn. The outside horse gave a shrill whinny and leapt forward as if it were attempting to jump a fence as its team mates curved off to the left, around the hundred and eighty degree turn; their weight pulled their airborne companion around with them but not so as it could keep its footing.

Down the beast went in a mad flurry of beating horse-limbs,

cannoning into its neighbour to bring it down, with disastrous consequences for the final two and sending Nero spinning from the disintegrating chariot, reins still wrapped about his waist. As the whole wreck skidded along the sand, quickly losing momentum, it became clear to Vespasian what he had to do, for he could not afford to pass Nero and be declared the winner. Grabbing the safety-knife from his belt, he steered his team straight at what was left of the chariot as if he himself was having severe difficulty in making the turn at such speed. As his bays attempted to leap the wreckage, Vespasian cut the reins and jumped to his right just as the wheels of his chariot hit the first of the debris and were catapulted up into the air. He crashed to the ground, belly down and arms outstretched with his chin ploughing an agonising furrow in the sand as his team cleared the floundering Arabs and, dragging broken shafts and flapping canvas behind them, pelted off in terror up the straight. With his eyes tight shut, Vespasian felt himself grind to a halt; the bestial snorts and shrieks of terrified horses was all he could hear. After a few moments he opened his eyes and his vision was filled with one object just a hands' breadth away: a foot; Nero's foot. He stared at it for a few moments and then, with a shock, realised that it was not moving. He heaved himself up, dirt clinging to his sweat-slimed tunic and skin and clogging his mouth and nostrils as senators jumped down from the stands and raced across the track towards their prone Emperor. The reins were still wrapped about Nero's waist but, fortunately, the Arabs were in no state to bolt and drag their driver to a red-raw death. He stumbled over to Nero as Caratacus and Burrus arrived and knelt down next to his head.

Nero's eyes flickered open and focused on Vespasian; he raised himself up, shaking the sand from his sunset hair and beard. He looked at Vespasian less than favourably as he rested an arm on Burrus' shoulder. 'You should get rid of that team; I've never driven one so lacking in unity and discipline. I find it extraordinary that they win any races in the Circus Maximus; no wonder I always beat you, as I would have done again today had you not crashed into me.'

'Indeed, Princeps; but you did, nonetheless, win again today and with the inferior team, such is your skill.'

'I did?' Nero's face brightened fractionally.

'Of course, you were in the lead when I crashed into you; therefore at the moment the race ended you were winning.' Vespasian swallowed hard and forced himself to carry on through gritted teeth. 'I shall get the twelve thousand I owe you from the Cloelius Brothers immediately.'

Burrus whispered a few words in Nero's ear.

Nero's mood seemed to change again, this time for the worse. 'Yes, do that, Vespasian, and bring it up to the palace where we shall discuss whether you deliberately collided with me in order to cause harm to my person.'

Burrus smiled at Vespasian with cold pleasure as he turned and helped the limping Emperor from the track.

'Yes, Princeps,' Vespasian said to Nero's back.

'That doesn't sound good,' Caratacus observed.

'I know,' Vespasian muttered, looking behind him to where his Arabs were being led away, all seemingly none the worse for their ordeal. 'Especially as I did collide with him intentionally.'

Caratacus nodded. 'And everybody saw that you did and will bear witness to the fact.'

Vespasian rubbed his chin; it was badly grazed and ingrained with sand. 'But they also saw that I hit him after he had gone over, in order that he should still win.'

'Do you think that will make any difference if Nero decides it was otherwise?'

Vespasian spat a curse as he felt the joy of the chase being replaced, again, by the fear.

'Twelve thousand denarii immediately?' Tertius Cloelius came as near to showing any sign of humour as he had ever done in his life; short, portly, bald and with sallow skin he was a creature of arithmetic and fact. 'We don't keep a sum like that just hanging around; you have to give us advance notice, fill in a request form, sign it, have it counter-signed and approved and then stamped with mine or one of my brothers' seals.' He held up his chunky signet ring to emphasise the point. His younger brother, Quadratus, nodded sagely as he listened to his brother's description of correct banking procedure, with a vague smile on his face as if he were relaxing to sublime music. 'It all takes time, you know.'

'That's as may be, Tertius,' Vespasian said as calmly as he could manage in the circumstances, 'but I *do* need it now as my life might well depend on it, seeing as I owe that amount to the Emperor himself and he is expecting it this afternoon.'

'Well, that is no concern of mine.'

'Is either Primus or Secundus here? Perhaps I could talk with them.'

'Both my elder brothers are away on business at the moment; and, anyway, they would say exactly the same as me, as would Quintus and Sextus who are busy upstairs.'

Again Quadratus nodded in agreement with Tertius' assessment; none of the Cloelius Brothers would ever go against banking protocol.

'Very well,' Vespasian said, getting to his feet and remembering what Caenis had told him. 'I have more than one banker in Rome; I shall try elsewhere and they can be the recipients of a very interesting piece of news. Good day, gentlemen.' He walked to the door.

'What news?' Tertius asked quickly.

Vespasian turned back to face Tertius. 'Beneficial news that you will now not know until long after one of your competitors does and so therefore you will find yourself at a severe disadvantage.'

'You've been with the Emperor, haven't you?'

Vespasian inclined his head in acknowledgement. 'And Caratacus.'

Tertius shared a fleeting look with his brother. 'It's Britannia, isn't it? Are we in or out?'

'That request form for the twelve thousand, Tertius?'

Tertius waved a dismissive hand; there was just one exception to the Cloelius Brothers' insistence that banking procedure be adhered to: when it got in the way of making more money or, potentially and worse, losing it. 'I'm sure that this one time the formalities can be dispensed with.' He clapped his hands and a clerk appeared in the door. 'Send down to our deposit for twelve thousand denarii immediately. I want the amount here within the hour.'

With a look of confusion the clerk nodded and scuttled away.

'So, senator,' Tertius almost purred, 'in or out.'

'Out.'

The brothers both looked startled.

'Surely not?' Quadratus whispered.

'Caratacus has been approached about being a client king after the legions begin withdrawing next year.'

'Next year?'

'That's what he said.'

Tertius looked with alarm at his brother. 'We need to get messages to our agents in Londinium to call in all our loans before this becomes common knowledge and financial chaos ensues as every other Londinium banker tries to do the same thing.'

Vespasian arrived, with the money loaded in boxes on a handcart, at the imperial residence accompanied by a heavily armed escort provided by the very grateful Cloelius Brothers. It had taken less than an hour to procure the cash; an hour during which Tertius and Quadratus had spent frantically dictating letters and making travel arrangements as they had both decided to journey to the province to make personally sure that they secured their considerable investment there before the news became public.

Giving orders for his escort to wait with the cart outside, Vespasian climbed the steps and submitted himself to the now routine search of anyone who wished to enter the complex.

'I've been looking for you,' Caenis said as he walked into the cavernous atrium.

'Have you been charged with taking receipt of my money?'

'No, my love; although I've heard about that. I hear that Nero is furious with you and has begun to exaggerate the incident.'

'That doesn't surprise me; he already had a new interpretation of events moments after he regained consciousness; Burrus seemed to be re-remembering for him as a spiteful piece of revenge for our blackmailing him. Have you come to warn me?'

'No; to fetch you. I've been charged with taking receipt of someone else's money and he wants you to come with me and he points out that, with Nero fuming, it might be as well for you to get out of Rome for a while.'

'But I'll need Nero's permission so I have to face him.'

'Don't worry; Seneca's had that attended to some time ago in preparation.'

'In preparation for what?'

'He's sending us to Britannia; me because I know his business and can represent him; you because you know the province. Now that it seems definite that Nero is withdrawing, Seneca is desperate to call in all of his loans; forty million in total; the largest of which is five million sesterces made to Prasutagus, the King of the Iceni.'

PART IIII

Britannia, AD 60–61

CHAPTER X

'WITH THE GOVERNOR away dealing with the druids on Mona, I am the man to ask,' Catus Decianus, the middle-aged procurator of Britannia, informed Vespasian, Sabinus and Caenis in the most unpleasant, smug manner. 'And then, of course, there would be some form of recompense for my trouble in taking the time to consider the case.' Plump, soft and pale, with a curled coiffure that was unmanly, he languished in his well-cushioned chair with an air of indolence enveloping him; he did not even bother to meet the eyes of the people he was addressing, seated on the other side of his desk. Behind him, through a window, could be seen the sturdy frame of the bridge across the Tamesis, the reason why Londinium had grown out of nothing and become so important in the seventeen years since the invasion.

Vespasian leant forward in his chair and pointed an accusatory finger, sporting his senatorial ring, at Decianus. 'Now listen to me, you—' He stopped mid-flow as Caenis squeezed his arm.

'I think what Senator Vespasian was going to emphasise, procurator,' Caenis said with a sweet smile and a honeyed tone, 'was that we don't need permission to travel to the lands of the Iceni as we have imperial letters of transit to go wherever we wish in pursuit of Seneca's business. We were just dropping in to ask permission of the Governor out of courtesy and, seeing as we have been shown none in return, we shall now leave.' She got up and smiled again. 'It's been such a pleasure meeting you, procurator; unfortunately our business is such that we simply do not have the time to accept that kind invitation to stay for a few days and recuperate in comfortable accommodation that you would surely have extended us. We shall, however, be staying a couple of nights here anyway as we have an appointment to meet with Seneca's financial agent in Londinium at the third hour tomorrow; I'll have your steward show us to our suite. We won't bother you for dinner either tonight or tomorrow but, rather, we'll have it served in our rooms.' With that, she turned on her heel and walked swiftly to the door, leaving Decianus with his mouth hanging slack and looking as if he had just been slapped.

Vespasian and Sabinus shared a quick look before following Caenis without saying goodbye.

'But you must have my permission!' Decianus blurted as they reached the door.

'Why?' Sabinus asked over his shoulder as he stepped out into the corridor.

'Because I'm in charge.'

'How lovely for you.'

'What a vile man,' Caenis observed as a slave closed the door behind them.

'He won't bother us now,' Sabinus said, grinning broadly at Caenis. 'You should have seen him as he watched you go; his face was as red as a spanked arse.'

'Yes, but it hasn't helped us in that it would have been nice to have the cooperation of the authorities in the province.'

'We'll enlist the goodwill of the city administration of Camulodunum when we get there in a couple of days,' Vespasian suggested as they continued along the corridor in the direction of the atrium where Magnus, Hormus and Caenis' two slave girls awaited along with Castor and Pollux. 'I'm sure if we're nice to the Urban prefect there he'll give us what we want. After all, a military escort to add a bit of lustre to our arrival at Venta Icenorum is not much to ask.'

It all came flooding back to Vespasian as he looked out of the window, the following morning, over a town swathed in a thick, damp fog. The bridge across the Tamesis and the river itself were lost somewhere within the miasma and Vespasian remembered just how much he hated the climate of this northern isle, which seemed, to his eyes, to vary little from one season to the next. But the changes to Londinium itself were far more marked than those to the weather: it was now a thriving port, more important even than the provincial capital of Camulodunum; here goods could be dispersed all over the province because of the bridge. So it was, then, that Londinium had become the natural place for merchants to set up business and with them had come the bankers. But the town had grown so quickly over the last thirteen years since Vespasian had last seen it, ever expanding north, west and east, with the thought only of profitable commerce and not costly defence and so, therefore, it was still an open town.

Vespasian shook his head at the results of greed. 'Fifty thousand people living, in a province that's barely pacified, in a town filled with goods and money with no walls to protect them is foolhardy to say the least.' He turned back to Caenis, still lying in the bed piled with blankets. 'The sooner we finish our business and we can get back to Rome the better, as far as I'm concerned; just the view out of the window, or lack of it, is a very strong argument for never having invaded and the lack of defences is an even stronger one for not staying.'

Caenis opened an eye. 'Come back to bed and keep warm; then perhaps you'll stop moaning. Our appointment with Seneca's agent isn't for another couple of hours; I'm sure we can amuse each other until then.'

'This is a complete list of all the loans made by me on Seneca's behalf in the last six years,' Manius Galla, financial agent to one of the most powerful men in the Empire, said with a deal of pride, taking a scroll from a cylindrical bookcase and handing it to Caenis. A ruggedly handsome, well-built man in his mid-thirties, Galla looked as if he should be in uniform, leading soldiery rather than engaging in money-lending to cash-strapped provincials. 'Names, amounts, interest rates, commencement dates and due dates.' The newly constructed forum, through the open window behind him, was teaming with traders of all sorts and their customers; at its northern end towered wooden scaffolding encasing the rising walls of the town's new amphitheatre.

Caenis scanned through the list, her eyes taking in the information at an impressive rate, as the cries and whiplashes of the overseers supervising slaves hauling stone blocks up the amphitheatre's scaffolding rose above the calls of the seagulls circling above the traders shouting their wares. 'So, eighteen loans are still outstanding including Prasutagus', which is by far the largest.' She passed the scroll to Vespasian. 'What did Prasutagus want the money for?'

'It wasn't just coinage but bullion as well. He said the money was to build up the Iceni's main town, Venta Icenorum, and the bullion was to strike his own coinage as the Iceni are technically an independent client kingdom. Since they rose against Publius Scapula when he tried to disarm them, they have been allowed a great degree of autonomy, basically because fighting the Silures and other tribes in the west makes it important for us to have if not overtly friendly then neutral tribes in the east. They still use our coinage as well as their own.'

'So we'll be asking Prasutagus to dismantle his people's currency when we call in the loan.'

Galla could not but agree. 'That'll effectively be what would happen, which would place a great strain on their economy and could well make for a very volatile situation.'

'Did Scapula succeed in disarming them?' Vespasian asked, passing the scroll onto Sabinus.

Galla sucked the air through his teeth. 'Yes and no. They agreed to destroy their war chariots and melt down their swords as the price of their independence; but how thorough they were at doing that has never been verified and the rumours are that all they actually did was disassemble the chariots and hide the parts and their swords in their thatched roofs. Then, of course, they still retain their spears and bows for hunting.'

Sabinus placed the scroll back on the desk. 'So, what you are saying is that if they were upset the whole Iceni tribe could be fully armed and ready for rebellion in a matter of days.'

'It would take them half a month or so to muster their strength in one place, but, essentially, yes.'

'Then we had better handle this very carefully,' Vespasian said.

'It would be best not to handle it at all,' Galla observed. 'Leave things as they are and just keep taking the interest; he does pay it regularly.'

Caenis shook her head. 'We can't do that as Seneca has decided that he wants to call every loan in the province back in.'

Galla looked at her, astounded. 'He can't be serious.'

'He is.'

Galla's eyes widened. 'Gods below; we're going to abandon Britannia.'

'You keep that to yourself, Galla; the fewer people who know about it the better for our business as we don't want to cause a stampede of creditors.'

'Indeed, Antonia Caenis; but I shall start to make my own arrangements, discreetly of course.'

'Of course. In the meantime you're to call in all the loans that you can; we'll deal with the four loans in Camulodunum as we pass on our way up to see Prasutagus.'

'As you wish.' Galla looked down the list. 'Most of these shouldn't be a problem; a million or so sesterces should be easy to refinance.' He looked up nervously. 'The news hasn't got out yet, has it?'

'Not yet, that's why speed is of the essence. A couple of the Cloelius Brothers are only a few days behind us; I think that once they start trying to claw back their money then it will become obvious what's happening and that's when the economy will start to crumble.'

'I don't have long then.'

'No one does.'

'What about Cartimandua up in the north? You do realise that calling in her loan could have a similar effect on the Brigantes and push them into rebellion?'

'But Suetonius is up there with the Fourteenth dealing with Mona,' Vespasian pointed out, 'so he could be on hand very quickly. Which legion is nearest the Iceni at the moment?'

'The Ninth Hispana, based just to the northwest of their lands at Lindum Colonia.'

'Ah! That's my son-in-law's legion. I can write to Cerialis privately and tell him to be on a high state of alert. Could you have the letter delivered for me, Galla?'

'Of course.'

'I'd be grateful for the details of the four Camulodunum loans,' Caenis said. 'Would you be good enough to furnish me with the details?'

'My pleasure. Although there is another loan there which does not appear on my list as it was done privately by Seneca back in Rome.'

Caenis was interested. 'Oh yes?'

'Yes, the Urban prefect of Camulodunum owes Seneca half a million sesterces; I only know because he makes his interest payments to me. He should be able to help you with the other loans there seeing as he acts as Seneca's agent in that town.'

'Well, we were going to see him anyway so we can wash two tunics in the same tub. What's the man's name?'

'Julius Paelignus.'

Vespasian sat up as if he had been stung. 'Paelignus?' he exclaimed, recalling the hunchbacked procurator of Cappadocia who had betrayed him to the Parthians, causing his two-year incarceration; the man he had sworn to kill. 'I wondered where he'd got to. I can see that I'm going to enjoy this trip much more than I thought I would.'

And Vespasian was not disappointed; the shriek of fearful recognition that Paelignus emitted when he barged, unannounced, knocking the doorkeeper aside, into the prefect's office in Camulodunum the following day warmed his heart.

'Y-y-y-you!' Paelignus stammered, dropping the wax tablet that he had been reading. 'What are you doing in my town?'

Vespasian gave his friendliest smile. 'I thought that I'd just drop in on an old friend, Paelignus; it's been such a long time.' He pointed to Paelignus' maimed hand; two fingers were missing. 'Remind me how you lost them.'

Paelignus looked at his hand in confusion. 'I ... er ... it was fighting the Parthians in Armenia.'

'Liar! You know perfectly well it's from when Magnus had to encourage you to divulge my whereabouts. And where was I, Paelignus? Can you at least remember that?'

'You were ... er ... you were ...' He trailed off, evidently unwilling to say where Vespasian had been.

'I was rotting in a cell in Parthia; that's where I was, Paelignus. Can you remember that now?'

With a feeble inclination of the head, Paelignus indicated that he could.

'And it was only through the loyalty of Magnus and my then slave, Hormus, that I managed to get out; otherwise I would still be there. A thing of filth and no consequence. Is that what you'd prefer, Paelignus, rather than me standing here now?'

Paelignus miserably shook his head, keeping his eyes averted.

'So, what to do, eh?' Vespasian mused.

'You've already had your revenge by giving that document to Seneca and ruining me.'

Vespasian threw his head back and laughed; he had supplied Seneca with the evidence, gained from Narcissus' private papers, that Paelignus had falsified his father's will, valuing his estate at far less than its true worth and thereby cheating the Emperor, who was named as co-heir, out of a considerable amount of money. 'That was nothing; that was just me warming up. Now, Paelignus, I'll tell you what we're going to do. I'm here with Seneca's secretary, Antonia Caenis, and my brother, Sabinus, to call in Seneca's loans from four people in Camulodunum and also from you.'

'Me?' Paelignus squawked, meeting Vespasian's gaze for the first time. 'You can't call in my loan with him.'

'Caenis has been asked to call in all Seneca's loans in Britannia.'

'But he gave me my loan in Rome.'

'And now you're in Britannia.'

'But I'm his agent here; he would have written to tell me about it.'

'But he sent us instead. I'm very sorry if you think we're misunderstanding our instructions, but they seem clear enough to us.' Vespasian turned to the door. 'Caenis!'

Caenis entered and, without asking permission, sat down opposite Paelignus and unrolled a scroll. 'So, Julius Paelignus, we believe that you owe an outstanding half a million sesterces to Seneca. As he has charged me with collecting all money owing to him in Britannia I'm serving notice that we will expect to receive the full sum on return from our journey to the lands of the Iceni, which should be at the beginning of next month.'

Paelignus stared open-mouthed at her. 'You can't do this, I'm the Urban prefect of Camulodunum; you can't make me pay.'

'Seneca is your creditor and he wishes to call in the loan.'

'Besides,' Vespasian said jovially, 'as Urban prefect I expect you can put a good squeeze on the locals and raise the money very quickly. Or perhaps you could take out a loan with one of the local bankers to help you with the cash.'

Paelignus was now incensed; he stood, leaning his hands on the desk, making the curvature of his back more prominent. 'Seneca just lent me back the money he had extorted off me in return for not telling Nero about my father's will. It's my money and I'll not pay it back.'

'I'm very sorry that you feel that way,' Vespasian said, his voice full of sympathy; once again he turned to the door. 'Magnus! Hormus!'

Magnus and Hormus came in, beaming recognition at Paelignus.

'Now, prefect,' Vespasian carried on, 'you recognise these two gentlemen, I'm sure.' He pointed at Magnus. 'This is Magnus, who severed your two fingers.' He then indicated to Hormus. 'And this is Hormus who held you down in order to make Magnus' task easier. Now, I can see that you've still got a few of your fingers left.'

Paelignus quickly put his hands under his armpits.

'It only took two for Magnus to get you to admit that you'd betrayed me to the Parthians; I wonder how many it would take to make you pay what you owe? What would you reckon, Magnus?'

Magnus rubbed his chin as if he were giving the matter serious consideration. 'Well, hard to say, sir. I can't recall him enjoying it the last time; in fact, if I remember rightly, he cried, real tears they were. No, he didn't enjoy it at all; not one bit. So I'd reckon he would agree to pay just by having his hand held down and me placing the blade on one of his fingers.' Magnus nodded to himself, his sagest expression on his face. 'I don't think that I would have to cut.'

Vespasian looked genuinely interested in that assessment. 'Really? Well, let's see if you're right, Magnus.'

Paelignus yelped and, seeing Magnus coming around one side of the desk and Hormus the other, nipped under it with surprising speed, and made a dash past Vespasian's legs to the door, which he opened only to come face to face with a smiling Sabinus.

'Is this the one you were talking about, brother?' Sabinus enquired, grabbing the wriggling prefect by the arm and hauling him back into the room.

'Yes, that's the one, Sabinus; how could you tell?'

'Because he's such a horribly bent little specimen; I seem to remember you mentioning that.'

'I probably did. Now, where were we? Ah yes, Magnus, you were going to see whether or not you needed to cut off one of Paelignus' fingers to get him to repay the money he owes.'

Paelignus howled as Sabinus dragged him over to the desk and Hormus grabbed the wrist of his undamaged hand, holding it firmly down on the surface.

'All right! All right!' Paelignus shouted as Magnus showed him the knife. 'I'll pay; I'll squeeze the locals and see if I can raise a tax of some sort on the ex-legionary settlers and then I'll get a loan to cover the rest of it.'

'Well, you can't say fairer than that,' Vespasian said in the most reasonable of tones. 'Magnus, you were right.'

'Normally am when it comes to that sort of issue, sir.'

'Yes, I wouldn't bet against you. Caenis, give Paelignus the list of the other four gentlemen in Camulodunum who owe Seneca money. They're minor nobles of the Trinovantes, Paelignus, so whilst we're away you can get them to pay, seeing as you act as Seneca's agent in this town; but use a bit of delicacy as they are no doubt proud men and influential with their people. And if you change your mind just remember, we know where to find you and should you decide to run the only place that you'll be safe from me is in the very prison cell that you condemned me to, as I don't fancy going back there. Now, if you'll excuse us, we're going to borrow a *turma* of your cavalry as, tomorrow, we have to visit the King of the Iceni.'

There was no road north, no Roman one at least, to the lands of the Iceni and the track that Vespasian and his companions followed instead soon became a morass in the steady rain, sucking at the hoofs of the thirty-two Gallic auxiliary cavalry and providing little support for the four wooden wheels of the *rhaeda* – the covered carriage – in which Caenis and her two slave girls travelled in some degree of cushioned comfort. Vespasian, Sabinus, Magnus and Hormus rode, hunched beneath thick travel cloaks, behind the rhaeda whilst their slaves, eight in all, trudged along on foot at the rear of the little column as it made its slow progress towards Venta Icenorum on the third day of the journey. Only Castor and Pollux seemed oblivious to the miserable conditions; their concern was their leashes, tied to the rhaeda, which prevented them from killing any more sheep. Magnus had already had to pay a couple of colonist farmers for the deaths of two of their flock and the mauling of a slave shepherd boy; this he had done with bad grace as he felt that it was surely the farmers' duty to keep their livestock protected and, after all, his dogs were only doing what was natural. The failure of this argument with even his friends had forced him to restrain the beasts in order to spare his purse; his mood had not been made better by the weather.

When they had set out it had been one of the rare clear days allotted to the miserably damp isle in November and Camulodunum actually looked tolerably pleasant in the thin sun. The brightly painted columns and walls of the Temple of Divine Claudius, which dominated the southern end of the forum, would not have looked out of place in Rome; nor, indeed, would the Governor's residence next to it, where they had spent the night. Vespasian had thought, as the escort turma of cavalry had clattered into the forum, that had it not been for the excessive number of men wearing trousers and sporting long hair and moustaches, a casual observer looking about the forum might be forgiven for thinking that this was a town in the north of Italia – until one took note of the countryside around the town, that was. One could not see any. It was flat and therefore invisible from the forum, or indeed, from anywhere inside Camulodunum's less-than-reasonable defences, a quarter of which were now made of brick that had begun to replace the broken-down wooden palisade that had originally formed the town's walls. It was only from the river port, to the southeast of the town, that any countryside could be seen and that was dreary marshland in the main, through which the river trailed on its way to the sea, just a few miles away.

Many of the townsfolk had gathered to see them off, curious as to what these high-status new arrivals were up to, and Vespasian noticed very few amongst the indigenous Trinovantes who had taken up Roman dress; it was only the colonists, discharged legionaries and their native wives, who looked Roman. Here, far more than in Londinium, Vespasian surmised, the pacification of the province was rudimentary. That fact was also emphasised by their short journey through the town to the north gates. In this part of the town, markedly more than around the western gates by which they had entered the previous day, the houses were native in construction: round with thatched roofs and a leather door-curtain. There were definitely two sides to Camulodunum and from what Vespasian could see, apart from trading in the forum, they did not mix.

And he had noticed the same thing as they journeyed north: small colonies of discharged legionaries living in brick-built houses with their native wives – who had been only too happy to get a husband after the mass killing and deportation to the slave markets of Gaul and Italia of so many Trinovantes men – contrasted with villages of round huts spiralling thick woodsmoke up through the holes cut in their thatched roofs. Again, the two never mixed. The further north they travelled, the more dominant the native villages and farmsteads became until by the end of the second day there was no sign of Roman occupation at all; it was as if the whole Claudian invasion had never happened and they were just a band of travellers journeying through a countryside dotted with damp, mist-wreathed farmsteads and deep woods as yet untouched by Rome.

Thus they entered the lands of the Iceni, the independent tribe whose domain was enclosed by the sea to the north and east, almost impassable fenland and marsh to the west and then the Roman-controlled Trinovantes to the south. Here the people lived under their own law. Yes, they traded with the Empire, paid tribute into its coffers and sent their young men to serve in its auxiliary cohorts, but it was to their chieftains and, ultimately, their King that they held loyalty.

'They were never conquered, did you know?' Vespasian said to Hormus, riding next to him. 'Sensibly, Prasutagus came to Camulodunum and submitted to Claudius without any blood spilt.'

'Did he not even take hostages?'

'He did but they had been returned by the time the Iceni rose against that idiot, Scapula, when he tried to disarm them. But now they are still technically independent, although I'm sure that won't last beyond Prasutagus' death seeing as he's only got a wife and three daughters to inherit. I don't know what the Iceni laws of inheritance are but in Rome they would not, in most circumstances, be able to inherit by themselves. They would need men named in the will, unless the Emperor gave a special dispensation – which is highly unlikely.'

'Besides,' Sabinus said, 'it's customary for client kings to leave their kingdoms to Rome in their wills. Atallus the Third of Pergamon did it and old whatshisname of Pontus.'

'Polemon?'

'I'm sure you're right. Anyway, I can't imagine us wanting to stand by and possibly let another Cartimandua take power over the Iceni; one Fury like that is quite enough for this island.'

'What is the name of Prasutagus' wife?'

'I've no idea but I'm sure we won't be able to avoid being introduced to the hairy beast.'

'What makes you say she's hairy?' Magnus asked, in a tone that implied interest; he had left his plump slave back in Rome in Gaius' household where he had supposed, rightly, that she would remain unmolested.

Sabinus indicated around them with an expansive gesture. 'Fog-bound marsh, dim forests all of little use for agriculture; only animals can live here and in my experience animals are always hairy.'

'Elephants aren't; they've got some hair on them but they ain't hairy.'

Sabinus sighed with irritation. 'All right, Magnus; if she isn't hairy she'll be huge.'

Magnus grunted, apparently satisfied. 'Fair enough.'

As it turned out Sabinus was wrong: Prasutagus' wife was both huge and hairy. It was to her that Vespasian and his companions, having sent their names on in advance, presented themselves in the marketplace the following day upon their arrival at Venta Icenorum.

'My name is Boudicca, wife of Prasutagus,' the Queen of the Iceni announced in a harsh voice, used to command; her russet hair was piled high on her head and fell in copious unkempt waves down her back, coming to her waist. She wore the tunic and trousers of a man, brightly coloured; a cloak was fastened around her by a bronze brooch, fashioned as a coiled serpent. About her neck she wore a golden torque, the sign of a warrior old in the way of war. Standing in front of the largest, by far, of the five hundred or so round, thatched-roofed huts clustered within the stockaded settlement, she fixed the visitors with a piercing glare, one after the other, as if assessing the threat posed by each one before continuing: 'My husband is unable to come and greet you personally as he is confined to his hall.' Her Latin was accented but reasonable.

Vespasian restrained an urge to snap at her, unimpressed by being treated in such an overbearing manner. 'It is with him that we need to speak.' He felt Caenis' hand on his elbow and tempered his voice. 'I suggest that we do so now.'

'You can suggest all you like, Roman, but I'm telling you that you cannot see him; he is on his deathbed. You will address any issues to me or you will leave. Rome does not rule here.' She folded her arms, the sleeves of her tunic riding up to reveal hirsute wrists. The warriors attending her shifted their positions to stand more firmly; here and there one rolled his shoulders as if limbering up. Other warriors could be seen through the haze of pungent cooking-fire smoke that wafted around the nearby huts.

Vespasian felt the turma of cavalry, standing behind him, tense.

Caenis stepped forward, looking up at the warrior queen. 'If we do not get to see your husband before he dies then I can tell you that there is no chance that I will do my business with you.'

Boudicca looked down at Caenis who was almost two heads shorter than her and well under half her body-mass. 'Do you speak for these men?' There was surprise in her voice.

'My name is Antonia Caenis; I speak for myself. I and my companions will speak with your husband.'

With their eyes locked, the battle of feminine wills raged in silence for a few moments.

'Very well, Antonia Caenis,' Boudicca said eventually, 'but just you and one other.'

'Seneca must think I'm stupid,' Prasutagus wheezed; his chest heaved and he hacked out a series of phlegm-filled coughs, spitting the bloody result onto the rushes covering the floor. He grimaced in pain as he lay back down on the pillow and gave a wan smile, wrinkling his thin skin even more than age had done naturally. 'But perhaps he's right: I was stupid to borrow that amount of money from him. It just seemed so easy, and at the time I didn't consider how I would pay it back as we didn't really have any concept of bank loans on such a vast scale before you Romans came and so didn't understand them.'

Caenis nodded her head in sympathy that Vespasian could see was put on. 'I'm sure that you understand them now.'

'Oh, yes; I understand them. I understand them well enough to know that the interest that I've been paying has stopped me from amassing enough to pay off the debt.' He wheezed again, this time through mirth. 'Seneca's been too greedy: he's not allowed me the means to repay him.'

Caenis crossed her legs and leant forward. 'Seneca doesn't see it that way, Prasutagus. His reasoning is that the King of the Iceni took out the loan so that the whole tribe would benefit; therefore the whole tribe is liable. So he suggests that you start collecting the taxes that you need to fulfil your obligations to him.'

The dying King looked at Caenis, his long grey hair lank with sweat. 'Or what?'

Caenis smiled sweetly at him. 'Or he has the influence to be able to send a legion to collect it and that will work out far more expensive for you and your people; especially bearing in mind that if the amount cannot be raised in cash and bullion, then slaves are getting quite valuable again after the drop in price when so many Britons were sold off in the first years of the conquest.' Caenis paused for a few moments to let this sink in. 'However,' she continued as Prasutagus acknowledged the possibility of such action, 'Seneca is not so greedy as to insist on repayment of the full amount, since he has, as you have pointed out, already made a considerable profit on the deal.'

Prasutagus fell into another bout of strained coughing; bloody saliva trickled from the corners of his mouth. 'How much does he want?' he asked once the fit had subsided.

'He's prepared to forget half of the outstanding interest if you pay by the calends of March; that gives you a little over three months to collect.'

This sent Prasutagus into a choking mixture of mirth and dry hacking, his chest convulsing with the effort.

'That's enough!' Boudicca's harsh voice cut across her husband's discomfort. 'You will leave him now.'

Caenis remained firmly in her seat. 'Not until I have an answer from him.'

'I am mistress here.'

Caenis turned hard, piercing eyes onto the Britannic Queen. 'That's what you might think, Boudicca; however, I make this offer only once, to him, the King, not to you. If I leave now without an answer, the full sum will be due the moment I walk out the door. Can you afford that?'

Vespasian again witnessed a silent battle of female wills, feeling relieved that he was not caught in the middle.

Boudicca blinked first. 'What say you, husband?' Her voice softened; there was considerable tenderness in it.

Prasutagus managed to get his chest under control. 'What can I say? I have to accept. Seneca dresses up a hard deal as a generous favour by threatening me with the immediate bankruptcy of the whole Iceni tribe to be paid for by the liberty of hundreds, if not thousands, of us sent to the slave markets of Gallia and Italia.' He looked back to Caenis. 'Come back in March and the money will be here; even if I'm not.'

'Then how can you guarantee that?'

'I'll make it a condition of my will. Seneca's loan will be paid off and then the rest of my estate will be divided equally between the Emperor on one hand and my wife and daughters on the other.'

Caenis tilted her head. 'Agreed, but with one change: you bring the money to me in Camulodunum.'

Prasutagus sighed deeply and nodded, too tired to argue any more.

Vespasian at last saw how he could be of use. 'Have the document drawn up now, Prasutagus, and I'll witness it along with my brother; as former consuls our signatures and seals would make the will unchallengeable.'

And so Caenis, taking the halting dictation of a dying man and in her ultra-neat hand, wrote down a will that favoured Seneca above all else. Sabinus was ushered into the hall and he and Vespasian witnessed the completed document under the glowering gaze of Boudicca. When it was done they took their leave of Prasutagus, leaving him emptying his lungs and cursing in equal measure.

'You know that in March it'll be with me that you'll have to deal,' Boudicca informed Caenis as they stepped out together into the chill, her breath immediately steaming.

Caenis did not look at the Britannic Queen. 'No, Boudicca; in March it'll be *me* that *you* have to deal with. And as far as I'm concerned, your husband has already made the deal, and if he's dead by March then I will expect you to honour it.'

'And if I choose not to?'

'Then it'll be the wrong choice because Seneca will have both the law and the military power on his side. If I were you I'd spend the next few months collecting the money.'

Caenis walked away leaving Boudicca seething, her fists clenching and unclenching. 'I should have you all killed, Romans,' she snarled at Vespasian and Sabinus as they passed her.

'And where would that get you?' Vespasian asked.

Boudicca stared at him with undisguised hatred, her towering frame tense as a strung bow. 'You think that you can come here and dictate terms to an independent king?'

'We just did, didn't we?'

Boudicca spat. 'No, *you* didn't, your woman did. You just sat there as if she were the man wearing trousers and you were the wife.'

Vespasian went for his *gladius*, ripping it from its scabbard.

Boudicca stood firm as her bodyguards surrounded her, their spears levelled. The auxiliary cavalry troopers, suddenly alert to the tension, leapt into the saddles; horses reared up in surprise at the abrupt activity. Castor and Pollux growled, deep and guttural, straining against Magnus and Hormus respectively.

Vespasian felt a hand grab his shoulder and another, his right wrist.

'Don't be stupid, brother,' Sabinus shouted in his ear.

'Do you expect me to let that insult pass?' Vespasian hissed, staring into Boudicca's mocking eyes.

'We're outnumbered; just look around you.'

Vespasian strained against his brother's grip, but knew that he was right. After a few moments he calmed, taking a couple of deep breaths, and then lowered the tip of his sword.

'Anyway,' he said, his voice tight with frustration, 'Roman men don't wear trousers.'

Boudicca sneered. 'Yes, I noticed.'

Again Sabinus had to restrain his brother, and it took Caenis turning and running back to grab his face in both hands, forcing him to look into her eyes, to calm him this time. 'Focus on me, my love; on me.'

Vespasian looked into her eyes and saw the strength within the sapphires; he gritted his teeth and did as she had commanded and then allowed himself to be led away.

With difficulty he ignored Boudicca's scoff.

'You make sure that you're there in Camulodunum with the money on the calends of March, Boudicca,' Caenis called over her shoulder.

'I'll be there, Antonia Caenis,' the Queen replied, her voice harsh in the cold air. 'On the calends or as soon after that as the tracks are passable, I'll be there.' She said something else, quieter, but neither Vespasian nor any of the others caught it as the words were drowned out by the neighing of horses and the jangle of tack.

'I wonder what they did,' Magnus mused, looking up at the bodies of four men slumped on crosses just outside the northern gate to Camulodunum; although their eyes had already become food for the crows there were faint signs of life in two of them.

Vespasian shrugged; he did not care, brooding, as he was still, upon the insult to his masculinity by a woman – albeit a very manly woman, but a woman nonetheless. What had irked him the most was the truth in what Boudicca had said: he had been nothing more than a bystander in the negotiations between Caenis and the King. And Caenis had dealt with the situation masterfully; he gave a rueful smile at the use of such a masculine word to describe her behaviour.

'Still,' Magnus went on next to him, seemingly oblivious to the fact that Vespasian was occupying his own internal world, 'I'd assume that it would have been serious seeing as they don't look to have been slaves.'

'Perhaps there's been a bit of tension whilst we've been away,' Hormus suggested, keeping his eyes averted from the grisly sight. 'It didn't feel like a very harmonious town when we arrived.'

Vespasian grunted. 'I agree; as soon as I've spoken with that little runt, Paelignus, we'll get back to Londinium and wait there for three months whilst the Iceni get the money together and the other loans are repaid.'

Sabinus smiled. 'In relative comfort, you mean?'

'In as much as anywhere can be comfortable in this arsehole of empire.'

'Talking of arseholes,' Magnus said, pointing ahead of them, 'there's a little one.'

Vespasian looked up to see Paelignus riding towards them with an escort of auxiliaries. As he got closer Vespasian could see that the prefect had the grimace that passed for his smile spread across his face.

'Ah, Senators Vespasian and Sabinus, it's a pleasure to see you both back,' Paelignus said in his most ingratiating tones as he pulled up his horse opposite them. 'I had people on the lookout for your party so that I could come and greet you myself.'

'What do you want, Paelignus?' Vespasian asked, well aware that their return was anything but a pleasure for the prefect.

'You'll be pleased to know that I've been entirely successful in my task of regaining the monies owed to Seneca.'

Vespasian hid his surprise. 'And what about the money that you owe him?'

The smile was sickening; it was as if Paelignus was trying to pretend that they were the best of friends talking about a thing of mutual interest that gave both of them joy. 'That is all in hand, Vespasian. I recently squeezed some more out of the colonists as a tax to go towards the completion of the walls, but seeing as we don't really need them I've appropriated that, which, along with what I have on deposit with the Cloelius Brothers' agent in Londinium, is over half the amount.'

The use of public funds for personal gain did not surprise Vespasian; he had seen it happen many times and was, frankly, used to it. 'And what about the rest?'

Paelignus' grimace cracked into a full-scale leer. 'Ah! Well, I thought that the easiest way to make the other creditors pay up was to use force; which, as I knew they were not citizens, seemed perfectly legitimate. So I had them arrested for plotting treason and, as Urban prefect and the highest-ranking Roman official here, I tried them myself.'

Vespasian felt the blood pound in his head; he gaped at the man he hated probably more than anyone else in the world, looking so pleased with himself, as he recounted what Vespasian was sure to be the most stupid thing that any magistrate could do.

'Of course, they were guilty and their estates forfeit. So I now have all the money that you came to collect for Seneca waiting back at the Governor's residence for you. Therefore, my ... er ... *friend*, perhaps we could forget all that has passed between us; take the money and go with my blessing.'

Vespasian felt sick as he looked back at the bodies hanging from the crosses. 'Are those the men, Paelignus?'

'Of course; I gave them a taste of good Roman justice.'

'No you didn't, you crooked little cunt; they were innocent as you yourself as good as admitted. What you've given them is a taste of good Roman injustice and in doing so you've managed to execute four men who were most probably held in respect by the rest of their people and you've therefore managed to piss off the entire Trinovantes tribe.'

CHAPTER XI

VESPASIAN SCREWED UP the letter he had just read and tossed it over the terrace balustrade of their rented villa, onto the muddy shoreline of the Tamesis – the place was an expensive luxury but better than running the risk of seeing the procurator, Catus Decianus, every day had they decided to stay at the official residence. 'Well, it was inevitable, I suppose.'

'What was inevitable?' Magnus asked, throwing a piece of meat high in the air for Castor and Pollux to fight for.

'Cerialis has written to say that Governor Suetonius Paulinus has ordered him to direct his attentions to the Brigantes in the north this coming campaigning season, rather than worry about the Iceni.'

Magnus lobbed up another hunk of pork. 'Why's that inevitable?'

'Because since Prasutagus' death last month, Paulinus doesn't consider the Iceni a threat seeing as they have a queen now rather than a king and she isn't officially the queen until Nero confirms her as such, which at this time of year will take a while.' Vespasian pointed at the dogs scrapping over the meat. 'Why are you feeding them just before we go out hunting?'

'I'm trying an experiment to see if they refrain from ripping the kill apart if they're not so hungry; it'd be nice, for once, to come back with a deer that's reasonably edible rather than something that looks like it's just had the starring role at the circus, if you take my meaning?'

Vespasian did and thought it not a bad idea, as Magnus' dogs had proved to be very enthusiastic hunters and seemed to build upon that enthusiasm with every succeeding hunt.

Magnus chucked another lump at the dogs. 'I suppose Paulinus is worried about the Brigantes taking him by surprise as spring approaches seeing as he's chosen to winter up there in the north.'

'He didn't choose to, he's been forced to; with Myrddin still unaccounted for and the few druids who escaped with him from Mona still at large somewhere up there, he had no choice. Add to that the new development of Venutius going back on his word to Seneca and stirring up trouble with the Carvetii to the north of the Brigantes then it makes sense for Paulinus to want Cerialis concentrating in that direction rather than towards the currently leaderless Iceni.'

'They do have a leader,' Caenis said, walking out onto the terrace with Sabinus, both dressed warmly, as were Vespasian and Magnus, in hunting clothes. 'Boudicca. Just because Nero hasn't confirmed her in her position doesn't mean that her people won't follow her; she's a very strong woman.'

'But even so, there would be nowhere to follow her to,' Sabinus pointed out. 'Assuming that Prasutagus' will is ratified and she can inherit, which according to Britannic custom she can but to Roman law she can't, she would be stupid to do anything provocative towards us once she's paid off her debt and the threat of having it collected by force has disappeared. If she lives peacefully then she'll wake up one morning later on in the year to the news that Rome is withdrawing and Caratacus is coming back to be king of the eastern client kingdom, which the Iceni would nominally be a part of but in practice will remain independent. If she does make a nuisance of herself then that event could well be delayed.'

'But she doesn't know that and nor can we tell her for obvious reasons.' Vespasian looked up at the low grey cloud laden with drizzle. 'Well, nothing's going to happen until what passes for spring in this damp shithole arrives, by which time we should be well away, provided she does turn up in Camulodunum in three days' time with Seneca's money.'

Magnus chucked the last piece of pork at his growling dogs and wiped his hands on his fur-lined cloak. 'Right, let's get going. Where's Hormus? Ain't he coming?'

'No, he's doing some business for Caenis and me with the Cloelius Brothers, now that they've returned from their trip to see Cogidubnus,' Vespasian said, heading for the steps down from the side of terrace, at the bottom of which their horses waited. 'We'll get going as he'll be a while.'

The road leading northwest out of Londinium was, as most roads were, straight as an arrow-shaft and cleared of trees and scrub for a hundred paces to either side. The hunting party clattered along it at a good pace, heading for a wooded hill just to the west of the road some three miles from the town. Castor and Pollux lolloped ahead, playing canine games of rough-and-tumble on the short grass to the side of the road. The all-covering cloud had begun to give up its ample store of moisture, but Vespasian, for once, did not feel gloomy in the miserable conditions as he knew that within a few months he could be back on one of his estates, having stopped off to see Titus in Germania Inferior on the way – provided the sea stayed calm enough for the short crossing to the mainland. But even if they were forced to wait until the end of April or beginning of May when the sea routes properly opened up, he would be happy to, in the knowledge that he would soon be away, never to return. And then, once back in Italia he would wait on his estate at Cosa for news as to how he stood with Nero and whether it was safe for him to return to Rome.

As the hill came into view they left the road and cut across country, past a couple of farmsteads where slaves struggled behind plough-horses tilling the thick clay soil in preparation for the season that, unbeknownst to them, would see an end to Roman rule in Britannia. Vespasian still thought it to be a move of the utmost stupidity, politically, but he could see that the economic arguments for it were beginning to stack up, especially bearing in mind Nero's increasing profligacy. In the three months that they had been waiting in the relative comfort of their riverside villa, it had become more and more obvious that, although the small corner of the southeast of the island was peaceful and reasonably pro-Roman, the rest most certainly was not. The Cloelius Brothers had arrived and immediately begun to send their agents around the province calling in their loans and causing massive resentment amongst the indigenous tribes. This, in turn, had led to a few beatings and a couple of murders of colonists and merchants; with the four legions in the province wintering on the frontiers to the north and the west and the auxiliary cohorts in the main garrisoning the series of forts along the roads that connected the four legionary camps, there was not much in the way of protection for Roman citizens and Romanised Britons.

The situation had worsened when the rest of the other Londinium bankers had realised what the Cloelius Brothers were doing. Then, when the rumour spread that Seneca had already called in his loans and the largest of these, the one to Prasutagus, was to be repaid without the full interest, a rush to get their money out of the province had begun in earnest, sucking the life out of the economy already damaged by war on the fringes of empire. Building work on the amphitheatre had ground to a halt due to lack of cash flow and local tradesmen who had provided the materials for it, and other stagnated projects, went unpaid. This, naturally, filtered down through the economy as coinage became increasingly hard to get hold of. Those that had it hoarded it, and those that did not have it fretted for it. Now it had reached the stage whereby those bankers who had not acted with alacrity were unable to recall their loans because there simply was not enough coin in ready circulation for the debtors to pay.

No one was letting their money leave their strongboxes and what was already a cold, damp winter had become even more miserable: unless a tribe or community had a reasonable amount of supplies they would start to go hungry as they would not have the cash to purchase more, and even if it had there was nothing to buy as no one would risk selling their winter surplus during a time of economic crisis.

Thus the new province of Britannia had come to an economic standstill. Many of the merchants had already left but there was another class that held too much of a stake in the province to be able to do so: these were the colonists, military settlers who had been rewarded with their own piece of land after serving under the Eagles for their allotted twenty-five years. If they were to leave where would they go? Back to their birth-towns to find work as a labourer or to beg? With no chance of being able to save enough to buy land elsewhere in order to keep themselves and their new families in dignity, they had no alternative but to stay and farm the land that they had been given. Therefore, in amongst the growing discontent of the local people was a large community that could be seen – wrongly – as being directly responsible for all the woes being visited upon them.

And it was this that Vespasian and his companions now saw direct evidence of; as they passed the second of the two farmsteads they plunged into a copse at the base of the hill, urging their mounts up the steadily rising ground. Castor and Pollux had ceased their play and now followed their noses, their pace increasing as a scent freshened. On they went, bounding up the hill swerving around the trees, following the path of their prey. Vespasian drew a javelin from the leather holster attached to his saddle as he kicked his mount forward, the thrill of the chase growing, once again, within him. Caenis, just behind him, let out an unladylike whoop, causing Vespasian to smile at the way she had taken to hunting in the last few months. The hounds cleared the trees and came out onto the heathland that covered the rest of the slope; in the distance, on the hill's crest, could be seen the three deer whose scent had attracted Castor and Pollux's attention. With deep-throated barks the dogs sped away.

But it was not the sight of the quarry that caught Vespasian's eye as he cantered onto the heath nor was it the scent of the trail that caught in his nose; it was a far more acrid smell, the smell of the pillar of dark smoke rising from a point about half a mile to the north.

Vespasian pulled up his horse, swinging it round in the direction of the fire; its source could not be seen, screened, as it was, by another copse. 'Call the dogs back, Magnus!' he ordered as Sabinus and Caenis pulled up next to him.

'Not much chance of that,' Magnus shouted as he sped after his hounds, which were by now brim with canine enthusiasm for the hunt.

'What do you think it is?' Caenis asked, shading her eyes so that the drizzle did not impede her vision.

'It's a veteran's farmstead,' Sabinus asserted, controlling his skittish horse. 'I'm positive; last time we were up here we went back that way chasing that doe which the dogs managed to dismember.'

'You're right,' Vespasian agreed. 'Let's take a look in case they need some help; perhaps their barn's caught fire.'

All three urged their mounts into a canter, traversing the hill; Magnus could be heard shouting at Castor and Pollux, now far in the distance, to desist.

Skirting around the top of the copse they started to descend until heathland gave way to pasture; but its scent was not sweet and it was not just the acridity of the smoke, there was another smell in the air, a smell that both Vespasian and Sabinus knew only too well: the stench of burnt flesh.

They came across the first body lying not far from the plough that he had most likely been using; of the horse, there was no sign. Nor was there any sign of the man's head. What could be seen from this position, though, was that it was not just the barn that was aflame; the whole complex was burning: barn, farmhouse, outbuildings, everything, including a couple of trees.

They approached with caution, on foot and using their horses as shields should whoever had done this prove to be still present and thirsting for more blood. More bodies lay closer to the buildings, all having fallen in the act of running away, lying on their bellies facing in the direction of the farmstead, if a headless man could be said to be facing anywhere.

'They've all been killed by sword slashes,' Vespasian pointed out, examining a couple of the dead.

'So?' Caenis asked.

'So they weren't killed from a distance, otherwise there would be spent javelins and arrows. It would seem that either their attackers approached them on foot and were right in amongst them before they started killing …'

'Which is unlikely,' Sabinus said, kneeling down and examining the ground.

'Which is unlikely,' Vespasian agreed. 'Which leaves a sudden, mounted attack.'

'Which it was; look.' Sabinus pointed to what were unmistakeably hoof-prints.

'So, we have a mounted attack by men who would have to be good cavalry to be able to kill from the saddle this efficiently; and, what's more, they were using swords, long swords that should all have been melted down under the terms of the peace agreement. They killed everyone in the fields and then took the house and set it on fire before coming back to remove the heads.' Vespasian looked in the direction of the conflagration. 'We'd better see what they've done with the colonist and his family.'

It did not take long to find him and his wife; they were not amongst the score or so of bodies, some on fire, some just smouldering, that littered the farmyard but, rather, they had been singled out for special treatment. For it was not two trees that blazed next to the buildings; it was two crosses. The crackling remains of the man and his wife hung, contorted and blackened, on the crosses, side by side, eyes, hair, noses and lips burnt away to give them rictus visages of pure horror staring out from the flames. At the foot of each cross lay sizzling chunks of meat that may once have been the bodies of an infant and a baby before they were dismembered.

Caenis put her hand over her mouth but it did not prevent the vomit from squirting out to either side.

'Come,' Vespasian said mounting up. 'There's nothing we can do here. We'd best be going as whoever did this is not long gone. I'm afraid that we're obliged to report this to the official authority.'

Vespasian knew that it would be an onerous task as it meant going to see Catus Decianus.

There had been no sign of those responsible for the atrocity as they had made their way back to the road, once Magnus had rejoined them. On the way through they had warned the other two farmsteads; the colonists had pulled their slaves in from the fields and had sent messages to all the nearby settlements.

By the time they reached Londinium, the short winter day was beginning to fade and it was in the half-light that they came to

Catus Decianus' residence. As their status was known to the guards, they were admitted without question.

'We must see the procurator immediately,' Vespasian informed the steward who met them in the atrium.

'Alas, master,' the man said, smiling with oily regret and bowing his head, 'the procurator is indisposed.'

'Well, un-indispose him then!'

'Alas, master, would that I could but his indisposition involves him not being here.'

'Well, where is he then? Send a messenger to have him brought back here right away.'

The steward paused for a sigh and an apologetic hunching of the shoulders. 'Alas, master, but by not being here I mean that the procurator is not in Londinium.'

'Where's he gone then?'

'Alas, master, I am not privy to that information; all I know is that he left yesterday morning soon after dawn with an ala of auxiliary cavalry. He didn't say where he was going, just that he would be back in seven or eight days.'

Vespasian wanted to hit the man but knew that would get him nowhere. 'Then find out as soon as you can; someone will know in the auxiliary camp. And tell me once you know.'

'It's so typical of a man like Decianus to go missing just when he might be of some use,' Sabinus complained as they reached their villa. Torches blazed to either side of the steps leading up to the front door. Slaves scuttled down to them to take their horses around to the stables as they dismounted.

'It's why he wanted to take an ala of cavalry with him that puzzles me,' Vespasian said as he climbed the steps. 'Almost five hundred men is quite a bodyguard.'

'Perhaps he had already heard about some unrest and had gone to suppress it,' Caenis suggested. 'What we saw this afternoon must have been a part of it.'

'No, if there was any danger involved you can be sure that Decianus would have sent a junior officer; he's not the sort to put himself in harm's way. No, what he plans to do might cause unrest so he thought it would be better not to take any chances.'

That moment Hormus came into the atrium to greet his master.

'Did the business with the Cloelius Brothers go well, Hormus?' Vespasian asked.

'Indeed, master.' He handed Caenis two scrolls. 'These are the bankers' drafts redeemable with the Cloelius Brothers back in Rome, mistress; the fee was twelve per cent of the total; Tertius Cloelius said that they had added a premium because of the growing tension in the province and the dangers of transporting cash over the sea.'

'I knew he would; but I suppose it's fair enough and, after all, it's Seneca's money not mine.'

'Well done, Hormus,' Vespasian said, 'you did a good job.'

Hormus coloured, unused to praise. 'Thank you, master.'

'Did Tertius tell you when the ship would sail with the cash?'

'Yes, master; he said in a market interval or so.'

'Why so long?'

'Decianus ordered him to wait for his return. He's gone to fetch some money and he wants it to be sent to Rome immediately.'

Vespasian frowned. 'Fetch some money? It must be a substantial amount if he wants it to leave the province immediately. Where's he fetching it from?'

'Tertius didn't know exactly; only that he's taken a large body of cavalry with him and he's headed northeast about four days' ride away.'

Vespasian, Caenis and Sabinus all looked at each other in alarm.

'That's a lot further than Camulodunum,' Vespasian said.

Sabinus nodded. 'Much further; you could get to Venta Icenorum in that time.'

'Yes, brother, you could. He must have heard about the Iceni collecting money to pay off Seneca. The bastard's going to steal Boudicca's gold.'

There was nothing to be done until the following morning and it was as the first glow grew in the eastern sky that Vespasian and his three companions headed in pursuit of the procurator, knowing that he was two days ahead of them. Hormus had been left in Londinium with their slaves as well as Caenis' two slave girls; Caenis had insisted on coming as she felt that the matter was very much of her concern.

To speed them up, each had a spare mount so that they could rotate horses every hour. In this way they were able to reach Camulodunum before midday. A brief enquiry of Paelignus, who looked terrified to see them and flinched every time Vespasian spoke to him, was enough to ascertain that Decianus and his men had passed through late afternoon two days before, without stopping. They were gaining on them.

Gambling on the fact that Decianus would be in no special hurry to reach his destination as the Cloelius Brothers' ship would not sail until he had returned and so therefore there was no point in blowing his escort's horses, they kept their speed at an easy canter knowing that they would steadily eat away at the procurator's lead. And so they retraced their path to the lands of the Iceni, sleeping that night a good distance from Camulodunum wrapped in damp blankets, with only Magnus being able to claim relative warmth snuggled between an exhausted Castor and Pollux. Rising with the sun the following morning they pressed on and, with every hour they travelled, the trail of the ala appeared fresher. As they came to Venta Icenorum at the tenth hour of the day, they arrived to find that the procurator had been in the settlement for only one hour.

But that hour had been enough; the settlement was sealed off.

'I don't care what your orders are, decurion,' Sabinus shouted at the officer commanding the turma of cavalry prohibiting entrance at the southern gate. 'My name is Titus Flavius Sabinus of proconsular rank, up until recently the prefect of Rome itself, and if you do not let us through then I shall personally see to it that you get a tour of the city ending up in the Circus Maximus.' He thrust his face, red with frustration, forward so that their noses almost touched. 'Do I make myself clear, little man?'

Sabinus had evidently explained himself adequately for the decurion swallowed, thought for a moment, and then snapped a salute; a couple of barked orders had his men on the gate open it and Vespasian and his companions trotted through into a town in the grip of a raucous chaos.

Although it was the biggest Iceni settlement, Venta Icenorum consisted of around five hundred habitations, therefore there were also roughly that number of fighting-age men and they were not necessarily all warriors; far from it, for most of the population farmed the surrounding land. Decianus had therefore chosen his escort well: the four hundred and eighty troopers of the ala had the town completely under control with groups of them riding through the lanes between the round huts shouting and threatening any of the population at large in order to keep them indoors.

The shouting continued as they made their way to the marketplace at the heart of the settlement where they had previously met Boudicca outside her late husband's hall. As they neared their destination, individual voices could finally be heard and they were raised in anger.

'You have no right!' The voice was harsh and deep and if Vespasian had not met Boudicca he would have thought it to be a man's.

'I have every right as Rome's representative,' Decianus replied as Vespasian and Sabinus pushed through the circle of troopers gathered outside Prasutagus' hall; Caenis and Magnus followed them, having tied Castor and Pollux to a post for fear of them attacking the wrong person in such a congested area. The commotion of their arrival caused Decianus to turn his head towards them as he sat in his curule chair, a symbol of his power; in his hand he held a scroll. Boudicca stood before him, her wrists manacled and her arms secured by two troopers as if she were a common criminal. The bodies of a dozen of her warriors lay bloody on the ground around her.

'What are you doing here?' Decianus demanded as he recognised Vespasian and Sabinus.

'I'm here to ask you the exact same question,' Vespasian replied, striding forward to place himself between the procurator and the Queen.

'I don't have to explain myself to you.'

'He's here to steal the money that we have collected to pay off Seneca!' Boudicca screamed, her voice a study in rage.

'Shut that bitch up!'

The trooper who tried to gag her with his hand was rewarded with deep teeth marks between his thumb and forefinger.

'That is not your money, Decianus,' Vespasian said.

'I'm the procurator of Britannia and therefore in charge of gathering taxes and the general financial wellbeing of the province. Just after the invasion Claudius lent all the highest ranking nobles substantial sums of money so that they would have senatorial status; lent, mind you, not gave. I am here to recall the loan and to show Claudius' successor just how good a servant I am to him.'

'By stealing Seneca's money?'

'No; Claudius lent to them first so his debt has priority over Seneca's. The Iceni have no right to dispute that now that they're officially a part of the province.'

Boudicca struggled against her restrainers but they held firm. 'My husband's will named me and my daughters as co-heirs with Nero.'

Decianus looked at the scroll he was holding and then ripped it in half. 'The will is worthless because under Roman law you cannot inherit.'

'Which law?'

'The *lex voconia* forbids testators in the first census class to name women as their heirs.'

'That law is a hundred years old,' Caenis said.

'But it is still valid.'

'Perhaps, but, as you said, only for people in the first census class.'

'Which Tiberius Claudius Prasutagus was; the Emperor Claudius placed him there the last time he held the censorship soon after he had lent him the money to give him that status.' Decianus smiled in triumph. 'As procurator I'm well aware of the status of the citizens in the province and Prasutagus along with Cogidubnus and Venutius are all in the first class. The will is invalid, therefore he died intestate and so his estate goes to the Emperor unless the heirs would wish to challenge it in the courts, which, of course, they cannot because of their sex. But even if they could they wouldn't succeed as Boudicca and the three daughters are named as co-heirs of half the estate or twelve and a half per cent each. As you well know, in law a husband *or* wife can only make a bequest to the other of no more than *ten* per cent of the estate's value. Again we have a cause to make the will null and void. Do you want me to carry on?'

'But this is Iceni land and not under the jurisdiction of Rome!' Boudicca screamed. 'We have our own customs and women have always been able to inherit.'

Decianus pointed down at the discarded will. 'Yet as a citizen, which no one can deny he was, your husband made his will under Roman law; he even got two men of proconsular rank to witness it.' He indicated to Vespasian and Sabinus. 'What am I to do?' He leant forward, teeth bared in a parody of a smile. 'I must enforce the law, of course; which means the will is worthless and everything goes to the Emperor and therefore this Iceni land is now part of the Roman province.'

This was too much for Boudicca; with all the strength of her huge frame she tore herself away from her guards and flew at Decianus, knocking him backwards off his chair and crunching her manacled wrist down into his face at the moment that the back of his head slammed into the ground. Cartilage was crushed and blood sprayed her hands; Decianus' nose was flattened to one side. His scream of pain was cut short as the Queen thumped her right knee, not once but twice, into his genitals causing him to choke with white, searing agony. Boudicca had time for one double-fisted punch that split both the procurator's lips before she was hauled off by half a dozen troopers.

'I thoroughly enjoyed that,' Magnus muttered next to Vespasian.

'I think we all did,' Vespasian said as Decianus was helped back to his feet clutching at his testicles and hyperventilating.

'Strip her and whip her,' Decianus wheezed.

'You can't do that,' Vespasian shouted as Boudicca was pulled away, kicking and hissing. Decianus, still hunched over as pain raged through his innards, looked up at Vespasian with half-closed eyes; blood poured from his crushed nose. 'Can't I?'

'No, her husband was a citizen.'

'Just watch me.' He raised a shaking, crooked finger towards Vespasian. 'Tie them up.'

Vespasian, Sabinus and Magnus all went for their swords but many hands grabbed them; hands that were unwilling to disobey a procurator, especially when the status of the arrested was unknown. And as Vespasian felt twine encircling and binding his wrists behind him, a sharp knife was ripped up the back of Boudicca's tunic and it was torn from her to expose great, pendulous breasts and wads of hair poking from under her arms. As her trousers were wrenched away she raised her eyes to the sky and screeched a curse to her gods in her own language; long it was and, as the first lash drew blood from her shoulders, it strengthened in intensity. Her body writhed in time to the whip but there was not one sound of pain; just the curse, intoned again and again, each repetition more venomous than the last as libations of her own blood poured into the earth of her homeland to seal her covenant with the deities of her people.

As the lash came down for the thirtieth time there was a scream, not of agony but of fear and it was not Boudicca: it was far more high-pitched and it was multiple. Into the ring of troopers three girls were dragged, all in their early teens and all naked.

Boudicca looked down at her daughters as they were thrown wailing to the ground. 'Stop that noise!' she shouted. 'Fight them, hate them, curse them but don't cry for them.' Another lash of the whip returned her to repetitive invocations as the three girls, now spitting curses in emulation of their mother, were pinned down, willing hands holding wrists and ankles. Even as the first troopers forced their way into each of them they did not cry out, nor did they submit peacefully during their ordeal and many an auxiliary had bite marks on his face by the time he had finished.

And so Vespasian watched as the mother was scourged and the daughters were raped again and again and again and he knew that what Decianus had done was irreversible and, with the legions busy in the north and the west, it was an act of such imbecilic foolhardiness as to take one's breath away.

The procurator had just pushed the Iceni nation into war.

Vespasian and his companions lay, still bound, on the damp earth as the auxiliaries loaded the strongboxes filled with Seneca's gold and silver onto a four-horse wagon. 'What about us, Decianus?' he shouted at the procurator. 'Are you just going to leave us here to be the objects of vengeance for your foolishness?'

Decianus looked down at Vespasian, a look of indifference on his battered and bleeding face; he wiped some blood away from his swollen mouth with the back of his hand. 'Calling me fool is, I would say, a foolish way to go about pleading for your life.'

'Forcing a peaceful tribe into rebellion is the act of a fool.'

'Rebellion? Now who's being the fool? They won't rebel; they wouldn't dare to. They haven't got the manpower; look.' He gestured around the settlement. 'This is their largest town; it's pitiful.'

'But how many other towns and villages do they have? I've seen a Britannic army, I've seen a few in fact, and I've seen how empty this land looks to be. But tell me, Decianus, where did the armies that I've seen come from? You're the procurator of the province; you know how many men from each tribe are subject to tax. Do you think the Iceni are any different? There are thousands of them; all they have to do is muster and then they'll be coming after you and every other Roman in this province and every Roman death will be laid at your feet.'

Decianus sneered as behind him his men started to mount up having finished loading. 'If that's the case then I'll leave you all here and make the first deaths yours, so you can't spread your tittle-tattle.'

'Killing us won't cover your tracks,' Sabinus said, struggling against his bonds. 'The Emperor will hear how this rebellion started, one way or another; the prefect of your auxiliary ala, for example.'

Decianus shook his head slowly as he smiled in mock regret. 'Nymphidius Sabinus knows how to keep his mouth shut because

I know what keeps it shut. Besides, the Emperor will care only for the millions that I bring him and he'll have that money within a couple of months; long before the Iceni manage to muster their entire strength, if your supposition is right and if they dare to. Two very big "ifs", Vespasian.' He turned away and strode, with a brief glance down at the semi-conscious bodies of Boudicca and her daughters, to his waiting horse. 'Pull out, Nymphidius! We'll travel as fast as possible.' He hauled himself up into the saddle and, without looking back, kicked his horse forward to join the column that was already streaming out of the settlement through the South Gate.

'This is not looking that good,' Magnus said, eyeing the warriors who were now emerging from the huts and narrow lanes between them.

'Try getting at the knot.' Vespasian rolled onto his side so that they were back to back; Sabinus was attempting to wriggle his wrists free whilst Caenis struggled to her feet and staggered towards the Queen.

The last of the auxiliaries rode out of sight and the build-up of warriors continued; there were now a couple of dozen men walking out into the marketplace, a few of them armed. Magnus struggled with Vespasian's knot, tearing at it with his fingernails but to no avail.

Vespasian adjusted his position. 'Here, let me try yours.'

Magnus held his wrists back so that the knot was available. 'As fast as you like, sir,' he urged as the warriors spotted them lying in amongst the bodies of their fallen comrades and royal family. 'Otherwise it'll be a pointless exercise in a few moments, if you take my meaning?'

Vespasian did but he was struggling as fast as he could and not having any success.

Caenis screamed as she was battered to the ground by the first warrior to reach Boudicca; the Queen stirred, moaning. A couple more of her men helped her up as another wrapped a cloak about her to cover her bloody nakedness; half a dozen more approached Vespasian, Magnus and Sabinus; spears and swords were in their hands and hatred on their faces.

Rough hands hauled the Romans to their knees and harsh voices shouted at them in their unintelligible tongue.

Vespasian felt a hand clamp itself on his skull and his head was pulled back to expose his throat. Next to him Magnus and Sabinus were in the same position.

'No!' Caenis shrieked, cutting across the growing shouts of outrage.

Boudicca's voice barked what sounded like an order and Vespasian closed his eyes, waiting for the blood to start flowing down his throat; the blood that would drown him. He felt the cool of the blade as it pressed against his skin and a short prayer to Mars flashed through his consciousness as Boudicca barked again. The hand holding the knife to his throat tensed and Vespasian felt a trickle of sweat roll down his back; the blade, however, did not bite but, rather, was withdrawn and then used to cut his bonds. He was helped to his feet; he opened his eyes and saw that his companions, too, were also being released.

'What the fuck happened there?' Magnus muttered, rubbing his wrists.

'I've got no idea,' Vespasian said as he watched Caenis being brought before Boudicca.

After a brief conversation Caenis bowed her head to the Queen and then walked back over to Vespasian. 'We're free to go,' she said, the relief she felt palpable in her voice.

Vespasian stared at her, incredulous. 'Why?'

'Because we both tried to stop Decianus; she wants to show us Romans the meaning of honour.'

Vespasian looked over at Boudicca who was kneeling by her daughters, weeping as women from the tribe wiped the blood from between their legs and comforted them after their ordeal. She sensed Vespasian's gaze and stood to face him. 'Tell the truth about what happened here, Roman; do not let that man give a twisted version of events. You know what I must do, what will happen; make sure, Roman, that your people understand why and know who is responsible.'

Vespasian walked towards her. 'You know you'll never win, don't you?'

Boudicca shrugged, wincing with the pain of her shredded back as she did so. 'Perhaps; perhaps not. But what I do know is that I will descend on your province like a Fury from your tales. You are the last Roman I'll ever talk to; from now on my blade is all that your people will get from me. Now go and tell your compatriots that to stay on this island is to die.' She pierced him with a glare of resolve firmed by hatred; nodded once and then turned away, walking upright with dignity despite the wounds to her back.

'I think we'd better find our horses before she changes her mind,' Sabinus said, retrieving his sword from the ground.

'She won't change her mind,' Caenis asserted. 'Not a woman like that; not with her strength.'

'Well, I ain't about to stick around and find out,' Magnus said, having retrieved Castor and Pollux.

Vespasian watched the Queen go. 'We're perfectly safe; Caenis is right: she won't change her mind. There's great strength in that woman; what stupidity for Decianus to have directed it against us. Let's go.'

'Which way should we head?' Sabinus asked as they mounted their horses. 'Decianus is on the south road and I don't much fancy getting captured by that little shit seeing as he's already tried to feed us to the Britons.'

Vespasian steadied his high-stepping mount with a couple of sharp tugs on the reins. 'South would be no good for us anyway; there're only a few auxiliary cohorts there and undefended towns. We go west and then when we've cleared the marshland we head north to the Ninth Hispana's camp at Lindum; Cerialis will be able to get a message to Paulinus. Unless the legions mobilise before the Iceni can muster, the province will be lost.'

CHAPTER XII

IT WAS EXHAUSTING because it was relentless, and it was relentless because there was no time to lose; the journey had to be completed as quickly as possible. They rose and retired with the sun, using all its precious light to navigate, pausing only to rotate the horses, fill their water-skins and relieve themselves; meals were taken in the saddle. The saving factor was that the way, for the most part, was flat; this made the going easier for the horses but, at the same time, did nothing to impede the passage of a cruel east wind that clawed at their backs as they drove west, hurling sheeting rain after them and inveigling its cold fingers into damp clothes, chilling them despite the exertion of riding. The terrain was low-lying and riddled with brooks, streams, drainage ditches and marshes, paradise for water fowl, of which there were uncounted amounts, but treacherous for the delicate legs of horses, and by the time they had made the passage south of the marshes and had begun to head northwest, two of the beasts had already succumbed to leg-breaking troughs; they had been put out of their misery and steaks had been cut from their rumps to be broiled hanging over the campfire in the evening. The meat was not to the Roman taste but outrunning, as they were, the rumour of rebellion, they had no wish to allow news of the Iceni's muster to overtake them for the sake of hunting game. Only Castor and Pollux managed to vary their diet but with creatures so mangled that they were not fit for human consumption.

On the third day they came to the road running north from Londinium to Lindum; their pace increased as they raced alongside it in the well-cared-for shorter grass to either side of the gently cambered stones, passing the occasional military supply vehicle but very little else and certainly not the thing that Vespasian and Sabinus were keeping a lookout for. Grim-faced and silent they rode, each immersed in his, or her, own thoughts or finding respite by retreating into the numbness of no thought at all, having allowed the ceaseless beat of horses' hoofs to drive all from their minds.

The miles sped by in pace but trudged by in time, each more painful on the raw thighs and bruised buttocks than the last; the sheepskins covering the saddles a torment now but far better than the hard leather and wood constructs that they protected against.

Magnus looked down at his dogs, bounding along beside them, tongues lolling from loose, saliva-flecked lips, exposing vicious teeth. 'My boys don't know how lucky they are,' he mused to no one in particular, shifting his position on the saddle for the hundredth time in the last hour. 'Not only they don't have sore balls and arses but even if they did they could lick them better.'

'They lick them whether they're sore or not,' Vespasian pointed out, truthfully.

'Yeah, well, that's because they can. I mean who wouldn't if one could.' He grimaced, sucking the breath between his teeth. 'Saving your presence, obviously, Caenis.'

'That's all right, Magnus,' Caenis said, adjusting herself and making a point of showing just how uncomfortable she was too. 'I'm just as sore as you and if I could I would too.'

Magnus muttered something unintelligible and would have gone red had his face not already been ruddy from exertion.

Vespasian essayed a laugh but found that his heart was not in it.

'Vespasian,' Sabinus said, peering ahead and shielding his eyes from the drizzle. 'Look!'

Vespasian stared for a moment and then looked with relief at his brother. 'At last.'

They stopped the imperial courier by lining their mounts across the road; the trooper was not amused. 'It's an offence to obstruct an imperial courier,' he said, looking Vespasian and his companions up and down and, unsurprisingly after their many days in the saddle, not liking what he saw.

Vespasian was not in the mood to explain himself. 'Where are you headed, trooper?'

The man stared in shock at his temerity and was about to give his opinion of such insolence when something caught his eye; he shut his mouth and saluted. 'Camulodunum, sir.'

Vespasian glanced at his senator's ring and made it more visible to the trooper. 'Good; you will go to the Urban prefect there, Julius Paelignus, and you will tell him that Senators Vespasian and Sabinus urge him to complete the town's defences in whatever way he can by the new moon and then look to the north. The Iceni are being roused and will fall upon him first. He should advise all the colonists in the area to gather in Camulodunum and then pray that they can hold out until the legions arrive; do I make myself clear?'

The trooper gawped at him and then saluted again. 'Yes, sir.'

'And he should send urgent messages to the Governors of Gallia Belgica and Germania Inferior telling them the situation and beg them to send whatever troops they can spare.'

'Yes, sir.'

'Repeat the message.'

'One more thing,' Vespasian continued once the man had done so to his satisfaction. 'You must stress to Paelignus that this is not a joke at his expense or a hoax but a genuine warning; tell him that I said that if it was just him there I would gladly let the Iceni arrive unannounced to carve him up, but in this case I'm sending him a warning in order to save other Roman lives, not his. Understand?'

'Yes, sir.'

'Good. How many miles is it to the next imperial rest post?'

'Seventeen, sir; the new fort of Durobrivae.'

Vespasian looked at the sky and judged that they could make that by dusk or at least soon after. 'May our gods go with you, trooper, and do not go near any bands of natives.'

The man swallowed hard, scanning the road ahead for any danger, saluted and then, as Vespasian and Sabinus moved aside for him, sped away.

* * *

That night Vespasian, with Caenis next to him, slept more deeply than he had for a long time such was his exhaustion; the modern facilities at the fort, designed to hold, at the maximum, a cohort, had done much to relax him. The prefect in command, Quintus Mannius, had been most generous – once he had found out who his guests were. The bath house had been reviving, the food and wine sustaining and Caenis entertaining – although her saddle-soreness did preclude some manoeuvres.

Rising before dawn, to the blare of *bucinae* sounding reveille, Vespasian wiped the sleep from his eyes and looked at his lover, curled up next to him, her skin aglow in the light of the night-lamp. 'I'm going to get Mannius to provide an escort for you back down to Londinium, my love.'

Caenis stirred and opened an eye. 'Hmm?'

Vespasian repeated himself.

'And what good would that do?'

'It would see you safe; Galla could get you passage to the mainland and you would be away before the Iceni head south.'

'What makes you so sure that they are going south? They could head west and try to cut all the north to south and west to east roads to prevent the legions from converging.'

Vespasian acknowledged the feasibility of such a strategy with a nod. 'They could do; and indeed that might be their best course. But they won't think in those terms. Boudicca's business is first and foremost with Decianus; she'll go for him and her warriors will support her in that. The men will see what was done to their Queen and her daughters as an affront to all their women; they'll want vengeance on the man responsible. No, she'll go south; firstly to Camulodunum and once her warriors have got the taste for Roman blood and loot they'll be hard to stop and hundreds more will flock to her every day. Londinium will be next and then Verulamium and after that probably Calleva and thus she will control all the roads north and west. If she does that before Paulinus has consolidated his forces, the best that we could hope for is that she allows our legions to embark peacefully, and the gods help the civilians and colonists left behind.'

'Do you think that will happen?'

'Yes, I do; there is more than a fair chance when you consider who would be in charge of the defence down here until Paulinus arrives.'

'Decianus; I see what you mean.'

'So go, then, Caenis; go to Londinium and take a ship out of here before panic starts to spread and ships become a rarity.'

Caenis smiled, her eyes reflecting the flame of the lamp. 'Not without you, my love; I'll go where you go. Having had a life almost exclusively confined to the palaces of the Palatine, this is an adventure that I wouldn't let go of for as long as we can be together; and besides, without me we would all be dead by now.'

'How so?'

'It was for me that Boudicca spared our lives; a woman thing, as it were. Had we all been men she would have flung honour aside, just as Decianus did, and probably have had us whipped to death. But because I'm a woman she didn't want to let down our sex in either her eyes or mine.'

Vespasian was incredulous. 'She let us all go so you wouldn't think badly of her?'

'Yes and no; it was more than that: she let us go so that I wouldn't think badly of her for stooping to the same level as Decianus and therefore justifying his broken sense of honour. She also wanted you and Sabinus to see just what an honourable woman she is before she ... what were her exact words to me? Ah, yes, before she tears the heart out of every Roman in this province and takes their heads.'

'So you still want to stay knowing that is what she intends to do?'

'Oh, yes, my love; I respect her and I'm looking forward to seeing how you men deal with her.'

Vespasian kissed her full on the mouth. 'Let's hope you don't have to wait too long; just time enough for Paulinus to assemble four legions.'

Cerialis did not look convinced as he paced around the newly constructed permanent praetorium of the VIIII Hispana's camp at Lindum Colonia; behind him the legion's Eagle, surrounded by its honour-guard, glistered in the glimmer of many oil lamps. 'How can you be sure they'll rebel, Father?' His words echoed dully off the plastered brickwork and high ceiling.

Vespasian struggled to conceal his impatience at his son-in-law's caution. 'Because she told Caenis that she would rip the heart out of every Roman in the province and I believe that she will do just that. What would you do in her position, Cerialis?'

Cerialis thought for a moment, looking between Vespasian and Sabinus, both sitting on very un-military, comfortable chairs, sipping heated wine. 'I would avenge myself even if it amounted to suicide.'

Vespasian blew into his cup. 'It'll only be suicidal if we manage to mobilise in time, which is why you must send a message to Paulinus telling him that you're marching south immediately and he should follow as soon as he can, otherwise there'll be no province left to govern.'

'But he's ordered me to look to the north so as to keep the Brigantes in order now that Venutius is trying to usurp his wife again.'

Sabinus had little patience. 'Fuck the north; the trouble is in the south right now and unless it's quelled quickly it'll spread to the north and west and then we'll all be fucked for lack of decisive action, Cerialis.'

'But my orders—'

'Fuck your orders!'

'That doesn't get us anywhere, Sabinus,' Vespasian cut in, putting his cup down on a table and standing in one movement. 'How long does it take for a messenger to get to Paulinus and back again?'

'If I'm lucky, two days.'

'Good. Now, do you remember what I told you about delay when we were listening to Corbulo's despatch being read out in the Senate?'

'Always speed in reaction. Hit the bastards before they get a chance to consolidate; or something like that.'

'Exactly, and that's what makes Corbulo such a good general: he doesn't dither. So write to Paulinus and say that you are marching south and should he wish to stop you the messenger will catch you up and you will turn the legion around immediately.'

Cerialis contemplated the suggestion. 'That way I suppose I'm covered: I can't be blamed for not acting precipitously and yet I acknowledge that I'm going against my standing orders but am quite happy to revert to them should the Governor require me to do so.'

Sabinus scoffed at Cerialis' transparent attempt to avoid any blame for his actions or lack of them.

'You'd think the same way, brother,' Vespasian said, 'if it were your career at stake. You know exactly how easy it is to make a miscalculation; that incident in the Pontus Euxinus when you let the Parthian embassy slip through your fingers springs to mind.'

Sabinus did not like to be reminded of his mistake whilst serving as the Governor of Moesia and Thracia. 'It was a fake Parthian embassy, anyway.'

'But you didn't know that at the time, no one did and it caused our family a lot of difficulties. If Cerialis, *my son*-in-law, is seen to have made as grievous an error as you did then the family will suffer again; so don't scoff, it's not helpful.'

But Cerialis was no longer listening to the brothers. 'Pasiteles!' he called and a thin, stooped-shouldered clerk, with ink-stained fingers, emerged from the shadows. 'Pasiteles, send word for the prefect of the camp.'

'At once, sir,' Pasiteles said, scurrying off.

'If we work through the night we could be ready to march at dawn,' Cerialis informed the brothers who had ceased their bickering. 'I'll leave a couple of my auxiliary cohorts here to garrison the camp and to watch our backs as we head south; Cartimandua or Venutius would both love to occupy this place.'

'Agreed,' Vespasian said. 'How many cavalry alae have you got?'

'There's one here and then there are another two ten miles to the west, plus the hundred and twenty legionary cavalry here in the camp of course.'

'Good, can we take half your legionary cavalry to escort us back to Camulodunum to make sure that little runt, Paelignus, is doing his bit?'

'Of course.'

'Thank you; we'll leave in the morning. In the meantime have the auxiliary ala here start to head back down the road as soon as possible to scout and report back; we need to know whether there is anything ahead of us.'

'They wouldn't dare stand up to a full legion.'

'It depends how many of them there are; but it's the possibility of an ambush that concerns me.'

Cerialis looked nonplussed for a moment and Vespasian wondered whether his son-in-law had what it took to make a good legate; his suitability to the job had not been something that he, Vespasian, had taken into account when manoeuvring to ensure that Cerialis got the position. Vespasian's only concern had been that his daughter should have a successful husband; he hoped that it too would not prove to be a miscalculation on his part.

'Yes, you're right, Father,' Cerialis agreed as a weather-beaten veteran resplendent in full uniform, topped with a crimson horsehair crest on his bronze helmet, stomped through the door followed by the clerk, 'I hadn't thought of that.'

'Prefect Quintus Ogulnius Curius,' Pasiteles announced causing Curius to crash out a salute. As the camp prefect he was the third most senior man in the legion after the legate and his second in command, the thick-stripe military tribune; both of these men were from the senatorial class and may well have had little or no military experience. The camp prefect, however, would have started his military career as the lowest of the lowest legionary and earned his promotion through the ranks becoming, eventually, the primus pilus, the most senior centurion, commanding the first century of the first cohort of the legion; after that he could become the legion's prefect of the camp. His knowledge and experience were therefore invaluable to the younger men set above him in rank – should they choose to listen to it; and there were many who were too proud to do so.

'Prefect,' Cerialis said, returning the salute without as much of a flurry, 'I want every tribune and centurion assembled here in half an hour.'

'Yes, sir.'

'And have the quarter-masters get ready to issue seventeen days' rations to every man at dawn.'

Curius did not so much as blink at this order. 'Sir!'

'And have them issue the tents, mules and carts ready for the march tomorrow.'

'Sir!' Another salute. 'Sir, may I ask where we're going?'

'You may, Curius. We're going south; if my father-in-law's information is correct we have a tribe of savages to put down.'

Curius' lined face cracked into a lopsided smile. 'Good, sir!'

'Good?'

'Yes, sir, good. The lads haven't had a decent scrap for a couple of years, not since that Venutius business; they're getting a bit soft. This should toughen them up.'

Vespasian did not like the sound of that; he would have preferred that they were toughened already.

In unison, an hour before dawn, almost five thousand men stamped to attention, guided by the bellowed commands of their centurions taking their cue from the primus pilus. The resulting crash of thousands of hobnailed sandals hitting the ground echoed around Vespasian's head clearing any last vestiges of the deep sleep that he had been roused from far too soon after he had fallen into it. He fought to control his horse, spooked by the noise, as he cast his eyes across the lines of grim faces, breath steaming from them, assembled on the torch-washed parade ground just outside the camp's main gates.

The crash died away leaving only distant barking from the camp's dogs, startled by the sudden disturbance to their peaceful night, and the flutter of thousands of cloaks moving in the breeze.

'Men of the Ninth Hispana!' Cerialis, flanked by the camp prefect and the thick-stripe tribune, declaimed from a dais. 'We march south to Camulodunum; what we will find when we get there I cannot say but be prepared for war.' He took a deep breath and then roared: 'Are you ready for war?'

'Yes!' was the thundered reply that further disturbed the dogs.

'Are you ready for war?'

'Yesss!'

'Are you ready for war?'

'YESSSS!'

Cerialis raised his arms in the air to keep the response going so that the word transformed into a prolonged cheer. Bringing his hands back down again he quietened his men with, what Vespasian considered to be, impressive control.

'We will march as if we are in hostile territory so there will be a stockaded camp built every night; this will slow our progress so to counter that we will march an hour before dawn every day and take fewer rests. We go to the aid of many of our brothers who served in this legion; we will not let them down! They will not stand alone. Legionaries of the Ninth, ARE – YOU – READY – FOR WAR?'

The resulting cheer to the affirmative beat any sound made that morning and sent the dogs into a renewed frenzy and caused Vespasian's and his companions' horses to skitter and snort nervously; behind them their escort of sixty of the legion's cavalry troopers fought to control their mounts as their infantry comrades started to beat their *pila* on their shields, firstly at random, producing a constant rolling rumble that gradually morphed into a steady, pounding, slow beat. Cerialis indulged his men, punching his fist in the air in time to their rhythm; slow, deliberate and menacing.

'That seems to have got the lads worked up,' Magnus commented. 'I wouldn't worry about Curius' assessment of their toughness, sir; I'm sure they'll make up for any deficiency on that front with keenness.'

'I hope you're right.'

'Yeah, well, so do I; we'll find out soon enough, I suppose.'

'Not for at least seven days, which will be the thirteenth day of the Iceni muster.' Vespasian bit his bottom lip, his strained expression exaggerated as he contemplated the timing. 'Paulinus won't receive the message until tomorrow so he cannot be expected to march until the following dawn; he has at least an eight or nine day journey. And as for the Twentieth and the Second Augusta, the gods alone know when we can expect them back in the south.'

'Then let's hope the Iceni take their time with their muster.'

Vespasian thought that to be a false hope. 'Would you?'

Magnus had to admit not. 'No, I'd fall on the towns as quickly as possible.'

'That's what I would do too; I've a nasty feeling that the next time we see this legion they could well be the only legion in sight and we'll have thousands of savages between them and us in Camulodunum.'

'He's done nothing, the little runt!' Vespasian exclaimed, outraged, as he surveyed the defences upon approaching Camulodunum at the seventh hour, three days later after a long, fast and hard ride south. 'Not one brick has been laid and he must have got our message at least three days ago.'

Sabinus cast a professional eye over the junction of the new brickwork and the old, unmaintained, wooden palisade that surrounded some of the rest of the town. 'That wouldn't hold a gaggle of squealing bum-boys for longer than it would take for them to do their make-up.'

'Four or five hours, then?' said Magnus, looking, without much hope, for any sign of workmen around the defences; there were none.

'You know what I mean, Magnus; we'd be lucky to keep a concerted attack out for more than half an hour. Let's go and find the little shit and kick him into action.'

'That's pointless, Sabinus,' Caenis said, letting her horse have a few tugs at the lush grass before it. 'Best we do it ourselves otherwise it will remain an open town.'

Vespasian urged his horse forward towards the north gate. 'You're right, my love; the sensible thing would be to ignore Paelignus and take command of the place. At least we'll take the threat seriously even if he won't.' He turned in his saddle to the decurion commanding their cavalry escort. 'Mutilus, leave me sixteen troopers to use as scouts and messengers, and get back to Cerialis. Tell him that there was no sign of the enemy and also there's no sign of any help, either.'

With a perfunctory salute the officer detailed two tent parties to remain and by the time Vespasian was clattering through the north gate the troopers were heading back towards their legion somewhere along the road north.

Vespasian made straight for the forum, which was operating as if there was nothing amiss; traders shouted their wares and townsfolk made purchases, exchanged gossip and behaved as if there was no possibility that the Iceni nation might appear, intent on their demise, at any moment.

'Get us some attention, Magnus,' Vespasian requested, jumping down from his horse and then mounting the steps of the Temple of Divine Claudius; Sabinus followed him up.

As they reached the top, canine anger and avian terror erupted from a stall at the foot of the steps as Castor and Pollux took advantage of Magnus opening the gate to a pen filled with geese. Guttural growls and high-pitched honks cut over the human noise from the forum. Feathers and blood flew as did the few lucky geese that escaped the pen; the rest succumbed to the jaws of the hounds. Outraged, the stallholder screamed abuse at Magnus before attacking him with a club he produced from under the table. Magnus laid him out with a straight right fist to the jaw and then called Castor and Pollux off their lunch. By now half the forum was staring in their direction.

'People of Camulodunum!' Vespasian shouted, his voice carrying over the whole crowd. 'The prefect of this town, your prefect, has put you in grave danger; in a couple of days you may well all be dead.' This got their full attention and Vespasian found himself being stared at by hundreds of pairs of eyes. 'Less than a market interval ago the Queen of the Iceni, Boudicca, threatened to rip the heart out of every Roman in the province.' He raised his hand to show his senatorial ring. 'I, Titus Flavius Vespasianus, of proconsular rank, and my brother, Titus Flavius Sabinus, also of proconsular rank, know this to be true because we were there when she made that threat. Some of you who served with the Second Augusta in the early years of the conquest will recognise me, as will those of you who served with the Fourteenth Gemina recognise my brother. We were your legates. We have your best interests at heart and we urge you to join with us and strengthen the defences of this town.'

'What for?' a voice from the crowd shouted. 'We could just leave and seek shelter in Londinium.'

'What's your name, soldier?' Sabinus asked.

'Former centurion Verrucosus, sir.'

'Well, Verrucosus, at least here you have some walls; Londinium has none at all. If the Iceni are not stopped by the time they come there they will sweep through the town like floodwater.'

There were discussions in the crowd that by their tone seemed to suggest that Vespasian's point had been taken.

'Nor will you stand a chance hiding from them in open country,' Vespasian continued, noticing that some of the native members of his audience had started to slip away. 'They will scour the whole land. Our only chance is to barricade ourselves in here. As I speak, the Ninth Hispana is coming south and should arrive in three or four days. Messages have gone to Governor Paulinus in the northwest with the Fourteenth. They could be here in six days as could the Twentieth and Second. If Paulinus can consolidate his forces in this area then he will crush this rebellion but he needs time; and you, former legionaries of Rome, you can give him that time. You can give your Governor what he needs to ensure victory if you can keep the Iceni out of this town and camped beyond the repaired walls whilst their destruction, in the form of four legions, makes their way *to this place*.' He emphasised the last three words, punching his fist into the palm of his hand as he did.

Silence greeted the end of the speech as all stared at him, open-mouthed.

'What's the meaning of this?' An all-too-familiar voice screeched. 'How dare you sow panic amongst these people?' Paelignus pushed his way to the front of the crowd and mounted the steps. 'The Iceni would never dare attack us; they haven't got any weapons since they were disarmed.'

'Disarmed did you say, procurator?' Sabinus sneered. 'Any man who hunts with a spear or a bow can kill a Roman. Did you not get our warning?'

'I had some rambling message from an imperial courier whom I assumed had been drinking so I had him thrown in a cell to sober up.'

Vespasian stared at Paelignus, unable to believe the man's stupidity. It seemed pointless saying anything, so, with a casualness that belied the sense of urgency he felt at commencing the work, he kicked the procurator between the legs and then kneed him in the face as his hunched form doubled over, laying him out on his back, unconscious. Turning back to the crowd, he asked: 'So what is it to be? Are you with me and my brother; will you help us strengthen the defences? Or are you as dismissive of the threat as this ... this ...' He pointed down at Paelignus. 'As this worthless piece of shit who is blinded by his own unwarranted arrogance?'

There was no immediate reaction either for or against but, rather, a mass outbreak of urgent chatter; groups formed and arguments broke out and it soon became obvious to Vespasian and Sabinus that a decision was not going to be reached by talking even though Verrucosus seemed to be arguing for them. In silent, mutual agreement they both descended the steps and, with Magnus, Caenis and their escort following, pushed their way through the crowd, heading back towards the north gate to the works on the wall so that they could lead by example.

Gradually the townsfolk, mainly veterans and colonists but also some Britons, joined them and by mid-afternoon there were over two thousand men and boys labouring to restore the original palisade in the many places that it was down as well as securing its segue with the new, and very incomplete, brick wall. Parties went out to cut down trees; others stripped them of branches; some dug holes and others raised the logs into position whilst their womenfolk gathered what food and drink could be found in the surrounding area and brought it back within the walls.

'So, Verrucosus,' Vespasian said as he and the former centurion packed the earth around the base of a newly raised section of the palisade, 'can we leave you in charge of this work while my brother and I put our minds to other matters?'

Verrucosus, stocky and bow-legged in his late fifties, grinned, exposing broken teeth. 'I'll keep them at it, sir; along with my brother former officers in the town. The lads respect us so don't you worry; we've already organised them into centuries.'

'What about if it comes to defending the walls?'

'We've all still got our swords and some still have shields and a few even have helmets. Some of us have slings and bows but it's javelins we need and they're scarce.'

'In which case detail some of the older men and younger boys to start making as many as possible; we need thousands. They don't have to be perfect, just as long as they have a sharp end and can be thrown.'

'Yes, sir!'

'And have piles of stones and bricks placed every few paces.'

Verrucosus saluted, smartly for a man of his age, his enjoyment of a military situation, after so long a civilian, evident on his face.

Leaving Magnus with the workforce, Vespasian, Sabinus and Caenis went back to the Governor's residence and there began to write a series of letters.

'This is your last chance, my love,' Vespasian said to Caenis as he handed two scroll-cases and a weighty purse to a fisherman, waiting in his boat, ready to set sail the following morning from Camulodunum's river port; his teenage son busied himself with the sail. 'You could be in Londinium by tomorrow morning then pick up Hormus and your two girls and either take a ship or be safe down on the south coast with Cogidubnus in three days or so.'

Caenis removed the scented handkerchief from her face that shielded her from the worst of the stench of raw sewage rising from the river. 'I wish you would stop going on, Vespasian; I stay by your side, for better or worse, and let that be an end to it.'

Vespasian shrugged, knowing he was never going to win the argument, and turned his attention back to the fisherman. 'Give both of these to my freedman, Hormus, at the house on the river that I described to you and then if you bring the answer back there'll be another purse this size.'

The man felt the weight and nodded, satisfied. 'Right you are, sir,' he said and he and his son began to cast off.

Behind them, further down the river, could be seen another boat, destined for Rutupiae, the main port in Britannia; it sailed slowly away, its sail billowing in the uneven breeze. It was in this boat that Vespasian had placed some hope. It contained three letters: one for the prefect of the port begging him to ignore the sailing conditions and order two ships to cross to the mainland, each with one of the other letters. One was for the Governor of Gallia Belgica and the other for the Governor of Germania Inferior, pleading with them to send what troops they could, as soon as they could. If they were to arrive within four days then it might just be possible to hold out in Camulodunum – if the walls had been repaired in time. He did not expect much joy from the letter he had sent for Hormus to pass onto Decianus asking him for troops; that had been sent more to protect himself from accusations of not warning the procurator and asking for aid, something he was sure the oily Decianus would do if they both survived the rebellion, whatever the result. Decianus would be sure to try to make certain that nothing was his fault. The other letters, sent via cavalry couriers, had been to Cerialis and Paulinus urging, quite unnecessarily, even more haste. The remaining cavalry troopers had been sent out on reconnaissance the previous day.

And it was one of these men who, as Vespasian and Caenis turned to go back to the Governor's residence, came striding towards them with Sabinus.

'Tell my brother what you saw,' Sabinus ordered the man as they drew close.

One glance at the fear in the scout's eyes was enough to tell Vespasian that whatever he had seen had not been good.

'Fifty miles or so to the northeast, sir. More than I've ever seen before.'

'More what, man?' Vespasian snapped.

'People, sir, people. The whole tribe is on the move, not just the warriors. Tens of thousands of them spread out on a frontage so wide that I could not see the ends.'

Vespasian looked at Sabinus in alarm. 'Mars' arse! If they're coming in those numbers it doesn't matter whether the walls are repaired or not, they'll just push them over and walk right in.'

'Perhaps we should think about leaving?'

'And go where? Londinium, with no walls whatsoever?'

'No, Vespasian,' Caenis said, 'he means what you've been suggesting that I do. Get somewhere safe.'

'If we're seen to run away from Camulodunum after what we said in the forum yesterday, no one will stand; they'll sweep through here and onto Londinium and the province will almost certainly be lost. Here is where we must stand; if we can get the walls repaired and the legions arrive then here is where we have a chance of defeating them.'

'If the legions arrive,' Sabinus said, 'and if they arrive in time.'

They began to come in later in the day, refugees, many of them; first in small groups, then in their scores and soon, by the following day, in their hundreds. Driven from their farms and settlements by the mass advance of the Iceni nation, the veterans and colonists, with their families, arrived with little more than their clothes and a few small possessions. In they came, ragged and exhausted; all had tales of horror to tell of impaling, burning, disembowelment and crucifixion and all who heard the stories repeated them, exaggerating the facts, until the town was swathed in dread. Of the new arrivals, those who could set to work helping on the defences, which, although they were progressing, were still not yet complete such had been the dilapidation that Paelignus had allowed them to fall into.

And still they came in, the refugees, in such numbers that by the time the first columns of smoke could be seen on the horizon, Caenis had worked out that there were over twenty thousand people crammed into the town – and each one was terrified. Of that number, only four thousand had served in the legions and could still bear arms. But that number, if combined with the VIIII Hispana and Paulinus' troops, would, Vespasian hoped, be enough, provided they could link up.

By the following day, two days after Vespasian had sent the letters, the columns of smoke were closer and had begun to meld with one another until, in places, they became sheets, a mile or so wide. Then, as the day wore on and the sun westered, the sheets began to join together; and then, as the first warriors appeared out of the oak woods, four miles away, and trampled across the farmland towards the town, they were backed by a continuous wall of smoke to the northeast of them as if the whole country was burning. Which, indeed, it was, for Boudicca had ordered that all trace of the hated invaders be expunged from the land and her people had taken that order very seriously.

Vespasian stood, amongst Sabinus, Caenis and Magnus with his hounds, along with many of the veterans, under the command of Verrucosus and his brother former centurions, on the top of the north gate watching the endless surge of Iceni appear, their arms and chests smeared with blue-green swirling patterns, their hair spiked and their moustaches flowing, filling up the cultivated land around Camulodunum. As their hope plummeted with every new war band coming into sight, something caught their eye coming south down the Lindum road: an orange glint, a reflection of the falling sun. Vespasian squinted and felt the bile rise in his gorge as he made out a body of cavalry; it was not a full ala, the amount that a sensible general would use as a vanguard for the legion in hostile territory but, rather, a solitary turma, a scouting party implying that Cerialis' legion was still on the road; the VIIII Hispana was close but would not arrive in time and nor would Paulinus. Vespasian now knew that they were on their own and massively outnumbered and could only hope to survive with a desperate defence of incomplete walls and palisade.

As this unwelcome news sank in with the veterans, manning the defences in their centuries, there was a swirling within the Britannic ranks now less than a quarter of a mile from the gate. The warriors parted; through the gap came a two-horse chariot and mounted on it, behind the kneeling driver, was a woman, huge in build with her copper hair massed upon her head. In her right hand she held a spear that she raised to the sky, its tip reflecting the setting sun, as she shouted the war cry of her people.

And her people answered.

Tens of thousands of voices roared the response but it was not the ferocious cacophony of hatred that sent a chill through Vespasian's heart; it was something completely different. Walking next to Boudicca's chariot was a figure in a long, dirty white robe; a matted, grey beard tumbled down his chest and Vespasian did not have to see his eyes to know that they could pierce, such was their intensity and power.

Boudicca had come south, intent on ripping out the heart and taking the head of every Roman in the province, and with her she had brought the one man whose hatred of Rome surpassed hers.

She had brought the chief of the druids in Britannia.

She had brought Myrddin.

CHAPTER XIII

'NOW THAT'S MADE it all worthwhile,' Sabinus said, staring at the man he held responsible for the death of his wife, Clementina, and his own incarceration suspended in a cage for months on end. 'The idea that Myrddin might be immortal by replacing him through the generations is down to their beliefs and perhaps the idea is true but that particular human version of him isn't immortal. I hope he's found his replacement because he's going to need him.'

'Who is Myrddin?' Caenis asked.

Vespasian felt the chill spread through him as the druid came closer; behind him were half a dozen other filthy members of his order. 'He's the latest in a succession of Myrddins. The druids believe that when they die, what they call their soul – their life-force, I suppose – is transferred into another body and therefore they have no fear of death. A Myrddin has always been the leader of the druids and they spend a lot of time looking for previous Myrddins who have been reincarnated to become their successor.'

'I see, so that's what Sabinus meant by the idea of Myrddin being immortal.'

'It's all bollocks obviously,' opined Magnus as Castor and Pollux seemed to sniff the air in the druid's direction and rumbled deep growls. 'He's as human as anyone.'

Sabinus gripped the hilt of his sword. 'And I intend to prove that by opening up his belly.'

'Take his eyes whilst you're about it, he owes me one plus interest.'

'You'll never get near to him,' Vespasian said. 'Do you remember that cold fear that they radiate? It clings to your limbs and makes it hard to move. What did Verica call it? *A cold power that cannot be used for good*; or something like that. Anyway, I've been close enough to it to know that I don't want to get near to one of them again, even if it was for revenge.'

'You might not have the choice,' Magnus said, his voice full of gloom as Boudicca's chariot stopped just out of bow-shot; in the distance, on the Lindum road, the turma had turned and was now making its way back north to report their sighting.

'Romans!' Boudicca shouted in a voice that would have done the most martial leaders of old proud; she raised her spear over her head. 'I have come to take back Camulodunum and I will have it.' She paused whilst dozens of men with sacks came forward. 'For too long we have been slaves in our own land. Today that stops. You have a choice, Romans: die or submit to us as our slaves for we shall not let you go free.' She brought her spear down and the men with the sacks spilled their contents upon the ground.

There was a groan from the townsfolk lining the walls.

'These are but a few of the hearts and the heads that we have taken,' Boudicca carried on as the grisly objects continued to be poured from the sacks. 'It is one to me whether I take your hearts and your heads from your bodies or whether you keep them and dedicate them to serving us as our slaves. But know this, Romans, one way or another I will possess them as I will possess this town. If you think that the Ninth Hispana will come to your aid you can forget them, they are too little too late. I shall crush them as they arrive and Rome will despair as one of her precious legions is wiped out for the first time since the great Arminius over fifty years ago in Germania.'

'She knows her history,' Magnus muttered.

'So what's it to be, Romans? Slavery or death? Either way, your world will end.'

The veterans lining the walls had no doubt which was the preferable choice and they roared their defiance at the Iceni Queen.

'I think that's a fairly obvious reply,' Vespasian said, looking left and right, his face grim as he registered just how incomplete the defences were; he offered up a prayer to Mars, god of war, that the centuries of veterans filling the gaps would hold off the Britons. 'But given the situation I think that we should be ready to leave if she breaks in. I don't think that she would spare us a second time.' He looked back down at the Queen; her words were lost in the din but her gesture, pointing her spear at the town, was obvious: she had ordered her warriors to assault the walls.

But her warriors were not just outside the town; as Boudicca ordered the attack, three or four sections of the palisade to both the east and west were pushed over and scores of men streamed through the gaps. The Trinovantes remaining in the town had now sided with the rebels and had left Camulodunum with even more gaps in its defences to the extent that it could still be said to be an open town.

'Verrucosus!' Vespasian called. 'Send runners to the reserve centuries in the forum and have them fill the new gaps. You know what happens if they get in.'

Verrucosus saluted and barked a series of orders that sent men sprinting back as the *carnyxes*, the tall, upright Celtic horns forged in the shapes of animals' heads, blared out the discordant drone that accompanied Britannic armies into battle.

Yet Verrucosus and his brother former centurions held their men steady as the Iceni tide rolled inexorably towards them, flowing out so that it lapped around the town, making Camulodunum a peninsula in a dark sea of hatred with just the river preventing its total isolation. On they came, their chieftains and champions mounted in two-horse chariots with their war bands around them, their shouted entreaties to their followers and their gods melding with the calls of the carnyxes, the war cries of the warriors and the cheering of another as yet unnoticed group: the women, the young and the old, for Boudicca had brought all her people to see her humiliation avenged and, as the attack advanced, they were left with the wagons cheering on their menfolk like spectators in a vast arena as the games begin.

'Has anyone seen Paelignus?' Sabinus asked, his eyes fixed on the oncoming mass, 'I'd love to see his expression watching this.'

'I haven't seen him since yesterday morning,' Vespasian replied, picking up a couple of javelins from a pile of the improvised weapons. 'I imagine that he sneaked out, somehow, during the night.'

All along the defences the veterans prepared their javelins, bawled at by the former centurions to whom they still showed loyalty as the right arms of the closest Iceni warriors were raised above their heads and they began to flick their wrists. And then the air fizzed with flying stone and lead as thousands of slingshots were released, augmenting the tone of the cacophony with screams of the wounded as bones were cracked, faces pulped and skulls split open, sending defenders tumbling back off the walls to lie broken at their base. But those who survived remained standing, braving the hail, as they waited for their chance to begin the killing.

'Release!' Vespasian roared as the Iceni sea washed to within fifty paces of the walls.

Centurions around the defences repeated the order, bellowing in their battlefield voices dredged up from the past; thousands of sleek missiles hurtled up through the air to reach their apex before plummeting down upon an unmissable target of soft flesh. The screams of the pierced and skewered rose up to the sky as swathes of warriors were felled by this lethal rain.

'Release!' was shouted again and again and the defenders hurled and hurled for they knew that their only chance of stopping this was now, because once the walls were reached it would be but a matter of time before they were breached.

And so javelins, some no more than sharpened, fire-hardened hafts, slammed into torsos, limbs and heads, reaping a ghastly toll in lives but doing very little to make any impression on the total number of warriors now surging towards the town, so great was it.

Missile after missile Vespasian, Sabinus and Magnus threw, all grunting volubly with the exertion as Caenis, along with many others of the women, ran up and down the steps to the carts laden with javelins awaiting at their foot to resupply the men braving the slingshot that still fizzed around; but soon the carts were empty and there was nothing else to throw at the encircling host other than the stones and loose bricks. By now, though, the

Britannic rebels had reached the defences; the defenders desperately hurled anything they could get their hands on upon the crush beneath them but the sheer weight of numbers tumbled down the embedded posts, surging over them like floodwater washing over a dam. Carried away were the grey-haired veterans who attempted to block the gaps, and in a few heartbeats all within Camulodunum knew that what had been a desperate situation was now hopeless and to stand was to die.

So they ran.

'The river is our only hope,' Vespasian said as they clattered down the steps from the gatehouse roof. 'Even if Cerialis and Paulinus arrive now they won't prevent everyone remaining in the town from being massacred.'

Sabinus ducked involuntarily as something unseen whizzed past them. 'We'll never get through now; the place will be crawling with the savages soon.'

'Then we find a place to hide and wait until dark.'

'What about the vaults in the Temple of Claudius?' Caenis suggested, hitching up her stola so that she would not trip.

Vespasian plunged into an alley heading in the direction of the river port. 'No; I imagine all the survivors will head there as it's the last place that could hold out for a while. We need something else.'

'The sewers!' Magnus shouted as they pounded down the alley, Castor and Pollux bounding behind them. 'There must be sewers and the Governor's residence is bound to be on the system at least.'

'You're right, there's an outlet in the river port; it stank when we were there the other day.'

They ran, now, with the speed of desperation, jigging left and right through the alleys, keeping away from the main thoroughfares as the Iceni poured in through the battered defences, intent on the death of every inhabitant in vengeance for their Queen and the affront to their honour. And the warriors set about their task with glee, breaking the last little pockets of resistance in a frenzy of slashing and stabbing that the innate discipline of the veterans could do nothing to counter.

From all around now came the death-screams of the men and shrieks of cornered women as their children were torn from them and despatched, their hearts ripped out before their mothers' eyes and their heads cloven from their shoulders; then, before the similar death was meted out to those same mothers, they suffered the combined fate of Boudicca and her daughters. They were scourged and raped repeatedly until they were things of blood; that death became a welcome friend, a light in this dark world, and they gave up their hearts and heads willingly for they had need of them no more.

It was the time that it took to commit such outrages that saved many of the people of Camulodunum, at least for a few hours; the business of rape and slaughter, systematically and comprehensively conducted, was slow work and as Vespasian and his companions finally made it into the forum there was not, as yet, any sign of the attackers; just hundreds of terrified townsfolk trying to barricade themselves into the complex of the Temple of Divine Claudius as the sun began to set on the town now abandoned by its founding god.

They raced past, on into the Governor's residence; the guards had gone but a natural respect for the building had seemed to keep the common people out as if even in this time of crisis they still knew their place.

Racing up the steps, Vespasian crashed through the doors and, once they were all in, slammed the bolts into place and was just about to wedge the bar across it when he realised the foolishness of his actions and slid the bolts back again.

'What are you doing?' Sabinus asked.

'If we barricade the door then they will know for sure that there is someone in here; leave it open and, well, maybe, maybe not.'

'Good idea, my love,' Caenis said, 'but what if someone else comes in and then locks the doors?'

'Then we'll just have to pray that it's them that get found and not us.' Vespasian began to walk with purpose through the atrium. 'The latrines are in the courtyard garden at the back; let's hope that the sewer is big enough for people.'

'And dogs,' Magnus added looking down at Castor and Pollux who had no idea what was in store for them.

The din of the sacked town, as they hurried across the courtyard in the half-light of dusk, was all pervading now and the screams and shrieks and sense of pure misery were such that Vespasian had come to the point where he no longer paid heed to it; Roman citizens were suffering and dying and that was that, there was nothing to be done about it – yet.

The latrine block was in the far left-hand corner of the garden, nearest the river, which gave them hope because although they had all made use of the facility many times, none of them had contemplated how, and in what direction, the waste was flushed away. But flushed away it was because unlike so many other latrines this one did not have too fetid a reek to it. Indeed, as they walked in, the sound of running water could plainly be heard coming from below the two long benches, set at right angles to each other along the two exterior walls. In each bench were six round holes so that a dozen people at any one time could make contented use of, what was, a surprisingly airy room; now, however, as Vespasian and Magnus went to lift one of the benches, it was only four people and two dogs that needed to utilise it and not in the way that it was designed for.

The yelp that greeted the removal of the bench almost made Vespasian lose his grip on it. 'Paelignus!' he exclaimed looking down into the trench to see the prefect squatting, ankle-deep in running water.

'You!' Paelignus sounded indignant. 'What are you doing here? This is my hiding place.'

'We thought that you would be long gone,' Magnus said, putting the bench down.

Vespasian reached in and dragged Paelignus upright by his ear. 'How come you're still here? I'm sure it's not to witness the results of your cunning strategy of doing nothing.'

Paelignus winced as Vespasian twisted his ear further, his eyes automatically searching for something on the ground next to him.

Vespasian broke into a grin as he followed Paelignus' look to a strongbox in the shadows. 'So that's it, is it? Couldn't take the gold with you so you thought you'd hide and wait for them to move on; well, you'll be waiting here a long time and you'll be waiting without your gold because we'll be taking it.'

Paelignus hissed as his hand jerked up; a knife flashed in it.

Caenis screamed as the blade tore towards Vespasian's shoulder; Sabinus and Magnus both dived at Paelignus but they were too late: Castor and Pollux leapt upon the prefect as his stabbing arm thrust up and the instant after the blade pierced Vespasian's flesh they took Paelignus down into the trench in a thrash of human and canine limbs to splash into the water that, a couple of growling rips and a curtailed scream later, ran red with blood.

Vespasian clasped the dagger's handle, inhaling sharply with pain; he looked at the blade and to his relief it was not deeply embedded, the dogs' quick reaction had prevented Paelignus from thrusting it all the way home.

'Are you all right, my love?' Caenis asked, gently touching the area next to the wound.

With a sudden jolt, Vespasian wrenched the blade free, dropped it and clutched the wound with his hand. 'I'll be fine.' He looked down into the trench as the hounds continued to savage Paelignus' body; his throat completely torn away. 'Which is more than can be said for that murderous, treacherous little runt.'

'That solved one problem,' Magnus mused, climbing into the latrine.

'What's that?' Sabinus asked. 'Our travelling expenses?'

'That as well, I suppose; but I was worried about how to persuade the dogs down into a latrine.' He lowered himself in and hauled the beasts off the body by their collars. 'Problem solved.'

A crash and harsh voices from the main house across the courtyard made them all turn in that direction.

'They're here,' Sabinus said. 'Quick.'

Vespasian, still clutching his shoulder, followed Magnus down into the reeking, brick-lined trench; Caenis picked up Paelignus' discarded knife, so that it did not act as a signpost, and tucked it into her belt before swinging her legs over the rim and lowering herself in. Sabinus lifted the bench so that it rested against the side of the latrine and then climbed down. Using Paelignus' body as a step, he reached his arms over the rim and grabbed the bench, pulling it up and sliding it over so that, after a few adjustments, it slotted back into place just as Britannic voices came from the garden along with the sound of doors being kicked open as the warriors searched for more victims.

In the dim light of the latrine Vespasian could see that the sewer ran off at the ninety degree junction of the two trenches; it was just tall enough to be able to crawl along. Magnus eased his way past him. 'I'll go first with the lads; it'll be easier to get them through if they follow me and you three block the way back.' With that he knelt down and disappeared into the pipe; after a bit of persuasion the dogs followed him in. Caenis went next; her stomach heaved but she managed not to vomit. Vespasian followed her with Sabinus taking up the rear, dragging Paelignus' strongbox behind him.

They had not gone ten paces when the shouts of the searchers became louder and clearer; they had entered the room above, the flicker of their torches illuminating the dozen circles. Laughter and ribaldry followed their discovery of what the place was used for and before long all twelve points of dim light were closed as the men of the Iceni decided to try out this novel Roman invention. Loud and prolonged were the sounds of their easing themselves, producing much mirth, as they sent turd after turd down onto the corpse of the man who had cost Vespasian two years of his life.

Vespasian did not give Paelignus another thought.

On they crawled through the blackness, their knees and hands squishing lodged waste, releasing stenches that Vespasian had not experienced since crawling up the sewage outlet to gain entrance to the Getic fortress of Sagadava in Moesia, all those years ago; he had been a military tribune and ordered by the Lady Antonia to retrieve the Thracian chief priest Rhoteces to be a witness to Sejanus' treachery. This time, however, the system was not three hundred years old and crusted with the excrement of thousands of Getic arses and, although there was no way that the experience could be called pleasant, it was far less overpowering. But what the sewage pipe may have lacked in aroma it made up for in length. On it went, past various junctions with smaller conduits flushing faeces away from the houses of the rich who could afford to be connected to the system.

The blood ran down Vespasian's chest from his wound as he could not clamp it with a hand; both were needed for crawling. He gritted his teeth against the pain and tried to consider himself lucky compared to the Roman citizens suffering above him. Still they crawled and slid on, keeping silent, not out of any need for stealth but, rather, because the conditions precluded conversation; even Castor and Pollux evidently felt the same and not a growl passed their flaccid lips as they too grimly pressed on.

Then the air started to freshen and their speed seemed to increase as the end of their ordeal neared and after a few more paces Magnus halted. 'I can see the exit. Stay here and I'll go take a look.' He crawled forward, his dogs following him.

Vespasian waited in the dark as, in front of him, Caenis lost her battle with her stomach and heaved copiously.

'Great!' Sabinus muttered behind him.

'It's clear,' Magnus called back to them.

'Sorry, my love,' Caenis said as she moved forward through her vomit.

Vespasian tried to think of a comforting rejoinder but nothing came to mind as the sour stink of what had been the contents of Caenis' stomach combined with the faecal reek of the sewer to make him gag. Caenis moved quickly and Vespasian kept pace; behind, Sabinus could be heard cursing as he too spewed as a result of the combined stenches.

A splash ahead of him alerted Vespasian to the reality of where the pipe came out and he braced himself for a cold dip that, when it came, was a relief; even though the water in this part of the river was polluted it seemed as pure as a spring after what they had just crawled through. He slipped beneath the surface and enjoyed for a few moments the absence of scent. When Vespasian surfaced, Magnus was helping Sabinus, who was now also in the river, with the strongbox; Castor and Pollux swam around near them as Caenis was treading water a few paces away from the outlet.

'It's no good,' Magnus hissed as they tried to lift the box out from the end of the pipe that was set into the concrete of the quay, 'the river's too deep to be able to carry it and we'll never manage to swim with it.'

'We'll leave it here then,' Sabinus said. 'We might get a chance to come back for it.'

'As if any of us will be wanting ever to come back here.'

Looking around, as Sabinus pushed the strongbox as far as he could back up the sewer, Vespasian could see no sign of a boat moored anywhere in the river port. He reached up and, kicking with his legs, managed to get his good hand on the lip of the quay; he pulled himself up and, with caution, peered over to see if there was one out of the water on the quay.

Glancing all around, he saw no boats on either side of the river. The clamour of terror still filled the night air and flames now flared all about; groups of warriors were silhouetted everywhere, chasing down victims, despatching them or participating in gang rape. As Vespasian watched he noticed that the flames were not always stationary and with a shock he realised that the Iceni had now taken to setting fire to their captives and then laughing at their antics as they tried to extinguish themselves. No mercy was being shown as was witnessed by the figure of a child of no more than five or six rolling along the ground, screeching as flames sprang out from his body, feeding upon the pitch in which he had been daubed. On the child rolled, straight towards Vespasian as its four tormentors, the swirling patterns on their torsos sheened with sweat, followed it, kicking it along if it slowed.

'Down!' Vespasian hissed, letting go of the lip. As he fell back towards the river's surface the screeching human torch received a mighty kick and flew over his head. Vespasian pulled himself close to the quay, along with Magnus and Sabinus, and turned to see Caenis staring in horror at the burning child heading towards her, her face illumined by the flames for an instant before she realised the danger and ducked beneath the surface.

But that instant was all that was needed for the danger to see her.

With whoops of triumph, the four tribesmen launched themselves into the river to land where Caenis had disappeared and the child's carcass sizzled, sinking slowly. Vespasian hurled himself forward, out from under the lee of the quay, to land on the shoulders of the nearest Briton, pulling him back with one hand on his throat as water sprayed into his mouth and nostrils. Magnus and Sabinus splashed to either side of him, lunging at two more of the attackers; water roiled with thrashing bodies as Castor and Pollux growled and barked, circling, unable to make out friend from foe.

With prodigious effort, half-choking and his wound burning, Vespasian forced his writhing victim under as, just two paces in front of him, Caenis burst through the surface, her eyes wide and her mouth agape, gasping for breath.

'Caenis!' Vespasian yelled, grappling and straining to keep the warrior submerged.

As Caenis sucked in the second breath she was yanked back beneath the river, her hand stretched towards Vespasian; reaching out for it, on impulse, he felt the warrior gain momentum in the struggle. He forced himself to abandon his lover to the depths as he continued his fight; Caenis' opponent surfaced, pushing down, gasping once, before plunging under.

Cursing, Vespasian renewed his efforts in the churning water.

Magnus and Sabinus wrestled their adversaries, each struggling to get secure holds on slick skin as the Britons squirmed in their grip, attempting to turn and face the threat tackling them from behind. Vespasian forced his man down, squeezing his hold around the Briton's throat, as the legs kicked without aim and the arms struggled to free him from the deathly embrace. He felt the struggling begin to ease and then slacken; letting go of his victim he surged forward to where he had last seen Caenis. Beneath his feet he felt the current swirl with the exertions of underwater combat; he dived down and hauled on the first thing he could find: hair. Lungs bursting, he kicked for the surface, pulling the struggling pair behind him, their battle not letting up. Breaking out into air he gasped a ragged breath as the body he heaved jerked with the spasm of death. Pulling it up in terror he came face to face with the dead eyes of a warrior in his teens; Caenis broke the surface, a wild look on her face as she filled her lungs again and again until she calmed enough to look in triumph at her lover and raise her right hand. 'I almost forgot I had it.'

Vespasian gasped in relief and let the dead warrior go as he saw the knife. 'Paelignus finally did something good.'

Caenis nodded, her chest still heaving. 'Without it I would have been lost.' She looked at the young warrior as he floated away; she started to shake.

Vespasian said nothing and pulled her to him as she contemplated taking life for the first time and coming so close within the reach of death herself.

'I don't suppose we get hugs for killing our bastards,' Magnus hissed as he released his drowned victim to be taken off by the soft current.

'You probably enjoyed it.'

Sabinus peered back over the lip, pushing himself up on the corpse of his opponent. 'They were all too busy having fun to notice,' he observed flopping back down into the water.

Vespasian let go of Caenis. 'Quick, let's go. We might be lucky finding a boat further downriver.' He kicked out with his feet and hauled himself along the wall, praying all the time that one of the human torches would not jump into the water bringing more of the macabre spectators with it. Only the dogs seemed to enjoy the river, swimming on ahead and then back as their four human companions edged their way slowly along in the lee of the quay.

The concrete ended after fifty paces or so giving way to natural riverbank and an un-dredged riverbed that they could, with the exception of Caenis, just reach on tiptoe. With Caenis clinging onto Sabinus they speeded up and soon the sound of misery was fading and the light from the human torches was just a glow in the distance. After a mile they were in near complete silence and darkness as the moon was covered by a thick and heavy layer of cloud.

'That's enough river,' Vespasian said, scrambling up the bank.

'At least we don't stink like a tannery any more,' Caenis pointed out as Sabinus heaved her out. 'I'm sorry that you had to crawl through my sick.'

'Just don't ever talk about it, my love, and I'm sure the memory will fade with time.'

Caenis laughed and tore off a strip from the bottom of her stola and gave it to Vespasian. 'Use that as a pad for your wound; how is it?'

'It stings but it isn't bleeding so much; I think the water was good for it.'

Magnus joined them on the bank pointing downstream. 'There's a light on the river.'

Vespasian squinted into the dark and, sure enough, there was a thin prick of light, some way off, but definitely either on or just next to the river. 'Let's go and see what it is; hopefully it's someone with a boat. Whoever it is I doubt they're part of the rebellion, otherwise they would be in the town; but you never know.' He drew his sword and moved off towards the light.

Closer to, Vespasian could see that the light was a fire that had burnt low; in its faint glow a couple of bodies could be seen wrapped in blankets, evidently asleep. A boat was tied to a tree just nearby.

'We're in luck,' Sabinus said, creeping forward with Magnus; as they neared the men one stirred in his sleep. Sabinus and Magnus froze and then once the breathing became more regular crept forward again. Standing over the nearer one, Sabinus put his blade to the man's throat. 'Wakey, wakey.'

The eyes slowly opened and then the body jerked with shock as the man registered what he saw. Magnus restrained the second man as he awoke.

'We need your boat.'

Vespasian stepped forward into the light. 'Let him go, Sabinus; I know him.' He looked down at the man. 'Did you find Hormus, my freedman?'

'I did, sir. I was on my way back to Camulodunum with a reply but then saw the smoke and flames as I approached so thought it best to wait until morning to see what was occurring.'

'Take my word, you don't want to go back there at the moment. What did Hormus say?'

The fisherman sat up now that Sabinus had withdrawn the blade from his throat. 'I don't know.' He rummaged about in a sack next to him and brought out a scroll; he handed it to Vespasian.

Squatting down next to the fire he broke the seal and unrolled it and began to read.

'Well?' Sabinus asked, impatiently.

'Well, things aren't looking good.'

'What do you mean?'

Vespasian looked at the fisherman. 'When did Hormus write this?'

'Midday yesterday. He told me to come straight back with it; we was lucky with the tides there and back again.'

Vespasian looked at his brother. 'That's not good at all. Hormus says he's heard that a messenger from Paulinus has told the garrison commander and the procurator that he won't arrive in Londinium for two days.'

'So that's tomorrow, the day we had hoped that he'd be arriving here; what kept him?'

'I don't know but he's not going to get here for at least three days.'

'Cerialis!'

'I know; he's got to withdraw tonight. You take Caenis and get back to Londinium in that boat. Tell Paulinus when he arrives tomorrow what's happened here but don't get into recriminations about Decianus; that won't help.'

Sabinus bridled. 'Don't patronise me, you little shit.'

'Sorry, but I know what you're like.'

'What do you mean, "what I'm like"?'

'This isn't helping either,' Caenis butted in. 'We'll just tell Paulinus the facts and then he can decide what to do.'

'Exactly,' Vespasian said, relieved that Caenis had averted a spate of bickering.

'What about me and the dogs?' Magnus asked. 'What are we going to do?'

'You're coming with me.'

'Where to?'

'We're off to find Cerialis tonight, alert him to the fact that he's on his own and advise that he withdraws to Londinium.'

'But he's on the Lindum road on the other side of Camulodunum with the whole Iceni tribe between him and us.'

'We'll skirt around to the west and then head north. If we don't find him by dawn then I very much doubt that his legion will see dusk.'

CHAPTER XIIII

'CAN YOU HEAR anything?' Vespasian whispered, standing just beyond the glow of a torched farm, listening to the soft sounds of the night.

'Just the horses,' Magnus muttered back, restraining Castor and Pollux by the collars, 'and the crackle of the fire, of course.'

Vespasian listened again; no human sounds came from the burnt-out farm. Smoke still wafted from smouldering timbers; here and there was the flicker of flaming wood but there was no sign of any Iceni in the firelight. Yet they must have been there because tethered in a small, still-intact orchard, twenty paces away, were half a dozen ponies of the shaggy sort favoured by Britannic horsemen; the saddles on the beasts confirmed the origins of their riders but of them there was no sign. 'They must be asleep.'

'Tiring work, all this massacring.'

Vespasian looked at the bodies of the former occupants of the house, nailed by their wrists to the trunk of an oak tree: a man and wife and their three young children. Their heads had been removed and, judging by the wounds to their chests, so had their hearts. 'I'd like to do the same thing to the savages that did that.'

'Another time, perhaps; let's just take the horses and get away.' Magnus moved forward at a crouch with his dogs.

Vespasian followed, drawing his sword as he did, praying that they would get away unnoticed. They had already been travelling for four hours, skirting around the south of Camulodunum, and had come across nobody in the night; they had begun to believe that the rebels had stayed in the town and that they might get through to Cerialis without incident until they had seen the burning farm. If it had not been for the ponies they would have given it a wide berth; however, the chance of quick transport had outweighed the danger of coming close to a small war band.

The ponies shifted about nervously in reaction to Castor and Pollux approaching; a couple of wickers and a snort made Magnus stop and let go of the dogs' collars. 'Sit!' he hissed and, to Vespasian's surprise, the dogs did as they were told. Magnus moved forward.

Vespasian moved past the sitting dogs and on into the orchard after Magnus; quickly they began to untether the ponies whose nervousness had not been abated by the dogs' halting. Another couple of snorts, a wicker and then a full whinny as the first beast untethered by Magnus kicked and bolted, its hoofs pounding.

'Juno's tight arse!' Magnus swore as he worked on the second tether in the dim light.

Vespasian tore at his knot with his fingers for a few moments and then shook his head in disbelief at his stupidity, drew his knife and severed the tether.

Another whinny came from the bolting horse; sharper this time.

Magnus followed Vespasian's example and swapped to knife-work.

A deep growl rumbled out and then both hounds started vicious barking as a shout came from out of the night.

'Shit!' Vespasian slashed at a second tether, cutting it, and then a third, keeping hold of it and control of the pony as the other two trotted off. Thankful that the beast was not a full-sized horse, he swung his leg over its haunches and hauled himself into the saddle as figures appeared, fifteen paces away, from close to the burning house, by which, presumably, they had been sleeping, warmed by their handiwork. Vespasian kicked his mount into action.

Slapping the rump of the final pony to be released, Magnus mounted his and urged it after Vespasian as Castor and Pollux, still barking, bounded after him.

A couple of javelins slammed into the ground to Magnus' right; furious shouting followed them.

Leaning forward, close to his mount's neck, Vespasian accelerated away, outpacing Magnus who had less skill in the saddle, but, due to the darkness of the night, he soon had to slow again as they got further from the burning house. The shouts from behind them continued and, rather than diminish into the distance, they seemed to stay constant and then, gradually, got closer.

They were being chased.

After another few hundred paces, Vespasian looked behind; Magnus was ten paces away with Castor and Pollux lolloping beside him, almost invisible in the dark. Behind were the silhouettes of at least two pursuers and they were gaining. He looked forward into the night and could see no way of increasing his speed without running the risk of being dismounted, and yet if they did not they would surely be ridden down. Not to get through could be the death sentence for a legion. 'We need to turn and face them,' he shouted over his shoulder to Magnus, 'otherwise they'll catch us.' He slowed and turned his mount, rearing on its back legs; Magnus managed the manoeuvre with less panache as the pursuit came on at speed, now less than twenty paces out. Drawing his sword, Vespasian urged his mount back towards them, slapping its rump with the flat of his blade. The two pursuers checked their pace, unsure of this confidence in their quarry; two dark shadows suddenly appeared, flying towards them, and, before they had time to register the attack, they were punched from the saddles. Castor and Pollux landed on their prey in a welter of ripping and growling; screams of abject terror of being devoured by unknown things-of-the-night issued from the Britons, long and hard, as they fought these monsters that could just materialise out of nothing.

Vespasian and Magnus both watched as the life was eaten out of the men, feeling that such a death was no more than their due; quickly, their struggles ceased and they were silent and still.

'Good boys,' Magnus purred with genuine affection for his pets as he dismounted and eased them off their feasts. 'But we haven't got time for a snack just at the moment.' He tickled each under its bloody muzzle and leapt back up into the saddle as the sound of pursuit on foot reached them.

Off they sped into the night, travelling as fast as they dared for the first quarter of a mile and then, once they had outpaced their pursuit, slowing down to a trot, heading ever northward.

With no care for the fatigue of their ponies, Vespasian and Magnus pressed on and soon, directly to the east, to their right, they could see the distant glow of Camulodunum.

'We're level with the town now,' Vespasian said. 'If we carry on for another mile or so and then head northeast we should hit the Lindum road and then we've got about an hour left of the night to find the Ninth.'

'Well, I hope they've got something good to eat; we haven't had anything since yesterday and that ain't good at my age. I'm starting to feel very weak.'

Vespasian said nothing on the subject; he was feeling the effects of hunger too and felt that talking about it would only make things worse. They rode in silence for a while.

In the distance the glow of the town grew, even though they were drawing away from it. 'They must have really put it to the torch,' Vespasian observed some time later, 'for it to be burning like that eleven hours later.'

'We shouldn't have stayed there,' Magnus said, 'it was almost suicide.'

'It was for a lot of people but had they had fled then they would have stood even less chance in the open. It was the Trinovantes within the walls breaking them down that really tipped the balance.'

'Bollocks it was; it was the sheer fucking size of their army. It'll take a few legions to stop it.'

'Which we'll have when they all converge.'

Magnus grunted and expressed no further opinion; they kept to their own thoughts until, a short time later, the sound of their ponies' hoofs on stone alerted them to the fact that they had finally reached the road.

And then a strange sound, faint and yet strong at the same time, floated on the pre-dawn air; Vespasian cocked his ear, frowning. 'What's that?'

They halted their tired ponies and listened.

It was a rumble that they could hear; a rumble not of inanimate objects but rather voices, male voices, thousands of them, in fact, tens of thousands of them. The Iceni army was on the move.

'They're heading up the Lindum road to surprise Cerialis!' Vespasian said, realising what Boudicca planned to do. 'If she takes us one legion at a time we're finished. There's not a moment to lose.' He kicked his long-suffering pony back into action and they raced away, their path along the road easier to see as the dawn glow in the east strengthened.

Behind them they could just make out a great shadow to the south, spread out to either side of the road. They thrashed their beasts north, hoping that Cerialis had already pulled back. But they did not have far to travel for, after half a mile, another shadow became distinct, this time ahead of them.

It did not take Vespasian too long to work out what it was. 'Cerialis, you fool. You're marching your legion towards certain death.'

But Cerialis did not know that he was marching towards annihilation, not because he was marching in the classic Roman fashion, without scouts; but because the scouts he had sent out had not, so far, returned. And so, Vespasian and Magnus were not challenged as they pelted up the road towards the VIIII Hispana.

'Where're his scouting units?' Vespasian wondered aloud as the cohort leading the legion's advance became distinct in the ever growing light. They swerved off the road and raced down the ranks and ranks of legionaries; past two cohorts they went until they approached the command position to see Cerialis, fifty paces away, sitting proudly on his horse with the legion's Eagle parading before him and his tribunes and his escort cavalry behind. The first rays of the newborn sun glinted pale off their helms.

'Cerialis, Cerialis!' Vespasian shouted, galloping towards the legate.

Cerialis looked towards his father-in-law but failed to recognise him in the dawn light with his unshaven face and dishevelled clothing. With a barked order to a decurion he sent him and four others of his escort against Vespasian and Magnus. Detaching themselves from the rest of the legionary cavalry they accelerated towards the two incoming riders.

'We're Roman! Roman!' Vespasian roared, slowing his pony and spreading his arms to show that he was not armed.

Magnus growled an order at his dogs to keep them in check.

'Roman!' Vespasian shouted again as the decurion and his men approached. 'Mutilus,' Vespasian cried, recognising the officer as the same man who had escorted him south from Lindum, 'it's me, Senator Vespasian; I must speak with the legate at once.'

Mutilus squinted at him and then recognition flooded onto his face. 'Of course, sir, right away.' The decurion spun his horse about and led the way back to Cerialis.

'Father!' The surprised legate exclaimed upon recognising Vespasian and Magnus. 'What are you doing here?'

'No, Cerialis, it's what you're doing here that is the question.'

'I'm coming to relieve you in Camulodunum.'

'Camulodunum fell yesterday evening; didn't your scouts tell you?'

'They told me that it had been invested so I thought that with swift action, like Corbulo, I could surprise the Britons this morning and we could crush them between us.'

Vespasian could not believe his son-in-law's folly. 'But you were meant to join up with Paulinus and ...' He stopped, realising that they were wasting valuable time discussing what Cerialis should have been doing. 'You have to deploy defensively, Cerialis, and make a fighting retreat back to your camp.'

'Why?'

'Because ...'

But Vespasian did not need to explain why, as just at that moment two factors combined: the sun rose and its light strengthened at the same time as the Iceni had a clear view of the VIIII Hispana. These two factors brought about the biggest roar that any in the legion had ever heard; on hearing it each legionary knew that it was baying to the gods of Britannia for every drop of their Roman blood.

'A hollow square is our only chance, Cerialis,' Vespasian urged. 'And then we fight step by step back to your camp.'

There was a distinct look of panic in Cerialis' eyes. 'Do we have time to deploy, though?'

'We're about to find out; if you don't give the order we'll all die anyway.'

Cerialis swallowed and nodded. '*Cornicern*! Legion hollow square!'

The musician put the mouthpiece of his G-shaped horn to his lips and issued four deep notes, each identical in pitch, and then repeated the alarm. All through the legion cornicerns relayed the rumbling call to their cohorts and then onto centuries. The repetitive drill of the Roman army was not done for nothing; every centurion, optio and standard-bearer knew his place upon hearing the signal, which was only sounded when the legion was in dire circumstances. Although none of them had ever had to react to the command in the field for real before, their innate discipline meant that they began to lead their men, with bellowed orders, to the correct place in the formation. The legion began to transform from column to defensive square with blocks of men fanning out, left and right, whilst the first and second cohorts formed up to the front, facing the threat.

But despite their efficiency, Vespasian could see that that it would be a very close-run affair; ahead of the VIIII Hispana the Iceni nation had broken into a mad charge, their chariot horses galloping and the warriors sprinting, keeping no order, all just intent on being the first to catch the legion in the middle of its manoeuvre, thereby ensuring its doom.

On they came as the legion's officers roared their men into more haste and precision, knowing that a hollow square with a gap in it was nothing more than a column with right angles and just as vulnerable.

'I don't like the look of this,' Magnus said, seeing how the first cohort had not yet completed its frontage and the space between it and the fourth cohort, facing west, was still considerable.

The sick feeling in his stomach, which Vespasian had experienced on that night, all those years ago, when his II Augusta had so nearly been caught mid-deployment, returned.

That night they had just made it; it was becoming apparent that this morning they would not.

The Roman horns rumbled, thousands of pairs of hobnailed sandals stamped, kit jangled and centurions bellowed, but all this did nothing to mask the sound of the Iceni as they savoured the scent of legionary blood.

With their Queen in their midst, the leading chariots, scores of them, swerved and tore across the frontage of the incomplete ranks of the first cohort, the warriors hurling javelin after javelin into the gaps within the formation, picking off the unshielded, punching them back and down to become an obstacle for their comrades behind to negotiate, hindering further their deployment. A few centuries were organised enough to reply with a volley of pila, the weighted heads ripping cruelly into man and beast alike bringing many crashing, legs thrashing, to the ground to skid along the grass, moist with dew.

Their javelins spent, the surviving chariot warriors, the élite and pride of the tribe, jumped clear of their vehicles; with hexagonal shields, resplendent with animal designs, and long, slashing swords whirling in their hands, they charged, heedless of personal safety, into the first cohort. But it was not with shield against shield that the battle was fought, in a contest where the individualistic Britannic warriors would always lose to the mutually supportive tactics of the legion; no, this time they did not have to throw themselves against a solid wall of wood, this time the mutual support was not there and the warriors crashed through the gaps that had been widened by their javelins and took on individual combats as, behind them, their brethren on foot closed with the fraying cohort.

Screaming their hatred to their gods, smeared in strange designs, their hair stiff with lime, the cream of the Iceni brought terror with their attack. Towering over even the men of the first cohort, they brought their long blades down from great heights or slashed them in broad arcs, outreaching the short gladii of their opponents.

And then the honed iron bit into the disorganised Roman ranks and, seemingly slow as if time had relented, the first head spun up into the air, spiralling gore, at the same instant as the first right arm slopped to the ground still gripping the sword hilt. And then time accelerated. Extreme violence had begun and it was on the Iceni's terms as they fell upon men trained to fight shoulder to shoulder and who were now unable to do so. As if crazed, the Britannic warriors twirled left and then right, forever whirling their swords in blurs of continual motion, their passage marked by sprays of blood, hurling their opponents back or down as the main infantry force of the tribe ploughed into the cohort and the second cohort next to it, forcing bloody furrows through, as the life was plucked from them and they ceased to function as units.

'They won't stand,' Vespasian shouted to Cerialis as the first cohort's standard disappeared down into the chaos of massacre. 'If you act now there's a chance that you can pull out with the rear six cohorts; they might get away if the Britons' lack of discipline keeps them massacring the unlucky bastards in the first four.'

'There's still hope, Father; I've ordered the fifth and seventh cohorts to form behind the first and second to limit the breakthrough.'

'If they get into contact you won't be able to extricate them and then that'll be another thousand men lost.'

'Not if we can stop them here and complete the formation; then we can stage a fighting retreat.'

Vespasian jabbed a finger to where the Iceni had started to lap around the sides of the Roman formation, eating into the fourth and third cohorts, facing west and east respectively, their formations already buckling. 'Look! Don't fool yourself, Cerialis; the best that we can hope for now is to save at least some of the legion whilst the rest are sacrificed.'

'The fifth and the seventh will stand.'

Vespasian bit back a stinging riposte as he watched the two cohorts attempt to form up at the rear of the disintegrating ones. File upon file raced forward, slotting into position in a wave effect; the fifth braced at ninety degrees against the backs of the fourth, and the seventh onto the third. But security only comes from those secure in themselves; this was not now the case. Death flowed freely through the legion and each man could feel its breath; eyes started to look nervously around rather than stay fixed to the front. Strict silence in the ranks was replaced by nervous enquiries as to the situation; old lags were asked their opinion and confirmed that they had been in far worse predicaments many a time but the tones of their voices were not convincing. Centurions started to look over their shoulders, looking for messengers with orders to begin the retreat; but none were forthcoming.

And then the dam burst: the first and the second cohorts could take no more; indeed, there were very few of them left to take anything at all, and those there were turned and fled. They crashed into their brothers forming behind; files opened to let them through ensuring the fresher cohorts were not swept away in the panic. Through these passages the fugitives ran, chased by their tormentors pressing them close. So close they pressed that the files did not close up in time and the Iceni penetrated the cohorts that were meant to hold them back with the ease and abandonment that Decianus' men had breached the bodies of their Queen's daughters; in they pushed, forcing themselves deeper, their weapons working constantly, blood spurting from the great gashes they hewed as more thrust in behind them, ever swelling their number and widening the passages as their sides were cleaved away, falling fouled by the slime of their own gore, faeces and urine so that cohesion entirely failed as the first warriors exploded out the other side.

In less than a tenth of the number of heartbeats, the nine hundred and sixty men of the fifth and seventh cohorts were either killed or swept away as the units were ravaged and left for dead; the Iceni were now fully within the hollow square and the same fate awaited the rest of the legion. To either side of them the warriors could see nothing but the backs of legionaries and the sight gave yet more heat to their lust for blood; as the rear ranks of legionaries began to turn, without any orders being issued, they set about them with a brutal efficiency so that they received hardly any strokes in return.

And their Queen joined them, standing tall in her chariot, arms raised, holding a bloodied spear that sheened in the sun, and beside her came her daughters, on foot and armed with long knives, attended by Myrddin and a dozen of his order. With them came an atmosphere: a fear, a cold dread that Vespasian had felt before and, even though he was three hundred paces away, he instinctively pulled his mount back as did Magnus, Cerialis and all the legionary cavalry behind them. They watched as the daughters prowled alongside their mother, roving about the fallen and upon finding legionaries, wounded but conscious, the druids would cut their armour from them as they screamed, futilely, for mercy; with eyes burning with revenge and to the accompaniment of druidical incantations the three girls harvested hearts, pulling them still pulsing from the chest cavities of shrieking men whose last moments were filled with the creeping terror instilled by the power of Myrddin and the abject horror of being slit open and feeling a hand inserted to rip out their hearts. As each victim's eyes faded, their last image was of their own blood falling towards them squeezed from that precious organ.

Now it was over; the four rear cohorts who had yet to be engaged could stand and watch no longer the massacre of their fellows nor could they bear the slow, steady advance of Myrddin and the druids of whom so many tales had been told, all of which had lodged within their superstitious minds. Ignoring the mantra that had been instilled in them since the first day of their training, as youths of sixteen or seventeen, that strength lies in solidarity, they broke and they ran, casting aside their shields and pila and thinking of nought but their own safety, which, in their stupidity, they had now put in the gravest peril. Their officers could do nothing, neither threaten, plead nor appeal to their loyalty or sense of pride, and rather than face the ignominy of seeking the

Ferryman with a wound to the back many of the centurions, optiones, standard-bearers and steadier old lags chose to hurl themselves at the enemy preying upon their comrades up ahead.

'Let's get out of here!' Vespasian shouted, swinging his pony around.

'I thought you'd never think of that,' Magnus said, following him, his dogs at his side.

'But my legion,' Cerialis cried, looking desperately at his father-in-law.

'Is gone, Cerialis. Now you have a choice: leave my daughter as a pregnant widow or ride with your cavalry back to your camp and muster as many survivors there as possible.'

'But my reputation?'

'Is in tatters; we'll worry about how to restore it if we all survive this. Now go!'

'Where are you going?'

'Londinium. We have to get a message to Paulinus. He needs to know that the Ninth will not be joining him because the Ninth is no more.'

CHAPTER XV

LONDINIUM WAS RIFE with rumour as Vespasian and Magnus arrived in the second hour of the night; but the rumour was of the uprising and the subsequent sack of Camulodunum. The obliteration of one of Rome's four fighting machines in the province had not been heard of, nor had it been even imagined. As they led their horses and Castor and Pollux through the crowded thoroughfares of the town, swelled by refugees, they heard much talk of the destruction of the province's capital and also optimism at the arrival of Paulinus, just before dusk, as his army made camp a quarter of a mile to the north. There was, however, no mention of the VIIII Hispana and that was because Vespasian and Magnus had ridden hard ahead of the news.

Having galloped away whilst the Iceni's attention had been on running down and butchering the fleeing remnants of the legion, Vespasian and Magnus had cut across country and made it to the Camulodunum–Londinium road by mid-morning. After a couple of miles they had managed to commandeer two fresh horses from a military way-station, advising the optio in command to pull his eight men back to Londinium and warn the occupants of every farmstead they passed along the way to do the same. Vespasian and Magnus did not have time for such niceties because, for all they knew, Boudicca might turn her gaze to the southwest and set off that very morning, with the corpses of the VIIII Hispana still warm. Two forced marches could bring her to Londinium by the evening of the following day by which time Paulinus needed to have a plan based upon all the facts; Vespasian was only too well aware that a decision cannot be made until all the relevant information has been received and once it has been it is best to have as much time as possible to process it.

Finally they came to the rented house on the river; Hormus answered the door with relief on his face. 'Master, I was beginning to worry what with the rumours of Camulodunum circulating around the forum.'

'Didn't Sabinus and Caenis tell you we were all right, Hormus?'

Hormus' confusion was evident. 'I'm sorry, master?'

'Sabinus and Caenis, aren't they here?'

'No, master.'

'We only left them last night around midnight,' Magnus pointed out, 'not even twenty-four hours ago. They may be having problems with that tide thing that they're so keen on here.'

Vespasian considered that for a few moments. 'You could be right; the fisherman did reckon two or three days for a round trip and only did it in two because he got the tides right. I'll have to see Paulinus on my own; I assume he's at Decianus' residence.'

'Yes, master, he went straight there and called a meeting with his tribunes and the two prefects of the auxiliary cohorts stationed in the town and a few men of status; it should be starting about now.'

'Good; pack, Hormus, and have Caenis' two girls do the same because one way or another we will be leaving tomorrow.'

The men of status, of course, included Procurator Catus Decianus who was speaking to the assembly as Vespasian pushed past the guard trying to bar his way into the audience chamber; he stopped in the shadows, out of reach of the light from four lampstands set in a square around the middle of the room, to listen to his version of events.

'So those are the reasons for this outrageous uprising. However, I can assure the Governor and the citizens of this town that Boudicca and her rabble pose no threat to Londinium.' The procurator had assumed an air of gravitas that sat at odds with his unmanly hair and the swelling and bruising on his face.

'And what makes you so sure, *procurator*?' Governor Suetonius Paulinus asked, seated on a curule chair at the far end of the room; lean and weather-beaten with an almost skeletal face and a grey wreath of hair semi-circling a shiny pate, he was the antithesis of the plump procurator and his antipathy to Decianus was made clear in the acerbic manner in which he pronounced his official title.

'They're an ill-disciplined band of savages who will, *if* the rumours are correct and they have managed to capture Camulodunum, which I doubt, take as much plunder as they can carry and then fall apart, like all Britannic tribes, as soon as they hear that a Roman legion has taken the field against them.'

'And that's your professional, military assessment, *procurator*? You seriously believe that every tribe of these warlike savages falls apart when they see a legion; if that's the case why are we still fighting them? Why have I just spent six months subduing the druids on Mona and the tribes on the mainland up there without noticing this phenomenon of "falling apart"? Tell me, *procurator*, in which legion did you serve during the invasion of this savage isle, that you have such a firm grasp of the martial capabilities of the Britannic tribes?'

'The Governor is well aware that I have not had the privilege of serving in any legion due to my health.'

'Your health! Since when has timidity counted as a health problem? Sit down, Decianus, and keep quiet until a subject comes up about which you have at least a modicum of knowledge; greed, for example.'

'But I'm the procurator, my opinion must be important.'

'The difficulty that we have, gentlemen,' Paulinus stated, ignoring Decianus' protests, 'is manpower. As you know, I'm here with the Fourteenth and a vexillation of three cohorts of the Twentieth plus four auxiliary cohorts. Now, taking into account the casualties we've sustained over the last campaign, what should be a force of around nine and a half thousand men is barely eight thousand.' He nodded at the two prefects of the Londinium-based auxiliary cohorts. 'With your men we're still shy of ten thousand. There is also another factor: what none of you here know is that the Second Augusta, which should have arrived here at the same time as us, has yet to move from its base at Isca.'

There were cries of disbelief.

Vespasian felt sick; the news he bore had just become twice as terrible.

'The legate and the thick-stripe had been recalled to Rome and their replacements have yet to arrive so Poenius Postumus, the prefect of the camp, is currently in command. He has refused my orders, why, I don't know and it gets us nowhere to speculate on the subject; we will, no doubt, find out at his trial after this has been settled. So, with our almost ten thousand, the two more auxiliary cohorts promised by Cogidubnus of the united tribes of the Regni and the Atrebates that are due to cross the bridge in the morning and then Cerialis' Ninth Hispana and auxiliaries, we can expect a force of something in the region of sixteen to seventeen thousand; with that we can stop them before they reach Londinium.'

'I'm afraid that won't be possible, Governor Paulinus,' Vespasian said, walking forward from out of the shadows.

'That's one of the men I was telling you about,' Decianus squawked, the surprise on his face showing that he had clearly thought Vespasian to be dead. 'That's Senator Vespasian.'

'I know who it is, you fool: he's a senator; a member of my class. But I thought you said he was dead.'

'He didn't lie to you, Governor,' Vespasian said, stopping in the centre of the room and pointing an accusatory finger at Decianus. 'He did think I was dead because he left me and my companions tied up at the mercy of the Iceni; and seeing as he had just stolen their gold, had their Queen, the wife of a Roman citizen and therefore considered to be Roman herself, flogged and had also allowed his men, all his men, to have their pleasure, in whatever way they chose, with her three unmarried daughters, he was quite right to consider me dead. Unfortunately for Decianus, the Queen of the Iceni, unlike him, has a sense of honour and she let us go as she could see that we had nothing to do with the outrage but, rather, tried to dissuade this rapacious idiot from his belligerent actions and prevent the rebellion that they have caused. She wanted us to tell the true story of what propelled her into her course of action; which I have now, before witnesses.' Stating all the facts plainly was too much for Vespasian's strained nerves and without thinking about it he spun around and landed a crushing right hook on the procurator.

Decianus twisted, arched back and slumped to the floor, stunned; his jaw would not have broken had his mouth been clamped shut but it had started to open as he had been about to try to defend himself from what he knew to be the truth.

'I'm sorry, Governor,' Vespasian said, looking down at Decianus who had begun to moan softly, 'but it's been a fraught few days and a lot of lives have been lost because of that shit.'

'No, no, don't apologise, Vespasian. I think that we all feel better after that; except for Decianus, of course.'

This observation caused the tension in the room to disappear, washed away by laughter.

'It's good to see you back from the dead; so what news do you have that tells you that my earlier arithmetic won't be possible?'

Vespasian looked the Governor in the eye. 'I'm afraid that there is no easy way to say this, Paulinus, but the Ninth Hispana was wiped out this morning.'

Vespasian drew to a close his recount of the events of the last few days since Decianus' folly; there was silence in the room and a variety of grim expressions.

'Gods above and below,' Paulinus whispered eventually. 'A whole legion this very morning and twenty thousand people yesterday in Camulodunum! She knows that after that she and her people can never expect mercy now. They have nothing to lose so they might as well commit the crimes that we will punish them for, in advance, tenfold. What do we do?'

'We stop them, of course,' Vespasian said, regretting it the moment the words slipped out.

'Of course we stop them, senator!' Paulinus snapped. 'Don't patronise me.'

'My apologies, Governor; I'm tired and I spoke out of turn.'

Paulinus waved the apology away. 'Forget about it. Now, the question is how do we stop them with perhaps a tenth of their number?'

'We may get more, Paulinus; I sent messages to the Governors of Gallia Belgica and Germania Inferior asking for reinforcements as soon as possible.'

'You've been stretching your non-existent authority quite a bit, senator: mobilising this province and alerting our neighbours.'

Vespasian shrugged. 'Someone had to; otherwise we would have lost the whole of the south before we knew what was going on. *He* was never going to do anything.' He gestured down to where Decianus lay to see that he had crawled off without anyone noticing.

'You're right, of course, and you have my thanks; but from now on the responsibility is mine.'

'Indeed, Paulinus.'

Paulinus stared at him for a few moments and then, satisfied that his authority would not be questioned, addressed the rest of his officers. 'So, what to do, gentlemen? We have ten thousand men and a Britannic army of probably at least a hundred thousand strong once it arrives here in what, if we're lucky, could be two days but is more likely to be tomorrow afternoon if Boudicca does the sensible thing and force-marches; and there's no reason to suppose she won't, judging by how she jumped on Cerialis. How do we defend Londinium and, more importantly, the bridge and how do we crush this rebellion whilst we're doing it?'

There was silence as every man in the room contemplated just how to do the impossible.

Paulinus tapped the arm of his chair with impatience. 'Come on, gentlemen, surely one of you might try to give me a bit of advice.'

Still nothing.

Vespasian cleared his throat.

Paulinus looked over to him. 'Go on then, senator; if the members of my staff are proving fruitless, you, perhaps, can make up for them.'

'You can't.'

'Can't what?'

'You can't defend Londinium and the bridge as well as crush the rebellion with this number of men; you can only do either or.'

Paulinus rubbed his chin. 'That's what I was thinking; I was just hoping that someone could see things differently. We either take our force into the town and defend it; if we started now, then by tomorrow afternoon, ten thousand should be able to make it defensible enough for the Iceni to move on after a couple of failed assaults and we could stay holed up until help arrives. But, by that time, Boudicca would have raised the whole province: Venutius and Cartimandua in the north would have settled their differences and joined her, the Silures in the west would have overwhelmed the holding force of the remainder of the Twentieth that I was forced to leave there, the Second Augusta would be pinned down in the southwest and probably trounced and the only useful aid would be ships to evacuate us.' He looked around the room at his officers. 'I think we can all agree that if we made it back to Rome, gentlemen, the Emperor would invite us to fall upon our swords only on the off-chance that he was feeling lenient.'

His men murmured their reluctant agreement.

'So therefore I have to do what good generals always do when faced with superior numbers: negate them as Alexander did at Issus or Leonidas at Thermopylae. I need to offer battle to Boudicca in a way that she won't be able to resist the opportunity given the odds; but I choose the ground. I believe I know the very place about fifty miles north of here, beyond the town of Verulamium; it'll suit our purposes well. Caninius, get a message to the camp. The legion is to strike and be ready to march upon my arrival by mid-morning.'

'Yes, sir,' Caninius, Paulinus' thick-stripe military tribune, said. 'And what about Londinium?'

'As soon as Cogidubnus and his auxiliaries have crossed the bridge we tear down a section making it impassable for the Britons, so they have to remain on the north bank, and then we abandon the town to its inevitable fate. All those fit enough to keep up with a legion's pace may seek our shelter; the rest ... well, I'm sorry, I can't wait for the young or the frail if we are going to reach the ground I've chosen and be ready for that Fury and her army. We inform the citizens at first light, destroy the bridge and then head north leaving a trail of stragglers for Boudicca to follow.'

'What if Sabinus and Caenis haven't arrived by the time Paulinus pulls out?' Magnus asked Vespasian as they stood, following dawn, on the bridge, staring downstream to the bend in the river, past Londinium's port; a single trireme was being loaded in the otherwise empty harbour.

'Then we wait here; they should arrive by mid-afternoon at the latest.'

Magnus pulled on his hounds' leads as they attempted to pounce, with a view to breakfast, on a passing small child. 'Boudicca could arrive by mid-afternoon at the earliest; did you notice a similarity there?'

Vespasian shaded his eyes as the sun rose. 'What? The mid-afternoon bit?'

'Yes, that bit; the bit that puts us in the same vicinity as one hundred thousand or more hairy-arse savages with a new-found taste for tearing out Roman hearts.'

Vespasian pointed down to the river. 'What's that?'

Magnus looked down at the murky brown water and frowned. 'It's a river.'

'Well done. And what floats on rivers?'

Magnus grinned, now playing along. 'Birds, logs and boats.'

'Excellent; and which one of those will Sabinus and Caenis be arriving in? I'll give you a clue: it's not a duck.'

Magnus pretended to think for a few moments as Pollux deposited a turd of admirable proportions on the wooden road; it was immediately subjected to Castor's close and vigorous scrutiny. 'So we just jump on Sabinus and Caenis' log, carry on upstream until we are safe to land and then cut across country to rejoin Paulinus.'

'Exactly.'

'And what if the Britons start sacking Londinium before the rescue-log arrives? Do you think that we'll be able to explain nicely to them that we're just waiting for our log which will be along at any moment and would they mind massacring someone else?'

'You could try doing that, if they could hear you.'

'What?'

Vespasian raised his voice. 'I said: You could try—'

'No, I meant: what do you mean?'

'Ah. I meant if they could hear you from the other side of the bridge over the gap that Paulinus is just about to make in it.'

Magnus looked south along the bridge. 'Of course; I'm a little slow this morning.' As he spoke a horse carrying a huge man in the uniform of a prefect of auxiliaries stepped onto the bridge: behind him marched rank after rank of auxiliaries in chainmail and with oval shields. 'Here comes our royal mate.'

'What?' Vespasian took his attention away from the river. 'Cogidubnus; I knew he would remain loyal.'

The Britannic King held his head high, his long moustaches fluttering in the river breeze, as he led his two cohorts, each eight hundred strong, across the Tamesis bridge. Centurions bawled out an order and the entire company broke step so that the wooden structure did not vibrate itself to destruction.

'Vespasian and Magnus, my friends,' Cogidubnus said, drawing near, his ruddy round face breaking into a broad smile. 'I wish it were in better circumstances that we meet again.'

'So do I, old friend,' Vespasian said, reaching up to grab the proffered, heavily muscled forearm; behind the King his men passed by, Britons in the uniform of Rome. 'What will happen to your people if this goes badly for Rome?'

'We have no wish to go back to the old days of constantly fighting amongst ourselves; it's bad for business, and business is something that the Regni and the Atrebates are getting very good at.'

'Really?'

'Put it this way: if Rome stays then all those estates and mines that I and others have bought back off Pallas for under twice what he paid us for them will be worth more than twice what we paid him. In just three months we would have doubled our money and my loan that the Cloelius Brothers called in last month will seem as nothing.'

'Pallas sold you back his investments! He was going to send me to negotiate that with you the year Agrippina died; I have to say that I'm pleased he didn't in the end.'

'I might have given him a better deal had you been negotiating for him rather than Paelignus.'

'Julius Paelignus?'

'Yes, a horrible little crookback; do you know him?'

'I did; the last time I saw him he was lying at the bottom of a latrine with his throat ripped out, being shat upon by a dozen of Boudicca's men.'

'How gratifying; I'm pleased to hear that the Iceni have done some good in amongst all this carnage.'

'But what was Paelignus doing working for Pallas?'

Cogidubnus shrugged. 'I don't know but you can be sure that he was getting a commission judging by his determined negotiation and bitter disappointment when I would go no higher than one and nine tenths of what Pallas had paid.'

'That would explain his strongbox that he was trying to take with him,' Magnus pointed out.

'It would,' Vespasian agreed, 'and I suppose it would be cheaper for Pallas to get someone who was already here to negotiate for him for a smaller percentage than it would have cost him to persuade someone like me to go but still it—'

'Prefect!' Paulinus' shout cut across Vespasian's thoughts. The Governor came striding onto the bridge with a bodyguard of a dozen legionaries fending off desperate-looking citizens shouting pleas, weeping and tearing at their hair; Paulinus acted as if they were not there. 'Welcome to you, indeed; your men are sorely needed.'

Cogidubnus saluted. 'The united tribes of the Regni and Atrebates will always be loyal to Rome, Governor.'

'I'm pleased to hear it. Now, I need your men to dismantle the bridge once they've crossed; it doesn't have to be pretty, just effective. Get as far as you can with the job by the sixth hour and then follow us north up the road, which should mean that you will be at least four hours ahead of Boudicca. Keep going at night until you catch up with us; we won't leave the road. I would hope to be—' Paulinus stopped abruptly and stared down towards the port; the trireme was under oars and heading out into the river. 'What the ... ? That's the last ship; it's not meant to sail until all my despatches are on board begging the Emperor and the Senate for help.' He put his hand to his forehead, rubbing it. 'And the letters to my wife and sons; how will they know if ... ? Who gave the order?'

But the answer to that question was obvious as, in the stern looking back towards the bridge, stood a portly man in an equestrian toga; he had a bandage wrapped around his face, holding his jaw in place. Procurator Decianus raised an arm in a farewell wave to Paulinus and the chaos that he had caused.

'I'll eat his liver,' Paulinus snarled.

By the look on the Governor's face, Vespasian could well believe he meant it.

'Governor! Governor! Don't abandon us!'

The shouts from the citizens trying to petition him impinged on Paulinus' conscience and he turned to vent his anger upon them. 'I have told you: we cannot hope to defend Londinium and crush Boudicca, and if we don't crush Boudicca, Londinium will fall eventually, so the logical thing to do is to let it fall now.'

'And march north to save Verulamium?'

'I will give the people of Verulamium the same choice as I've given you.'

'But our livelihoods, our property, our wives and children!' The shouts were mixed and emotional, growing in clamour; but they failed to move the pragmatic Governor.

'Come with us, if you want to, or cross the bridge before it's destroyed or stay here and defend yourselves; I don't care what you do as long as you do it now and leave me alone.' He turned back to Cogidubnus as the last of the auxiliaries left the bridge. 'See that it's done.'

Cogidubnus pointed to a couple of centuries who were stripping off their chainmail at the middle of the bridge. 'I've just given the order.'

'Good. I shall see you later tonight.' Paulinus nodded, satisfied, and then looked at Vespasian. 'Are you coming, senator?'

'No, Governor, not yet; I have to wait here for my brother and my ... er ... Antonia Caenis; they'll be here soon in a boat. We'll follow you as best we can.'

'Well, good luck, Vespasian; may the gods of your family hold their hands over you.'

'Thank you, sir; and I wish the same of yours.'

Paulinus gave a curt nod and turned; his bodyguards ploughed into the crowd surrounding him and cast them aside, strewing them on the ground so that the Governor walked freely as if he were completely alone.

'You had better get across,' Cogidubnus suggested as the first planks were ripped up from the centre of the structure.

Vespasian saw Hormus coming through the crowds, loaded with luggage, followed by Caenis' two slave girls and the other slaves, equally as laden. 'I'll see you on the north road, my friend.'

'I hope so; it's been a while since we drew our swords together.'

They grasped forearms again and then, once Magnus had said his farewell, they crossed the bridge, along with surprisingly few refugees, to wait for Sabinus and Caenis, praying they would arrive before Boudicca.

Although the gods had, in the past, listened to many of Vespasian's prayers, they did not listen to that particular one and by the time Cogidubnus had been gone for a couple of hours, having torn up fifty paces of the bridge and pulled four of the great piles from the riverbed, the first fires appeared on the northeast side of the town. Soon the screaming could be heard and the fires broadened. Vespasian sat with Magnus and his dogs on the southern bank of the Tamesis wondering at the folly of those who had chosen to stay in the town when to do so could only mean certain death.

'I suppose they'll have nothing if all their property is destroyed,' Magnus opined after Vespasian had mentioned to him that one of the refugees had told Hormus that he thought that there were upwards of thirty thousand people who had decided to throw themselves on Boudicca's mercy or just hide until the storm passed over.

'They'll have their lives,' Vespasian said, still trying to get his head around the size of the massacre that was about to be perpetrated.

'But what good is that if there is no way to feed and clothe yourself, let alone your wife and children? If you've got nothing you've really got nothing in this world and that includes chances; it's something that people of your class find impossible to see the reality of and then comprehend it. Nothing is exactly what it says and it's very bleak indeed.'

Vespasian thought on that for some time as the people on the further bank who preferred to chance death rather than face the reality of nothing began to die in droves, judging from the clamour of death that floated across the river. And then they appeared, hundreds of them, running to the bridge to find that it really had been cut and it was not just some cruel joke being played upon them. More emerged on the shoreline along half a mile to either side of the useless structure as fires grew behind them so that a thick grey pall hung over the town as if put there by the gods so as to shield their eyes from the atrocities happening below. And Vespasian could see that what was happening below was truly terrible as the Iceni flooded in their hundreds through the streets and buildings down to the shore and trapped thousands of the populace between them and the river so that the massacre could really get under way.

Pitiless they were as they turned the waters of the Tamesis red.

In their thousands the Iceni butchered the citizens of Londinium, regardless of age or sex. Novel ways they found to massacre, so that it would not become too repetitive for them. Vespasian watched with macabre curiosity as they nailed children to the bridge's upright supports, hung old men from its beams, sliced off women's breasts before impaling them on the water's edge; they disembowelled, ran-through, bludgeoned, severed, strangled, flayed, hacked, ripped out hearts and then decapitated at will in an orgy of death that even the most avid fan of gladiatorial combat in the circus could not, for one moment, have imagined.

The few who could swim managed to save themselves by taking to the river, others who could not tried anyway and drowned in the attempt for the tide was nearly at full height. Many chose this death in preference but the majority lacked the necessary strength to end their own lives and, instead, died screaming on the vengeful blades of the Iceni. As the piles of heads and hearts grew and grew so did the fires in the town strengthen, driving even more victims from their hiding places down to the shore that soon became the only place safe from the conflagration, for Boudicca had surrounded the entire town with the best part of her hordes so that none could escape by any other way. But death waited for them there as sure as it did in a cellar beneath the inferno and, for what seemed to be endless time, Vespasian and his companions watched the horror unfold on the north bank. Silent and grim they were, unable to take their eyes from the slaughter as the warriors of the Iceni stained themselves red with the blood of the Roman citizens of Londinium. For a whole mile along the river frontage of the town, red monsters roamed, killing at will, knowing that they would be punished for what they had done, for Rome would not forgive so great an outrage, so better, therefore, to make the crime as great as possible. And that they achieved in a spectacular manner and by the time the four transport vessels, under full oars, appeared around the river bend Vespasian had seen more death in one day than he felt he had ever seen in his whole life; he gazed at the ships for a while unable to register what they were and their significance, so full was his mind with the images and sounds of brutal murder.

'Cavalry transports,' Vespasian said eventually.

'What?' Magnus asked vaguely, unable to tear his eyes away from a screaming, naked girl as she sank lower and lower onto the upright stake between her legs.

Vespasian repeated himself.

Magnus turned his head as the girl lost her struggle against gravity. 'So they are; what are they doing here?'

'Don't you see? They must be the first part of the reinforcements from the mainland. I sent the messages to Germania Inferior and Gallia Belgica five days ago; two days to get there, a day to react and then two days to get back. Come on.' Vespasian began to walk at pace east, towards the ships that had begun to steer towards the south bank now that the crew had seen the situation in Londinium.

For half a mile they walked until the ships were less than a hundred paces away and then they hailed them, proclaiming their Roman citizenship across the water that even here bore the unmistakeable hue of blood. But there was no need to stress who they were for they were recognised; the lead ship veered towards them and in the bow Vespasian saw Caenis standing between Sabinus and another man in the uniform of a military tribune, his helmet resplendent with its red horsetail plume.

As the ship backed oars and came to a gradual stop, twenty paces from the shore, the tribune took off his helmet.

'Hello, Father,' said Titus.

CHAPTER XVI

'SCRIBONIUS RUFUS, THE Governor of Germania Inferior, allowed me to come with half an ala of Batavian auxiliary cavalry,' Titus explained as he helped Vespasian aboard. Down the centre of the deck the hold was not covered over and it was filled with horses; their riders stood on the starboard rail watching Londinium burn. 'He only granted that favour because I'm your son; he's sent a letter to the Emperor asking permission to send more and it will, obviously, be at least fourteen days before he can expect the reply.'

'The province may well be lost by then and every Roman butchered,' Vespasian said as he landed on the deck; he indicated to the massacre upstream. 'Just look at it.'

'I know; we were in Camulodunum yesterday; there was no one left alive and not a complete building left intact. The Temple of Claudius had been stormed and everyone holding out in there massacred.'

Vespasian embraced his son.

Caenis kissed Vespasian as he let Titus go. 'Titus came across us a few miles back; we'd had a terrible time fighting the tide both yesterday morning and this morning.'

Vespasian returned her kiss. 'I'm glad to see you safe, my love.'

'Why aren't you with Cerialis?' Sabinus asked, scratching at his stubble as Magnus began supervising the lifting of Castor and Pollux aboard; there were many volunteers to help Caenis' girls and only Hormus seemed to be without aid.

'Because his legion was wiped out yesterday morning.'

'Wiped out?'

'Pretty much so; all but the cavalry. Cerialis got away with them back to his camp and Magnus and I came to warn Paulinus here but there wasn't much time to do anything because Boudicca has moved with frightening speed. He had to abandon Londinium and go north to tempt her into a battle in a place where her numbers will not be so significant. If we're to join him we need to get upriver, otherwise we'll find the rebels between us and Paulinus; and I was expecting to do it in a small fishing boat which could have slipped under the bridge on the southern side and not have to go through the gap.'

They all looked at the gap in the bridge; where the four piles had been torn down there was just enough room for a ship to pass through but, above on the remains of the north side of the bridge, the Iceni were rampant and would be able to hurl weapons and fire down on them as they negotiated the passage.

'Ah!' Titus exclaimed. 'This is going to take careful timing. Jorik!'

An auxiliary decurion, young for his rank, stepped forward and saluted. 'Your orders, sir?' His Latin was accented in the manner that Vespasian recognised from his last dealings with the Batavians almost twenty years previously.

'Have the lads fill all the buckets on board with water then put blankets and anything else that might help to protect them on the horses' backs and relay that to the turmae on the other three ships.'

Jorik saluted and strode off.

Titus took another look at the gap. 'Right. I'm going to speak to our trierarchus.'

The approach of four Roman vessels had not gone unnoticed, even by the most blood-crazed of the Iceni, and, as they neared the gap with the stroke-masters' shrill pipes sounding a fast beat, many of the red-stained apparitions gathered on the bridge, well aware of the opportunity that was going to present itself should the ships be foolish enough to try for the gap.

'Ramming speed!' the trierarchus shouted from his position between the steering-oars.

The stroke increased to the fastest possible rate, maintainable only for a couple of hundred pulls.

On went the four ships in single file, headed straight for the gap, a hundred paces between each of them; on their decks knelt the sixty-four troopers of the two turmae they each carried, shields poised, javelins in right hands and a spare grasped in their shield hand.

The first arrows from the bridge slammed into the bow with vibrating reports and slingshot fizzed through the air and thwacked into the hull; on the shore the massacre continued with groups of victims now herded together, many accepting their fate, dully awaiting the inevitable as the warriors despatched them in batches with cold-blooded, methodical efficiency. Behind them the town burnt pumping thick smoke into the already laden sky.

The ships powered on and the missile hits increased, juddering into deck and shields and clinking off helms; in the hold the horses skitted, their nerves taut.

Fifty paces out, forty, thirty. Javelins began to hail down; a horse bucked and screeched with a sleek missile embedded in its rump. Panic spread amongst its neighbours to either side.

Twenty paces.

'Loose!' shouted Titus.

The troopers jumped to their feet, hurling their javelins in one fluid movement at the bridge and then, without pause, let fly with the second; many of the scores of missiles hit home, punching men back or sending them howling into the river below.

Ten paces.

'Oars!' the trierarchus roared.

With remarkable precision all sixty oars were brought inboard and the vessel glided on into the gap as missiles, fire and the mutilated bodies of the dead were hurled down onto the deck.

Shieldless, Vespasian crouched in the lee of the mast, his arms around Caenis, protecting her. A couple of the more reckless warriors jumped down onto the ship but were despatched as they tried to regain their footing. Half a dozen troopers dashed around with buckets, dousing flames before they could take hold. A trooper fell back, a javelin in his eye, the point, bloodied and brained, protruding out of the back of his helmet. A scream as another was crushed under the dead weight of a headless cadaver. More burning timber was hurled down and just above head height part of the bridge's supports had caught fire.

Another hail of missiles from above and two more deaths, skewered to the deck, and then it stopped, suddenly. They were through and the warriors had turned their attention to the next ship.

Vespasian took his arms from around Caenis. 'Are you all right, my love?'

She looked about and then back at the bridge as the order to reset the oars was shouted. 'Yes, I'm fine.'

'Jorik!' Titus shouted. 'Calm the horses and then get this mess cleared up. I've never seen such an untidy deck; what are you thinking of?'

The decurion grinned and saluted. 'Yes, sir!'

'He's got a good way with his men,' Caenis commented.

Vespasian nodded thoughtfully. 'I was just thinking that myself.'

Through came the next ship, its deck smouldering and stuck full of embedded arrows and javelins; and then the third appeared through what was now becoming thick smoke as the fire in the bridge supports had strengthened and it would only be a matter of time before what was left of the northern section of the bridge would collapse into the river and likely block it. Beyond the smoke the fourth ship could not be seen and Vespasian waited with drawn breath for its outline to materialise.

'Come on,' Titus urged in a tight whisper, peering into the pall as their ship gradually increased its speed now that it made its way upriver.

'There she is,' Vespasian said with relief as the bow of the vessel broke through the smoke.

But the further it came through the more it became obvious that all was not as it should be: the deck was a mass of combative figures all engaged in dispersed fights, some single duels and others in groups. There was no formation as the Britannic warriors had jumped, en masse, onto the deck as the ship had passed through the gap beneath them, so that they covered its full length. Fire had taken a firm hold amidships as the troopers were too busy trying to repel boarders to deal with it.

The oars were spread and the stroke began as the fighting grew in intensity in proportion to the fire.

In the chaos and thickening smoke it was impossible to make out who was getting the upper hand. Bodies fell to the deck or tumbled over the rail to bounce off the oars and down into the river. The clash of weapons, shrieks of agony and the bestial screeching of panicking horses drifted across the water, louder even than the clamour of the massacre that still continued on the shore, this side of the bridge. On the four ships went with the battle still raging in the rearmost; and then suddenly it slewed to the starboard as the larboard oars fouled and then were dropped. The fire had burnt through the deck and red-hot timbers were falling onto the rowers. The starboard oars ceased rowing and figures could be seen clambering out of the oar-ports. Above them, on the deck the fire had grown in intensity, fed by the sizzling bodies of the fallen.

The third ship had turned, ready to pick up survivors as the oarsmen, clad only in their tunics, thrashed in the water; those who could swam towards the returning ship, others just cried choking prayers to their gods as they tried to pull oars out of the floundering vessel in the hope that they would float well enough to support their weight.

The fighting had suddenly ceased on the deck as both sides realised that the ship was doomed. The horses had realised it too and their terrified screeching rose in intensity as the gate at the top of the ramp to the hold was hauled open. Up they streamed onto the deck and then, seeing the flames, made the easy choice of clearing the rail; the first few crashed into oars, breaking them off and clearing the way for their fellows behind as, with mighty splashes, they hit the water. With them came their riders, expert swimmers as Vespasian knew from the early days of the invasion when Aulus Plautus had used Batavians to swim a river in order to take a hill; a feat they had accomplished despite being in full armour. Man and beast now swam together, making for the south bank and relative safety as the Britons left on the burning deck now faced a choice between immolation and taking their chances in the river; in they went as the rescue ship neared. Vengeful troopers hurled javelins at the floundering warriors, picking them off with ease as others reached down with boat hooks to haul rowers to safety.

'They'll be able to keep pace with us on the south bank,' Vespasian said as he and Titus watched the forty or so surviving troopers swimming to safety with their mounts. 'If I remember rightly the terrain is mainly flat. They can swim over to us when we land on the north bank.'

Titus looked over his shoulder at the north bank; the fire raged in all parts of the town and on the shore bloody murder was still being done, but the ships were now pulling away from the carnage and were in full view of the main part of Boudicca's army camped outside Londinium, sealing off all chance of escape. 'I believe that'll be harder than you think, Father.'

Vespasian turned; a large war band of warriors, over three hundred of them, all mounted on their shaggy ponies had detached itself from the main army and was now keeping pace with the ships. 'Ah! I see. It looks as if they want to discourage us from landing on the northern bank.'

'In which case we'll oblige them.'

The horses' hoofs made a hollow clatter as they were led down the ramp onto the southern shore and Vespasian was certain that it would be audible in the night air to the Britons if they were indeed just over a quarter of a mile away on the north bank. But no one knew for sure whether they were or not.

Titus had ordered the ships to press on under sail and oars as fast as the exhausted rowers could manage for as long as possible in order to tire the Britons' ponies as they struggled to keep up. Then, as dusk fell, he ordered the oars in so that the vessels carried on under sail in relative silence; with no lights burning and staying as far as possible from the northern bank, the ships were almost invisible in the night with thick cloud overhead. Sharp-eyed lookouts were stationed in the bows but the river was wide and the speed of the ships under sail slow. For five hours of the night they had edged forward in silence with no idea whether or not the Britons still tracked them until Titus ordered the disembarkation.

'You and your girls are going to have to stay on the ship, my love,' Vespasian said to Caenis as the last few horses were led down the gangplank.

'I know,' Caenis replied, taking his arm. 'There is no way that I'll be able to swim the river, even if I'm holding onto a horse's saddle.'

'It's not so much that; we could find a way of getting you across.'

'A woman's place is not in a battle?'

'What do you think?'

'I think Boudicca might have a different opinion on the subject. But I saw enough in Camulodunum to know that I don't want to see more so I won't argue this time.' She grinned up at him. 'Besides, I've killed my man. What are the ships going to do?'

'They'll wait until the Britons pull out of Londinium and then sail back through the bridge and on to Germania Inferior. That's the reason why you can't come with us: I need you to go to Germania Inferior and emphasise the gravity of the situation here to Governor Rufus; your eyewitness account may be the difference between him waiting for orders from Rome or acting on his own initiative. It's so vitally important that you make him do that, my love, if we're to stand any chance of retrieving the situation.'

'Now, that is something I can do, if he's prepared to listen to a woman's assessment of a military situation.'

'He'd better for all our sakes. Even if Paulinus does manage to defeat Boudicca in one set-piece battle we'd still find ourselves in a precarious position in a partially conquered and restless province with a population that has now witnessed the destruction of a legion and knows that it could be done again. We need reinforcements soon and the nearest legions are on the Rhenus. You must make him act.'

'I'll do my best.'

'I'm sure you will; I've seen how persuasive you can be with Burrus. I've ordered Hormus to stay with you for protection; he can be very handy if he needs to be. I'll see you in Germania Inferior once this business is done and we can get back to Rome.'

'Why don't you come with me now? This is not your fight and surely Rufus would be more persuaded by your word rather than a woman's?'

'And not go to war with my son? What would he think of me?'

Caenis pursed her lips, shaking her head slowly. 'I hadn't looked at it that way; you're right, you have to go.' She stood on tiptoes and kissed his cheek. 'May Mars Victorious hold his hands over you; both of you.'

'Over us all, I pray. We're certainly going to need him to in the coming days.' He kissed her in return, full on the lips, and then followed the horses down onto the bank, praying that it was not to be their last.

Decurion Jorik issued a stream of quiet orders in the strangely harsh language of the Batavians that always made Vespasian think that they were trying to clear their throats mid-sentence. The troopers emptied their water-skins and then blew them up, tying the top in order to seal in the air so that they were left with a leather balloon which they then secured to their shield handles.

Vespasian had done the same and now stood next to his mount, one of the surplus from the fourth ship, the survivors of which had rejoined them as they disembarked. Another quiet order and then, holding on to one of their saddle horns with the right hand and the buoyed shield in the other, Vespasian, Titus, Sabinus and Magnus, with an excited Castor and Pollux in tow, walked their mounts into the water along with the rest of the half ala.

'My bollocks have just disappeared,' Magnus complained as the water submerged the area in question.

Vespasian gritted his teeth and forced himself onward; as he got deeper he placed his shield on the surface, with the improvised buoyancy bag underneath, and lay on it still holding onto his mount. As the beast started to swim it pulled him along on his little raft and so, in the dark of the night, the half ala crossed the Tamesis in almost total silence.

However, the silence could not be maintained when they got to the northern bank as the horses emerged from the water and the troopers swung up onto their backs in a jangle of equipment and the metallic rings of drawing swords. The suddenness and intensity of the noise woke the sleeping Britons, who had, indeed, managed to track them. But newly waken men are easily confused and the sight of more than two hundred cavalry horses surging from the river, water exploding about their hoofs and flowing from their manes and tails, in a line as if they had galloped along the riverbed, was too much for the Britons' dulled minds to comprehend; as the throat of the first man to his feet was sliced open, they still could not fully understand what they were facing.

Howling the war cries of their ancestors, now that silence was not an issue, the Batavian troopers set about the rousing warriors, giving them no time to arm themselves or to organise a defence, and with blade, point and hoof they brought death to those who would have killed them. Vespasian worked his mount and sword in unison, turning and slashing as panic quickly spread through the Britons and they began to flee rather than face these horsemen of the deep. And as they ran the horsemen followed, sending them to the afterlife bearing the shame of a wound to the back. So with the few surviving warriors scattered and the ponies sent bolting, the Batavian half ala headed north, without fear of pursuit, to join Governor Paulinus for his desperate stand against the masses of Boudicca.

For the remainder of the night they pressed on mainly at a walk, bearing, as far as they could judge, directly north on Sabinus' suggestion as it had been this part of the province that he had been responsible for subduing with the XIIII Gemina in the first years of the invasion. However, navigation in the starless night had proved reasonably simple: all they had to do was to keep the orange glow in the sky to their east; Londinium still burnt. By the time the sun crested the eastern horizon, they had reached the road running west to Calleva and were a dozen or so miles north of the river and twenty west of Londinium. But even at that distance, as the light grew, so did the clarity of the pillar of smoke climbing to the sky from the ruins of the town, backlit by the dawn sun, glowing with the same hue as the flames that produced it.

The growing light also revealed another unusual sight: the country was alive with people, either in family units, hoping that their small size would render them less visible, or in larger groups bound together in the belief that safety would lie in numbers. All were heading for the Calleva road and then following it into the southwest, away from the storm that had roared out of the east, for rumour did not need to travel by word of mouth now that the smoke, rising for all to see from the stricken town, proclaimed the hatred that approached.

'It would seem that the whole south of the island is on the move,' Titus observed as he surveyed the countryside speckled with refugees, many driving their livestock before them.

Vespasian winced as he shifted his sore backside in the saddle. 'Are you surprised after what you saw in Londinium and Camulodunum?'

'But where are they going?'

'They probably don't know themselves; anywhere where Boudicca isn't would be enough for me were I in their place.'

'As for us,' Sabinus said, taking no interest in the refugees, 'if we carry on heading directly north we should hit the northwest road in about thirty miles, soon after it's passed through Verulamium. Paulinus' choice of ground must be somewhere where the road passes through hill-country just before Veronae. If we keep moving we should be there in two or three days.'

With no one other than Sabinus having any experience of this part of the province they accepted his assessment and, with tiredness eating away at them, pushed on, pleased to put themselves into Sabinus' hands and not to have to make any decisions.

It was after they had been travelling up the northwest road for a couple of hours the following day, keeping just to the side of it due to the carts and wagons fleeing the rampaging Iceni, that there came a moan, like a communal sharing of grief, from the refugees as many of them halted and turned to face back down in the direction whence they had come.

Vespasian looked behind as Titus halted the half ala. It was unmistakeable: although not yet as large as the one that had risen from Londinium, it was a column of smoke, grey and growing fatter from the combustion feeding it below.

'Verulamium,' Sabinus muttered.

Vespasian wondered how many people had elected to stay with their property rather than follow the example of the thousands on the road. 'How far is that from Londinium?'

'About twenty miles.'

Vespasian did a rough mental calculation. 'She must have pulled her army out from Londinium yesterday at dawn to have got there by now. She's moving as fast as she possibly can with that huge host.'

'She has to,' Titus said, turning away from the macabre sight. 'How else can she feed them?'

Vespasian nodded thoughtfully, pleased with his son's logic. 'That may be our best weapon against her.'

With a hand signal, Titus restarted the column and they carried on their journey northwest in search of the army of Suetonius Paulinus.

'And you say that the road is still clogged with refugees?' Governor Paulinus asked, pacing to and fro in front of a map set on a board, hanging from one of the posts supporting the massive leather tent that was the XIIII Gemina's campaign praetorium.

'Not clogged, but busy,' Vespasian replied. 'Most of them were continuing up to Veronae and beyond.'

'Only about a fifth left it following your trail,' Sabinus said.

'That should be enough,' Paulinus stated, stopping to consult the map yet again, and then looked over to Cogidubnus, seated on a campaign chair gnawing a chicken leg. 'Do you think she'll know yet that I didn't retreat to Veronae but left the road early?'

'She has her spies,' the King replied through a mouthful.

'I suppose it doesn't matter if she does or doesn't, just as long as there's a goodly number of refugees that she can follow to lead her here.' He turned abruptly and addressed Titus. 'You said just now in your report that you saw the smoke from Verulamium at the beginning of the third hour of yesterday?'

'That's correct, sir.'

Paulinus contemplated the information for a few moments. 'It's forty miles from there to here, so assuming that she lets her men have their fun for the remainder of the day and overnight, she would have pulled out this morning. A disorganised rabble like that won't build camps, they'll just sleep where they drop, so if she marches eight hours a day and spends four foraging, she'll—'

'With respect, sir, she won't,' Vespasian interjected.

Paulinus looked about to shout but then controlled himself. 'What won't she do?'

'She won't march eight hours a day; she'll do twelve and won't stop to forage.'

'What makes you think that, senator?'

'I saw the size of her army at Camulodunum, sir; a conservative estimate would have put it at sixty thousand with at least the same again of families. It was the whole Iceni nation on the move, not just the warriors. Now, thanks to Paelignus, the Trinovantes have joined them; I saw her army again as we sailed past Londinium and it can now only be described as monstrously huge, almost double the original size. She can't feed them and the countryside can't support them; they have to rely on what they bring with them. They burnt Camulodunum and Londinium before they had time to loot them properly for food and I imagine that they did the same with Verulamium; and what with the whole countryside fleeing before her taking all their supplies and livestock with them, well? What's the point in stopping for four hours a day to collect what isn't there?'

Paulinus stroked his chin; his eyes widened. 'You're right, Vespasian: she has to get this over as quickly as possible so that she can disband. She has to force-march, to catch us quick before her warriors start to get too hungry.'

'Exactly, sir; so instead she'll opt for making them tired. She'll march before dawn and carry on until at least sunset.'

A smile crept onto Paulinus' face. 'Minerva's crusted minge, you're right. She'll be here tomorrow evening and her men will be exhausted; I'll make sure that mine aren't.'

The XIIII Gemina and the two cohorts of the XX legion plus their auxiliaries amounted to a little over ten thousand men, giving a frontage of just over half a mile if deployed eight deep, and Vespasian could understand exactly why Paulinus had chosen this ground: it was a sloping valley between two very steep hills that, at the opening, were a mile and a half apart but then the gap gradually closed, as the ground rose, until they converged. Just before their junction, Paulinus had built his fortified camp on the eaves of a thick forest that sealed the valley and would preclude any rear assault, just as it would prevent any retreat; it also provided shelter for the thousands of refugees that had sought the protection of the army, for Paulinus would not allow them in the camp. All in all the valley was a place where ten thousand men could stand a chance of defeating many times their number as they were funnelled uphill towards them, or die in the attempt.

What it was not, however, was a field for cavalry because Paulinus' strategy was based on infantry standing shoulder to shoulder and killing the man in front of them again and again until there were none left. To that end he had, during the time remaining to him before Boudicca's arrival, ordered the ground for a couple of hundred paces in front of where the Romans would stand to be strewn with stones and tree branches to disable the Britannic chariotry and their small number of cavalry. This had been done on a cohort by cohort rotation basis so that at any one time most of the army was resting or eating.

'There's no way that I'm going to fight mounted,' Magnus said after Titus had told him, Vespasian, Sabinus and Cogidubnus the news that his Batavians and the rest of the cavalry were to act as reinforcements for the infantry line, having come from Paulinus' briefing the following afternoon.

'I didn't think you'd be fighting at all,' Vespasian said, 'considering your age, that is.'

'Now don't you start mocking me again, sir; there's plenty of fight and fuck left in me yet.'

'You're seventy; you should be dead.'

'Well, perhaps tomorrow I'll get the chance to put that right. Anyway, I wasn't thinking of getting nice and snug in the front rank; I'll leave that pleasure to the younger, keener lads. I thought that somewhere near the rear would suit me fine; you know, do some pushing on the back of the man in front of me, a bit of finishing off the wounded as we go forward, give Castor and Pollux a chance for some nice breakfast and all that sort of thing. Nothing too strenuous to start off with as I'm sure there'll be plenty to go round and I'd rather have my share when they're a bit less fresh, if you take my meaning?'

'I'm sure you'll get as many of them as you can manage,' Sabinus said, pointing to the mouth of the valley.

Cogidubnus gave a low whistle. 'More in fact than you might want, my friend.'

Vespasian, Magnus and Titus looked up to where Sabinus had indicated: there, in the distance, a black shadow was materialising, extending across the complete mile and a half width of the valley's opening.

Boudicca had, indeed, travelled fast and had, as she saw it, cornered Paulinus with her speed. She led the Iceni and Trinovantes nations onto the ground of Paulinus' choosing with thoughts only of victory, never of defeat.

CHAPTER XVII

For the last two hours of daylight the Romans watched the Britons arrive and, even as the sun fell, there was no sign of an end to the black shadow creeping up towards them.

Immediately the sighting had been reported to Paulinus the *cornu,* the horn used for signalling on the field of battle, had sounded and the entire army had formed up across the valley. But Boudicca was not in a position to attack straightaway upon arrival as her army was so spread out; she halted her chariot a half mile from the Roman line and there her army began to build their cooking fires and erect what small amount of tentage they had. As night fell, Paulinus withdrew to his camp and the valley lit up with thousands of points of firelight as if it were a giant mirror reflecting the firmament above.

An hour before dawn the soldiers of Rome, having slept well and breakfasted on hot food, marched out of their camp and reformed the line. As the light grew, the Britannic warriors saw Paulinus' army waiting for them, a short thin line compared to their horde's massive bulk, and they laughed as they smeared their war-patterns over chests and legs and spiked their hair with lime. Those who had to go without breakfast, and there were many due to lack of supplies, did not complain or even mind as they knew that the whole business would be over within the hour as all they had to do was run up the hill and sweep the thin line of wood, flesh and metal away; and none in that immense host doubted their ability to do that.

'I'm starting to think that Caenis might have been right,' Vespasian said as the sun's rays revealed the size of the task they faced; his throat had just dried. 'Perhaps I should have gone back with her to Germania Inferior as this is not my fight.'

Titus, astride his horse next to him, reached over and put his hand on his father's shoulder. 'And let me face my first set-piece battle without the benefit of paternal advice, Father?'

'That was roughly the argument that I used with her.'

'Well, I wish you hadn't,' Magnus grumbled, 'even Germania Magna, let alone Germania Inferior, sounds better than here at the moment.' He had relented about fighting mounted on account that it may well be less tiring on his knees; Castor and Pollux sat next to his horse, watching the confusing human spectacle with some interest.

'We'll be fine,' Sabinus assured them with uncharacteristic optimism, 'at least we're in the reserve line.'

Magnus looked left and then right to the only other three small units positioned behind the main line to plug any gaps. 'What there is of it.' Paulinus had used his three cavalry units as reserves and the Batavians were one of them; the legionary cavalry and an ala of Gallic cavalry that had been divided into two units were the others. Each had a little over two hundred paces of frontage to cover, or three and a half tightly formed cohorts; the Batavians were to the right of the centre behind the first three cohorts of the XIIII Gemina. 'Just over two hundred men to act as a relief for almost two thousand including the élite cohort.' Magnus hawked and spat to illustrate just what he thought of the situation.

'My men have the right wing,' Cogidubnus, who had ridden over to wish them luck, said. 'That's not going to be fun with the Iceni trying to get around our flank.'

Sabinus looked over to the right-hand hill. 'The hill's too steep.'

'Do you think that will stop them trying? You just think yourself lucky, Magnus, that you're not going to be used until later, if at all.'

Magnus did not look convinced. 'My point is that if we are used it will be in a very nasty situation where a breakthrough has occurred through a legionary cohort; and I can tell you that if something punches a gap in the first cohort it'll take a lot more than a couple of hundred cavalry to stop it.'

Vespasian had to concede that Magnus had a point and looked nervously at the seemingly limitless body of men that now approached with menacing intent. Deep they were and their limit could only be judged by the multitude of wagons in the distance, halfway down the valley, stretching from one hill to the other, where their families waited to watch their menfolk avenge the insult to the women of the Iceni.

In the centre of the horde stood Boudicca in her chariot; her daughters, brandishing their long knives, walked next to it with Myrddin and a dozen more of the filthy, matted creatures. There were no other chariots in evidence; scouting parties in the night had evidently found the obstacles deterring them. At two hundred paces out, Boudicca punched her spear, two handed, above her head and they stopped in a shambolic manner and raised a roar to the heavens.

In silence the Romans watched, each man busy with his own thoughts, envisaging just how he was going to get through this day, as Boudicca's chariot turned ninety degrees and started to travel along the front of the haphazard Britannic line. The roar stopped and she began to address her people in her harsh and loud masculine voice that carried far over the field.

'What's she saying?' Vespasian asked Cogidubnus.

'She's talking in their uncouth dialect, but from what I can make out she's saying that it is normal for Britons to fight under the command of a woman but she's not seeking vengeance for her kingdom or possessions taken from her as a woman descended from great ancestors. No, she seeks it as one of the people, for her liberty lost, for the unjust flogging she received and for the rape of her daughters. If the Romans, in their cupidity, cannot even let our bodies go undefiled, then why should they be expected to display moderation as their rule goes on, when they have behaved towards us in this fashion at the very outset?' Cogidubnus stopped translating as he cocked an ear.

'Well?' Vespasian asked.

Cogidubnus put his hand up signalling that he was listening.

Eventually the Queen finished and from beneath her cloak she produced a hare; she set it on the ground and it immediately ran towards the Roman line. There began a series of mighty roars; the omen was good.

'That was very eloquent, what she said,' Cogidubnus remarked. 'Tell us.'

'It was a good speech and would have got them roused; it was something like this in translation: "But, to speak the plain truth, it is we who have made ourselves responsible for all that has befallen us, in that we allowed Rome to set foot on this island in the first place and didn't expel them at once as we did their famous Julius Caesar, and in that we did not deal with them while they were still far away as we dealt with Gaius Caligula and made even the attempt to sail here a formidable challenge. As a consequence, although we inhabit so large an island, or rather a continent, one might say, that's encircled by the sea, and although we possess a world of our own and are separated by the ocean from all the rest of mankind so that we believe we dwell on a different earth and under a different sky, we have, notwithstanding all this, been despised and trampled underfoot by men who know nothing else than how to secure gain. They have brought with them laws that take precedence over our customs, the tax-farmers who bleed us dry and then the odious bankers who pretend to offer wealth with one hand but give poverty with the other in order to enrich themselves without a care for the consequences. However, even at this late day, though we have not done so before, let us, my countrymen and friends and kinsmen – for I consider you all kinsmen, seeing that we inhabit a single island and are called by one common name – let us, I say, do our duty while we still remember what freedom is, that we may leave to our children not only its name but also its reality. For, if we utterly forget the happy state in which we were born and bred, what will they do, reared in bondage to our eternal shame?" Good stuff I'd say; it's just a pity that it's so misguided.'

'I'd say she'd made a few reasonable points,' Magnus said, tugging hard on Castor and Pollux's leads as they reacted enthusiastically to the clamour coming from the Britons. 'From what I can make out this whole thing has been caused by Seneca's, the Cloelius Brothers' and the other Londinium bankers' greed. Not that greed is a bad thing, mind you, it's just when you fuck off a whole nation rather than a few rivals it ain't so clever.'

Vespasian, despite all the atrocities he had witnessed, was forced to agree. 'But don't forget Decianus as well as the bankers.'

'Procurators? Bankers? What the fuck's the difference? It's all about getting rich on other people's wealth, which, as I say, is no bad thing until … well.' He gestured to everything around. 'Well, something like this happens and I happen to get caught up in it.'

Vespasian's thoughts on the subject were cut off by Paulinus addressing his troops from horseback.

'Soldiers of Rome!' Paulinus declaimed in the high voice favoured for speeches to large audiences. 'I know your valour for together we have recently subdued the Isle of Mona. You will not fear this horde, this rabble, made up, as it is, of more women, children and old men rather than fighting-fit warriors; and of those warriors many seem to be young men of a new generation who have never been tried before in battle. You have heard what outrages these savages have committed against us; indeed, you have even witnessed some of them. Choose, then, whether you wish to suffer the same treatment yourselves, as our comrades have suffered, and to be driven out of Britannia entirely; or, by achieving victory here today, avenging those who have perished and, at the same time, display to all others who would take up arms against us an example of the inevitable severity with which we deal with rebellion. For my part, I'm sure that victory will be ours; first, because the gods are our allies; and second, because courage is our heritage, since we Romans have triumphed over all mankind by our valour. And let us not forget we have defeated and subdued these very men who are now arrayed against us so they are not antagonists, but our slaves, whom we conquered even when they were free and independent. Now, one word of warning, soldiers of Rome: if the outcome should prove contrary to our hope – and I will not deny the possibility – it would be better for us to fall fighting bravely than to be captured and impaled, or to look upon our own entrails cut from our bodies, or to be spitted on red-hot skewers, or to perish, screaming in boiling water or any other manner of torments these savages enjoy inflicting on civilised men. Let us, therefore, either win or die on this ground. You all know your places at the sound of the first cornu signal. So, soldiers of Rome, are you ready for war?'

As the reply was roared back and the question re-asked, Vespasian was relieved that Cogidubnus' men were right to the far side of the field and would probably not have been able to hear all that well Paulinus implying that they were Rome's slaves. Judging by the shadow that passed over the Britannic King's face, Cogidubnus was not impressed by Paulinus' rallying speech. 'I'll return to my cohorts, and see if they're still in the mood for killing their fellow countrymen, as Boudicca put it.'

'It was tactless of Paulinus,' Vespasian affirmed.

'Tactless? Of course it was tactless; it was pure Roman.'

Vespasian gripped Cogidubnus' forearm. 'May your gods hold their hands over you, my friend.'

Cogidubnus touched the four-spoked wheel of Taranis that hung on a chain about his neck. 'My gods will be busy today; they have to answer prayers from both sides.'

And then the carnyxes blared.

Discordant barks filled the air, issuing from the animal heads of the tall, upright horns that sprouted from the Britannic host; bronze wild boar, ram, bull or wolf figures mounted on poles, the standards of individual war bands, were shaken above the heads of their followers, as well as wheels of Taranis, coiled serpents and leaping hares. Boudicca made one more length of the Britannic front, holding out her spear so that it rattled along the tips of the weapons or their shafts held up to her for her blessing in a metallic and wooden clatter that gave percussion to the carnyxes' cacophony.

By the time she had returned to her place in the centre, the hundred thousand plus horde of warriors was at fighting pitch, urging each other on to great deeds and stories of valour. Behind them, their families, in similar numbers, roared on their menfolk, eager to see the field running with Roman blood. With one last flourish of her spear above her head, Boudicca brought it down and pointed it at the heart of the Roman line; her warriors took their first steps forward, gradually accelerating, jumping the obstacles, until they were at a run.

And then the cornu rumbled.

Suddenly the cohorts all along the line sprang into action.

'What the fuck are they up to?' Magnus exclaimed.

Vespasian, Sabinus and Titus were equally nonplussed.

Files of legionaries from the outsides of each cohort raced to its middle, gradually building it up, evenly, so that protrusions of men appeared, lessening until at the tip there was the primus pilus of the cohort, acting as the biting point of the wedge. The Roman line had transformed itself into a series of sharp teeth in the time it had taken the warriors to cover half the separating distance.

Each primus pilus, resplendent with transverse horsehair plumes across their helms, raised their sword in the air and looked along the line to their superior at the apex of the first cohort. Down came the legion's senior centurion's sword arm; his brother officers followed. In unison, ten thousand shields were struck by pila – just once; sudden. The resulting crack thundered down the valley as if Jupiter himself had cast a mighty bolt along the length of the field. Warriors deep within the crush who could not see its source looked up to the sky as the shock of the noise made them falter in their step. The carnyxes wavered for a couple of beats and almost, for an instant, there was silence.

And that silence remained on the Roman side; mute and grim were the wedges of legionaries as they watched, with hardened eyes, their foes regain their steel and their pace and their volume.

'Why weren't we a party to that little trick?' Titus asked.

'Spooking the enemy evidently isn't a privilege extended to reserve formations in Paulinus' army,' Vespasian hazarded, his nervousness dissipating, having witnessed more than a hundred thousand men falter.

Paulinus, seated upon his horse, with his staff, to the rear of the first cohort, nodded to the cornicern stationed near him; the man pressed his lips to the mouthpiece and issued a two-note rumble that, because of its booming depth, carried beneath the clamour approaching. The signal was repeated throughout the army and, as the Britannic mass came to within fifty paces of the Roman teeth, the legionaries in the front four ranks and down the sides of the wedges stamped their left feet forward and pulled their pilum-wielding right arms back, keeping their shields up as the javelin rain started to fall.

Vespasian watched Paulinus calculating distance in his head, thinking of all the times he had to do the same thing when he had been the legate of the II Augusta. He glanced back at the approaching horde. 'Three, two, one,' he muttered to himself. 'Now.'

Sure enough the cornu sounded and a black cloud of pila rose from the legionaries. It was not continuous because the rears of the wedges were not yet in range, but it was lethal. Lead-weighted iron shafts tore from the sky; at thirty paces out the warriors facing the thinning parts of the wedges were pounded backwards in explosions of blood, screaming, bodies arched and pierced, arms flailing, to crash into those behind, taking them down to entangle the feet of yet more following.

Indentations appeared along the Britannic front and, as they were filled, fifteen paces out, another dark hailstorm slammed into them, pulping faces, pinning shields and shield-arms to bellies, slicing into ribcages to explode out through backs in sprays of crimson that splattered the faces and torsos of the men behind the instant before they impaled themselves on the razor-sharp, protruding points. Down went hundreds more in the limb-thrashing agonies of death; many others were tripped or pulled to the ground, there to die trampled by so many feet that their bodies split open and their offal warmed the earth.

But what were hundreds or even thousands amongst the tens of thousands as Boudicca's army surged on, howling bare-toothed hate, swords and spears held high, their long moustaches flowing back in the wind of their haste?

With shoulders jammed into shields and heads hunched low, the legionaries braced themselves for the impact, sword in hand, blade protruding beyond shield-rim.

The pilum clouds now erupted from the rears of the wedges, pummelling down hundreds more, but still that made no difference.

And then the horde hit the leading centurions and flooded down the sides of the wedges so that it seemed to Vespasian, further up the slope looking down, that the wedges themselves were moving forward, penetrating the Britannic body with the ease of a needle into an eye.

But, as they pushed in up to the hilt, the wedges took the velocity out of the massed charge for the impacts were spread and the weight of more than one hundred thousand was dispelled so that what could have been a hammer blow that sent the Roman line reeling back did no more than bow it slightly. A massed grunting and groaning erupted from both sides as the strain shifted back and forth until equilibrium was settled. And it was at this point that the Roman war machine roared into action. Cocooned behind their shields, held firm against the shock of impact, the legionaries down each side of the wedges had room to wield their blades so that the teeth themselves sprang teeth. Swift and sure they worked them through the gaps between their shields and their comrades' next to them, slanted at the same angle of the wedge to present a smooth surface. Stab, pierce, twist left and right, withdraw again and again, no matter if they killed the same flesh twice or thrice as the grinding of the war machine continued.

Pressed together in the crush of the attack the Britannic warriors had not the room to wield their blades with the freedom that they relished in individual combat; they could do little more than hack, in downward strokes, with their long swords or jab, overarm, with spears at heads and shoulders. These, however, were protected by the shields of the legionaries behind them and the warriors did no more than scar the legion's emblem blazoned on boards or blunt their blades on bosses. And upright they died and upright they remained long after their deaths, oozing fluids as their cadavers were pierced again and again for want of fresher flesh, held fast by the press of the tens of thousands behind desiring only to sweep the Romans to their doom.

But the men of Paulinus' army had no intention of letting that be so; now they had absorbed the impact, now they had started to kill and feel the warmth of the blood and urine of their enemies splatter down their legs and onto their feet, now that their comrades around them still stood firm and fought as one, now that they knew that they had not been driven back by the headlong charge and now that they realised that there could not be another; now, because of all those factors, the men of Paulinus' army started to believe that they could triumph and that the field would end the day carpeted with the bodies of their foes and not their own. And so they doubled their efforts, not only now working their swords but punching also with their shield-bosses to clear away the upright, lolling dead and expose new targets. Down the corpses slithered, leaving trails of dark slime smeared on Roman shields; second rank legionaries stabbed into them in case a vestige of life remained in one, enough to punch a knife up into the groin of the man straddling them as, without any signal but rather from the collective consciousness of every component of the war machine, the Roman formation took a step forward.

Now it was with joy, not fear, that they worked their blades and Vespasian sucked in a lungful of air, realising that he had been holding his breath since the first contact a couple of hundred racing heartbeats ago. 'We can do this,' he said to no one in particular, and probably no one heard for the din of battle raged and no one looked at him because it was virtually impossible to tear eyes away from the wondrous sight just down the hill.

Vespasian glanced over at Paulinus; the Governor sat bolt upright in the saddle, both fists clenched, pulled tight to his stomach, his jaw jutted and his eyes staring so intently at his men as he willed them on that they seemed to be bursting from their sockets.

With another phenomenal effort, Paulinus' army took another step forward and the first signs that warriors in the forward ranks of the Britannic mass were having second thoughts about remaining in combat started to manifest themselves: individuals turned their heads to see if a way clear was possible, some here and there even tried to force their passage back, receiving wounds to their kidneys from the relentless swordwork of men who just wanted to kill in revenge for the fear that they had been made to feel by the sight of so vast an army.

On the Roman blades worked, sheened dark with blood and faeces, slicing into Boudicca's army, instilling terror where there had once been confidence. Whether Boudicca was aware of this or whether it was some other power who ordered it forward, Vespasian knew not; but what he was suddenly conscious of, as was every other man, friend or foe alike, was a cold dread approaching from the heart of the Britannic horde, a cold dread that he had felt before and it was close again. He looked up; dead centre between the tips on the first and second cohorts' wedges was a swirl in the enemy mass as warriors, despite the crush, shoved each other out of the way to make room for a group of filthy, matted beings surrounding Boudicca. Myrddin was coming at the call of the Queen and he had summoned his powers channelled from the dark gods of the indigenous people of this isle; gods for whom the great henges had been built long before the Celtic tribes' arrival with their druidical priests more than twenty-five generations before. Gods whose secrets the druids had rediscovered and whose powers, now, only the druids understood; and Boudicca had chosen to wield them.

Through the mass of warriors came the sacred band of druids surrounding the Queen, brandishing writhing serpents and symbols of the sun and moon, wailing invocations to the gods of the Celts and the darker gods of those before, adding fervour, as they progressed, to the warriors already in combat and a desire to engage in those who were not. Wherever they passed, the intensity of the fighting grew as they inspired the Britannic warriors, imbuing within them a new strength born out of the chill fear they had conjured. With Myrddin leading, they went in a straight line for he was heading for the weakest point at the centre of the Roman formation where two wedges segued together, a place where the line was only two men deep. It was a place, Vespasian knew, where Myrddin, inspiring the warriors around him, could cause the Roman army to be riven in two.

And Paulinus knew that too for he pulled his horse about and raced back to the waiting Batavians. 'Tribune,' he said, in a calm voice but edged with tension, to Titus as he pulled up, 'I need your men to reinforce that weak spot. My lads won't stand for long against Myrddin, they know of his terror from Mona, which is why we couldn't capture or kill him. But he can die like any other man and perhaps your boys have as good a chance as any having not yet learnt to fear him.'

Titus saluted and then looked down at the advancing druids now just twenty paces from the junction of the wedges. 'We'll do our best, sir.'

'We'll do more than that,' Sabinus said, his eyes locked on the cause of so much suffering, 'we'll take his heart and head.'

Doubt registered on Paulinus face. 'Do you know what you're up against, senator?'

'Yes; and the reason why I came back to this shithole was to have a chance of completing my unfinished business with him.'

Paulinus nodded and turned away.

Titus barked the order to advance at Jorik; the decurion repeated it in Batavian and the signaller blew a shrill note on his *lituus,* the long cavalry horn with an upturned end. The standard dipped and the cavalry unit moved forward at a walk.

Vespasian judged the distance between them and the crucial point. 'We need to hurry, Titus.'

'Sound the trot,' Titus ordered Jorik as they moved on down the hill.

A series of shrill notes quickened the Batavians' pace as Myrddin and Boudicca approached the join between the first and second cohorts; around them warriors fought with the abandonment of fanatics, pressing the legionaries hard, pushing them back, stretching the bow. Across the rest of the field the Romans still made progress, advancing step by step, thus making this push in the centre so much more likely to succeed as the line was being strained. On the far right there were signs of the Britannic warriors fleeing in large numbers as Cogidubnus' Regni and Atrebates auxiliaries triumphed against their fellow countrymen; but all that success would be for nought if the centre broke. Should that happen the entire army would soon be enveloped and then it would just be a matter of meticulous slaughter. And that was what Boudicca had realised; this, now that the initial charge had not swept the Romans away, was her only hope.

Vespasian felt his heart pumping as, with another blast of the *lituus*, their speed increased to a canter down the hill. Myrddin was less than fifty paces away and already the legionaries before him had started to give ground, so furious now was the assault by warriors inspired by his and Boudicca's presence.

As they came to twenty paces from the rearmost legionaries the line bowed even further so that they were now no longer shoulder to shoulder, working as one, but, rather, becoming isolated, a target for the individualistic combat so favoured by the Britons. The Roman formation was cracking and, with a chilling series of imprecations, Myrddin cast his serpents over the heads of his warriors and onto the wavering legionaries; and with them he cast the fear of his power, a cold power that cannot be used for good, and it froze the heart of all who felt it and the soldiers of Rome within its net either turned and ran or stood transfixed with fear to be cut down by merciless slashes as Boudicca screamed her followers on.

Britannic warriors now began to pour through the gap and turned left and right onto the rear of the legionaries to either side.

A shudder went through the first and second cohorts.

'Release and charge!' Titus screamed at the top of his voice and the two hundred troopers under his command thundered towards the breech, hurling their javelins at the densely packed flesh as they did, as more of the Iceni flooded through.

His javelin spent, Vespasian drew his sword and felt the cold fear of Myrddin creep towards his heart; he wanted nothing more than to turn and escape the dread that he induced but his mount carried him on, unmoved by fear of human gods. Thus every horse in the half ala carried the charge home, despite their riders' terror; they piled into the warriors and the Batavians forced themselves to use their swords. Down their blades flashed; Vespasian's arm jolted at the first impact, slicing through a collar-bone. To his left, Titus reared up his horse so that the beast's forelegs thrashed out, cracking a skull and snapping an arm. To his other side, Sabinus, leaning forward, hacked his way on, his hatred bare and overcoming the cold aura emanating from his target, now just ten paces away. Magnus, never one for mounted combat, had hung back with his dogs, waiting for a chance of work more to his liking. A bestial screech from next to him, as Vespasian cleaved open a baying man's helm, and Titus' horse reared up even further, a spear deep in its chest; upright it was in its agony and Titus clung to its mane but could not keep his seat. He slithered down the dying beast and hit the ground, feet first, just managing to dodge out of the way as the horse arced over and collapsed onto its back. Warriors, keen to take advantage of a dismounted officer, surged towards him as Vespasian desperately tried to turn his mount left, towards his son, but found himself having to defend to the right; a quick glance over his shoulder told him that Titus was struggling to hold off the attack; a sword swiped at neck height but Jorik forced his mount forward to take the blow on its shoulder. The beast went down, toppling its rider into the mass of warriors and blocking them from Titus, leaving Jorik to perish beneath the blades of the Iceni as the Batavians slogged forward.

Slashing and stabbing, the Batavians held their nerve and filled the gap as the legionaries, to either side, tuned to face the Iceni who had made it through and between them they began to grind the warriors down into the bloody meat of the arena floor.

But before them still stood Myrddin and no one dared approach him; even Sabinus as he cut down the last warrior between him and the druids, opening the man's face in a splash of blood and teeth, baulked at the prospect and pulled his horse about as Vespasian hacked his way to his brother's side. Myrddin stared hard at the brothers, eyes piercing, as his brethren kept up an atonal chant to their dark gods; recognition flooded onto his face followed by the joy of having hated enemies within one's power and Vespasian felt his limbs freeze as Myrddin turned his full attention onto the siblings. The druid raised his hand, pointing his finger at Vespasian, and screeched a sentence full of loathing; as he bayed the final syllables, lifting his face to the sky, a black streak shot through the air and clamped itself onto his exposed throat as another chomped onto his extended wrist. For, as with the horses,

Castor and Pollux felt no fear of gods conjured by men; no dread nor creeping cold paralysis; they saw only a threat to one of their humans and, with unquestioning canine loyalty, they went for that threat. Vespasian and Sabinus jumped from their mounts and ran to where the druid lay fighting the beasts off as, beyond him, the rest of the filthy creatures backed off at the combined sight of the chief of their order down and torn and then of more Batavian horsemen coming through the gap, now that the spell was broken. Pulling the dogs off, Vespasian and Sabinus looked down at the ravaged body, blood oozing from great wounds.

Myrddin's eyes flickered and then opened and Vespasian felt a faint voice calling him but he took no notice. 'Do it, brother.'

Sabinus did not need a second invitation. As he raised his sword, what was left of Myrddin's mouth twitched into a smile and his eyes told Vespasian that this meant nothing to him. Down the sword flashed and, with the wet and hollow crunch of a butcher's cleaver, it sliced through the gorge and the spinal column and struck off Myrddin's head, burying itself in the bloody ground below. For an instant all seemed still. Leaving his sword embedded, Sabinus grabbed the matted hair, lifted the severed head and screamed out 'Clementina!' over and over; as Boudicca and her warriors saw it, they despaired.

The men of the first and second cohorts began to wield their swords with renewed vigour as the warriors facing them lost heart by degrees. The men of Boudicca's household closed about her and the Queen disappeared back into the crush. Vespasian jumped back onto his horse and turned, looking towards the place he thought he had last seen Titus. Now there was just corpse-littered ground as the Batavian line had moved forward and was now past Vespasian, following up the surviving warriors who had been beaten back through the gap.

'He took my mount, if it's Titus you're looking for,' Magnus said, nonchalantly walking through the debris of battle as it still raged not twenty paces from him.

'It was; I saw him get unhorsed.'

'And I helped him get up again; he looked to be quite enjoying himself, from what I could see of his expression under all that blood. Pity about Jorik, though, he was a good lad. Ah! There they are.' Magnus bent down as Castor and Pollux came bounding up to him, slavering and licking the blood from their chops and furiously wagging their tails in evident self-satisfaction. 'Good boys, did you get the nasty druid, did you? Goooood work; I'm proud of you I am.' Magnus accepted their blood-tinged licks and ruffled their sticky coats as they wagged their tails, pleased at the praise.

Vespasian stared down at the incongruous scene and wondered for a moment if he was dreaming and there was not a battle of epic proportions taking place just a few paces away; then the reality of it became obvious with a mighty cheer from Roman lungs as the Britannic line crumbled and panic, mixed with shame, began to set in to the fleeing warriors. 'Did you just ask your dogs if they got Myrddin?'

'I did.'

'You set them onto him, then?'

'Of course I did. I came down with the charge, hanging about at the back, but, as you know, I just don't hold with fighting mounted, it ain't natural, and I can't work up an appetite for it. Anyway, I saw Titus go down so I thought he might as well have my horse seeing as I wasn't really putting it to good use and me and the boys could wander along on foot, just behind you and Sabinus, bringing mercy to Boudicca's wounded, if you take my meaning?' Magnus pulled a particularly fine silver torque from his belt. 'I saw this just after I noticed that mess Myrddin start to take an interest in you so I sent the boys to help you out whilst I helped the former owner of this fine piece become dead.'

Vespasian, despite himself and all that was going on around him, found himself laughing.

'Senator, we haven't got time for idle conversation and amusing anecdotes,' Paulinus said, pulling up his horse, his face a study in relief. He smiled and proffered his forearm. 'You and your brother have my thanks for everything you've done, not least plugging that gap and taking Myrddin's head.'

Vespasian grasped the arm as Sabinus drew up, Myrddin's head tied to his saddle.

'There's one more piece of business, other than the massacre of as many of these savages as possible.'

'Boudicca?'

'I want her alive. Ask your son to get her for me.'

'We'll both go,' Vespasian said, looking at his brother.

Sabinus inclined his head a fraction; he understood.

With no quarter asked for or expected, the army of Paulinus followed up the Britons' rout, hacking and stabbing at the backs of the warriors; down they fell in their hundreds and thousands as they tried to flee from the moving wall of iron, muscle and wood steadily driving them back south. However, their numbers precluded speed and the slower legionaries were well able to keep in contact, causing such high casualties that the individual soldiers found it hard to keep a tally. Here and there pockets of resistance did turn to defy their tormentors only to be swept aside with brutal ease, holding up the line for a few moments. And the line was kept, the army advanced as one knowing that to do otherwise would be to offer the possibility of victory to the vanquished. The new primus pilus of each cohort – not one of the originals had survived fighting at the tip of the wedge – kept their commands rigid as they rolled inexorably down the hill. But soon the valley widened enough for the pressure to be taken off the Britons' numbers and for their speed to increase so that they gradually broke contact with their pursuers, who nonetheless pressed on, expanding their formations as they did so that none could get around the flanks.

So it was that Vespasian and Sabinus soon caught up with Titus' Batavians as they picked their way through the anti-chariot obstacles and the dead and dying lying in their thousands.

'So we've got to carve our way through there, Father?' Titus said, looking nervously at the seething mass of retreating Britons, having been apprised of what was expected of his half ala.

'We wait until they get more spread out. Then it'll be safer and easier.'

But then the Britannic confidence of their inevitable victory came back to haunt them: just as they were starting to really pull away from the legionaries they came across the multitude of wagons and carriages that had been placed across the valley upon which their families had expected to observe their crushing victory. The families had mostly fled but the laager remained, entrapping the Britons just at the moment they had thought to escape from the relentless Roman blades. As they climbed over, pushed through and crawled under the obstacle, the logjam became such that the army of Paulinus regained contact and if they had sown terror before then this time they doubled it as they killed now not out of vengeance, but for pleasure, knowing that this was their last chance to reap Britannic lives.

And they laughed as they slew, joking with their comrades at the antics of those who had by now lost all pride and were scrambling to save themselves at the expense of others. Vespasian and Sabinus joined in the slaughter with glad hearts, the Roman citizens of Camulodunum, Londinium and Verulamium in their minds: the young girl slithering down the impaling stake, the children nailed to the bridge, the women with their breasts hacked off, the human torches in the river port; all the atrocities they had seen. By the time the barricade burst open and the Britons could flood out from the valley, almost eighty thousand lay dead along its length. One man for every Roman citizen slaughtered during the rebellion.

With urgency Vespasian and Sabinus rode, accompanied by Titus and his Batavians, avoiding the bigger clumps of Iceni and cutting up the few fools who turned to try to hinder their passage. Speed was imperative as Boudicca was no more than a quarter of a mile away, her chariot plainly visible amongst the cluster of household warriors jogging beside her. Beating their mounts with the flats of their blades, the Batavians gained on the slower-moving chariot; the household warriors looked nervously over their shoulders and increased their pace. But a horse can go faster and for longer than a man, especially a man who has just suffered defeat in battle, and within half a mile the cavalry had overhauled Boudicca and her household warriors, just fifty or so of them left; they turned and formed up to face the Batavians, ready to die for their Queen.

Vespasian raised a hand and Titus gave the order to split and the Batavians streamed around the clump of Iceni, surrounding them so that they could go no further. The two sides stared warily at each other as Vespasian eased his horse forward. 'Boudicca!'

The Queen had her driver turn her chariot about and she drove through her household warriors and up to Vespasian; Sabinus had now joined him.

'You two!' the Queen growled. 'Perhaps I should have killed you.'

'That's why we're here,' Sabinus said, 'because you didn't.'

Vespasian checked his frisky mount. 'Paulinus wants you alive, and you know what that means?'

The Queen's expression showed she knew exactly. 'And you outnumber us, yet you don't take me; why is that?'

'We both owe you our lives.'

'So you wish to give me mine in return?'

'To dispose of now, as you please.'

'And my body?'

Vespasian nodded to her warriors. 'If they can get away with it then it will be theirs to bury as they will.'

'My daughters?'

'Have suffered enough and have had their revenge; there is no further score to settle.'

Boudicca looked between the two brothers. 'Why do you do this?'

'To show you that not all Romans are without honour.'

She nodded slowly and then called her daughters and the leader of her warriors forward. There followed tearful words in the tongue of the Iceni as farewells were said.

'I'm ready,' Boudicca said eventually.

'How will you do it?' Sabinus asked.

Boudicca looked down at the grisly head dangling from his saddle and pulled a vial from inside her tunic. 'Myrddin gave me this against being captured alive; he was a master of death, so this will be quick and relatively painless. You know, of course, that you haven't defeated him? He's already back in another form.'

Sabinus reached down and patted the head. 'Believe what you want; all I know is that I've had my vengeance and this skull will sit very well on the shrine of my household gods in memory of it.'

'Vengeance is a sweet thing and I have taken mine.'

'If you hadn't then you would have been free later this year,' Vespasian said.

'What do you mean?'

'Nero was planning to withdraw from the whole island because the province was a drain on his finances; that's why Seneca and all the other bankers started to call in their loans.'

The Queen thought about that for a few moments and then burst into laughter. 'That is beautiful! I shall die content. Nero wanting to pull the legions out to save money was the catalyst that caused the rebellion; what delicious irony. Now, of course, after such a rebellion and so many dead, Rome can never leave without seeming weak. I've just cost your Empire untold millions in the coming years. But more than that, I've caused your defences along the Rhenus and Danuvius to be stretched because of the troops that you will be forced to keep here; perhaps, one day, that will be your downfall.' She raised her vial in a toast and looked first at Sabinus and then Vespasian. 'I said that you would be the last Roman I spoke to.' She downed the contents in three great gulps and then sat on the floor of her chariot to wait.

She did not wait long.

Nor did Vespasian and Sabinus wait long after she had gone, but, rather, turned their horses about and, with Titus and the Batavians following, rode back north, leaving Boudicca's warriors to carry away the body of the Fury who had defied Rome.

EPILOGUE

Rome, AD 62

ROME HAD AN air of menace hanging over it as Vespasian and Magnus followed the Via Aurelia, leading their horses, through the Trans Tiberim, on the west bank of the Tiber, and then crossed the Aemilian bridge to arrive in the Forum Boarium in the shadow of the Circus Maximus. Large groups of citizenry paraded all around holding up statues of a woman decked out in flowers. Punching their fists in the air, they chanted her name, 'Claudia Octavia!', over and over again as they converged on the Palatine.

Here and there were other statues, tumbled off their plinths, shattered on the ground, their painted life-like eyes staring sightlessly to the sky.

'Poppaea Sabina,' Vespasian said, reading the inscription on one plinth.

Magnus pressed a finger to the side of his nose and cleared a nostril. 'She seems to have pissed people off.'

'More to the point, what are her statues doing up anyway? She's Nero's mistress, not the Empress.'

'A lot changes in eighteen months,' Magnus observed, clearing the other nostril; Castor and Pollux both examined the produce as it hit the ground.

'Yes, but we would have heard if Nero had divorced Claudia Octavia and married Poppaea in that time; after all we've only been fifty miles up the Via Aurelia in Cosa for the last four of them; news like that doesn't travel that slowly.'

'Your uncle will no doubt inform us.'

Vespasian did not doubt it but, nevertheless, what was of concern to him was that the citizens of Rome were behaving in such an aggressive way towards the Palatine and therefore, by extension, the Emperor and yet nothing seemed to be being done about it; there was no sign of either the Praetorian Guard, the Urban Cohorts or even the Vigiles.

Nothing.

And what was even more concerning was that there did not seem to be anyone of the equestrian or senatorial classes on the streets; no purple-edged togas, no litters, lictors or red leather sandals, nothing at all to indicate rank. The streets had been taken over by the mob and Vespasian felt very glad of his stained travel clothes. He was aware of most of the news in the eighteen months that he had been away, but this was a mystery. He pulled his hood far over his head and walked with pace towards the Quirinal.

It had taken a long time to get back to Rome, longer than Vespasian had hoped. Immediately after the battle, once he had got over his fury at the brothers allowing Boudicca to take her own life, Paulinus had sent Vespasian down to the southwest, to the II Augusta, to give the prefect of the camp, Poenius Postumus, the choice between immediate suicide or a shameful trial in Rome for cowardice in refusing to bring his legion to Paulinus' aid. Having expressed his deep regret at depriving the legion of a share in the glory of Boudicca's defeat, Postumus obligingly fell on his sword at Vespasian's feet. He had then been forced to wait down in Isca until midsummer and the arrival of the new legate. With no Imperial Mandate he could not officially command the legion; however, Paulinus was anxious that he should advise the young thick-stripe military tribune – a patrician youth just out of his teens – to whom the command fell when he arrived at the legion a few days after Poenius' suicide, on the mopping up operations in the wake of the revolt, which were considerable and province-wide. The tribune was far out of his depth but refused, with patrician pig-headed arrogance, to recognise the fact until he managed to lose most of a cohort and all of his right arm as they helped the XX legion to repel a series of serious incursions by the Silures who had been emboldened by Rome's weakened presence in the west.

Upon the arrival of the new legate, a few days after that incident, Vespasian and Magnus had headed back to the ruins of

Londinium to find a flattened, charred landscape with not one building intact. They had found the same at Camulodunum when they went to retrieve Paelignus' strongbox from the sewer outlet, before sailing back to Germania Inferior with Sabinus, Titus and his Batavians to be reunited with Caenis and Hormus. Cerialis, however, stayed, the remnants of his legion, numbering just under a thousand, bolstered by reinforcements from Germania where Caenis had been successful in getting Governor Rufus to act with alacrity. Cerialis' reputation was, in part, restored by the brutality with which he slaughtered any surviving Iceni war bands and then ravaged their tribal lands to the point that it would take generations for them to recover their strength.

And so Vespasian had left Titus in his province and travelled south to his estate in Cosa where he, Magnus and Hormus had spent a convivial winter. Caenis and Sabinus had both carried on to Rome whence they, along with Gaius, sent him regular reports and it was the latest one of these, received just a few days previously, which had told him that he could return to Rome: Burrus had fallen and was dead. The man responsible for keeping the memory of his collision with Nero in the circus had been poisoned by the Emperor who, according to Caenis, was so keen to pretend that he had done nothing that he actually came to Burrus' deathbed to ask him how he was; Burrus replied: '*I'm* all right.' He then refused to talk to the Emperor any more – partly because his throat had swollen up – which left Nero fretting that Burrus would go to his grave thinking badly of him.

It was with relief that Vespasian arrived at Gaius' front door as, throughout their passage across the city, the air of menace had increased and the gangs of citizenry had grown more vocal in their support for Claudia. But there had also been something else going on and it was not just Claudia who had caused the unrest: not only had there been freeborn and freed on the streets but also a substantial proportion of slaves were about and they and many of the freedmen shared the same grievance.

'Pedanius,' Gaius informed Vespasian and Magnus, sitting in the sun of his courtyard garden around a table amply supplied with wine and honeyed cakes.

'The prefect of Rome?' Vespasian asked.

'The very same; although we should say that he's the ex-Urban prefect.'

'He stepped down from the position?'

'No, dear boy; he was murdered.' Gaius selected his next treat. 'By one of his slaves,' he added just before the cake disappeared, whole, into his mouth.

'No!' Vespasian was appalled.

'Yes,' Gaius assured him, spraying crumbs over the table.

'We haven't had an incident like that for decades. How did it happen?'

'I believe he reneged on his agreement to give the man his freedom after the price had already been negotiated and then, to add insult to injury, he started using his slave's favourite boy in the most provocative manner. The man crept into Pedanius' room whilst he was otherwise occupied with said boy and stabbed him.'

'Is the law being invoked?'

'It's not certain yet as there are more than four hundred slaves in his household in Rome and on his country estate and in law they are deemed to be all equally responsible for their master's murder and should all be crucified. There have been arguments for and against it for the last few months since the murder happened; however, it should be Nero's final decision but he can't make up his mind. He's worried that the common people will think badly of him if he says yes so he's decided that the way out for him is to give the matter over to the Senate; there's due to be a debate about it in the House tomorrow.'

'No wonder the slaves and freedmen are protesting,' Magnus said, helping himself to more wine. 'There's always a certain amount of sympathy in these cases.'

'I agree, Magnus. No one likes to see babes nailed to crosses on the Via Appia; but the law is the law.'

'I shall certainly go to the debate tomorrow,' Vespasian said.

'Yes, it'll be interesting because what with all the unrest about Nero divorcing Claudia Octavia and marrying Poppaea—'

'He's married her?'

'Not yet; the ceremony's set for the day after tomorrow and the whole Senate is expected to attend. Poppaea's a few months' pregnant and likely to go to full term so Nero divorced Claudia last month on the grounds of her being barren, which is no surprise seeing as, from all accounts, on the very few times he's been near her since their marriage he's used her like Pedanius did that boy; now, I may not know much about women but I do know that won't get them pregnant. The people are up in arms about it because they see Claudia as having all the virtues of an upright Roman wife and she has their total support. They're demanding that he recall her from exile and remarry her. The pro-Claudia sentiments have been growing and they're now being fuelled by this slave debate and Nero doesn't know what to do. He's terrified and hasn't been seen for a couple of days; meanwhile, the Praetorian Guard are refusing to move until they get a largesse to make up for Burrus' murder. Also the Urban Cohorts are leaderless because Pedanius is dead and Nero hasn't appointed a new Urban prefect yet and the Vigiles don't know who to take orders from because Tigellinus has been made the new prefect of the Guard. It's a mess that Nero shows no sign of sorting out.'

Vespasian's mortification was plain. 'Tigellinus is Praetorian prefect! That's almost as bad as Burrus still being alive.'

'I know; there was nothing that anyone could do to prevent it. Nero insisted upon promoting his playmate to the highest position; call it a reward for bad behaviour if you like. It's put everyone in mind of Sejanus. But worry not, dear boy; for the first time in his life, Seneca has done something for the good of all and not just his purse: he persuaded Nero that he should go back to the times when there were always two prefects on the basis that Tigellinus will be too busy with the administrative work to be able to give his full attention to him. Obviously it had never occurred to Nero that there was any work connected to the position so he agreed with Seneca and now the most honest man in Rome is co-prefect with Tigellinus.'

'What do you mean by honest?' Magnus asked with genuine interest.

'In that he's been prefect of the grain supply for the last seven years and hardly took any advantage of it financially.'

'Ah, so you really mean stupid.' Magnus lobbed a cake towards Castor and Pollux, neither of whom took any interest in it, preoccupied as they were with a bone each.

Vespasian nodded thoughtfully, seeing the sense in this. 'Faenius Rufus; he's a perfect balance to Tigellinus.'

Gaius beamed his agreement. 'So you see, if Tigellinus tries to make trouble for us over the Terpnus affair then we just protest our innocence to Rufus—'

'And the honest man believes us,' Vespasian cut in, finishing the sentence.

'Precisely; and what with his support and then Paulinus' very flattering report of both yours and Sabinus' conduct during Boudicca's revolt, which was read out in the Senate in front of Nero, I think it's reasonable to assume that we're safe from Tigellinus' venom.'

'For a while, at least. But I wonder if Seneca was acting for the good of all when he put Rufus forward.'

'What do you mean?'

'It's just that it's strange that Seneca's decided to put someone in charge of Nero's personal safety who is, perhaps, less than completely devoted to it. Remember Rufus and Piso implying that they assumed that Sabinus had given his tacit approval to the attack on Nero and Terpnus and not condemning it?'

Gaius cast his mind back, looked at Vespasian in horror and then quickly fortified himself with another cake. 'You're right, dear boy. Do you think he's ... ?'

'No, Seneca's far too clever for that; he's trying to secure his fortune and his position. Let someone else go for the top prize and then perhaps Seneca can advise and influence him.'

'Who?'

Vespasian held his palm up as a warning. 'It's best not to speculate as we don't want to be involved should it fail.'

'Quite right.'

'Anyway, it may be just a coincidence and Seneca doesn't know Rufus' true feelings. I'll mention it to Sabinus and have him pay close attention to any informers he may have,' Vespasian said, rising to his feet. 'Meanwhile, I'm off to see Caenis.'

'Not Flavia?'

'No, I'll stay with Caenis tonight, seeing as Flavia couldn't be bothered to visit me whilst I waited in Cosa, on the grounds that there is nothing for her to do in the country; besides, I'm not that keen on having to see Domitian, just in case he's got worse.'

Gaius shuddered. 'I don't blame you, dear boy; from all accounts, he hasn't improved. I steer well away from the brute even though he's your son. A boy like that makes me seriously question my choice of lifestyle.'

Vespasian declined to comment further on the subject. 'When Hormus arrives tell him to leave Paelignus' strongbox here and then take everything else over to my house; I'll see him there in the morning for my salutio before we go onto the Senate together.'

'You're not trusting Flavia with the contents then?'

'With two thousand aurei? Would you?'

'Pallas guessed that you would come here first,' Caenis said, reaching up to link her arms around Vespasian's neck as he walked into her atrium.

'What do you mean?' Vespasian asked, nuzzling her hair and savouring her scent.

Caenis broke away and retrieved a wax tablet from a table. 'I mean he sent a letter to you here; it arrived a couple of hours ago.'

'Curious.' Vespasian took the tablet, broke the seal and opened it. As he read, his face fell.

'What is it, my love?' Caenis asked.

'He's asked me to visit him tomorrow after the House rises and to bring you, Gaius and Magnus; also, he wants us to come in a carriage.'

'All the way down to Baiae?'

'No; he's staying at his villa just outside the city on the Via Appia. He came to try and present himself to the Emperor to congratulate him on his new bride.'

'Still trying to get back into favour?'

'Evidently; but it's not worked. Quite the opposite in fact: Nero replied to his request for an audience that if he really did want to please him on the occasion of his wedding he would do well to be dead; that way the Emperor would only take nine tenths of his fortune leaving him to decide on how to disperse the remainder.'

'I suppose that concentrates the mind. Are you going to go?'

Vespasian gave it a few moments' thought. 'Yes, I think I will. No matter how much he's tried to manipulate me throughout my career, I think that, on balance, I owe him more than he owes me; I'll go and pay my respects before he takes his life.'

'And so will I.' Caenis took his face in both hands and, going up on tiptoe, kissed Vespasian full on the lips. 'Meanwhile, we haven't got any appointments until the Senate meets tomorrow morning. I'm sure we could find something to do.'

Vespasian returned the kiss and then, with some urgency, led Caenis on through the atrium in the direction of her bedroom.

'I give the floor to Faenius Rufus,' Lucius Asinius Gallus, the presiding consul, announced after he had declared the auspices good for the business of Rome that day. 'He will speak on behalf of leniency.'

There were murmurs of outrage from those senators of the more conservative persuasion as Rufus got to his feet. Some, Corvinus amongst them, went further, growling and gesturing threateningly at him. Through the open doors of the Senate House the Forum Romanum was packed with thousands of citizens and slaves awaiting news of the debate.

'This should be interesting,' Gaius whispered to Vespasian and Sabinus. 'The honest man asking why over four hundred slaves should be condemned for the actions of one of their number.'

'Conscript Fathers,' Rufus declaimed, head held high with his left hand across his chest, clutching his toga, and his right hand down by his side, holding a scroll; the image of a republican orator. 'The law is the law! But does it follow that the ways of our ancestors will always suit us in this modern age? In this instance I would argue no. In this instance we have a set of circumstances that our ancestors never had to think about. It is a religious issue.' He paused to look around the chamber; that had gained everyone's attention. 'Most of us are aware of this new Jewish cult that has been slowly creeping into the city; we know it because it infects many of our slaves. This perversion, this denial of the gods, this religious intolerance has been growing also in the underclasses, bribed by the lie of a better life in an imaginary next world when we all know what really awaits us when we cross the Styx.' Rufus gestured to the crowds outside. 'There is the proof of it in our Forum; not all of them are followers of this crucified Jew whom they call Christus; however, those who are have managed to stir up sympathy for Pedanius' slaves, especially amongst other slaves and also the freedmen who were once slaves themselves. Why? I hear you ask; because many of the condemned slaves are followers of this cult. Since becoming prefect of the Praetorian Guard, I have had more than a few of them questioned under torture. Atheists! And they are encouraged by a Roman citizen, Gaius Julius Paulus; a man of no honour, a man of ...'

'I'd forgotten about that little shit,' Vespasian said as Rufus went on to list Paulus' many failings.

'I haven't,' Sabinus said. 'He's here.'

'Here?'

'Yes, dear boy,' Gaius assured him. 'He arrived soon after you both left. He'd been imprisoned for agitating in Judaea but, as he's a Roman citizen, he has invoked his right to appeal to Caesar.'

'And from his house arrest,' Rufus continued, his outrage growing, 'this agitator writes to his followers, stirring them up even more, breeding religious intolerance and extremism; he claims that the followers of Christus amongst the condemned slaves are being martyred by the heavy hand of Roman law, whilst he hides behind the protection of that very law in order to work against our state. And there is nothing that we can do because, as a citizen, he does have the right to appeal to the Emperor.'

'The trouble is,' Gaius muttered, 'that Nero can't be bothered to see him.'

'So therefore, Conscript Fathers,' Rufus continued as out in the Forum the crowd began to part for a litter to make its way through, escorted by lictors, 'let us not create martyrs, even false ones, for this abomination; let us show leniency. We should take away the argument that Paulus is using against us and spare all but the murderer; the rest can live out their lives in the mines. If we don't do this then this poison will continue to spread throughout the poor of the city and I need not remind you, Conscript Fathers, that there are many more of them than there are of us.'

'No!' Corvinus shouted, jumping to his feet as Rufus sat down. 'Pedanius was one of our own! How will the common people ever trust us to implement the law fairly for them if we can't even do it for a member of our own order? The law is the law and it should not be changed because of the agitation of a religious extremist.'

'I have to say that I agree with him,' Gaius said, as Gallus called for order and invited Gaius Cassius to take the floor.

'But you don't know Paulus, Uncle,' Vespasian said as the elderly Cassius struggled to his feet, 'his ambition to control people is great.'

'Conscript Fathers,' Cassius declaimed in a strong voice that belied his grey hair and wrinkled skin, 'I have on many occasions been present in this House when demands were made for new decrees of the Senate that contravened the laws of our forefathers; and I did not oppose them ...'

'That must be Nero,' Vespasian whispered to Gaius and Sabinus; outside the crowd grew more agitated as the litter neared the Senate House steps. 'I thought he didn't want to be associated with the decision.' Vespasian watched as the crowd grew more vocal forcing Cassius to raise his voice as he concluded.

'We now have in our households tribes of foreigners who have different rites, alien religions or, as we have heard, no belief in the gods at all. You will not hold scum like that in place except by intimidation. Yes, and when you consider that every tenth man in a disgraced legion is beaten to death by his comrades, you will realise that brave men also draw the lot. Every great deterrent involves a measure of injustice but wrongs done to individuals are counterbalanced by the common good.'

Cassius sat down to silence as the senators, none wanting to make a decision until they had heard what the Emperor had to say, watched Nero's litter be set down at the door. With slow menace, Nero pulled back the curtain, stepped out and, brushing aside his lictors, entered the building; with him came the fear.

Nero stood in the middle of the floor, turning slowly, his eyes almost crazed, his hands outstretched appealing to each man within, as his gaze passed over them. 'My person has been abused.' The voice was thick; then: 'Abused!' Senators jumped as the word cracked around the high marble-clad walls. '*My* person!' He looked down at his body – now grown far more corpulent than when Vespasian had last seen him – and stared at it in disbelief. 'My person abused! And more than my person: my dignity! I heard common people call me names. Me! I who do nothing but serve them, called the most foul names; names and lies! I was on my way here, Conscript Fathers, to throw myself at your feet and weep. Yes, I would have wept and begged for you to show mercy for those slaves as my gift to the common people; a gift in return for the gift of understanding that they will give me tomorrow when I take my new wife. But they have abused my person and called me names! I shall not weep, Conscript Fathers, and neither shall I beg and nor shall I expect their understanding or care for what they think. No, not any more will I care for the feelings of the common man; from now on I will live as I wish, as is *my* right as a human being!' He stopped, panting, and scanned the rows of mesmerised senators.

Vespasian felt his gaze pass over him and then quickly return, only to carry on to Sabinus.

'Titus Flavius Sabinus,' Nero croaked. 'You will resume your former role as Urban prefect. Your first task is to clear the streets and crucify the slaves. All of them! Send to Tigellinus for a cohort of the Guard to protect my person as I go back to the Palatine and then find a hundred of the people who insulted me; they shall appear at the games to celebrate my marriage. Understand?'

'Yes, Princeps,' Sabinus said, getting to his feet. 'Thank you—'

'Go!'

Sabinus did not need to be told twice.

On the other side of the House, Vespasian noticed Corvinus looking at the Emperor and then the retreating Sabinus in horror.

'And you, Rufus,' Nero rasped, turning to the new prefect of the Praetorian Guard as Sabinus' footsteps, the only other sound, echoed around the chamber. 'You are to send immediately to Anicetus: he is to provide me with a wedding present for my new wife; he knows what would please her best. Now go!'

For an instant, Rufus paused but, knowing better than to defy Nero when the fear was so heavily upon him, saluted and walked out, the regular twitch in his jaw muscles the only evidence of his inner thoughts.

Nero then turned his attention to the rest of the senators, his look steeled. 'You will stay with me here until the Guard arrives and think of ways to make me the happiest of men on my wedding day because after such abuse only the finest gifts will help me to recover. And it would not do for me not to recover.'

Vespasian knew exactly what he must do, such was the fear.

Emitting raw-throated wails, a girl-child, not long from the womb, writhed on the nails transfixing her wrists and ankles to her cross, as her mother, hanging next to her, stared in disbelief, screaming silently, at her offspring, tiny on the wooden structure, enduring such torment so soon after entering the unforgiving world. Screams and hammer blows rent the air as Urban Cohort soldiers held down and fixed to crosses the condemned slaves of Pedanius' household. Others, already mounted on the crosses that lined the Via Appia, as Vespasian, Gaius, Caenis and Magnus passed by beneath them, hyperventilated, shrieked, muttered prayers or pleaded to be let down; those still to be dealt with shuffled in their chains, staring up in terror at their fellows, tears flooding down their cheeks, arms around womenfolk and children, shaking with fear, as they made their last journey in a world in which they had never held a stake.

Amongst the condemned and the soldiery were many who were there to comfort, although what comfort there could be against the piercing of the nails was unclear to Vespasian as he rode in the carriage driven by Magnus.

'What are they doing?' Gaius, sitting opposite him, asked, pointing.

Vespasian looked over to a group of people kneeling. 'I think these followers of Christus pray on their knees.'

'How very uncomfortable.'

Magnus spat in the group's direction. 'No self-respect, that's their trouble; kneeling as if you've been defeated.'

'I suppose in a way they have,' Caenis suggested, 'by life, seeing as they are the lowest of the low. I had to have one of my girls whipped the other day when my steward reported that she had drawn a fish above her bed.'

Gaius frowned. 'A fish?'

'It's their sign. I won't have it in my house; I'll sell the girl once her wounds have healed and she's worth something again.'

Vespasian put his hand on Caenis' knee. 'There's a difference between punishing slaves for a crime they've committed and one they haven't.'

'You don't approve of this, my love?'

Gaius winced at a teenage boy's shrill wails as he watched a nail being beaten through his body. 'The law had to be upheld.'

Vespasian turned his eyes away from the agony. 'But tell me, Uncle, if these were your beautiful boys, what then?'

'They're not, though.'

'Just imagine if one of your new purchases took exception to what you were doing to him as you were breaking him in, shall we say?'

'It wouldn't happen; I'm very gentle first time. Besides, at my age one can't be too vigorous.'

'But say it did and all your boys were nailed up, what would you think?'

'I'd be dead.'

'Yes, Uncle; but in principle: if all your beautiful boys were nailed up because of the actions of one of them, what would you think?'

Gaius looked down at the teenager who now stared at the sky in catatonic terror. 'A waste of perfectly good bum.'

Vespasian sighed. 'That's one way of looking at it, I suppose.'

Magnus slowed the horses as the carriage approached Sabinus, overseeing proceedings with a couple of Urban Cohort tribunes.

Seeing their arrival, Sabinus broke off his conversation and walked over to them, breaking into a broad grin. 'I'm told that Seneca's face when he was told that I had been reappointed Urban prefect by the Emperor was a study in horror; apparently he'd just taken receipt of Corvinus' marker for eight million to get him the post which he's now going to have to return.'

Vespasian could but enjoy his brother's good fortune. 'Well, Corvinus' face watching you leave the Senate was a match for Seneca's, I can assure you.'

Gaius chuckled, his jowls and chins wobbling furiously. 'I saw that look too; so that explains it. How gratifying.'

'It was the final blow to Seneca,' Caenis informed them. 'I was there when he was told this morning; and no, his face wasn't so much a study in horror but, rather, resignation. He now completely accepts that he has lost any small influence he still had over Nero. As influence equals money he doesn't see any point in continuing as Nero's chief advisor.'

Vespasian was far from astonished; the appointment of Rufus now really made sense. 'I think he might already be arranging his way back. How is he planning on persuading Nero to let him retire in the first place?'

'He's hoping to buy his way to it using his money that Decianus stole off Boudicca; the Cloelius Brothers have agreed to give it back to Seneca – for a substantial fee, of course – now that Decianus has not been heard of for a year.'

'I wish him luck; I'll be very pleased to see the back of him after all the damage he's done with his banking.' Vespasian turned to Sabinus. 'So, brother, is there any last message you would like me to give to Pallas?'

Sabinus thought for a moment. 'Tell him I'll always be grateful for my life.' With a cheerful wave he turned and went back to supervising the execution of the rest of Pedanius' household.

'His life?' Pallas said, looking closely at the bark on the trunk of a walnut tree in his garden and stroking it. 'He has a lot more to be grateful to me for than that; but who am I to criticise or quibble when I shall be dead before sundown?' He turned to face Vespasian, Gaius, Caenis and Magnus who stood in attendance to their host on the central path through the gardens; his hair and beard were now almost white but his eyes remained bright and his expression as neutral as it had ever been, despite his impending suicide.

Colonnades, statues, fountains and arches, all brightly painted – strong yellows, deep reds and azure blues predominating – enhanced the manicured natural elements of the garden, neatly divided up by gravel paths and channels of running water. It was not a bad place to spend one's last hours, Vespasian had reflected as Pallas' steward had shown them out of the villa and into the freedman's little paradise.

'No matter,' Pallas said, clasping his hands behind his back and leading them further away from the villa, 'a little gratitude is better than none at all; and you all have things to be grateful to me for.'

'You've always been very good to our family,' Gaius said, sweating as he tried to keep up with the leisurely pace.

'That is because you never disdained to talk to me when I was merely a slave.'

'There's never been anything "mere" about you, my friend.'

'I have moved in the highest circles all my life, I grant you that. I made my patron, the Lady Antonia's son Claudius, emperor and secured his position and it was I who manoeuvred that ungrateful, untalented and unhinged deluded maniac, Nero, into succeeding him. I now see that was a mistake as, despite my … er … helping to free, shall we say, myself and him at the same time from his mother, Agrippina, I have not been allowed back into a position of influence. And now he demands my death and nine tenths of my property; well, he's welcome to it. Forty million sesterces will be ample for my wife and two children to live on.'

'Wife?' Vespasian questioned.

'Children!' Gaius exclaimed.

Vespasian was astounded. 'I never knew you had a wife.'

'Well, you never asked and I never brought them to Rome as it's best not to advertise a weak spot; this villa was the closest they ever came. But they are the reason that I've asked you here: I want you to look out for them after I'm gone. My two boys are eight and ten; they're both freeborn citizens of Rome and with even an equal share of just a tenth of my fortune will easily qualify for senatorial status. My wife will bring them to you for an introduction when they each come of age. Help them up the Cursus Honorum; if my hunch is right then you will be the best placed to do that.'

'What do you mean?' Vespasian asked, playing the innocent.

'Let's just say that Nero won't last for ever: I'm sure that you've noticed Nero's appointment as the second prefect of the Praetorian Guard; things have now started to move. When my mistress, Antonia, gave you her father's sword, the sword that she had promised to give to whichever of her grandsons she thought would make the best emperor, I think she had made a shrewd guess.'

Vespasian remained non-committal. 'Claudius took that from me in Britannia.'

'I know, I was there. But now you can have it back.' He reached under his toga, unhitched and then brought out the sword of Marcus Antonius, once the greatest man in Rome.

'Thank you, Pallas,' was all that Vespasian could manage as he took the perfectly balanced weapon in its battered scabbard from the freedman; it was the sword of a fighting man and not that of a parade-ground soldier.

'Use it well.'

Vespasian went to say something but Pallas held up a hand, stopping him. 'Just look after my sons and acquit yourself well in Africa.'

'Africa!' Gaius exclaimed, jowls a-wobble.

'I've deposited the necessary funds with the Cloelius Brothers in the Forum in your name.' He addressed Caenis. 'Who will take over from Seneca?'

'It'll be Epaphroditus.'

Pallas nodded. 'I thought as much; get in with him early, Vespasian, tomorrow at the wedding, if possible, and Africa will be yours next year. He's Nero's freedman so has the influence; and you never know, you might not need to use a cash incentive in the negotiations.'

Vespasian wondered if Nero's nuptials were the right place to make such a deal but agreed, nonetheless.

'Gaius,' Pallas continued, 'I know you've been disappointed in your ambitions for the consulship.'

Gaius dismissed the comment with a gesture. 'Not enough push in my youth and entirely forgotten about now.'

'And an opportunity for enrichment missed; go with Vespasian to the Cloelius Brothers and you will find that redressed, as will you, Magnus, to a lesser degree. Both bankers' drafts are, like Vespasian's, in your own names and therefore cannot be traced to me; so they are safe from Nero.' As Gaius and Magnus both expressed their thanks, Pallas turned to Caenis. 'I know the currency that you prefer, so you'll find the reason why I told you to bring a carriage already loaded into it when you leave, which I'm going to ask you all to do now as I wish to spend my final couple of hours with my sons and my wife.' He indicated to three figures seated beneath a pergola some distance away. 'I wish you all a better end than mine.' He embraced Caenis and then took Magnus', Gaius' and then Vespasian's forearms in a firm grip. As he turned away towards where his family were seated, Vespasian got one final glimpse of his face and, as always, it remained neutral.

The crucifixions had been completed as the carriage passed back up the road towards the city gates and now there were but a few Urban Cohort soldiers on duty to deter anyone from trying to cut down the agonised wretches hanging off their nails. A few gawkers gaped in fascination at the smaller bodies on the crosses and some children, laughing, pelted a victim their own age with faeces and stones, making his wails even more pitiful; the soldiers did nothing to halt this but, rather, smiled benevolently at the gang's antics. But Vespasian, Caenis and Gaius hardly noticed the suffering as Magnus drove them past, too busy were they with Pallas' gift to Caenis.

'In one crate he has given me power over so many people,' Caenis said, scanning a scroll. 'This one details Pallas' dealings with Seneca when they colluded over Agrippina's murder.'

Vespasian shook his head in disbelief. 'This one is about how Pallas secured Tigellinus his post as prefect of the Vigiles in exchange for information on Seneca and Burrus which he is still receiving. So that's how he seemed to know that Seneca was trying to get out.'

'Is there anything of interest to me?' Magnus asked over his shoulder.

'I'm afraid that Pallas moved in far higher circles than you, my friend,' Gaius said unrolling a scroll.

'And yet he was a slave and then a freedman and I am a free-born citizen; I sometimes wonder if it is time to have a little tinker with the system, if you take my meaning?'

No one did.

'Dear boy,' Gaius wheezed, 'this one's for you, if Caenis would let you have it.' He handed the scroll to Vespasian who read it with Caenis leaning over his shoulder.

'So that's what he meant when he said that I might not need cash for the negotiations with Epaphroditus; this details how Pallas blackmailed Nero's freedman to pass on information about the Emperor's intimate habits by threatening to reveal that he was already doing the same for Seneca.'

'Give that to me, my love,' Caenis said. 'I think that I can use this best.'

'I'm sure you're right.' Vespasian handed Caenis the scroll and grinned at his uncle. 'I think that I might almost enjoy Nero's wedding tomorrow, after all.'

The ode to love growled on. All stood, sat or reclined transfixed in an act of adoration that the élite of Rome now performed to perfection, so used had they become to hearing their Emperor sing.

And none performed it better than Poppaea Sabina: her eyes never left her new husband, sitting next to her, grating out his own composition whilst accompanying himself on the lyre, which he had mastered with the same degree of aptitude as the voice. One hand on her swelling belly and the other resting on Nero's thigh, she gazed at him with the fervour of a devout worshipper in the presence of the deity and all but swooned at every discord and missed note.

In the midst of the adoring crowd of senators and their wives, Vespasian stood next to Flavia, his eyes constantly straying to her, ensuring that she was keeping control of her feelings as she witnessed the phenomenon of a singing emperor for the first time; despite a couple of winces, he thought she acquitted herself tolerably well. Even Seneca, standing on the other side of her, had dressed his face with a look of wonderment and Faenius Rufus and Calpurnius Piso, beyond him, made efforts not to let their disapproval show. Gaius and Sabinus were both seated next to Vespasian: Sabinus with his head in his hands so that his face was obscured and Gaius making use of a large handkerchief, mopping up the sweat on his face in a good imitation of one drying tears of joy.

And joy was soon genuine as the last stanza withered and died, instantly forgotten, bringing the ordeal to an end; the audience burst into rapturous applause and Nero wept with the emotion of it all: the wedding ceremony, the consummation of the marriage – with a young boy, looking curiously like Poppaea, standing in for the bride due to her pregnancy – and now the wedding feast which he had opened with the ode, dedicated to himself, that he had spent the last month composing.

As Nero soaked up the adulation, Vespasian glanced over to where Caenis stood next to Epaphroditus and caught her eye; she smiled and inclined her head fractionally. By the look on Epaphroditus' face, Vespasian could surmise that a financial inducement had not been needed to secure him his province; relief surged through him as he knew that soon he would, once again, be able to escape the fear that all who came in contact with the Emperor were daily subjected to.

'She's done it,' he said out of the corner of his mouth to Flavia.

'Who's done what?'

'Caenis has secured me the province of Africa next year.'

Flavia snorted. 'Well, if you think that I'll be accompanying you, think again. I didn't marry you just to go back to the semi-barbarous place where I was brought up; now I'm in Rome I'm staying here.'

Vespasian did not respond as the arrangement suited him well and he was afraid that he might be unable to keep the satisfaction out of his voice.

'My friends,' Nero rasped, standing and extending his arms as if to embrace all in the high-ceilinged, botanically frescoed chamber, designed to seem as if it were an extension of the gardens blooming beyond the windows. 'My friends, it grieves me that I do not have the leisure to play for you more but the time has come for you to offer me your gifts in celebration of my marriage and in turn I may grant you a request.' He signalled to Seneca. 'My old friend and tutor, you shall be first.'

Seneca stepped from the crowd. 'Princeps, it is my pleasure, no, my honour, yes honour—'

'I don't care what it is, just get to the point.'

'Yes, Princeps. It is my honour to present you with the total of all my investments in the province of Britannia. Now that you have decided not to abandon the province it is only right that we, your subjects, help in the financial burden that you have placed upon yourself for the good of Rome.' He handed Nero a scroll. 'Since the crushing of the revolt I have reinvested much of the money that I had taken out; this is a list of those investments, they are all yours.'

Nero took the list and handed it to Epaphroditus. 'And what about the money that Decianus took from the Iceni causing the revolt?'

'I was coming to that, Princeps; the Cloelius Brothers will transfer the five million sesterces, in gold, to the treasury … your treasury in two days.'

Nero's face lit up, exaggerating the flesh now accumulated on his cheeks. 'A handsome gift, my friend; and what would you have me grant you as a mark of my favour?'

'No more than what your great-great-grandfather granted his loyal servants, Marcus Agrippa and Gaius Maecenas: retirement from public life. They had received their rewards, large indeed, that were in line with their service. In my case …'

As Seneca launched into what was obviously a prepared speech, Vespasian steeled himself for his gift, consoling himself with the sure knowledge that if he did not give it then it would soon be taken from him by the Emperor who considered everything within the Empire to be his own personal property.

'Should you, who have such an abundance of stamina,' Seneca concluded, 'and who has, over the years, wielded supreme power effortlessly, allow me my repose in my gardens and country homes then that will be counted to your credit.' Seneca bowed his head.

Nero struck a pose of magnanimity, one hand extended to the supplicant before him. 'The fact that I can respond immediately to your prepared speech is what I consider to be your gift to me; you have helped to bring out in me the impromptu as well as the prepared …'

No one in the room was moved to argue as Nero expounded on his own delusional talents, occasionally giving his tutor a peck of credit, all knowing that there was nothing impromptu about the Emperor whatsoever and that this too was a prepared speech.

So the last great farce between Nero and Seneca was played out in public and, as it came to a close and Seneca offered half his remaining wealth to Nero to let him retire peacefully, Nero surprised all by departing from the script: 'It will not be your moderation that will be on the lips of all if you return the money that you've made from exploiting your position, nor will it be your fortunate retirement they will discuss if you take your leave of your Emperor. No, Seneca; rather, it will be my greed in demanding the fortune and fear of my cruelty that made you leave my service that will be spoken of. Your retirement will make me look bad, *old friend*.' Nero paused to look at Seneca without a trace of friendship on his face and all in the room knew that the most powerful man in Rome after the Emperor was caught in a prison of his own making: he had no influence and yet could not leave. 'Surely a philosopher would not want to make a friend look bad?'

Nero opened his arms and Seneca submitted himself to an embrace and kiss.

'Go,' Nero commanded, pulling away, 'and wait until such time as I might find a use for your life.' A cruel smile. 'You will hear from me by letter.'

Seneca hung his head. 'As you wish, Princeps.' A broken man, he turned and walked back to his place in the crowd.

As Seneca passed, Vespasian asked: 'Was it worth it? All those lives lost for money that can't even guarantee your life?'

Seneca paused and looked at him. 'Guarantee my life? How? How can anyone guarantee their life in this court? We're dying every day.'

Seneca moved on as Piso, Rufus and the rest of the senators began to come forward with their gifts and then to receive, or not, the boon they asked. Piso and Rufus soon returned to their places, their dislike of the situation becoming evident as their backs were turned to the Emperor. After Gaius had just promised a brace of his Germanic slaves, it was Vespasian's turn.

Epaphroditus looked at him with loathing as he approached the Emperor and then whispered something in Nero's ear.

'Princeps,' Vespasian said, 'I have one thing worthy of you.'

'I know it and you have chosen well, Vespasian; your Arab team will make a fine gift. I was anticipating no less from you. As you have fulfilled my expectations you shall have what I'm informed that you want: you shall have Africa next year.'

'My thanks, Princeps; I shall serve you and Rome to the best of my ability as governor.'

Turning and trying not to smirk as he caught an outraged-looking Corvinus' eye, Vespasian took his place next to Flavia who pointedly refused to congratulate him.

'Well done, dear boy,' Gaius said as the last few senators began to go forward. 'Governor of Africa and Urban prefect; things are looking good for our family – if we can survive in this fear.'

'I shall be hundreds of miles away across the sea, Uncle; I won't feel the fear for all of next year.'

'But we shall live with it constantly,' Sabinus said, 'and it will intensify as he gets worse. His brother, his mother, the prefect of the Praetorian Guard, countless senators and equestrians and now his former tutor and chief advisor just waiting for the letter demanding his suicide; who next? No one is safe.'

'Not us if we give him what he wants.'

'He wants everything.'

'Then, dear boys,' Gaius said as Tigellinus entered the room, 'I suggest we let him have it.'

'Is he here?' Nero asked, a look of excitement on his face.

With his snarl-of-a-rabid-dog smile, Tigellinus nodded.

'Then bring him in!' As Tigellinus did his Emperor's bidding, Nero took Poppaea's hand. 'My dearest, your present has arrived.'

'What is it, husband?' Poppaea purred. 'What more can you give me? What more than this child and to make me your wife?'

'A present born out of love,' Nero replied as Tigellinus escorted Anicetus into the room; he carried a wooden box. 'Bring it here, Anicetus.'

Nero took the box, beaming with delight, and, holding it in one hand, pulled open the lid. 'I give you your security, my dearest.'

Poppaea looked inside and then smiled, cold and cruel; she stuck her hand in and pulled out her wedding gift by the hair. With a howl of triumph, shriller than that of any Fury, and with one hand pressed on the new life growing within her, Poppaea spat in the lifeless face of Claudia Octavia.

All who witnessed it felt a chill; a chill so deep that it froze the heart. Vespasian looked in horror at the Golden Emperor, the man with ultimate power over all, the man who thought nothing of murdering a third member of his family merely as a gift and, along with everyone else in the room, he, Vespasian, shuddered under the weight of the fear.

AUTHOR'S NOTE

THIS BOOK IS based on the works of Tacitus, Suetonius and Cassius Dio. Unfortunately, however, none of them tell us what Vespasian was doing during the timespan of the story; so, once again, I have had to insert him into the events of the time.

Suetonius and Tacitus both tell us of Nero's rampages through Rome at night disguised in a wig, raping and murdering for amusement. Tacitus mentions the unfortunate case of Gaius Julius Montanus who was forced to commit suicide after putting up resistance to one of Nero's assaults.

Nero did study music under Terpnus who was considered the greatest lyre-player of the age; during the timespan of this book he kept his 'talent' a secret, singing only to a privileged few. My take on his voice comes from Suetonius telling us that, despite his lying with weights on his chest and using enemas and emetics as well as refraining from eating apples, his voice was 'feeble and husky'.

Venutius was captured by Nasica and the VIIII Hispana in AD 58 after rebelling first against his wife, Cartimandua of the Brigantes – who had replaced him with his armour-bearer, Vellocatus – and then carrying the rebellion against Rome; his being sent to Rome is my fiction but not entirely impossible.

Sabinus was the Urban prefect at this time and, conveniently so that I could get him to Britannia, was replaced by Pedanius for a year in AD 61.

It is my fiction that Seneca and Pallas conspired together in Nero's murder of his mother, Agrippina. The matricide would have taken a long time to prepare as Anicetus did build a collapsible ship – it being fashioned like a swan is my fiction. I have taken a combination of both Suetonius' and Tacitus' accounts of the shameful incident and, apart from inserting Vespasian and Magnus into the action, have not embellished it that much. It was the feast of Minerva; Nero did make a show of reconciliation with his mother even – as Suetonius mentions – going so far as to kiss her breasts as she embarked onto the doomed ship. She escaped just as Magnus described and Nero was paralysed by fear of retribution. Seneca and Burrus advised him to act first so Nero did then throw a sword at the feet of her freedman, Agermus, and accused him of being sent by Agrippina to assassinate him and then despatched Anicetus, Herculeius and Obartius to kill her. She died inviting her murderers to stab her in the womb that bore Nero. Both Suetonius and Tacitus tell us that Nero examined the dead body of his mother remarking on her beauty; you do not need to make this stuff up!

Nero did steal Otho's wife, Poppaea Sabina, and banish his one-time friend to Lusitania to be governor. Corvinus being replaced in the post is my fiction; however, he was awarded a stipend by Nero to help him out of his poverty.

Tacitus tells us that Nero used to practise chariot racing in a circus at the foot of the Vatican that had originally been commissioned by Caligula. The obelisk that still stands in St Peter's Square is a remnant of that construction. Suetonius mentions Vespasian taking a drive as his morning exercise once he had become emperor so I feel justified in having Vespasian race in this story.

Corbulo was conducting the war against Parthia in Armenia at the time and his despatch is taken from Tacitus' report of events that year.

Seneca, like a lot of wealthy men of the time, did invest heavily in Britannia, charging exorbitant rates of interest. If you fancy a great read on Seneca then I recommend *Dying Every Day: Seneca at the Court of Nero* by James Romm. Cassius Dio says that he had as much as forty million sesterces lent out in Britannia alone. Cassius Dio also tells us that Seneca calling in all his loans in Britannia was one reason for the uprising; the other was Decianus claiming that money lent by Claudius at the beginning of the occupation had to be paid back. Suetonius tells us that Nero considered withdrawing from Britannia, and Tacitus says that Boudicca was flogged and her daughters raped after Prasutagus' will was rejected and his kingdom seized by Rome. I've combined all three sources by making Nero's intent to pull out the catalyst that forces Seneca to call in his loans. Decianus insisting the Iceni pay back Claudius' gift and then being responsible for the flogging of Boudicca and the rape of her daughters is the final factor that pushes Boudicca into rebellion. The course of the revolt happened much as described and, again, I've not embellished that much: Camulodunum, Londinium and Verulamium were all destroyed; Cassius Dio tells us of women having their breasts cut off and being impaled on stakes. Eighty thousand Roman citizens were butchered as well as Cerialis – Vespasian's son-in-law – losing most of his legion. Suetonius tells us that Titus served in Britannia and it's possible that he did come as part of the reinforcements from Germania where he also served; his arrival in time for the Battle of Watling Street is my fiction.

The battle itself was a masterpiece by Suetonius Paulinus. Tacitus tells us that he negated Boudicca's far superior numbers by positioning his army between two hills – the location is still unknown – and formed it into wedges as Boudicca's men closed. He also mentions the families in their wagons hindering the Britannic retreat and leading to many of the eighty thousand deaths that he reports with the loss of only four hundred Romans.

Cogidubnus' presence is my fiction – I needed someone to translate Boudicca's speech for us! Both Boudicca's and Paulinus' speeches are a mixture of the versions reported by Tacitus and Cassius Dio.

Tigellinus and Faenius Rufus did replace Burrus who, Tacitus tells us, was poisoned by Nero. Rufus did have the reputation for honesty after his tenure of the prefect of the grain supply over ten years.

Tacitus tells us about the murder of Pedanius by one of his slaves. There was much sympathy for the plight of the four hundred slaves in his household who, according to Roman law, would all be executed. Gaius Cassius' speech is abridged from Tacitus and this won the day; all four hundred were crucified.

Tacitus reports Pallas' enforced suicide in AD 62 and the fact that he died having amassed a fortune of four hundred million sesterces. He must have left children as a descendant of his became consul in the second century.

Nero did divorce Claudia Octavia on the grounds of being barren and then married Poppaea once she became pregnant. Claudia's head was sent to Poppaea to gloat over; it being a wedding present is my fiction but I would not put it past Nero!

My thanks again go to my agent, Ian Drury, at Sheil Land Associates, along with Gaia Banks and Melissa Mahi in the foreign rights department. A big thank you to my editor, Sara O'Keeffe at Corvus/Atlantic, for her great input that considerably sped up the narrative and for making me realise, once again, that a story cannot just be in my head if others are to enjoy it too! Thanks also to all the people at Corvus/Atlantic who work so hard on my behalf and to Will Atkinson for encouraging them to such great efforts. And thank you for all the posters! Thanks also to Tamsin Shelton for her incredible eye for mistakes and disastrous sentences during the copy-edit.

To my shame I've never acknowledged Tim Byrne for his atmospheric cover designs that add so much to the story; thanks, Tim, I love every one.

Finally, my thanks and love to the two people who always join me for the story: my wife, Anja, and you, dear reader.

Vespasian's story will continue in *Rome's Sacred Flame*.